# GREATER
# THAN ALL

# GREATER THAN ALL

## TORTH BOOK FIVE

## ABBY GOLDSMITH

Podium

*This book is dedicated to my dad, Dr. Michael Carl Goldsmith, who set an example of breaking free from majority consensus in order to excel.*

This is a work of fiction. Names, characters, places, and incidents are either products of the author's imagination or used fictitiously. Any resemblance to actual events, locales, or persons, living, dead, or undead, is entirely coincidental.

Cover design by Jeff Brown

ISBN: 978-1-0394-4293-1

Published in 2025 by Podium Publishing
www.podiumentertainment.com

**Podium**

# GREATER THAN ALL

# STORMED BY HOPE

Byiyi was especially good at the job of toweling.

Other slaves in the Grand Spa claimed she had an easy job. They said she was lucky, and they said it with envious authority. Byiyi answered those remarks with an apologetic, good-natured smile, but deep inside, she was not so sure they were right.

Every time a dripping, naked god stepped out of a marble pool, Byiyi was obliged to rush across wet tiles with a clean towel.

Every time she gently blotted a god dry, she remembered the sisters and brothers she used to bathe and take care of, whom she would never see again.

The gods—the Torth, everyone called them—had ripped her away from her family. They had punished her for screaming and crying about it. Byiyi had suffered so many pain seizures during her first moon in this city, blood had poured from her ears.

A Torth had punished her for that, too, for making a mess.

Byiyi had learned to bury the screams inside her heart. She supposed other slaves buried their screams, also. One did not make a sound in front of the gods. Slaves only spoke in slave zones, where they pretended that life was bearable. Everyone learned to keep silent in this cloud-shrouded, floating city and never complain, or else they did not survive beyond their first three lunar cycles.

A well-muscled Torth stepped out of one of the mineral pools. Byiyi dared not keep him waiting.

When she enfolded the muscled god in her fresh white towel, she imagined that she was caring for a strong child of her own. A healthy son.

As an exotic sapient, Byiyi was unlikely to encounter another one of her kind, anyway. There were no other spindly, long-faced Athpinari on this world.

And if she did meet another Athpinari?

Well, she would never dream of disobeying the law. City slaves were not permitted to have children. Sexual activity meant execution by torture. She could never be a mother. She could never care for her own children the way she used to dress and play with her siblings, whom she still missed and mourned for.

Only when she toweled a Torth did she allow herself to imagine the family she yearned for.

That was what made her so good at it. She wanted to stay immersed in her daydream.

But the god was dried off. Another slave began to dress him in a white spa robe.

Byiyi fiercely missed the pretend-adolescent in her arms whom she had loved. She had felt so proud of him, so whole, with that child who . . .

Well, who did not exist.

She trudged to the towel rack and picked up another folded towel, ready to do it again.

Every day felt anemic and feeble. Byiyi knew that her love-filled daydreams were not enough to sustain her forever, although this was the best life she was capable of having. She was unsure if she would survive for another six lunar cycles.

If only she could believe in silly legends, like some of her bunk mates.

They kept each other up late with tales of heroic runaways. Lately, all they talked about was Kessa the Wise, an ummin elder who supposedly rode on storm clouds and conversed with the gods in their silent tongue.

What nonsense.

Byiyi found it much easier to imagine her nonexistent children than to imagine a nonexistent hero. A child could, theoretically, be real. But a runaway slave? That was nothing but an impossible, wistful, foolish fantasy.

Something crashed in the distance.

Crystalline orb lamps glowed due to a sudden absence of sunlight. The Torth in the spa looked abruptly alert. They all sat up in unison, some with soapy hair, their blank white eyes more open than usual.

A thunderhead towered beyond the huge windows and sky domes.

Lightning arced over the floating city.

Byiyi had never seen a storm roll in so fast, and this was the sunny season. Strange. But a storm was none of her—

Action exploded around Byiyi.

Torth leaped out of pools, splashing water. They ignored proffered towels and robes and lunged toward their clothes, reaching for blaster gloves. Many slipped or skidded on the wet floor. Torth in a hurry were ungraceful.

Thunder cracked. The concussive sound was so close and loud, Byiyi jumped.

A titanic god fell out of nowhere, seemingly from the air itself.

He wore black armor that bristled with immense, jagged spikes. Lightning snapped across his massive chest plate and shoulder caps and thorny gauntlets. He landed on his feet with a terrific thud. The air smelled freshly seared.

The titan straightened to his full height, which was overwhelmingly tall. He was massive enough to blot out some of the storm-dark sky.

If he had a face, it was hidden. The faceplate of his helmet was as black as night.

A loose collection of electricity gathered in his armored hands. The electric glow grew denser, brighter, evolving into a weapon.

A spiked mace.

The Torth were panicking. What sort of colossal god could cause its lesser brethren to act like frightened slaves? Byiyi hurled herself beneath a towel rack and tugged towels around herself. She folded her spindly arms and legs, ratcheting her many joints closer and closer, trying to keep them out of harm's way. Other slaves claimed that she looked like a bug, but that was an insult. She was as sapient as any slave. She just happened to have more joints than the common species.

Nude Torth sprinted for the exits. One slipped on the soapy floor and slammed down.

An unseen force yanked that Torth off his feet.

Byiyi hardly paid attention to the violence, because she noticed a small person—a slave?!—aiming a blaster glove at one of the fleeing Torth. She stared. Slaves were not allowed to touch weapons.

Yet this one wore a weaponized glove, like a god. He even wore armor.

The slave thumbed the trigger.

His target reacted as if struck by a metaphysical blow and fell to his knees in a defeated pose.

The slave triggered the glove again and again. More Torth gave up and dropped. A few of the fallen Torth tried to crawl away, but mostly, they sat in puddles and looked hopeless.

Byiyi stared at the slave with the blaster glove, which looked custom-tailored for his three-fingered alien hand. Instead of wearing rags, or a gray spa uniform, this ummin was padded with embossed armor. A half helm with leatherwork flaps framed his beaked face.

Most striking of all: he was not afraid.

Several Torth took aim at the ummin slave.

The armored colossus slammed his mace into the threats, knocking them away. He struck so swiftly, one of the gods ended up embedded in a marble wall. The impact made the room shake.

That Torth was dead. Actually dead! He was smashed and barely recognizable as a formerly living being.

Other Torth scrambled away. One of the naked gods held out a hand, and a blaster glove hurtled into her grasp, as if magnetized.

Byiyi supposed she should not be surprised that Torth hid mystical powers. As gods, they possessed untold secrets of the universe . . . yet even so. She had never seen Torth cause water to rise and twist, freezing, into icicles as sharp as blades.

Torth should not be able to raise their hands and cause ice to fly at an enemy.

Torth should not be able to somersault through lightning, unharmed. Or make fire out of the air, causing puddles to mist into sizzling vapor.

Although their attacks were impressive feats of magic, none of them were able to harm the armored titan. He dodged or whirled as if he could predict everything. He threw ropes of lightning. He used invisible powers to seize each Torth and hold them in the air, one by one, while they kicked helplessly. The armored slave neutralized them.

Some of the ice daggers did hit the titan. But nothing pierced his armor.

He must be a more powerful god than any Torth in this city.

The spa shook. Walls cracked. Pools flooded across marble floors or steamed away. Torth got dropped, injured and defeated, or dead.

Slaves hid or scurried away, and Byiyi cowered. She stayed hidden until, finally, the explosions and the roaring flames quieted.

Even in the relative silence, she trembled. If the armored colossus decided to collect trophies to celebrate his victory . . . well, she was an exotic slave. Torth seemed to believe that her many-jointed limbs and her bioluminescent facial colors were pleasant to gaze upon. Or perhaps they valued her because she was so good at toweling? Byiyi did not know. She could only guess at why the gods treated her with more care than the common species of slaves.

She tried to be extra still, behind piles of fallen towels.

"The slaves of this city are now free."

The speaker must be exceptionally large, because her gentle tone reverberated around distant corners.

"I am Kessa the Wise." That was what the distant speaker said. "Your city, known to us as Equatorial Quartz Sprawl, is under my protection. The Torth who used to rule you are now prisoners. They will serve you as slaves."

That was impossible to believe.

Byiyi listened carefully. The distant speaker went on, saying incredible things. If she truly was the legendary Kessa, she must be extraordinarily powerful as well as wise. How else could she get away with speaking out loud? Any slave, especially a runaway, would be punished for making a speech.

Kessa the Wise explained more things about the conquest, which Byiyi did not quite understand. There were other liberated cities? Powerful allies? Enslaved Torth?

The announcement paused and then began again. It replayed with the exact same words, tones, and cadences.

Byiyi began to suspect that it was as false as holographic window displays. It was an auditory illusion.

Was this a trap, designed to weed out the stupidest of slaves?

Such a fanciful message would lure slaves out of hiding. But anyone with a sliver of sense knew that hope and self-confidence meant death. Byiyi remained still.

The colossus used his powers to drag defeated Torth together onto a relatively intact square bathing platform. Byiyi could not guess what his purpose was. She would wait until he finished, and then, once he was gone, she would dare to sneak out of the ruined spa. She would hide in slave zones until this madness was over.

"I can remove your slave collar."

It was the ummin in armor. He crouched to peer at Byiyi. Despite his outlandish garb, he had kind eyes. His face looked a bit like one of her bunk mates'.

"My name is Choonhulm," the ummin said, introducing himself. "Please do not be afraid."

Byiyi hesitated. She wanted to respond to his friendliness, because every slave knew how rare and valuable friendship was. One should make an effort to talk whenever one was in a slave zone.

But this was not a slave zone.

"Freedom is real." Choonhulm waved his gloved hand, and Byiyi gasped when her slave collar snapped open and slid off her neck.

The collar should have been aglow, to show that she was still on a work shift. Instead, it was broken and dead.

Byiyi began to believe.

"Is Kessa the Wise a real person?" she asked.

"I know her," Choonhulm said. "She came to my slave farm and set many of us free."

Byiyi boggled at that.

"I must go." Choonhulm straightened. "The Torth of your city are rendered powerless, but we still have much to do. I will remove other slave collars. Please be assured that you are safe. If you want answers to your questions, please seek one of Kessa's clerks. They wear black head covers with white circlets." He gestured. "And Kessa herself will give a speech later today."

Byiyi unfolded herself as the ummin walked away. She scanned the niches of broken stonework, fearing that a Torth would pop out and try to reenslave her.

"Choonhulm," she called.

He glanced back.

Byiyi attempted to sort out the big questions crowding her mind. She could wander the city in search of those clerks, but first she had to know . . .

"What does freedom mean?" she asked.

Choonhulm smiled with more confidence than a slave should have. "It means you are your own master," he said. "You can lounge like a Torth. Or you can learn how to free other people." He held up his blaster glove. "You can fly transports. Or command prisoners. Or start a family. Whatever you want."

Byiyi let him walk away. She was stunned.

Then, filled with wonderment and beauty and love and delight, she walked out of the wreckage.

# PART ONE

*"Join Me if you want happiness. Join Me if you are afraid.*
*I accept you as you are; the Majority never will. Come to Me."*

—Thomas the Conqueror broadcasting to anyone orbiting his mind

# CHAPTER 1
# BATTLING EXTINCTION

Cherise sat curled up in a stone window seat, gazing at the rain-sodden city.

Few hovervehicles or electric lights graced this neighborhood. At night, the maze of alleyways looked a lot like the Alashani underground, each storefront dotted by the glow of a gas lamp. Hand-painted signs marked the doorways of a toy shop, a jeweler, a tea café.

Except the streets were mud instead of stone.

The air smelled fecund, like New Hampshire in early summer. Alien frogs chirruped in eerie, overlapping songs from gardens and gutters.

"All this water." Flen joined her by the window. He spoke in the slave tongue, since that was the language they had in common. Cherise had not learned the shani language, and Flen had no time to learn English.

He inhaled the night air with a look of wonder. "It's potable?"

"It is," Cherise confirmed.

Flen held out his palms to catch rain. "It just pours and pours from that . . ." He gazed upward. "Sky?"

His people had no native words for the sky, or weather, or anything related to oceans, or a lot of things. They were too proud to admit ignorance, but they were beginning to infuse slave words into the shani language.

"Yes." Cherise had overheard some albinos attribute rain to the Lady of Sorrow lamenting their lost loved ones, ignorant of the fact that Evenjos had actually wrought the destruction of their homeworld. "It is called *rain* in my language, and it is as natural as stalactites."

"This rain situation happened in paradise?" Flen was incredulous.

Cherise giggled, although she wished Flen would come to one of her classes, just once. His conceptualization of Earth was so wrong it bordered on comical.

"Our houses had better protection than this," she explained. There were no glass manufacturers on this planet, and she didn't want to get into a debate about the merits of human versus Torth technology.

A pathetic coughing sound came from the courtyard below.

Four zombified Torth stood down there. As far as Cherise could tell, sentry duty was the only thing they did. She had never seen them take a break. When she had asked Flen whether they ever slept or used a bathroom, he had scoffed. "*What are they, infants? We should not have to care for them like they are invalids.*"

Cherise had almost argued.

But she and Flen were arguing too much, lately. Anyway, Flen was not responsible for the zombified minions. Their deplorable state was not his fault.

And he had good, valid reasons for wanting to hurt Torth.

"Have you heard any news about my mother and sister?" Flen sat on the stone ledge beside Cherise, his black armor creaking.

Dozens of albinos were being rescued from slavers. Apparently, Thomas had teamed up with Garrett to locate and rescue the missing family members of Alashani Yeresunsa. Orla had been reunited with her siblings. Shevrael had regained his elderly parents, and more.

Everyone heard their celebrations. Happy albinos praised the *rekvehs* as heroes.

Flen pretended to be glad for his fellow warriors, but his smile dropped as soon as he was alone with Cherise. He begged for his mother in his sleep. Whenever he woke up weeping, Cherise would hold him, letting him cling to her, wishing she had a power to work miracles.

Or to make Thomas work yet another miracle.

"I heard news," she admitted, "but it's not good."

Flen gazed into her eyes. "Tell me."

Cherise hesitated, but this was too important to hold back. "According to Vy, every shani who could have been rescued has been rescued." Cherise saw Flen's devastation, and quickly added, "That doesn't mean they're dead. But they've been shipped to one of the enemy supergeniuses, the one known as the Death Architect. Her lair is hidden from the Torth Megacosm, so not even our mind readers can learn the location."

"Our mind readers." Flen's tone was dark with sarcasm. "You mean the *rekvehs* that rule us?"

Cherise did not try to persuade her boyfriend that Thomas and Garrett were freedom fighters. She had no desire to retread the ground of past arguments.

But really. How many times did Thomas need to win battles and save cities to prove that he was on the side of the good guys? She had plenty of concerns about her ex–best friend, but his loyalties were obvious, even to her.

"So that's it?" Flen asked. "They've given up on rescuing my mother and sister? They're going to let them die?"

"They haven't given up," Cherise said defensively, tripping over her own resolve to avoid an argument. "I'm sure they're still searching. But you must understand, they'd have to search the whole galaxy."

"Lies," Flen said bitterly.

"No!" Cherise said. "I heard this from Vy, and she asked Thomas directly."

"Your sister is a pawn of the *rekveh*," Flen said in a tone of suffering tolerance. "She'll say whatever words he puts in her mouth."

Cherise tried to remind herself that Flen was hurting, in mourning for his family. She took a bracing breath. She needed to just let Flen's bitterness wash over her, like the sound of rain. It shouldn't affect her.

But it did stir up her own self-doubts.

What did Flen truly see in Cherise, if he believed her human family members were all a bunch of gullible fools? He claimed to love her. He said that he was infatuated with her angelic beauty. Clearly, he had no problems making love to a human from paradise. And when they were in bed together? He was good at making Cherise feel like a goddess.

But apart from their bedroom activities, he acted just like all the other superstitious albinos.

Alashani mothers dragged their children across a street in order to avoid Cherise. Every time that happened, Cherise would painstakingly reassure them. *"I'm not a mind reader."* She had said that once—only to realize it sounded like she was reading their minds. *"I am a human and I teach classes at the academy. Please come, and I will teach you about a world without Torth or mind readers."*

Flen claimed to love her, yet even so . . . it was as if part of him, deep down, believed that he was dating a weirdly friendly penitent Torth.

Not that he would admit that out loud. The one time Cherise had brought up her suspicion, Flen had furiously defended himself. That had been their worst fight ever. They had been screaming at each other, tears streaming down their faces.

"Do you think I'm nothing but a pawn of the . . ." Cherise trailed off, interrupted by choking, wheezing sounds from the courtyard.

One of the zombified Torth down there had fallen.

It looked like a female, clad in a bodysuit, now curled on her side in the mud and apparently choking. She looked and sounded exactly like a suffering human.

Cherise raced for the doorway, inwardly cursing her own misguided sympathies. It was a Torth. Not a human. Not a person.

And yet.

"Where are you going?" Flen seemed unaware of the distant, gasping sounds.

"I'll be right back," Cherise called.

She barreled through a corridor of rough-hewn stone, then down a spiral ramp, wide enough for two or three nussians abreast. Everything Ariock built was cavernous. The war complex looked like a collection of squared-off mountains from the outside, much like the academy buildings.

Cherise considered tapping her wristwatch to dial emergency medical services. But who would lift a finger to help a zombified Rosy Recruit or Servant of All?

It would do no good, Cherise knew. Any medic would take one look and refuse to render aid. If she asked a medical team to rush out here, in the rain, through alleyways, perhaps appropriating a hovercart from someone who actually needed it . . . they would blame the human for a false alarm that wasted precious time and resources.

That would likely pile on more nasty rumors about humans. Some people thought Cherise and Vy were secret mind readers, with secret hidden powers.

Cherise splashed into the muddy courtyard. Three zombies remained standing, their faces gray, their lips swollen and discolored. The fourth lay unmoving.

Cherise knelt by the fallen one.

She had seen friends blown to bits or devoured alive. Even so, she recoiled from the fallen Torth. Her face was gruesome. No visible pupils or irises. The woman appeared to have choked to death on her own swollen tongue.

Cherise checked the zombified woman's neck for a pulse. Nothing.

Then her wrist.

The woman was dead.

Cherise stood, her hair and woolens drenched with rain. It felt awkward to be sympathetic toward an empty shell of a person who used to think of herself a god. Servants of All tended to be merciless. The fallen zombie had probably murdered people for no reason other than her own sadistic whims, back when she'd had a working brain.

Her fate here was probably karmic justice.

Maybe that was what Thomas told himself when he twisted minds. Did he believe his victims no longer deserved enough freedom to make personal decisions? Did he think that robbing them of free will was somehow better than outright killing them?

Executions would be more merciful.

"Cherise?" Flen rushed into the rain, protected by his wide-brimmed hat and his lithe body armor. He wrapped her in a protective embrace. "What are you doing?"

Cherise looked around for a pail, or anything that could be used to gather rainwater. "The zombified victims must be thirsty," she explained. "And tired. Who's in charge of them?"

Flen let go of her.

"How long have they been standing in the rain?" Cherise asked. "I've seen them here for days. Has anyone thought to command them to take breaks?"

"The *rekveh* said they would be self-sufficient enough to survive," Flen said.

"They don't have free will." Cherise wondered if the zombies were even capable of sleep. "They still need commands for certain things."

"They're more trouble than they're worth," Flen said with disgust.

"If you want to use them," Cherise said, "then they need basic necessities. They're living people, not—" She hesitated, since the slave tongue lacked any word for robots. "Not vegetables," she finished.

Flen faced the remaining three zombies, exasperated. "Drink sky water!"

The zombies tipped their heads back. Rain fell on their tongues, and they made swallowing sounds.

"Isn't that pathetic?" Flen put his armored hands on his hips. "I've heard of one that went blind because no one told it to blink. They relieve themselves like animals unless we order them not to. And we lose them because they keep taking orders too literally."

"That's sad." Cherise stared at the zombies as they struggled to drink rain.

She used to be able to defy her ma in small ways. These zombified victims were worse off than that. One of them had just died of thirst in a downpour.

"You are too kindhearted," Flen told her. "The only person who wants these useless creatures around is your skinny little *rekveh*. He is secretly puppeteering everyone in power!"

Cherise rolled her eyes. She had problems with Thomas—he had never apologized for torturing her—yet she doubted he was evil. He had saved her once.

Well, maybe more than once.

Anyhow, Thomas was a hybrid, like Garrett, not wholly a Torth. His unknown biological father—a victim of Torth rape, no doubt—must have graced him with some non-negligible amount of human compassion.

Flen saw her unspoken defense of Thomas. He tightened his jaw, no doubt suppressing his own arguments.

"I agree that what he is doing to the Torth prisoners is wrong," Cherise admitted in a placating tone. "It's sick. No one deserves to become . . ." She gestured at the zombified victims. "What they are."

"Oh, they deserve it," Flen said.

Cherise lowered her gaze, aware that Flen had powers. Sometimes he caused things to float when he got enraged.

"This is the exact same sort of demon that enslaved my mother." Flen pointed at one of the gaping zombies. "And my sister. This is the evil that murders everything good. This is the reason I don't have a family anymore!"

He drew back his leg, looking mighty in his compact armor. And he kicked the nearest zombified Torth.

Hard.

The helpless victim staggered. Yet she continued to gape at the sky, mindlessly catching rain on her tongue.

"Stop," Cherise said. "You're beating up someone who's already a victim."

"This is a monster." Flen slammed his armored fist into the woman's stomach, hard enough to make her fall, doubled over.

"Stop, Flen!" Cherise wondered if he was aware that the victim he was beating up looked somewhat like his girlfriend. The zombified Torth had black hair and a skin tone that was similar to Cherise's.

"Kill yourself!" Flen yelled at the fallen victim. "Choke yourself, the way your evil slave collars choke slaves to death!"

The victim obeyed, of course.

Cherise could not imagine what thoughts, if any, went through the victim's damaged mind. The command was stronger than whatever survival instincts her body had left. She wrapped her hands around her own throat and began to gag.

"What is wrong with you?" Cherise screamed at Flen. Her rage surprised even herself. "They're helpless! And they feel pain! You need to tell her to stop!" She shifted her attention to the victim. "Stop!"

But Thomas had brainwashed this victim, like all of them, to only obey warriors. The zombie would not, and did not, obey Cherise.

"They deserve suffering." Flen spoke as if his words were more important than life. He ignored the woman dying at his feet with her own fingers digging into her throat.

Cherise whirled and stalked away through the mud. Flen was not the only warrior who treated the zombified prisoners as if they were still capable of doing harm, but Cherise didn't care. She would never approve of brutalizing a helpless person, no matter what sort of monster that person used to be.

Maybe she should teach a class on why her culture had abandoned torture and excessively cruel punishments. A lot of people in Freedomland could use education about human rights.

Flen never imagined that he was doing evil things. To him, the bad guys were always Torth and the good guys were always Alashani. There was no nuance.

Yet he had the nerve to accuse Thomas of being callous and unfeeling. Was Flen really that much better?

"Flen," a female voice called from the echoey darkness of the foyer. "See that the remaining zombies get a rest break."

Jinishta stood in the archway, arms folded, her black civilian garb blending in with the shadows. She watched with a mild expression.

"Is this how you take care of your war assets?" Cherise said coldly.

"Vedlor was supposed to care for them tonight," Jinishta explained. "He took the night off without bothering to ask anyone to cover for him. I just found out." She called to Flen, "After they have something nourishing to eat and drink, direct them to dispose of the dead bodies."

How pragmatic.

Justifications for abuse were easy. Cherise's ma used to pretend to be the suffering mother of a spoiled brat. Ma would say anything to justify hitting or neglecting her own children.

Cherise hurried past the premier of premiers. She had nothing to say except criticisms.

"Cherise?" Jinishta called. "I know it is wrong."

Cherise stopped on the ramp upstairs. She had never heard a warrior sound ashamed.

"This is not how I ever imagined battles against Torth," Jinishta said. "I did not think we would use prisoners like this. It is dishonorable."

They regarded each other in the dim foyer.

"Flen is angry," Jinishta said. "He lost his family. And his world."

"I know," Cherise said. "But brutality like that"—she pointed to the corpses— "is wrong."

Flen shepherded the surviving zombies toward a bench. They might live another day, maybe two, but there was no mercy in that.

"Anger is all we have left." Jinishta's luminous eyes were anguished. "Cherise, I know Thomas is not the evil *rekveh* my people believe him to be. None of us would be here without his aid."

That was definitely an unpopular sentiment among Alashani. Cherise stared at Jinishta, wondering why she was confessing such a heretical opinion.

Jinishta climbed the ramp, coming close enough to lower her voice. "We lose warriors in battles. There are fewer than eleven hundred of us left. And we are not replaceable."

Cherise knew how overworked the warriors were. Flen barely had enough time to get intimate between battles and fleeting hours of sleep. Although they had won every battle so far, anyone who understood the scope of the galaxy knew that this was only the beginning of a major war. There would be many bloody battles ahead.

"We are being carved away to nothingness," Jinishta said. "I fear that we have lost our future as well as our world."

Although she spoke with the poise of a warrior, fear underlaid her words. Fear was in her eyes.

And Cherise understood. There were no Alashani in other cities. Most of the surviving Alashani lived here, in Freedomland. The albinos were a stark minority in contrast to ummins, nussians, govki, and even some of the more exotic sapients.

They had not been a large population to begin with. Extinction was on their minds.

"I am afraid the zombified prisoners give us our only chance for survival," Jinishta said, her shoulders bowed in shame. "We need them. We need even more of them."

Cherise felt sick, imagining armies of shambling, brain-damaged victims.

"I don't like what they are," Jinishta admitted. "I am ashamed to use them. But we are learning to take better care of them. We can make them last longer."

This was a matter of survival for the Alashani. Cherise could not fault Jinishta for grasping at straws, but she still wondered if there was any alternative. Was this truly the best path to winning the war Thomas could think of?

"If Thomas would speed up the production of them," Jinishta said, "then the Alashani have a chance of survival."

And warriors such as Flen would not have to die in battle.

"But Thomas refuses to zombify more than ten prisoners per day." Jinishta's tone became bitter. "He keeps making excuses. My people are not his top priority."

Cherise hated herself for thinking that Thomas might be right.

She loved the Alashani, at least a little bit. She liked Flen when he wasn't ranting or kicking zombies. But . . . well, she supposed the stakes of this war were higher for slaves and for Alashani than for humans.

So far.

"Would you please ask Thomas to zombify more prisoners for us?" Jinishta asked.

Cherise stared at the premier of premiers. Jinishta ought to ask for the opposite.

Someone powerful should beg Thomas to quit making zombies. Didn't Kessa see how wrong it was? What about Ariock? Why wasn't he putting a stop to it? Or Vy?

Was Cherise truly the only one who thought Thomas should be stopped?

"Or," Jinishta said, seeing her unspoken protests, "could you ask Vy to ask him? Please?"

Begging was not in Jinishta's nature. This was serious.

"You can help the Alashani survive." Jinishta gently squeezed Cherise's arm. "Just as we are trying to help your people, and all the enslaved people in the galaxy."

Jinishta walked into the rain-drenched courtyard, leaving Cherise to wonder if suffering was the only way to right the wrongs of the universe.

# CHAPTER 2

# THE TRAUMA OF TORTHHOOD

"What do you think of the salad?" Kessa nibbled a cactus slice topped by Reject-20 lizard caviar. "Is it to your taste?"

Thomas sat across from her. He speared a slice with his fork and took a bite. "It's . . ." He considered. "Interesting."

They sat on an open-air balcony that overlooked the sprawling oceanside city of Freedomland. A long table separated them. Kessa wanted to stop feeling disadvantaged, and the distance prevented any chance of Thomas probing her memories or reading her intentions. It was a small measure of equality.

"Interesting?" Kessa prompted.

The salad bore no resemblance to the rotting slop piles that slaves had no choice but to dine upon. For most of her life, Kessa could not have imagined a delectable meal such as this, beautifully arranged with a garnish and presented by a friendly chef.

Thomas ate another bite, chewing thoughtfully. "Well, these aren't flavors that humans or Torth would normally put together. But it's good."

Kessa watched him eat, making mental notes for later analysis. She wanted to make a regular habit of inviting Thomas to dine with her, but she wasn't confident about her knowledge of humanoid culinary tastes. Vy liked herbal beverages. Cherise preferred spicy treats. Ariock and Garrett were indifferent to those things, but they ate like nussians when presented with seared meats. Jinishta, predictably, liked mushrooms prepared in a variety of ways.

As for Thomas? When he had been dying from his neuromuscular disease, even the act of eating had been a chore for him.

Now he seemed like a new person.

He no longer resembled an emaciated skeleton devoid of muscles. The purple mantle he wore rested easily on shoulders that were no longer quite so narrow. He was able to lift his own fork and his own glass of water. Kessa had heard, through reports, that he ate whatever was on the menu for the research annex.

"You look a lot stronger," Kessa said, aiming to put Thomas at ease before she dived into her questions.

He seemed flattered. "Thanks."

Kessa finished the last bite of her salad. "How is the zombifying going?"

Thomas's smile became a troubled frown.

Kessa pretended not to notice. She poured more water for herself and for Thomas. "I have heard," she said, "that they die very easily."

She had heard much more than that about the zombified Torth. According to her informants, they were as delicate as sea scum. They forgot to blink. They forgot to hold their bowels. Some forgot to breathe. Warriors had taken to using them for target practice rather than taking them into battle.

"They require micromanagement," Thomas admitted. "I'm refining a list of baseline operational instructions to load into each one. But their main purpose is really to be a deterrent, not a fighting force."

Kessa sipped from a crystal goblet. "Are they working as a deterrent?"

Anyone could make the inference. Ever since Thomas had begun to twist the minds of prisoners, the Torth Empire had gone into full retreat mode. They seemed to be the reason for Ariock's victories.

Thomas confirmed it. "Yes, they're the reason why we don't see many Rosies or Servants in battle anymore, and why the Torth evacuate cities when we show up."

"Yet they don't retain their powers?" Kessa asked.

"Zombification entails massive brain damage," Thomas said. "They lose a lot."

Kessa made a mental note to ask more about that later. She remarked, "You don't own any, yourself."

"I don't want any." Thomas's voice had an edge. Candles flickered, and the air temperature dropped.

Kessa let that line of questioning go. She was secretly gladdened by his obvious discomfort about the topic of zombified Torth. It could be difficult to gauge Thomas's humanity, since he never shared his feelings. He hardly confided in anyone.

But he had promised to answer any question that Kessa asked, as long as they were in private.

"The Torth will take back all the cities we've won if we let up the pressure, even for an instant." Thomas studied a slice of cactus as if it held secrets that he wanted to crack open. "They have the military capability to attack a hundred planets simultaneously. We can't fight them with numbers or technology. So we need to make their military champions terrified to face us."

Kessa understood that. Yet . . .

"This is a temporary solution," Kessa observed.

"Yes." Thomas gave her a look of respect. "I know."

Ariock was well on his way to conquering Umdalkdul, but he did not have the bandwidth to hunt and kill every individual Rosy throughout the galaxy. He could not singlehandedly conquer every planet. Sooner or later, the Torth would grow bold again. Or they would invent a new advantage for themselves.

"Zombification is not our path to victory," Thomas said. "I never imagined it would be." He picked at the remains of his salad and selected a tangy bit. "How is your work with the penitents coming along?"

Kessa offered a taut smile. She was not ready to capitulate control of the conversation. "How many prisoners do you zombify every day?"

"Ten," Thomas said.

Kessa knew that Thomas could zombify anything that had a brain. He could probably zombify a lot more than ten per day, but she did not blame him for setting limits. It was a particularly dangerous power.

"It's an evil power." Thomas gave her a frank look. His purple eyes picked up evening light from the cloudy sky outside. "I don't like using it."

Kessa inwardly agreed. She rarely saw the zombified minions, but rumors were enough to make her feel uncomfortable about them.

"What about the prophecies of Ah Jun?" she asked. "Is your zombification of the Torth featured in the book?"

"Garrett has not seen fit to share the prophecies with me," Thomas said.

That was not really an answer to her question.

"Yes, I think it's in there," Thomas said, likely seeing that she meant to dig further. "But I'm sure the other heroes must play a role in defeating the Torth. Otherwise Ah Jun wouldn't have made such a big deal about there being four. And I assume we also need heroes like you."

Kessa clicked her beak at the flattery. She doubted she counted as a hero.

"I think you're the key to getting real Torth on our side." Thomas adjusted his utensils on the table. "Willing Torth. Who aren't brain damaged."

There was a trace of sadness in his gaze, and Kessa suspected he was remembering the one and only Torth he had persuaded. The Upward Governess had been assassinated moments after she'd volunteered to go renegade and become a penitent.

"Do you still visit the Megacosm every day?" Kessa asked.

"Yes." Thomas sounded cynical. "For all the good it does."

Kessa could imagine many reasons why a secretly emotional Torth would be reluctant to give up godhood. If they agreed to kneel, they would lose many luxuries—and they would put themselves in terrible danger. They might end up shot, either by vengeful slaves or by their own peers.

"I suppose it is very dangerous for them." Kessa studied Thomas, wondering how well he acknowledged the risks he was asking many Torth to take.

"We have a safe haven for them." Thomas gestured at the city, with its bustling alleyway bazaars and stone tenements. "Freedomland."

Freedomland must seem like a strange place to any Torth.

An adult sky crocodile soared lazily overhead, its immense shadow flitting over buildings. The beast could probably swallow a nussian in its gigantic beak. Hazards like those were the reason why the Torth Empire had rejected this planet for colonization.

That, and Reject-20 was far from any temporal stream.

Any Torth who approached this world would need to travel for seven days through local space. They would have to hail the makeshift Freedomland spaceport for clearance to land. And they would need to show up unarmed, prepared to serve former slaves.

"The Torth Majority keeps a very close watch on all Torth citizens," Thomas conceded. "They don't have privacy. But . . ." He sounded frustrated, almost offended. "I took risks. I managed to escape, despite being watched constantly." He gestured at the sprawling city on the cliffs below them. "And unlike me, they actually have somewhere to go."

Freedomland's planet was unique in that it was protected by Ariock, Evenjos, and Garrett. All other planets—including Earth and other so-called wilderness preserves—were owned by the Torth Empire. Reject-20 was a true safe haven.

At least for now.

"Other Torth are not you," Kessa gently pointed out. "They may not be as brave."

Thomas made a dismissive face.

"You had a human parent," Kessa reminded him. "He gifted you with human emotions."

Thomas looked annoyed, as if she had pointed out some trivial, inconsequential fact.

But having emotions was not trivial or inconsequential. It made all the difference between being a penitent and being a human. It was something to be proud of. Surely he knew that?

"What do you object to?" Kessa asked him.

Thomas gave her a look, perhaps surprised by her perceptiveness. "Well . . ." He hesitated, ashamed. "I've never felt very human. I fit in better with the Torth."

Kessa felt a chill, hearing him admit that. She hoped he would not say such a thing in public, or within earshot of anyone else.

Thomas went on. "It's always been easier for me to not deal with emotions. Even talking this way?" He threw up his hands in frustration. "It's awkward."

Kessa heard the unspoken implication. Avoiding emotions, or repressing them, was how he preferred to live. Was he saying he preferred to be a Torth?

Although . . .

Kessa had known slaves who shut their emotions off. The most traumatized of slaves became dreamers. They sleepwalked through life, forgetting their own names and stories. They allowed others to push them around, or to assign names to them.

Wasn't that very much what Torth did? Individual Torth allowed their inner audiences to make decisions for them. An individual's orbiters collectively assigned their name-title, their mentor, and any privileges or punishments.

Did that count as trauma, though?

Kessa had trouble imagining the average mind reader as a victim of abuse. Torth did not get ripped away from families who loved them. Torth were not beaten or killed for failing to complete menial chores. Torth weren't victims.

Were they?

Kessa began to wonder. Torth civilization looked utopian from the perspective of slaves—but whenever Thomas or Garrett described the Megacosm and the peer pressure of Torth society, they described a nightmare. That was one of the few topics they actually agreed on.

The Torth Majority had collectively voted to outlaw their own intense emotions.

They self-medicated by wearing tranquility meshes.

They had essentially voted to act like traumatized slaves, to reject pain and anything they associated with pain.

Only a handful of people knew the story of the origin of the Torth species. Kessa mulled over what Evenjos had explained about the rise of the Torth Empire— the earliest generations of mutant mind readers used to be downtrodden peasants. All they had wanted was a better future for their children.

What did downtrodden and damaged people do, upon gaining power and privilege?

Kessa realized that she was actually qualified to answer that herself. She touched her neck. She still had her scars. She still woke from nightmares. She still hated any Torth who might oppress her.

Damage did not magically go away.

Twenty-four thousand years later, it seemed the Torth still had to grapple with emotional damage they had never collectively healed.

They'd even retained their hatred of Yeresunsa.

"I want to be proud of my human heritage," Thomas was saying, unaware of her thoughts due to the distance between them. "But I guess I didn't see much human kindness when I was growing up. Maybe that's why I feel more like a Torth than a human."

Kessa wanted to ponder that. Were humans unkind?

That seemed wrong. Vy was wonderful, and Delia and Cherise had never seemed tyrannical. Although . . .

Well.

Cherise had obvious psychological scars that predated her time as a slave. She reveled in art and storytelling, but she had nothing to say about her birth family or her human friends. She did not reminisce. She never painted pictures of her past.

In fact, Cherise embraced alien cultures as if eager to shed her human cultural heritage. She acted and dressed like a shani. She spoke the slave tongue fluently.

What, exactly, had drawn Thomas to Cherise and vice versa? Hadn't they been best friends on Earth? Hadn't Cherise once idolized Thomas, promising that he would rescue her from slavery, no matter the odds?

They had stuck to each other like traumatized orphans.

Or like penitent Torth.

Many penitents refused to speak out loud. They refused to emote. They co-cooned themselves in an uncaring attitude, which made them seem arrogant . . . but what if Kessa and her lieutenants were misreading the situation?

What if the penitents were bonding over shared trauma?

"Thank you," Kessa said.

Thomas looked curious. "For what?"

"You have given me a new idea," Kessa said.

# CHAPTER 3

# ZOMBIFIED

*No don't hurt Us (leave Me alone) stop go away (We don't want You) turn around (go away) no (no) no (no) We don't want . . .*

Wet, white eyes gleamed in the dusty light of the Mirror Prison. Fear reached Thomas like a stench.

"Could you try to do twelve today?" Jinishta said. "Instead of ten?"

Thomas longed to be in his sunny laboratory, coaching Varktezo on capacitors. That was where he belonged. Not in this grimy underground facility.

But hub cities throughout the galaxy were emptying because of what he could do. The Torth Majority was no longer able to think of Thomas as a mere betrayer. His forces had taken too much territory and enslaved too many Torth. His name-title had morphed into something more threatening: the Conqueror.

And they were terrified of him.

The Torth Majority kept urging their military ranks to fight, but not even their galactic peer pressure could overcome the sheer panic that most Rosies and Servants felt when faced with the prospect of being taken prisoner. None wanted to be zombified.

So Ariock was busy taking over Umdalkdul. With the threat posed by Thomas, it was easy to conquer cities. All Ariock had to do was show up with an army. The Torth were in the process of evacuating the entire planet, letting Ariock and his forces dominate city after city.

"We have a finite number of prisoners," Thomas said. "We can't afford to burn through them quickly."

"So start zombifying penitents," Garrett suggested.

"No." Thomas made it a flat statement. "Penitents are under Kessa's jurisdiction. She'll send me any that she deems beyond redemption."

"She's not sending enough of those," one of the warriors said.

"I won't zombify anyone who can be rehabilitated." Thomas had to keep reminding them of that point. "Only—"

"Yeah, yeah," Garrett grumped. "We know. You're completely inflexible."

Why was Garrett here? Thomas wished the old man wasn't so fascinated by zombification. Garrett did not attend every session, but he showed up more often than not.

"Let me get this over with." Thomas floated toward a ragged victim behind the bars of the holding cage. He plunged into her mind.

That was how he thought of them—not as prisoners or enemy combatants, but as sacrificial victims.

He was not an executioner. He was worse.

*Please no.* The imprisoned Servant of All whimpered wordlessly. *Please spare Me. I will do anything You want (Great Mind) (Conqueror). I will be Your slave forever. Just please, will You deign to show Me mercy?*

From the perspective of mind readers, the Conqueror was a colossus of incomprehensible mental size and fierce complexity. His physical frailty was inconsequential. Torth paid attention to the psyche more than appearance. They saw the Conqueror as a tyrannical, godlike monster who contained almost a million lifetimes.

He was even more terrifying than the Giant.

He was destruction incarnate.

The Conqueror did not downplay his own mental stature. It was nothing but the naked truth. He was not going to drag out this process by pretending to reassure the victim. He just wanted to get his quota over with.

So he inhaled her fear and wrestled it downward. He shoved himself into the depths of her mind.

He tasted hidden sorrows. Dark moments. Abuses. Indulgences.

Shining moments rose to the top like clouds.

Injustices lumped in a heavy gloop.

The Conqueror grabbed salient memories the way a diver might grab sunken coins from a treasure chest. He weighed and sorted everything he sucked up. His internal scales of justice tipped back and forth, judging cruelties against kindnesses.

This Servant was not quite as cruelly sadistic as most victims, but she was no innocent lamb. She had tortured slaves. She felt nothing for them. No pity. No empathy.

She had never done anything good or kind.

Her thoughts wrenched in a terrified scream. *NOOOOO!* Her terror caused her to whine out loud.

*I'm sorry*, the Conqueror thought to his first victim of the day.

He wrenched her mind.

Memories vaporized. Individuality was gone. The will of the Conqueror seeped into her broken mind, overriding everything else.

Vacancy replaced her terror. The zombie no longer understood that she used to be a Servant of All, or that she used to have free will. Her mind was reduced to an echoing cave of neediness.

She blinked when Thomas blinked. She swallowed in sync with Thomas and looked wherever Thomas focused. To Thomas, it felt like having double vision, only multifaceted. It was double everything. He had an extra body.

Easy for a supergenius to handle. Impossible for anyone else.

Thomas silently listed subroutines, giving the new zombie a bunch of priorities to follow. It was a laborious process. Zombies with ordinary mental capacity could only remember so many instructions per second, nowhere near as fast as he could process information.

At least he could ensure that these latest zombies would swallow and blink without instruction. They would perform the basics of self-sufficiency.

"Who wants this one?" Thomas sounded hollow. It was difficult to act kind or friendly while his subconscious sifted through innumerable irrelevancies.

"Tchensi," Jinishta commanded.

The named warrior stepped forward, looking ashamed. None of them liked to babysit zombified Torth.

They might have felt differently if they were mind readers, comfortable with sending commands at the speed of thought. But the albinos were superstitious about letting the zombies get within telepathy range. They insisted on speaking every order out loud. What a drag.

Thomas silently layered more priorities into the zombie's broken and readied mind. The zombie should henceforth obey the warrior known as Tchensi. The zombie must ignore any command from a Torth. Thomas attached extra importance to that command, embedding it at the root of the zombie's instructions so that no one else could override it.

Last but not least . . . the zombie must detach herself from the Conqueror's direct control.

That broke the synced-up feeling.

The zombie silently awaited instructions from her newly assigned owner, while Thomas was glad to be rid of the excess sensory input.

He dared not tell anyone that the zombies were like extensions of himself. Garrett suspected it, but Thomas was not going to confirm the old man's suspicions.

"She's yours," Thomas said.

He rotated his hoverchair to face the next cowering victim, while the warrior named Tchensi tested out her new minion with a routine of exercises.

"Hopefully this batch will last longer," a warrior muttered.

"They would be much more effective if you let them get within telepathy range," Thomas pointed out. "Thoughts are faster than words."

Thoughts were clarity. A mind reader would never misinterpret a command, provided they were close enough.

It was no wonder that Audavian had begun to zombify his own loyal telepaths all those eons ago. Telepaths were perfect minions. They were better than robots, able to fully absorb the intricacies of someone else's will. With a billion expendable proxy bodies, the Conqueror could do just about anything, seize anything . . .

A chill rippled over Thomas.

No.

That was certainly not what he was going to do. He might be on a path toward fulfilling Migyatel's prophecy, but he did not need to become a power-mad tyrant. He would rather be known as the Wisdom than some terrible mental octopus.

"What are you waiting for?" Garrett asked, oblivious to his thoughts, standing beyond telepathy range. "We haven't got all day."

No one dared to go near Thomas when he was doing this kind of work.

He went on, acting as judge, jury, and executioner. He tore through the mind of a cruel Servant who had never felt anything for slaves. This one's life had been full of vapid pursuits, without a care for the harm and pain he caused.

Another victim.

Another.

The Conqueror weighed their consciences and their histories, all while enduring their pleas for mercy and their perceptions of his power. His victims screamed like people being fed to a hungry god. A few of them even tried speaking out loud, using the scraps of English they'd soaked up from his mind and the Megacosm, just in case it might stir up some vestigial shred of human mercy.

If only they had felt mercy toward their slaves.

If only they had joined the Conqueror. They regretted not doing so now, of course. Too late. They should have exhibited willingness when it would have made a difference.

"Please," the final victim whispered, her voice raspy, her eyes pink. "Please let me die."

The worst thing about twisting minds was not the garbage he absorbed or the cruelty of obliterating their souls. The worst thing—the real reason he felt morally bankrupt—was the act of destroying knowledge.

One individual mind was only a droplet of knowledge in comparison to the vast cache inside the Conqueror's mind. And his capacious mind was but a droplet next to the Megacosm. Even so, droplets could add up to an ocean. The only way to preserve their knowledge was to absorb and absorb and absorb.

*I'm sorry,* Thomas silently told the final victim of today.

He dived into the primal depths of her core mind and wrenched it with practiced ease.

The victim ceased pleading. She became a mere echo of the Conqueror's every thought and reflex.

His mind churned with sadistic experiences from his victims. He would need an hour to assimilate most of what he'd absorbed.

"Why don't you take this last one for yourself?" Garrett suggested.

The Conqueror needed a millisecond to process the suggestion. Once he understood what Garrett had said, he wished he had misheard.

"I don't want one." Thomas braced himself for a fight.

Garrett put his hands on his hips. "What you want," he said, "is some common sense. You're a high-value military target, and I expect the Torth Empire will start getting crafty soon. You have zero battle experience. I think it's obvious that you need round-the-clock protection."

Thomas bristled with more misgivings than he could put into words.

"Garrett," Jinishta said with disdain. "We agreed that no mind readers should own zombies."

They had agreed. A whole war council had been held, and they had all agreed that zombified Torth did not belong under the command of anyone who used to own slaves.

"We all need to be able to sleep safely." Garrett pointed to Thomas. "Remember, if we lose him, we lose the war."

How flattering.

A gulf already existed between Thomas and everyone else. Did Garrett want to exacerbate that? People mistrusted them both. One zombified body shield could easily become two or three, and then more. Thomas could end up commanding an army he didn't want. And how would he look, with an army of brain-dead minions following him around?

"I have bodyguards," Thomas pointed out. "I'm safe."

That might be a bit of an exaggeration.

Shingyu and Yanalthram resented the job of guarding Thomas. As far as the two nussians were concerned, Thomas and his lab assistants lounged about like princelings. Most soldiers believed scientists were a bunch of weaklings who chatted about esoteric matters while braver people fought and died in order to protect the Freedomland way of life.

There was some truth to that.

In any case, Thomas never complained about his council-appointed bodyguards. He pretended to be grateful. He wanted to seem weak and mostly useless. That was better than the alternative: proving to everyone just how dangerous he could be.

"*Rekvehs* have enough advantages without owning zombies," one of the warriors pointed out.

Several warriors glared at Garrett.

The old man looked ashamed, unused to criticism from his fellow warriors. He usually pulled off the swaggering, boastful attitude of an Alashani warrior—enough to be accepted as one of them, in spite of his evil power to read minds. Garrett was literally a cousin to Jinishta. He was family.

Jinishta shot the offenders a stern look, but then she fixed her glare on Garrett. "The Torth are fleeing every city we target. I do not think Thomas or you need any extra power."

Thomas added his own stare. If the old fool insisted on forcing him to own zombies, the next war council might turn into a mutiny.

"All right, all right." Garrett showed his empty palms, placating. "But we do need to discuss these matters."

"Yes," Jinishta said in a dangerous tone. "Agreed."

"In the meantime," Garrett said, "let's work on productivity." He turned to Thomas. "Do you think you can try to zombify an extra five today, boy? The warriors really could use more of them."

The Alashani turned their stares toward Thomas.

"You have a good number for now," Thomas said. "How about if you work on making the ones you have last longer?"

"We need more of them to practice on," a warrior argued.

"I have important work to do in the research annex." Thomas backed away. His excuses were weak and he knew it. "I'm researching the inhibitor and ways we can attain immunity to it. I really can't afford to spend a lot of time each day on prisoners."

He had already completed the superluminal communications network. He oversaw other projects, but science was slow.

"Meanwhile," another warrior growled, "we fight and risk our lives every day. Your zombies are disposable. But we are not."

The warrior was right.

The Twins and the Death Architect were out there, scheming. Industrious. As disabled children on the losing side of this war—for now—they were easy to underestimate, but they had all the resources of a galactic empire at their beck and call.

The people of Freedomland took Ariock's strength and victories for granted. Ariock himself took his strength for granted, growing more confident with every fresh victory. But overconfidence could prove fatal. Any supergenius knew that.

"Prisoners are just a drain on resources," Jinishta said. "As zombies, though, they serve us."

"Zombification ought to be a top priority," Garrett added. "In fact, I'm making it a command. I want you to zombify fifteen per day."

Jinishta studied Thomas. "Can you do that?"

Thomas felt trapped, unwilling to lie.

A little piece of his soul withered.

He was the evil stuff of nightmares. The Torth understood that, even if his allies did not.

"I'll try for fifteen," he said. "But no more than that."

# CHAPTER 4

# ANOTHER ORPHAN

The overcast day was far too bright for Thomas. He squinted as he floated up the ramp and out of the Mirror Prison.

*Dangerous*, one of the nussian sentries thought upon seeing him.

*Should not be allowed so much freedom*, the other sentry thought.

Thomas gave no hint that he overheard their judgments. He told himself he didn't care. Besides, he had no room to process anything extraneous.

He wanted minimal sensory input. It would be best if he could just sit alone for a few hours. In silence. And darkness.

An assistant awaited him on the boulevard. Today, his assistant was the tawny govki who used to serve him as a personal slave. Nror was pacing on all six stubby limbs. He wore a net over his furry body, the govki version of clothing. Upon seeing Thomas, Nror reared to a quadrupedal arrangement. He dusted off his hands, opened the satchel he carried, and unfolded a wide-brimmed sun hat.

"Was everything all right in there?" Nror asked.

Thomas didn't think he could be civil right now. Not even to someone who was trying to be his friend. Lately he kept waking up with a sensation that his bed was actually a heap of Torth corpses.

"Oops, let me put your hat on." Nror sped after him.

Thomas tolerated the kindness. He quelled the part of himself that insisted that he did not belong in a dusty street among inferiors *(slave species)* who made noises to communicate. His sense of superiority was superficial. It came from the lifetimes he had just absorbed.

Mostly, he just felt numb. Flattening his emotions was the only way to endure terrified victims without falling apart and weeping.

The academy was uptown, which meant uphill. Pedestrians crossed to the far side of the street upon seeing Thomas. Nror trotted by his side, keeping up a companionable stream of one-sided prattle. Thomas feigned interest by saying "hm" or "ah" at appropriate pauses.

Multistory buildings lined the earthen streets, their ground floors lined with shops and restaurants. Hovercarts whooshed up or down the central lane like cars. Passengers did double takes when they saw Thomas. He sensed their reactions. At a glance, Thomas looked like a disabled Alashani who was brave enough to use the evil technology of a hoverchair. Their moods curdled as soon as they realized that he wasn't an albino.

Thomas figured he could pass as an Alashani teenager if he tried harder. He wanted to build up his strength so he could walk unaided.

Ahead of them, a flying sky crocodile landed on the overhead barbed mesh that protected pedestrians from carnivorous megafauna. It emitted a piercing caw of pain. Instead of flapping away, the beast slipped between wires and plummeted.

It was a hatchling, merely the size of an Earth alligator. Adult sky crocs were far too big to fall through the rooftop meshwork.

"Oh!" Nror interrupted himself.

The hatchling became entangled amid clotheslines, flapping and clawing against the side of a building. It wrenched free—only to slam against the ceiling meshwork.

That sent it falling again. This time, the beast crashed into a shop sign and landed hard on the packed dirt street, scaring pedestrians.

It made another attempt to fly away. But it was too exhausted.

A nussian butcher rushed toward the tired beast with a raised cleaver, yelling threats.

Thomas figured the sky croc must have smelled the meat racks in the butchery. That explained why it had attempted to land in the first place. Nussian shopfronts were broad and open to the air.

"Uh, let's take another way home." Nror backtracked a few steps. "I would have liked to pick up a roast for tonight, but not now."

"Wait."

Thomas knew that the mob of onlookers would kill the hatchling even if the butcher did not. Sky crocs were apex predators. They looked like alien pterosaurs—sort of like dragons. They had been known to swoop down and attack people out in fields. There were rumors that a whole chain gang of penitents had been devoured by a pair of the adult predators.

And yet.

Thomas could see that this hatchling was frightened and alone. It kept trying to launch skyward, as if in search of missing parents.

Ariock had relocated all the indigenous megafauna away from the coastal city, but sometimes sky crocs found their way back. Local animals had yet to learn to avoid people with guns. Soldiers and transport pilots tended to shoot wildlife as a means of target practice.

A well-cared-for hatchling would not have ventured into city airspace. Only a starved animal would take major risks.

This beast was clearly too young to catch prey on its own. It looked scrawny.

Sky crocs formed close family units. Its parents would have attempted a rescue if they were alive.

"Excuse me." Thomas floated into the crowd. "Will you let me through?"

The reactions ranged from *!!!* surprised to fearful. People would shuffle aside for a shani warrior, but they leaped out of Thomas's way. No one wanted to be within his range of telepathy.

Their fear and resentment distorted the atmosphere like heat waves. Thomas saw himself reflected in their minds. Unlike his victims in the prison, these people viewed him as terrifyingly ordinary. He wore drab woolens. His face was shaded by a hat that any typical albino would wear. Many people wished he looked more monstrous just so they could more easily steer clear of him.

"Thomas, what are you doing?" Nror scurried to catch up.

"Don't!" Thomas yelled at the butcher.

The nussian paused, one immense arm raised with a cleaver. The blade was large enough to slice through the hatchling's long neck.

"What is your objection?" the butcher rumbled.

The hatchling fluttered its black wings. Its glossy black scales rippled.

"Let the injured animal live," Thomas said.

The butcher goggled as though he'd heard only gibberish. "I don't understand. We can't let a deadly beast roam free in the streets." He launched into a long explanation, defending the good people of Freedomland, his shop's reputation, and the fact that sky crocs were good for nothing. Besides, the animal was injured and orphaned. It would die anyway.

All very good reasons for killing it.

"Please." Thomas held out his hand. "Let the animal go. I'll guarantee that it will stay away from your shop, and it won't bother you again. Can I buy a family-size cut of sauropod steak? You can scan my credit code."

Thomas held out his wristwatch. Much of the city had shifted to a currency system of legal tender war credits, enabled by trust in the current leadership.

Disbelief surrounded him.

Thomas was painfully aware that he did not have any logical, rational reason for aiding a wild predator. Some of the surrounding people guessed he wanted to torture the hatchling. Some feared that he would zombify it, then use it to wreak havoc on anyone who defied him.

On top of stoking unwanted rumors, Thomas wasn't sure he could actually help an orphaned beast. Could he even trust the animal not to bite his head off? Its toothy, scissorlike jaws would easily fit around his head. It could swallow an adolescent boy like Thomas in four or five shakes of its long, powerful throat.

But it was shivering with pain and exhaustion.

The hatchling lay in the dirt, too weak to fight, cocking its head to glimpse the faraway sky.

Thomas sensed its yearning. The hatchling awaited a rescue that would never come.

He knew exactly what it was going through.

He knew—not just from absorbed knowledge, but from bitter, firsthand experience. Thomas was an orphan, too. He had been alone and trapped amid strangers on Earth. He had waited desperately for his birth mother and father to show up and rescue him.

They had never come. Nor would they ever come.

He was alone, neither human nor Torth. He was like this sky croc hatchling: neither crocodile nor pterosaur, but reviled by everyone.

Thomas was not going to turn his back on an orphan like himself. Wild creature or not, he could at least offer the animal something other than hatred.

"One salted family-size roast." The butcher offered a ham-size cut of meat rolled in protective layers of burlap. He eyed Thomas's weak arm with skepticism.

"I can't lift that," Thomas admitted. "Will you please put it in the compartment on the back of my chair?"

"Sure." The butcher loaded the ham onto Thomas's hoverchair, all the while emanating incredulity and a perverse sense of anticipation. He wanted to see what the *rekveh* would do with a wild predator.

The whole crowd wanted to see. They stood back, watching.

"You want us to just . . ." The butcher looked pained by his own doubts. "Let the animal go?"

"Yes," Thomas said. "Please."

While the butcher backed away, Thomas hovered farther into range of the hatchling sky croc. Not that he particularly wanted to absorb yet another lifetime . . . but if he was going to attempt to befriend this thing, then he needed to understand the way its alien mind worked.

He drilled down into its core.

He went beyond its fog of fear and pain and found the things it loved. Like the freedom of flight. Days full of wonder. Sailing on thermal currents.

Food, of course. It preferred soft, slow prey. It had the instincts of a raptor.

And curiosity, too, like that of a wolf pup. It was primed to learn.

The hatchling's life was simple and light, like a refreshing dessert after the serious heaviness of all the Servants of All and Rosy Recruits. Thomas was surprised to find that he enjoyed it.

"Come to me." Thomas offered words in the slave tongue, then followed that up with a hissing, clicking sound, similar to a croon made by the hatchling's parents.

Onlookers stared. To them, Thomas had uttered a bestial, alien sound.

The baby sky croc snaked its neck and flapped its leathery wings. It scissored its long, beaklike snout, displaying sharklike teeth in a terrifyingly hungry grin.

Thomas sensed the sky croc size him up as possible prey.

He held his ground and met the gaze of the animal. A prey animal would back away or flee. Instead, Thomas invited it to observe how he floated on air.

He rotated his hoverchair, offering the food. He emitted the inviting click-hiss sound, and repeated, "Come to me."

"He's crazy," someone in the crowd said.

Perhaps they were right. Thomas didn't like having his back to the hatchling. Especially when he heard it launch into the air.

It landed heavily on the back of his hoverchair, the way it might cling to its mother or father.

Thomas did not turn around, but he kept an eye on the hatchling through the visual perceptions of the butcher, who stood within his range. The beak was very close to his head.

The hatchling tore into the ham, swallowing the meat whole and leaving the burlap empty.

Thomas prepared to use wildfire just in case he needed to defend himself from the enormous toothy maw.

But he sensed that the hatchling was no longer hungry. Now it only wanted to feel safe and cared for.

Only Thomas could sense that. No one else.

He click-hissed and loosened his arms. That made his body into a nestlike shape.

Onlookers gaped in shock when the hatchling crawled over the hoverchair's backrest and folded itself across Thomas's lap.

Instead of snapping his head off, or stabbing him to death, it folded its wings and neck. Most of its weight rested on the armrests. It was being gentle, careful not to crush the being that it now regarded as a surrogate parent.

Perhaps Naglitay or Vy would be willing to wrap the animal's wounds with herbal poultices and pain-killing drugs? Thomas would refrain from asking Ariock or Evenjos for the favor of healing. They were always busy, and they might not approve of his new friend.

Besides, he did not want to fuel rumors that he forced the most powerful people in the universe to do his bidding.

"What are you doing with that beast?" Nror asked. "It's a dangerous wild animal."

Disturbed by Nror's tone, the sky croc uncoiled its long neck. The govki leaped back.

Thomas smoothed the shimmery black scales. Contentment radiated from the animal, and it folded back into a sleepy position.

Nror was right, of course. Adult sky crocs were larger than most transports. This animal's jaws would grow to more than twelve feet long.

Thomas figured he could teach it what meals to avoid—people—and then release it back into the wild.

Or . . .

Well, Thomas had secretly toyed with the idea of experimenting with brainwashing. A mild form of compulsion should be possible, according to the ancient knowledge he had soaked up from Evenjos. Zombification was fifth-magnitude telepathy. That meant Thomas was also capable of fourth magnitude. He should be able to lightly brainwash victims without completely destroying their free will and individuality forever.

*Not this animal*, Thomas decided.

"I might train it," he told Nror.

A gigantic, dragon-like predator wasn't a suitable pet . . . except, well, Thomas could detect its intentions before it acted. He felt sure that he, of all people, was perfectly suited to raising a monster.

He knew how its alien mind worked.

He was a monster himself.

# CHAPTER 5

# AN AGE OF WAR

Ariock awoke in a palatial bedchamber. Glowing orbs and panels of sea glass softened the black granite walls. Curtains billowed around the veranda, delicate gauze bordered by silver and gold thread. The intricate embroidery matched the starbursts and wheeling spirals and shock waves that decorated Ariock's armor, depicted in diamonds. Cherise had designed his signature galactic theme.

A pleasing fragrance completed the atmosphere. Vy had ordered custom aromatherapy oils for the lamps, with an approximation of fresh pine, plus a hint of ozone after a thunderstorm.

Ariock stretched on the enormous bed he had put together with his powers.

Someone stirred beside him.

Ariock's eyes widened in surprise. He saw a feminine waist and hip in his peripheral vision, as nude as he was.

This was a first.

Vy had her own suite across the hall. Whenever she visited Ariock, she was always dressed. She owned satiny pajamas that barely clung to her curves. The skimpy outfits exposed her thighs and some midriff and cleavage, but that was supposedly what upstanding Alashani ladies wore to bed.

And if Ariock tried to remove the pajamas?

She'd only laughed softly. *"No. I'm not giving you easy access."*

She was not ready for sex. She would cuddle with Ariock, and she would kiss him, and she might move with pleasure when he touched her, if she was in the right mood. Yet she would leave if Ariock got anywhere near insistent.

*"I won't do anything you're uncomfortable with,"* Ariock had told her, more than once. But he wasn't sure he could even believe his own comforting words. How could he guarantee safety? Any intense emotion triggered his powers. His control was tenuous and they both knew it.

Safety was best. But . . .

Maybe now?

Ariock rolled onto his side and covered her hip with one huge hand.

When she cuddled into his warmth, he moved his hand, stroking. Down her naked leg.

She laughed softly with pleasure, inviting him to keep going.

Ariock's throat tightened in anticipation. Another part of him swelled, tightening in another way. He could hardly believe his good luck.

His caressing hand brushed a shapely calf . . .

Which did not feel like her prosthetic.

He froze.

The woman next to him raised herself up on one elbow, her purple hair a cascade around her face. Her expression was sultry and utterly devoid of Vy's kindness.

Ariock leaped off the bed. He grabbed a satin sheet and held it over his waist, hiding his arousal, which was fast wilting.

Evenjos emitted a throaty laugh.

"Why—? What—?" Ariock looked around. "Where is Vy? Is she okay?"

Evenjos shoved the last of the sheets away. She was stark naked, her bodily proportions verging somewhere between real and impossible. Her enormous, sensually curved wings shone like blades dipped in syrup.

"Your Violet Hollander is not very accommodating for you." Evenjos said that in the most judgmental way possible. "She is attending to errands or something." She waved one languid hand at the archway.

Ariock remembered visiting Vy last night. They had talked halfway until morning, and then he had tucked her into her bed and gone to his own suite.

And then? Evenjos must have lurked in his bedchamber, unseen, her incorporeal dust unaffected by the ocean breeze. Spying on him while he slept.

Was this what Evenjos did between healing injured soldiers?

Instead of learning how to dismantle warships in space, or getting to know warrior captains, she was wasting time, invading Ariock's private life.

"Get out." Ariock was torn between glaring at Evenjos and averting his gaze. She looked like a naked goddess on his bed.

He reminded himself that she was all artifice. Her true form was corpse dust.

Evenjos nestled deeper into the pillows, making her body a soft invitation.

Ariock turned away with a growl of disgust. He had given Evenjos multiple hints that he was uninterested in having a vain shapeshifter as a partner, even as a friend. She refused to take a hint.

Maybe it was time to be more direct. That was what Vy suggested.

And Vy was right. Ariock's soldiers needed heroes they could respect. Evenjos had yet to prove herself worthy. The Yeresunsa warriors whispered that she was a coward. The regular troops barely knew that she existed.

"We have a busy day today." Ariock used his powers to twist warm water out of the adjacent bath spa. "We're planning to take over three major cities. I want us to fully take control of Umdalkdul within this month."

He dropped the sheet and used his powers to splash his naked body. He used several bars of soap and washcloths to clean himself as efficiently and fast as possible.

"Are you going to bother to come along and help?" he asked Evenjos.

She looked frustrated.

Ariock rinsed. He sent the used water outside, across the veranda and upward, where he dissipated it across the sky, adding to the morning clouds.

At the same time, he connected to the folded underclothes that one of his valets had prepared. Using his powers, he pulled those on in a few seconds.

"You're not welcome in my private suite," Ariock said. "Do you have something to tell me? If not, then get out."

Evenjos sat up. She lingered, like she wanted to say something.

It had better be an apology.

Ariock held out his bulky arms and caused armored pieces to fly into place, fastening onto each part of his body. He didn't particularly like having so many mirrors around, but they were advised by Thomas. Apparently, mirrors warded off clairvoyants. Ariock had tested that theory, and it was legit. For some reason, mirrors confounded his disembodied self when he was in a ghostly state.

He couldn't ghost into a star, or a black hole, or a temporal stream, either. Something about the effects of refraction or bent light made it impossible.

So he could not directly teleport into his own bedchamber. He had to appear on the veranda, or else walk in like a normal person.

It was a good security measure. Even so, Ariock felt self-conscious with so many mirrored angles showing his reflection. He could not avoid seeing how dangerous he looked, especially in his spiky, thorny battle armor. He looked like someone who might crush a normal-size person by accident.

Was it any wonder that Vy wanted to escape whenever he got carried away with lust?

Was he crazy to think she would ever feel comfortable with him?

Maybe that was a question he should bring up to someone wiser than he was. Except he didn't feel comfortable asking Thomas. Or Garrett. He didn't even want to ask Kessa.

His relationship with Vy was no one else's business. He didn't want friends and soldiers judging his personal life, or getting intrusive with Vy, or putting pressure on her to "loosen up" or behave in a certain way. Nor did he want to deal with awkward questions or rude insinuations. Interference like that would take away from his focus in battles.

"I don't know what you plan to do all day," Ariock said to Evenjos. He tested his armor's integrity, making sure he could make fists and move his fingers independently. "But I never want to catch you in my bedchamber again."

He strode out toward the veranda.

"Why do you hate me?" Evenjos begged.

She must have become a cloud, then re-formed, clad in a snug, sparkly dress and clinging to his arm. That was her way of moving fast.

"I don't hate you." Ariock pulled out of her grip. He normally wanted to avoid provoking Evenjos, or confronting her. But she kept misinterpreting his lack of interest.

Was it because she wasn't very good at mind reading?

Or did he need to be less polite and more direct?

"I don't want you." Ariock stated it firmly, leaving no room for misinterpretation. "I am not attracted to shallow, self-absorbed divas. I value people who want to accomplish what I want—winning battles against the Torth."

Evenjos looked as if her soul was crushed.

Guiltily, Ariock recalled that Evenjos was a victim of torture. She had suffered more than anyone in the universe. She was powerful, but there was a delicateness about her.

Maybe Evenjos had not realized that she was crossing a boundary when she spied on Ariock? Or when she tempted him by lying naked in his bed?

He was probably expecting too much from the deposed goddess-empress. She deserved pity.

"I'm sorry," Ariock said.

He turned away and used his powers to summon one of his favorite proximity weapons. The double-headed battle-ax slammed into his waiting grasp.

He had designed the weapon himself. Its ionic blades could slice through Torth armor and bone, and the weight of the weapon ensured that few Torth could lift it, let alone swing it. Its size and shape made it perfect for energy enhancements, offering Ariock trajectory lines for his extended awareness. He had learned that he was even more deadly with such a weapon. No Torth could stand against him.

"Can I do anything to please you?" Evenjos asked. "Other than battle. You know that is deadly for me. If I put myself in the path of the inhibitor . . ." She sounded ragged, older than her youthful face implied. "I am dead."

Ariock thought of all the times he had taken deadly risks.

He thought of his best warriors and soldiers. Jinishta. Weptolyso. Nethroko. Garrett, of course. In addition to those friends, he had other favorites—exceptionally fierce fighters who would face danger with the odds stacked against them in order to score another victory against the Torth Empire. He particularly liked Guradjur and Zenzaldal and Choonhulm.

People like that did not waste time simpering.

They were not obsessed with their own personal safety.

They took the time to get to know their fellow soldiers, because that was vital. They understood that the freedom of the galaxy was at stake. They did not have to be lectured about why winning every battle was so important.

Evenjos trotted closer, as if hoping Ariock might bend down and kiss her. "I want to serve you, Ariock Dovanack." Her voice was a seductive whisper. "Please, tell me your heart's desire."

So fake.

Ariock stepped back. "You come from a different era." He searched for a way to make his point with kindness and diplomacy. "You're from a time of royal balls. The people you knew were less violent than the people of today. They were polite." He reconsidered. "Well, I guess they made a show of being polite, anyway."

Evenjos had told Ariock that the Yeresunsa of her era never got their hands dirty. They had worn gowns adorned with gemstones. If they had scars, they hid them. And if they were violent, they would never dare admit it around their fellow nobles.

"Maybe someday," Ariock said, "we'll have an era like that again. But for now?" He hefted his battle-ax. "This is an age of war."

He needed serious warriors. Not prissy empresses who played games in palaces.

"If you refuse to devote yourself to this cause? Then stop bothering me."

Ariock stepped up onto the stone balustrade, towering over Evenjos for a moment. Then he walked off the veranda and connected with the wind. His army was assembling on the teleportation flats in preparation for another day of battle.

# CHAPTER 6
# DYNASTIC

Evenjos condensed into her phoenix form and flew up into the crisp morning air. She soared past cottony puffs of clouds, climbing away from Ariock's city, stretching toward the banded sphere that dominated the sky of this planet.

She would gladly fight battles. But only if someone valued her. Only if someone cared about her.

Of all the people in the universe, Ariock ought to value her as more than a mere soldier. They were special! Did Ariock truly believe they were nothing but weapons to be used up and thrown away? Didn't he understand that elite individuals such as themselves should not have to work until they broke or died?

Perhaps ongoing loneliness was Evenjos's penance for ignoring the warnings of Ah Jun all those millennia ago.

She felt as if she was sealed inside that pitch-black tomb, neglected for a duration that could only be described as eternity. Could she escape the gnawing emptiness inside herself if she rocketed to another galaxy?

Let Ah Jun rot. Let her prophecies go unfulfilled.

Let Ariock fail in his futile war. She ought to reject him the way he had rejected her. Except . . .

Evenjos still cared for Thomas. He was her friend. She wanted him to win.

And she supposed she did owe her help to all the people of this brutish era. She owed a debt to the entire galactic population for her part in enabling the Torth Empire to rise.

Evenjos dipped her wing through a cloud and thought about brutality.

Ariock had made a good point, as painful as it was to hear. She kept thinking in terms of the people she used to know. But Ariock and his warriors were not the types to lounge on divans and bicker about high fashion. Ariock did not see himself as a god-emperor. If he feared the inhibitor, he faced it anyway, just like his soldiers did. He saw himself not as a royal, but as a soldier with a job to do.

Perhaps Evenjos needed to adjust to a new paradigm.

She arced in a new direction, heading toward the grassy series of plateaus that everyone called the teleportation flats. She didn't care what the soldiers thought of her, but she really wanted Ariock's respect.

Hovercarts bused soldiers through narrow streets, past decorative archways lit by lanterns. The flats themselves were unadorned. Fluffy clouds reared like the tropical mountains. Beneath the colorful sky, the eighty thousand soldiers looked grim.

Evenjos would have chosen a more lighthearted color scheme for the army.

But she understood that black represented the opposite of oversaturated Torth decadence. Black was the traditional garb of Alashani warriors. It was the color of their ruined homeworld, and the eternal night where they had hidden from the Torth Empire during all the time that Evenjos had been imprisoned. Black represented freedom.

Ariock loomed in the center of the orderly, square formations of soldiers. When he raised his immense battle-ax high above his head, soldiers cheered. They yelled as if they could not contain their pride.

"We are going to take Ambient City!" Ariock said, his voice booming. "Happenstance City! And Treatise MetroHub!"

He outlined the battle plan Thomas had given him. Advance teams had already infiltrated the target cities, spreading rumors about freedom and rigging an intercom system.

Choonhulm was in charge of sneak operations. That unit was all former slaves. Armed with blaster gloves, they were ready to disable the powers of any Rosy or Servant. The Torth were so used to overlooking ummins, govki, and other slave species, they rarely saw a covert soldier until it was too late.

The regular soldiers worked themselves up while arranging themselves into square formations. Squares enabled Ariock to mass-teleport the army more easily.

Evenjos soared past the rear of one quadrant, where nussians blocked her from Ariock's line of sight. She landed unobtrusively and resumed her default winged-goddess form.

Heads turned to watch her. Everyone recognized her metallic wings and purple hair.

The Torth had already evacuated much of Umdalkdul. They were even fleeing the moon bases. Their overworked supergeniuses were desperately trying to invent something now, now, now. What were the chances that they would slam Evenjos with their deadly inhibitor?

She might never get a more opportune time to prove herself in battle.

The Megacosm made all the difference in intergalactic power dynamics. Evenjos had not feared the spacefaring Jodinak civilization during her reign, despite their greater level of technology, because their use of temporal streams had been limited. They could not have coordinated a war from so far away.

Now Thomas was inventing superluminal communications technology. The galaxy would soon be knitted together in new and frightening ways.

This war could only escalate.

The next planetary conquest would be more of a challenge. The planet after that would be worse.

Some of the soldiers gave Evenjos disdainful looks. She tried to ignore them, but she wanted to scream in their faces. Would they be so self-righteous if they risked collapsing into an inert pile of dust for the rest of eternity?

Well. Perhaps they did take risks like that.

Maybe she should mindlessly follow orders like they did? Maybe she should pretend to be as worthless as they saw themselves?

"Your Highness!" Garrett called.

He approached, leaning on his silver walking staff. His crooked leg gave him a limping gait. "Will you do me the honor of walking with me, Your Eminence?"

Garrett Dovanack knew the right honorifics to use for an empress. His royal etiquette was like a breath of refreshing cleanliness in a zoo filled with wild brutes. Dressed in his polished armor, he looked impressively gallant.

Yet Evenjos shook her head in refusal.

She did not trust this crafty old mind reader. After all, if the common soldiers disdained her, then Garrett must be even more keenly aware of her low status here. His flattery was all false. He simply wanted to use her power, like so many other people.

"Please." Garrett offered his arm. "I would like to chat with you about my great-grandson."

Ariock.

It was the only topic that Evenjos might wish to discuss.

She offered the barest hint of a nod in acquiescence. Garrett must be baiting her, but she would stay on guard.

"I'm pleased you're here." Garrett indicated the gathering army. "You are very brave to consider joining us in battle. I understand the potential cost to you."

He spoke in her archaic language, protecting her from the shame of being overheard.

Evenjos scanned his mood for any hint of ridicule, but there was none. Garrett was showing her a rare glimpse of honesty.

"I am uncertain if I can show up every time," Evenjos admitted.

"Of course." Garrett spread his armored hands in a gesture of acceptance. "Look, I have an idea. Why don't you stay aboard an armored transport? That way, you can pick up soldiers who need healing while staying safe from the inhibitor yourself."

The notion appealed to Evenjos. Hidden like that, she would likely be safe during the battles.

But Ariock would judge her a coward.

If she remained safe on Reject-20, as she had been doing, she could excuse herself by saying that she was protecting and bolstering the city. She was always busy healing people in the local hospitals.

"You are not a coward," Garrett said. "And really, anyone who thinks that is a fool. I include my great-grandson in that statement."

At least Garrett wasn't full of sneering disdain, like the common soldiers. And like Ariock. But why did Garrett care so ardently about her safety?

He must have Ah Jun's prophecies memorized. He was probably trying to steer Evenjos toward a specific destiny, or something along those lines.

She shivered in disgust and walked onward.

"I'm not trying to manipulate you." Garrett sounded frustrated. "You've endured worse suffering than anyone in this galaxy has the capacity to imagine. I'm aware of that, even if nobody else is. I'm aware that no one has earned the right to tell you what you should or shouldn't fear. Or what risks you should or should not take."

Evenjos stopped. He really did sound as if he cared about her, the way no one else in this era did—except, perhaps, for Thomas. Was it possible?

Garrett radiated sincerity. It was as fragrant as the pipes he liked to smoke.

"You're not a coward." He sounded certain. "The inhibitor won't be a problem forever, you know. The boy is working on an antidote. Once we have that?" He shuffled closer. "You and I, and Ariock, will be invincible."

And safe.

Evenjos studied the elderly man, trying to discern his motives. Was he sympathetic to her plight? If so, why?

Garrett was a lot like Ariock. Both of the Dovanacks regularly slashed their way through cities full of Torth who might destroy them with a microdart. They took huge risks every day.

Evenjos no longer believed that either Dovanack respected her.

Why should they? Even the lowliest soldier was braver than Evenjos. She looked down in shame.

"Your Highness," Garrett said. "I have seen you fight fearlessly. Ariock might have forgotten. But I was there, too." He looked at her with helpless admiration. "When you're angry, you are a sight to behold."

As if monstrosity was something to value.

Unthinking rage was inexcusable in a Yeresunsa, especially in one as powerful as herself. Evenjos had emerged from her imprisonment with all the pent-up rage and anguish of millennia. She had no wish to transform into a deadly behemoth ever again.

She gave Garrett a stern glare of disapproval. If he wanted her to go berserk with suffering, then he did not care about her at all. Nor did he care about the deadly blunders she would make in that uncontrolled state.

If he admired the powerful monster instead of the sorrowful woman, then he admired the wrong thing.

Garrett must have sensed her thoughts, because he looked alarmed. "No," he said. "I don't want you to lose yourself in rage. I understand what that's like. And I would never wish it on anyone."

He emanated regret as well as shame.

Evenjos realized that Garrett must have done something. He had blundered with his powers, perhaps in a similar way. He had caused trouble. Perhaps he had harmed or killed innocent bystanders?

As had Ariock.

Evenjos had doubts that Ariock had accidentally killed his own mother, though. He tended to take more blame than was warranted. He even blamed himself for catastrophes he had not directly caused, such as the destruction of the Torth Homeworld. He blamed himself for Vy's amputated leg. He seemed halfway willing to blame himself for every slave who suffered at Torth hands. He was determined to save the universe—and he had turned the war into a personal matter.

"Ariock understands power." Garrett's shoulders slumped. "He is far more self-aware than I was at his age. His way of thinking might be self-destructive, but it also ensures that he is careful. It keeps the people around him safe."

Evenjos supposed there was something to that. If she had been as cautious and as guilty as Ariock, perhaps she would have been a more competent empress.

"Ordinary people believe that wielding power is easy," Garrett said. "But power amplifies every action we take. I think we live with larger heartaches than most people. Our joyous moments might be intense, but our griefs and regrets are multiple times worse."

The conversation reminded Evenjos of strolling through the crystal gardens, when she had discussed philosophy or epistemology with a peer or two. Garrett would have felt at home among the royalty of her era, just as easily as he waged urban battles in today's war. He truly was a remarkable man.

Sorrow was etched into his wrinkled face. When Garrett spoke of grief and regret and the dangers of power, it seemed personal.

"Who did you hurt?" Evenjos made a guess. "Was it your wife? Or your daughter?"

Garrett turned away. *Both.*

He emanated so much pained guilt, Evenjos felt her own buried guilts stir up. She had watched her top adviser starve to death. She hadn't been able to do anything to help him, chained to that throne in the prison of mirrors.

Evenjos had stayed young and beautiful while her brothers grew old and died. She had outlived better people than herself. That entailed its own guilt.

"I used to be so afraid of drawing attention to myself," Garrett said, "I failed to learn real control over my powers. You once expressed disgust that I am self-taught. Well, you are right. I needed a teacher. But even so, that's no excuse for the accident I caused."

Evenjos did not ask for a confession. She did not need to learn the exact details of what Garrett had done to his wife, or how his daughter had reacted, or the fallout. Whatever had happened, it had clearly been an accident.

Garrett was carrying a lot of guilt—perhaps even more than Ariock carried.

And she sensed an unspoken question. Was Garrett seeking absolution? Or did he want lessons on the finer points of self-control?

"I am not a teacher," Evenjos reminded him.

Garrett looked disappointed.

"No Yeresunsa has perfect control," Evenjos admitted. "That is a truth the Yeresunsa Order did not advertise. But it is a truth nonetheless."

Throughout the flats, soldiers rushed to finalize their square troop formations. They straightened, chests puffed out.

Ariock levitated, excess focus rolling off him in snapping crackles of electricity. He gave a final round of instructions, his heavy voice amplified by power. Soldiers pumped their fists in the air.

"The people of this era try to blur the line between royalty and commoner," Evenjos observed. "But this is dangerous."

In her time, no one except Unyat had tried to blur hereditary lines. Most people had known better. They had known that if royals and peasants intermarried, it would entail vast power differentials within families. There would be husbands with frightening power over their wives, or vice versa. Royal children would accidentally destroy their powerless parents. Such imbalance would unravel the very fabric of civilization. It was abominable.

That was why royals married royals and commoners married commoners. That was how it should be.

"I know." Garrett spoke with quiet pain.

She looked at him, wondering.

"I married a commoner," Garrett said. "So to speak. I married someone whose power was vastly different than my own."

And he regretted it. That was clear, judging by the sorrow that suffused his mind. He had accidentally hurt his commoner wife.

Perhaps he had even killed her by accident.

Tentative, Evenjos reached for Garrett's grizzled cheek. She stroked his face, exploring the craggy, sorrowful depths.

It was comforting to know that a brute of this era could accept the price of power: the bitterness of inequity. This man was not the thug she had assumed him to be. Not at all.

Evenjos imagined Ariock, titanic and afraid of nothing, wielding that ax in battle, and then pretending to be meek and mundane for his human girlfriend.

What a hopeless fool.

Maybe Evenjos ought to seek love from someone wiser?

Garrett was more seasoned with life experiences. He was closer to her own biological age. Although he lacked the astronomical raw strength of Ariock, he was powerful enough, and noble enough in spirit, to match any royal from her era. He had the impressive Dovanack boldness. Yet his boldness was tempered with attractive, hard-won caution.

"I, too, loved a commoner." Evenjos trembled, admitting one of her secret shames out loud. "I outlived him. He died."

That secret love affair was not the sort of thing she would have admitted to her peers. But in Garrett's company, Evenjos felt as if she was speaking with a friend. She wanted to get to know him better.

"I'm sorry." Garrett grasped her hand.

Evenjos sensed a yearning in his mind that echoed her own. He yearned to remove his armored glove so he could caress her skin.

Instead, he let go of her hand and said, "I know how much you care about Ariock." His chuckle was regretful.

A ghost lingered in his mind. Garrett was determined to remain devoted to that ghost of his wife, no matter what, as if he owed her his love even beyond the grave. Garrett still loved that commoner.

Evenjos stepped back, frustrated. Were all Dovanack men fools in the same way? Commoners were just fragile creatures. Commoners died easily. How could they be worthy of the love of someone with majestic powers?

Well, she used to be just as delusional.

Evenjos swept aside the ache in her heart, or she tried to. She never should have allowed herself to fall in love with someone so fragile, so mortal. He had died eons ago. Yet the ache of missing him never ended.

"I understand," Garrett said, responding to her thoughts. "Perfectly."

Evenjos swallowed a lump in her throat. Garrett truly did understand. She sensed that he was damaged in the same way she was.

"That is why I know Ariock needs you," Garrett said.

Ah. So here it was. Garrett had probably seen a prophecy, maybe something along the lines of Transformation saving Strength. He had no interest in Evenjos for her own sake. He just wanted—

"You misunderstand," Garrett said. "Evenjos, I'm not talking about the prophecies right now. I am talking about dynasty." He grasped her shoulders, gentle with his armored hands. "You and Ariock are made for each other. You can't hurt each other. You can found a new civilization—one where Yeresunsa rule, the way they did in your time."

Ah. How tempting.

Ariock could only be dragged down by a powerless commoner such as Vy. He deserved someone who was in his league of power and strength.

"He will come to his senses." Garrett stepped closer, as though he couldn't help gazing into her lavender eyes. "I mean, look at you." He gestured up and down. "Not only are you a goddess with superpowers and the most perfect sense of beauty I've ever seen, but you care deeply about justice. You're the avatar of Transformation. Any man who rejects you is a complete moron."

He emanated so much admiring certainty, Evenjos could not help but smile.

Her pleasure was tinged with bitterness, though. Garrett and Ariock had both rejected her. Did that make them both morons?

"I've chosen loneliness," Garrett said. "I don't have room in my heart for . . ." He clenched a fist over his chest. "Look, I'm an old man. I don't have much of a future left. My death is preordained."

Evenjos studied him, wondering how true that was.

"But Ariock?" Garrett went on. "He's founding an empire. He has a future, and he needs help from you."

Evenjos sensed Garrett's enormous love and concern for his great-grandson. It seemed he had repurposed all the love he used to feel for his family and channeled it toward his sole heir.

That was honorable, in a way. Royal families did that sort of thing. Garrett was trying to secure a legacy.

Evenjos flexed her wings and thickened her dress from gossamer to armor. She could not bear children for Ariock, but she thought that Garrett was correct, in terms of what his great-grandson needed. Ariock should learn a thing or two about ruling planets. She could act as his tutor.

And perhaps Ariock could stand to learn a few other things. Such as the fact that a breakable commoner was not a suitable love interest for someone with cosmic power.

"That's right." Garrett's gaze lingered on Evenjos with approval. "You're perfect." He seemed to realize there might be room for misunderstanding, and clarified. "For Ariock."

# CHAPTER 7

# MUSHY MALCONTENT

Flen loosened his blood-spattered armor, trying to look less like a thuggish warrior and more like a pleasant man. That wasn't easy to do these days.

Maybe that was why Cherise wanted to spend all day teaching rather than put her arms around him?

She seemed to believe her frivolous lessons were just as important as killing Torth. Her students were even more mystifying. Liberated slaves could mate or party without repercussions . . . and instead, they wanted to sit around and practice reading and writing?

It was so boring!

Well, they were aliens. At least shani showed more common sense.

"Hey, war hero!" a flirty maiden called to Flen from a balcony. "This decanter is too fizzy for us to finish alone."

Her companion giggled. "Want to join us?"

The first one shrieked and gave her a slap on her bared shoulder.

Flen paused, shielding his eyes from the sun with one hand. He ought to go home and have his reedy old chambermaid bathe him and dress him in clean clothes. Tall buildings kept the streets in shadow, but even so, Flen disliked the huge, bright sky. Skies like this could burn one's skin.

"I'm heading home," Flen called back.

Even so, he hesitated. Not that he would betray Cherise—he had pledged himself to her, with a candlelight ceremony that he wished his parents and sister could have attended—but he had plans to go to the Mushy Grove Tavern after sundown.

Perhaps one casual drink beforehand would not hurt?

The maidens on the balcony wore big, fashionable hats to ward off the sunlight. They were as pale and as plump as mushrooms.

Sometimes Flen wondered if he had made a mistake in promising himself to an exotic angel from Earth, instead of an upper-class Alashani maiden. Sometimes he had second thoughts about Cherise.

The ladies upstairs were likely insipid and dull. Most people seemed that way to Flen. But at least they would be fully comprehensible to him. They would speak his language. They might even agree with his particular views about the war, and about what should be done with *rekvehs*. Cherise only got quiet and refused to talk about such matters.

He decided to check out the bar on the ground floor, just to see if he recognized anyone.

"Welcome to the Extra Notch." The bouncer, a nussian, snorted and lowered his head in a sign of deference. "We do not charge war heroes at this fine establishment."

Flen stopped cold in his tracks. Why had this tavern hired someone who wasn't even a proper Alashani type of nussian?

The alien's accent made it plain he came from one of the newly liberated cities of Umdalkdul. He likely knew nothing about Alashani cultural values, despite working deep in a neighborhood full of albinos.

If this establishment was willing to hire non-Alashani, then they probably served fusion cuisine. Ugh. Flen was simply not in the mood for alien flavors. He had to consume fruit salads and stringy white meat for his meals between battles. When he came home—or to this approximation of what home used to be—he wanted comfort food. He wanted fungus and cave fish. Why else would he stay within the borders of the main Alashani district?

"I just remembered something important I forgot to do," Flen said politely. "Perhaps I will visit later. Thank you."

He left.

The Mushy Grove, at least, adhered to unspoken rules in favor of Alashani purity. There were no aliens—former slaves or otherwise—in the tavern that Flen favored. If anyone entered who did not belong, a whisper network brought out the bouncers, and they would politely usher out the intruder.

Flen went home first. He took care of personal hygiene with help from the old woman who used to be among his family's household staff. He did not use his powers. After a battle in which he had killed two Torth and helped to collar more than five hundred of them, he wanted to be careful about depletion. His powers needed a chance to recover so he could be fresh for yet another battle tomorrow.

And the day after that.

And the day after that.

With his hair trimmed and his skin clean, he left the war-fortress complex. He slouched through narrow streets, ignoring the creepily silent vehicles known as hovercarts. His frock coat was dark purple, matching the hue of his Yeresunsa mantle. People offered respectful greetings. Flen responded with rote politeness.

At least the people of this neighborhood understood what he was. Newly liberated slaves sometimes mistook him for a Torth, or some kind of strange Torth-like alien. They were never aware of how insulting that was.

The Mushy Grove Tavern evoked underground neighborhoods that no longer existed. Salt-rock columns divided the counters into sections. Hammered gold plates and trickling waterfalls reflected a wide array of flickering lamps and chandeliers that dripped with silver and gold. The multiple bar counters and shelves were illuminated by lamps carved to approximate the gills of mushrooms.

Flen took his usual place on a barstool along the counter at the far back wall.

"Your usual, Flen?" The bartender, a matronly lady in traditional aprons, slid a mug his way.

"Thanks." Flen appreciated a tall, fizzy ale, even if it was brewed from the substandard mushrooms farmed on Reject-20. Its cap of foam puffed outward.

He tried not to think about *rekvehs* harvesting the fungus he liked, touching it with their evil, stinking hands.

Jobs like that still needed to get done. If only the overseers would get brave enough to simply shoot all the penitents and replace them with a more wholesome labor force of former slaves and low-class albinos.

No one was that brave.

Flen sampled his drink's foam, pondering his own paradoxical courage as a war hero weighed against his utter lack of courage when it came to speaking up to Jinishta, or any of the battle leaders.

"I'm glad you are still finding your way here, Flen." That mellifluous voice belonged to Councilor Yarl.

Like everyone, Yarl had lost his wealth in the destruction of the Alashani homeworld. Unlike many of them, Yarl had regained some of his former riches by forging deals with friends of Kessa and various mayors and merchants. He had a knack for figuring out who needed what and how best to provide it.

Yarl was easy to underestimate since he lacked Yeresunsa powers. But Flen thought Yarl could read the currents that underlaid society.

"Word is," Yarl said, "our forces liberated TriSolstice City today." He studied Flen. "Another easy victory?"

"Easy," Flen said darkly.

Nothing in battle was as easy as it sounded in summary. One careless moment and a warrior might get stung with an inhibitor microdart. Flen had to keep his awareness expanded constantly while in enemy territory. One could never be careful enough, even around liberated slaves.

That much wariness was draining. Only here, in his home district, could Flen finally relax and feel almost as normal as he used to feel.

"Well." Yarl waited for the bartender to refill his drink. He took a surreptitious look around, surveying who might be within earshot.

Flen did the same. Unlike Yarl, he did not have to move his head or his eyes. He simply flared out his awareness.

Every Yeresunsa on the planet could detect the baseline power level that meant Ariock or someone in his league was on this world. Ultrapowerful Yeresunsa distorted and disrupted the ordinary detection of life sparks. Even so, Flen could tell that he was the only Yeresunsa in the Mushy Grove bar. He was intimately familiar with his own personal sphere of influence. He would sense if anyone extraordinary moved into range.

He gave Yarl a nod. They were safe from eavesdroppers.

The tall councilor relaxed slightly. "Have you heard Henshta's proposal?"

"I have," Flen said. The loudness of the tavern masked their conversation, so he spoke his opinion with only a little caution. "Henshta is not thinking clearly. It is a relatively simple matter to find a cave system on this planet in which we might make a new home. But finding caves is really not the obstacle we face." He adjusted his Yeresunsa mantle, trying to convey what the obstacle truly was.

"The messiah." Yarl nodded with a grave expression. "You are saying that he will not simply let you and other warriors go. That is what I think, too."

Flen laughed bitterly. The scope of the problem seemed much larger than Ariock. "It is not just him. It is everyone in power. Jinishta. Kessa." He sniffed, tasting dissatisfaction that was more sour than his ale. "And those *rekvehs* who pull their strings and make them dance."

Yarl peered into his drink as if searching for a solution.

Flen took a gulp of ale. How could someone as intelligent as Yarl—a councilor, no less—believe that escaping this war would be easy? There would be no reclamation of "lost cities," as the ancient prophecy predicted. There could be no new home. Jinishta and Ariock and others had broken the Warrior's Pact. They had failed to guard the sacred relics. They had failed to kill a *rekveh* in their midst.

Because of their failures, the Alashani were doomed. They were being whittled down, mere pawns in the scheme of a particularly dangerous and vicious *rekveh*.

"Well," Yarl said. "What if the *rekveh* pulling the strings was . . ." He lowered his voice. "Gone?"

A lot of Alashani must secretly think that assassinating Thomas was an excellent idea. Yarl was not the first person to suggest it within Flen's earshot.

Flen sipped more ale. "How?"

Yarl looked taken aback by the logistical question. People would ask the councilor about matters of shipping and manufacturing, not questions about killing. "Uh . . ." He thought about it. "How about an inhibitor microdart?"

"The *rekveh* is surrounded by protectors at all times," Flen explained. "He won't even take a piss alone. And he zombified a wild animal, one of those sky serpents, and it patrols the airspace around his tower. It obeys his every command."

Yarl shuddered.

"He is preternaturally perceptive," Flen went on. "No one dares to make a threatening move against him in public. He is inaccessible in private. No one with nefarious intentions can get close to him."

"What about poison?" Yarl asked. "In his food?"

"He is an expert on chemical compounds," Flen said. "He will be aware of any out-of-place odor or taste. And he eats the same food as everyone in that annex building. It is prepared all at once. He is also very likely to notice a suspicious person in the building."

Yarl considered the problem. "I suppose it will have to be a spear thrower, then? From a distance? Perhaps when the *rekveh* is distracted?"

Flen remembered stalking lone Torth through ancient ruins that dripped with toxic grime. Back then, his greatest ambition had been to collect a mind reader's head as a trophy. He would have been proud to kill the *rekveh* known as Thomas.

Only now, Jinishta would condemn him for it.

Cherise would have a problem, too.

"I fear that anyone who takes on that mission," Flen said, "will almost certainly fail. That *rekveh* dodged the very bomb that killed his obese mentor from the Torth Empire. He has absorbed an obscene amount of intimate information about every shani alive, so he would figure out who threw the spear. There is no question. They would be condemned."

Yarl thinned his lips, clearly perturbed. "You think he is unassailable?"

"There are warriors who would take the risk," Flen admitted. "Guresh of Hufti, and Densaava of Ellonch. But yes, I do think the attempt would fail and end in their execution."

"Your points are well taken." Yarl waited for the bartender to pass by, out of earshot. "Are you a target, do you think?" He gave Flen a look of pity. "Considering who you are betrothed to . . . are you afraid the *rekveh* is angling to get you killed, in particular?"

Flen snorted. "You give *rekvehs* too much credit. They do not have souls. They have no feelings."

Yarl made a gesture of concession.

"But I think it is clear," Flen said, "that he is angling to get us all killed."

Yarl gave him a troubled, attentive look.

"What do you hear on the war council?" Flen asked. "Is it all good news? We are winning? We keep winning and winning?"

"I suppose so," Yarl said. "There are logistical matters that we discuss, such as what must be included in the next import or export on the schedule. And we discuss city magistrates and military mayors. But yes. Every battle is a win." His tone became skeptical. "Ariock says that we owe all our victories to his mind-reader friend. The young *rekveh* is a military mastermind."

"Of course." Flen thought of his brutal schedule. He hardly had time to visit taverns. Meanwhile, what did that *rekveh* do all day?

"Are you saying we are not winning?" Yarl studied Flen. "Have we lost any cities?"

"No, not yet." Flen took a sip that was mostly dregs. "But I have seen a galactic map, Yarl. Have you?"

"No," Yarl admitted.

Cherise had shown Flen a glowing disk on her data tablet. She had zoomed into various points, showing him different worlds. Every world had cities. They seemed as numerous as water droplets in the ocean.

"We have only conquered the barest fraction of a fraction of Torth lands," Flen said. "And every warrior is working double shifts." He gestured around, indicating the whole district. "We cannot defeat the Torth Empire. Not with so few warriors. Our numbers are diminishing. Not rising."

Yarl frowned. "If that is so . . . that sounds like a very poor plan."

"It depends on your goals," Flen said with sarcasm. "All I know is this war was planned by a telepathic supergenius."

They drank in silence for a while. Both ordered another round and shared a bitterness that needed no words.

Anyone with sense could see that the *rekveh* known as Thomas was leading everyone off a cliff. He was supposedly a human hybrid, yet he hoarded power, safe in his stone fortress, surrounded by slavish ummins and other people who worshipped him. He was setting up his own miniature empire right here, on Reject-20, with himself at the top of society. He ruled Ariock. And Ariock ruled everyone else.

"Something needs to be done," Yarl said.

Flen silently agreed.

He and Yarl were undergrounders, members of a secret society dedicated to resurrecting the Alashani sense of dignity and destiny. It was a comfort to not be alone in fearing extinction.

Many Alashani seemed to be rejecting their old way of life. They adopted alien myths and culinary tastes. They discarded Alashani prayers and traditional clothing in favor of floppy sun hats and slave songs.

But the undergrounders knew that mixing with alien cultures was poison.

There was a reason the Alashani had survived beneath Torth notice for countless generations. It was wrong to toss away ancient rites and values, as if tossing out the chaff from mushroom meal. Their long legacy of freedom was unique in the galaxy—not something to be casually thrown away.

They were not a slave species. They were not victims. They were, and always had been, better than slaves.

"You're a good man, Yarl." Flen clasped the councilor's arm in a gesture of friendship after they finished their drinks.

"You, too, Flen." Yarl returned the friendly arm clasp.

They said their farewells and parted, knowing they were likely to meet again in the Mushy Grove. Undergrounders favored this tavern. This was where unsavory ideas got discussed, away from anyone who might be an undercover informant for Kessa.

As Flen slouched out of the tavern, hands in his pockets, he felt somewhat ashamed and cowardly about giving up so easily on the matter of killing Thomas.

There was something about being a warrior that people like Yarl failed to understand. Life-threatening risks could drag on a person until life itself began to feel dull and pointless and the end of life began to seem like the very point of it all. It became difficult to care about anything.

Flen remembered a different way of existing. He remembered his lovable, laughing sister, and the warm embrace of his mother, and his affable father, who collected jade and turquoise knickknacks.

He remembered lamplit balls and sneaking into palace grottoes. He used to spar with his Yeresunsa friends without a single worry about Torth or blaster gloves or the inhibitor serum or extinction.

Flen wanted that life back.

He would do anything to regain a semblance of that life.

# CHAPTER 8

# BRINGER OF HOPE

Dead children floated in the swimming pool.

This entire subterranean facility was room after room of dead toddlers and children, amid bouncy balls and other toys. Water trickled down waterslides. A decorative mobile hung from the ceiling, lazily twisting and sparkling with glitter.

Tiny, pudgy bodies were blasted into bloody chunks, contrasting with the pastel colors of the underground low-gravity waterpark.

Ariock had not been alerted fast enough to hear the screams. He heard them anyway, ringing inside his imagination.

"S s s o r r y."

"P l e a s s s e f f f o r g i v v v e U s s s?"

Four adult Torth cringed inside a makeshift cage of debris that Ariock had thrown together with his powers. These were the only survivors of the spate of suicide-massacres throughout the moon colonies of Morja and Jerja. He had flickered to Lunar Vantage and other baby farms just to double-check.

Gangs of adult Torth had apparently yanked toddlers out of playpens and broken their necks.

They had smashed amniotic sacs, spilling fetuses onto laboratory floors.

Unable to evacuate the moons fast enough, the Torth Empire had left assassins behind to murder every baby and child that Ariock's forces might claim. And then they had turned their blaster gloves on themselves.

Only the remaining dregs—the cowards who couldn't bring themselves to commit suicide afterward—begged for mercy.

"Should we collar them as penitents?" Choonhulm asked with uncertainty.

Ariock stared at the sorry bunch of prisoners. Their inner audiences must be fleeing their minds in droves. These were not Yeresunsa, so Ariock would normally consign them to Kessa's lieutenants.

But could he trust such murderers to work toward absolution?

What if they savaged their fellow penitents? They might murder mind readers who had genuinely earned redemption.

"Please." One of the dregs spoke out loud, gazing up at Ariock with beseeching iridescent-yellow eyes. He was a teenager, barely old enough to have graduated from a baby farm himself. "I am so sorry. I did not want to."

"Then why did you do it?" Ariock's voice was cold.

The teenager sank down, hands clasped. "They made me. The audience in my head."

The Torth Majority. Of course.

What sort of psychotically intense peer pressure could induce this acne-faced boy to murder children? Whichever Torth was responsible for the initial suggestion, Ariock figured they deserved to have his fist punched through their skull.

"The idea had an origin," another prisoner whispered. She was middle-aged, just like Ariock's mom had been. "The Death Architect suggested it."

A disabled child. The Death Architect was twelve years old, and she had apparently commanded hundreds of Torth to murder tens of thousands of children. Ariock wanted to sort out his feelings about that, but the teenage pawn spoke up again. "I can be a good boy. Can I be a penitent?"

All four murderous pawns prostrated themselves on the floor of the shrapnel cage. "L e t t t   U s s s   s s s s e r r r v e   t h e   C o o o n q u u e e r o o o r."

Ariock took a breath and regretted not cleansing the air first. It stank of chlorine and slaughter. Other pawns sprawled nearby as headless corpses. Most of the adults had triggered their blaster gloves in their own faces after reducing children to meat and garbage.

This carnage was reminiscent of Ariock's failure to save the Upward Governess. Just like that situation, Ariock might have saved these children if he had taken stronger preemptive measures.

"I just don't understand." Choonhulm's beak had a sad, frustrated twist. "Was this meant to shock us? Or scare us?"

"Neither," Ariock said. "It was done to prevent us from having a full victory."

He had smashed so many Torth combatants in recent weeks, the Mirror Prison always had cells full of freshly captured Rosies and Servants of All. The quicker Ariock took victories, the more scared the empire seemed to become. They had actually fled the moons of Umdalkdul, leaving luggage and slaves behind, as well as their children and babies.

The planet Umdalkdul and its moons were safe as of today. This was a huge milestone. It was meant to be a celebration. Ariock knew there were already celebrations in Freedomland and several major hub cities.

He should have guessed the Torth Empire would not allow his first planetary conquest to be a clean victory. The Majority wanted him uncertain and reeling.

"But why target their own offspring?" Choonhulm asked.

The reason seemed obvious to Ariock. Maybe he was spending too much time with Thomas. "Fewer than forty percent of Torth children are able to pass their Adulthood Exams. Most baby Torth have emotions." He gestured around. "Basically, their children might be willing to join us without even needing to become penitents."

"Really?" Choonhulm's eyes grew round with incredulity. "Are you saying most Torth offspring are like humans?"

That was a comparison Ariock would rather not have faced. But he nodded. "I think so."

Older children would probably have trouble emoting and speaking out loud. But Ariock could imagine baby mind readers alive and burbling. Or crying. Or babbling in baby talk, just like any human baby.

He pictured Torth toddlers playing with hatchling ummins under Kessa's caring guidelines. It was hard to imagine. But perhaps in time, Kessa's system would raise a generation of mind readers who behaved like humans.

"I am not sure our side would embrace Torth children easily." Choonhulm's brow ridges knitted in a frown. His mate was incubating an egg, so he would have his own hatchling in the near future.

Ariock felt brutish even discussing the future of families while the blood of children stained walls and floors everywhere he looked.

"Well . . ." Choonhulm raised his blaster rifle. "I guess it's too late for these kneelers to become penitents. They desecrated Kessa's main law."

Penitents were forbidden from committing acts of violence. The punishment for violating that law was death or zombification.

"Should I kill them?" Choonhulm asked. "Or do you want to bring them to the Mirror Prison?"

The four Torth spoke in sync. "W e e e  a r e  s s s o o o  s s s s o o o r r y."

Ariock considered the kneeling pawns. Were they entitled to mercy? They had not shown their victims any such thing.

Part of him wanted their death screams to reverberate in the Megacosm. He wanted to teach the Torth Majority that his side of the war had zero tolerance for atrocities.

But he already knew that he and his friends could not influence the Torth Majority. Thomas kept sending welcoming invitations to any renegades who might secretly exist in the Megacosm. So far, none had risked a journey to the makeshift spaceport in Freedomland or to any of the safe harbors on Umdalkdul. None had surrendered their weapons to Kessa's lieutenants. None had proclaimed themselves friendly to Kessa or Thomas or Ariock.

Brave Torth renegades did not seem to exist.

Or if they did, then Torth peer pressure must be beyond anything a sane person could imagine.

Ariock began to say that the four kneeling Torth would serve his troops as zombified minions.

A tear rolled down the cheek of the teenager.

That emotionless face, combined with that tear, and that youthfulness . . . this boy might as well be Yellow Thomas. Ariock's supergenius friend had sentenced him to death by crucifixion because of pressure from the Torth Majority.

Ariock himself had torn apart innocent animals with his bare hands.

He wanted to forget those awful days in the gladiatorial arena, but he remembered the disturbingly decadent audience and their judgmental silence.

"I want to let Kessa decide their fate," Ariock realized. Kessa had ideas about how to integrate penitent Torth into society, as well as how to incentivize them to act more human. Ariock motioned Choonhulm to lower his weapon. "This isn't our jurisdiction."

"Kessa will just sentence them to death by zombification." The stocky ummin looked skeptical as he holstered his blaster rifle. "They're too dangerous to let loose in a city."

"Maybe." Ariock felt lighter now that he did not feel obligated—or pressured—to kill anyone. "But it's not my place to tread on Kessa's authority."

He did not always need to mete out justice and death. He could outsource the decision-making to Kessa the Wise. That was some relief.

Ariock gave the kneeling Torth a stern glare. "When you arrive at an intake camp, you need to tell Kessa's lieutenants what you've done. Don't hold anything back."

The four Torth pressed their foreheads to the ground. Only one of them spoke. "Agreed."

Ariock turned to Choonhulm.

The ummin gave him a businesslike nod. "I'll make sure they're delivered with a detailed report. As for the carnage?" He glanced around with disgust. "This is worse than the aftermath of most battles. I'll request penitent laborers for the cleanup."

Ariock imagined dead babies and children dumped down garbage chutes. They had never been named. They had never been loved.

"Please ask the laborers to treat the remains with respect," Ariock said. "These were not enemy combatants. Have them buried or cremated."

Choonhulm saluted. "Got it."

"And go for fresh air if you need it." Ariock wished he could clap Choonhulm on the shoulder, but he would have to bend down to do that for an ummin. It would be awkward. "You'll be notified when I return."

The liberated slaves of Umdalkdul had yet to form their own space fleet. Ariock was the only method of interstellar transportation for Choonhulm and other soldiers. He would bring them home later.

Very few Yeresunsa had enough raw strength to even approach the possibility of teleportation. Ariock was the only one who could do it with passengers, or on a casual whim.

He put himself in a clairvoyant trance. Soon he was zooming away from the moon Morja, past the beat-up scraps of metal that used to be Torth warships. He had familiarized himself with the route to Reject-20, and he leaped across hundreds of light-years within seconds.

It was predawn in Freedomland. Ariock ghosted through the war palace, past late-night parties. He considered dropping in on Vy and her eclectic group of friends, but he didn't want to ruin her happiness. Vy was always too patient and understanding when he complained.

He located Thomas in a manufacturing facility adjacent to the research annex, where a few technicians stood at workstations. Thomas hovered alone at his own executive workstation. He seemed engrossed in inspecting a tiny device.

Ariock targeted the empty space behind Thomas's hoverchair. That seemed big enough for his body.

Pulling himself across the galaxy was an instantaneous act. It felt like flipping upside down and then pulling himself psychically through a knothole, but it was a process that Ariock was used to. He dropped out of thin air and landed on his feet.

Thomas twitched in startled surprise. "Jeez, Ariock! Don't do that."

Ariock took his usual half a second to acclimate to the different gravity, atmospherics, and directional compass. He felt much heavier on this planet than he had on the moon Morja.

"Oh." Thomas's tone softened. He rotated to face Ariock, and his purple eyes were pained. He must be absorbing the recent horrors that clogged Ariock's memory.

"Yeah." Ariock tried not to sound accusatory. If Thomas had even remotely guessed that the Torth would slaughter their own children . . . well. Surely he would have warned someone? Surely he would have recommended preventative measures?

Thomas set aside the device he'd been inspecting, giving Ariock his full attention. "I didn't guess the Torth would do that. I, uh, did consider it as a remote possibility, but . . ." He trailed off, probably sensing Ariock's dismay. "Sorry. I miscalculated. I'm going to need to stop underestimating the Death Architect."

Thomas had dark circles under his eyes. He looked overworked.

Ariock nodded, recalling that Thomas was tasked with upgrading all the technology for their army. Thomas also planned the tactics and strategies for every battle. That was on top of his physical therapy regimen, war council appearances, and his daily zombification quota.

Garrett probably made those tasks even more unpleasant than they needed to be.

But Garrett's life experiences might actually have made him wise in a way that Thomas was not. Whenever Ariock looked at adult Torth—even penitents—he saw unrepentant entitlement. He saw murderers who were willing to shove blaster gloves into the faces of babies. He saw evil.

Where were the millions of friendly Torth allies that Thomas had promised?

"We could have benefited from preadolescent Torth." Thomas looked haggard. "I'll bet Kessa would have converted them to our side. That's why the Death Architect ordered them killed."

"I hope we'll get the chance to find out." Ariock had trouble imagining a future where happy children of all species played together. Wouldn't there always be an insurmountable chasm between nontelepaths and mind readers?

"Oh, let me show you what I'm working on." Thomas picked up the device in one hand and rotated it between his fingertips. "This is going to revolutionize communication and equalize the gulf between Torth and everyone else. I'll need your help to set up relay satellites, especially near temporal streams. That's a project for later this week." His voice cracked.

Thomas was fourteen now. The heroes had held a small, private birthday celebration a few months ago, and even then, Ariock had noticed that regeneration healing seemed to have broken a spell over Thomas's body. Thomas never mentioned it or complained, but he was clearly dealing with rapid-onset puberty on top of everything else.

Thomas cleared his throat. "Once we're done, people on different planets will be able to talk to each other. So we'll be a lot less likely to be blindsided by random acts of Torth cruelty."

Ariock wanted to feel enthusiastic.

Instead, he thought of social media and the Megacosm and insane amounts of peer pressure.

He thought of disabled children commanding armies. And commanding people like Ariock himself.

"That's great." Ariock reminded himself that he had won an entire planet, including its populated moon colonies, thanks to Thomas's planning and tactics. One little sliver of the galactic empire now belonged to Ariock and his friends. They had scored hundreds of victories without a single defeat. That was something.

He should be celebrating.

So should Thomas.

It seemed neither of them was feeling victorious.

"By the way," Thomas said, "Garrett should have alerted me about the baby farm massacres as soon as the vote was held. He didn't. So I'm guessing the Death Architect timed it to happen during his sleep window. Either that or he's slacking off."

"I'll ask him," Ariock said. Immersing oneself in Torth culture must be awful, but Garrett was the only one of them who could do it without detection.

"In the future," Thomas said, "it will be prudent for us to time any potentially risky conquests for when Garrett is awake and able to spy for us. That will work until the Majority gets even more secretive. Anyway, I'll take it into account." He gave Ariock a look of concern. "You've been doing an outstanding job. If I can help . . . even if it means more zombifying . . . I believe Garrett could link with me and give me enough of a power boost to, uh, get more of them done. And faster."

Hordes of zombies could soften up a targeted city even before Ariock showed up. He might be able to win another planet. Maybe he would even be able to liberate a baby farm or two, if he could pull off a surprise attack.

Ariock thought of the teenage boy with a silent tear rolling down his cheek. Did he deserve zombification?

Did anyone?

"That's an idea." Ariock patted Thomas's hoverchair, not wanting to seem ungrateful. "I hope you can take a break to celebrate."

"Same to you," Thomas said.

"I will." Ignoring his friend's troubled look, Ariock shut off his communicator with the click of a switch. He put himself into a clairvoyant trance, making himself unreachable, despite the thousands of soldiers that relied on him and the millions of liberated people who praised his name.

He ghosted to a region where there were no cities or worshippers.

He found a plain full of wheat grass rippling in the breeze. It was midafternoon. Peaceful. Good for a moment of personal reflection.

Ariock teleported into the endless grass. He had to show up above it, since he could not displace solid matter, but he'd gotten good at landing on his feet.

He straightened.

The only life sparks within a hundred miles moved without the purpose of sapient beings. They were alien critters.

Ariock withdrew his awareness and allowed himself to be truly alone beneath the cloudless sky.

Right now, he knew, there were triumphant parades and festivals and important speeches going on in the cities he had liberated. An entire planet was freed from slavery. When people learned about those baby farm massacres? It wouldn't diminish their joy at all. They would shrug and say those victims were merely Torth.

Ariock's reputation would remain untarnished. People called him the Bringer of Hope. Son of Storms. The messiah. They considered him to be a cosmic sorcerer, a great liberator.

But what was he, really, if crimes happened on his watch, under his rule?

Who was he, if he could not protect the innocent?

Ariock waded through grass that was so tall, a child could have gotten lost in it. But he saw all the way to the horizons. The prairie was an endless vista of purity.

# CHAPTER 9
# A FIERY FRIEND

After days spent visiting fields or sweatshops where penitent Torth labored, Kessa thought the academy looked jarringly clean. Everyone in the hallways was well-groomed.

Penitents were not allowed to mingle with students, of course, and they were not allowed near research scientists. They could not be allowed within range of anyone who possessed potentially sensitive military intelligence.

Kessa visited acquaintances who worked in Thomas's laboratories. She interrupted technicians at workstations. Once she had said her hellos, she gained directions to the tower where Thomas lived.

There were sentries. There was an intercom. The vault-like gates looked thick enough to withstand a grenade.

"Come on up," Thomas's voice said once he had been informed of his visitor.

The pair of nussian sentries looked overawed as the gates slid apart. They might feel honored to meet Kessa the Wise—or perhaps they were shocked that someone actually dared to visit Thomas.

Kessa walked through a cavernous private lobby. She wore a pastel-colored outfit sewn with lacy puzzle patterns, which made her feel delicate and out of place. Her reflection was a meager blur on burnished-meteorite wall panels and pillars.

She climbed an echoey spiral ramp that was wide enough to accommodate mated nussians. She doubted that many nussians went into the so-called Dragon Tower. Their hands were too big for Torth-designed lab equipment, so they couldn't really become lab technicians. She had heard that a group of nussian students were creating their own workstations so they could participate in scientific endeavors.

After poking her head into dozens of cluttered storage rooms, she located Thomas in the tower-top aerie, with its open-air archways. Decorative tapestries moved in the breeze. Beyond, the banded gas giant filled the sky, its faint reflection playing upon the tranquil ocean.

"Hey, Kessa." Thomas flexed a hinged device that Kessa recognized as Torth gym equipment.

He was painstakingly working out.

"Hello, Thomas." Kessa leaned against the doorway, arms folded. She made no comment on what he was doing while soldiers fought to win cities according to his plans, and while technicians worked in his laboratories. Thomas, of all people, deserved some downtime. "It has been such a long time since we last spoke. You give us so many penitents to work with, it is a full-time task just to stay organized."

"That's mostly Ariock."

Kessa wondered if Thomas was trying to appear humble. Sure, he never went into battle himself, but his strategies translated to constant gains of liberated people, prisoners, and penitents.

What about his superluminal communications technology? That was having a massive effect. For the first time, former slaves were able to talk to each other spontaneously across a gulf of light-years. They were almost on par with the Torth Empire. Everyone realized it.

Nowadays, entire fleets or armies could be stationed in alien metropolises and Ariock didn't have to constantly move them around. Battle captains and warrior premiers could interact with the war council from anywhere in the galaxy.

"I just make the plans." Thomas flexed his arms against the resistance device. "Ariock executes them."

Perhaps Thomas wanted to distance himself from responsibilities? He rarely left the research annex of the academy. Whenever he did venture out, it was either to the Mirror Prison or to the cliffside fortress where war councils were held.

He avoided the dingy places where penitents worked. He never even looked at them.

"Perhaps you could visit a barracks full of penitents, sometime?" Kessa asked, getting straight to the point of her visit. "I am sure I could benefit greatly from your analysis of them."

Thomas stopped exercising long enough to grimace at her.

"Why not?" Kessa asked.

Thomas let the hinged, weighted device rest in his lap and gazed out at the ocean. He looked reluctant to answer.

But he was obligated to answer.

He was not obligated in the same way as a penitent Torth, yet nevertheless, he was caught in the honor of his promise. Kessa waited.

"I soak up enough abject fear whenever I visit the Mirror Prison," Thomas said, breaking the lengthy silence. "I get it from the Megacosm, too. The Torth have mental mantras to remind each other to watch out for the temptations I offer. They're on high alert."

"The penitents are not in the prison or in the Megacosm," Kessa pointed out. "They might be welcoming to you."

"I'm their Conqueror." Thomas sounded ironic. "As far as most penitents are concerned, I'm a horrific tyrant with no oversight. I'm sure they hate me."

Kessa clicked her beak in consternation. Thomas almost seemed to welcome hatred. He never defended himself on war councils; he never acted friendly in public. He was aloof and ominous.

She stepped farther into the room, closer to Thomas. "Is that how you wish to be seen? Remote and dangerous?" She gestured around the tower top. "Is that why you avoid potential friends and spend so much time alone?"

Thomas gave her a frustrated look, as if she was failing to grasp an essential fact. "I can twist minds."

Kessa nodded, urging him to explain why he wanted to be seen as a monster.

"The penitents and other Torth are afraid I'll mind-twist them," Thomas said. "They're afraid I'll zombify everyone they know—maybe the entire the Megacosm."

If Thomas could casually end the Torth Empire with a thought, he would have done so. Nevertheless, Kessa was too curious not to ask, "Is that something you think you are capable of?"

Thomas laughed. Kessa chuckled, pleased that he had picked up on the wry humor in her question.

"That certainly makes me sound dangerous," he said. "But no. The only way I can twist minds through the Megacosm is if my victim allows it. And I could only do it to one at a time. So it's a self-defeating proposition, something the humans of my homeland call a catch-22. If I went around tricking Torth into letting me into their core minds, then twisting them . . . soon no one would allow me in. I would lose access to the Megacosm."

Kessa had not even known that Thomas could zombify Torth in the Megacosm. He was more dangerous than she'd realized. He might actually be able to seize an army of loyalists before the Torth Majority kicked him out of the Megacosm, depending on . . .

"How many Torth can you zombify in quick succession?" Kessa asked.

She immediately regretted asking. She ought to avoid learning military secrets, since she inspected penitent Torth on a regular basis.

"Never mind," Kessa said. "Don't answer that."

Thomas gave her a gracious nod. He began to flex the hinged gym equipment again, trembling from the effort.

Kessa wandered the room, gazing at tapestries and contemplating the fact that Thomas could singlehandedly create his own army, despite how feeble he looked. He was only limited in speed and raw strength.

Except . . .

Well, linking was possible.

If Thomas asked his powerhouse friends, Ariock and Evenjos, to imbue him with their raw power, would he gain exponential strength? How many Torth could he enslave if he was boosted like that? Thousands?

Millions?

Kessa suspected the idea had already occurred to Thomas. It was natural for him to consider factors no one else remembered. She could see him hiding the idea, like a winning game piece he might flourish when all other options had been exhausted.

"So," Kessa said, "you dislike being feared. Yet you keep making more zombies." She kept her tone gentle and nonaccusatory.

"It's what Garrett wants," Thomas said.

Kessa knew his enslavement to Garrett was superficial. "Do you agree with him?"

Thomas looked defensive. "We have little choice as long as Torth keep refusing to join us. Besides, Ariock and Garrett keep capturing defeated Rosies and Servants. What else can we do with them, other than flat out kill them?"

Kessa began to suggest keeping them imprisoned and on the inhibitor.

But Thomas forestalled her. "It's best not to let the Mirror Prison get too full of high-value prisoners," he said, "or else the Torth Empire might try to liberate them."

Kessa imitated a human snort of derision. The Torth Empire couldn't invade Freedomland. Their warships could not approach the planet without running a major risk of being caught in Ariock's periodic clairvoyant sweeps. Even if a rogue jumper shuttle got through, the only place to land was the Freedomland spaceport, which was active at all hours.

"Never underestimate the Torth," Thomas said, putting his exercise aside and resting. "Their Rosies and Servants want to teleport across the galaxy. It's only a matter of time before they figure it out."

Kessa recognized that as good advice.

"We're winning for now." Thomas gazed outside at the city sprawl. "We're slicing away rot, exposing how feeble the empire was. But we're going to strike bone at some point. The Torth Majority will find its spine."

Kessa knew the Torth well enough to suspect he was right.

"They'll do something I fail to predict," Thomas said. "It's bound to happen sooner or later."

Below them, pedestrians flowed through the streets, relaxed and talkative. The people of Freedomland felt safe. But Kessa could imagine enemy supergeniuses inventing new weapons, or telepathic champions figuring out galactic teleportation.

Or what if the Majority simply voted for their military ranks to take bigger risks?

Alashani warriors used to carry suicide pellets in their teeth. Wasn't it only a matter of time before Rosies and Servants took similarly drastic measures?

Thomas swept the city with a protective gaze. He must value Freedomland as much as any freed slave.

Which made sense. Thomas had chosen this planet and selected this exact site for his stronghold. Every major street and plaza was arranged according to Thomas's blueprints. He had instructed Ariock on what to construct and what supplies to import. Ariock led the war councils, but he deferred to Thomas. Ariock kept winning battles, but every battle was strategized by Thomas.

Many residents lovingly nicknamed this beautiful new homeland Ariock's City. But Kessa thought it would be far more accurate to call it Thomas's City.

She ambled around his hoverchair, giving it a wide berth, staying clear of his range of telepathy. "I would like to return to the topic of penitents. A few of them show promising signs . . ."

She lost her train of thought, frozen in midstep as she became aware of an enormous beast eyeing her from the shadowy depths of the room.

A sky croc.

It raised its bony head on a sinuous, graceful neck. Its yellow-orange eyes were avid and watchful. The beast scissored its immense jaws, revealing a grin with needle-sharp teeth.

Kessa lost her words and her sense of safety. She stepped back and back again.

This sky croc looked like a juvenile. It was smaller than the monsters that soared over distant cliffs, but it was still big enough to chomp her in half. Its kind were known to snatch ummins and albinos and, most often, penitent Torth, and fly off with them. Victims were never seen again.

"Don't be afraid," Thomas said. "Kessa, that's my friend. He won't hurt you."

Kessa dared not take her eyes off the wild beast. It lay in a makeshift nest, its leathery body folded amid shredded boxes and blankets. It must have been watching her throughout the whole conversation.

Its snout was longer than the beak of a mer nerctan. It had so many teeth.

"Please don't leave." Thomas sounded anxious. "I want Azhdarchidae to learn who my friends are."

The beast's enormous eyes had slit pupils.

Kessa became aware that it was merely watching her. This animal could easily jut out its long neck or fly. Instead, it seemed content to assess her from a distance.

"As Dark a Day?" Kessa wondered at the multisyllabic phrase Thomas had named his friend with. It sounded like a Torth name-title to her.

"Azhdarchidae." Thomas pronounced it in a way that blended the syllables together. "The word derives from a human reference to fire-breathing monsters with long necks and leathery wings. It's used on Earth to refer to extinct predators that looked somewhat like my friend here."

"Fire-breathing?" Kessa hoped sky crocs could not exhale flames.

Thomas interrupted her thoughts. "Well, watch this."

He floated to a refrigerated container, lifted the lid, and pulled out a chunk of frozen red meat. Kessa blinked in amazement. Thomas would have been unable to heft that item a month ago. He really was getting stronger.

The beast stirred. It looked ready to lunge at the meal.

"Stay put," Thomas told it in a firm tone.

To Kessa's surprise, Azhdarchidae settled down. The animal seemed uncaring of the fact that Thomas was the size of its typical prey and unable to stand up. It seemed curious, like a child, rather than the predator it was.

Thomas placed the steak onto a spring-loaded catapult mounted on a swivel.

"Northwest," he told Azhdarchidae in a commanding voice.

Kessa jumped as the enormous beast lunged out the window toward the mountains, snaking its neck and snapping its bony jaws. At the same time, Thomas swiveled the catapult in that direction. He pressed a button to release it.

The frozen steak hurtled away with a whooshing sound.

It also caught on fire. The steak became a fireball engulfed in white-hot flames.

Azhdarchidae banked in midair, ready to catch the fiery meal. By the time the steak vanished into his huge maw, the flames were gone. The air smelled faintly of barbecued meat.

"He loves cooked food." Thomas sounded like a proud parent bragging about his child. "It's a special treat for him."

Kessa found the display unsettling. She could not guess why Thomas had befriended a carnivorous wild animal, but he had a purpose for everything he did.

Azhdarchidae landed on a balustrade and clambered back inside the tower room, apparently content to settle down in the nest. The animal was definitely not a zombified victim. It—or he—was too curious and too alert to be brain damaged.

"I'm training Azhdarchidae to steer clear of the city when he flies," Thomas explained. "He follows my signal flares in midair."

Kessa supposed that might keep people in courtyards or on rooftops safe.

Thomas looked sheepish. "I'd appreciate it if you keep quiet about my friend. Just for a while. I'm not exactly keeping him a secret, but . . ." He looked embarrassed. "There are already rumors. I don't want people to think I'm zombifying animals."

Kessa nodded.

"And I'd rather not have Garrett find out right away," Thomas admitted.

Mind readers made everything complicated. "I can avoid the range of penitents for a few days," Kessa said. "But it is my job to work with them, Thomas."

"I get it. Thanks." Thomas gave her a grateful look. "By the way, friends are welcome to meet Azhdarchidae. It would be nice if . . ." He hesitated, shoulders hunched defensively. "Well, I would like Cherise to meet him. It's best if Azhdarchidae recognizes who my friends are."

It felt good to be counted among Thomas's friends.

And it was interesting that Thomas had casually mentioned Cherise after many moon cycles of never seeing her or speaking with her. How often did he think of the Earth girl?

Thomas plucked the exercise device off his lap and placed it on a countertop with other equipment. "I know you want me to vet penitents for you," he said. "I just don't feel ready."

Kessa wanted to question his reluctance. What was more important than meeting former Torth and trying to gain their willing allegiance?

It seemed Thomas would rather play with a juvenile sky croc than meet people who feared or hated him.

Or who worshipped him. Kessa had a sense that a few penitents admired their Conqueror.

Before she could think of how to phrase her concerns, Thomas said, "It's too bad you never got an influx of underage mind readers to work with. I hope we'll be able to free a baby farm or two. Maybe on the next planet we conquer."

Kessa imagined it. Thomas was an underage mind reader. Might others be as . . . well, not emotional, perhaps, but as kind as him?

She doubted it. Torth hatchlings surely did not go around befriending slaves and sky crocs. Thomas was one of a kind.

"Your work is vitally important," Thomas told Kessa. "We need to win hearts, not just bodies and minds. We can win battles with zombies, but not forever. We need Torth willingly on our side."

Kessa hid her doubts. There were so many generations of injustice between former Torth and former slaves, she kept wondering if her work would matter at all. Even if she succeeded, soldiers would refuse to fight alongside penitents. Families would refuse to adopt Torth children. People would be unable to trust mind readers even if they miraculously began to act as human as Vy.

And they were a long way from that.

"You have to make progress." Thomas gave her a look fraught with hope. "Otherwise? Our freedom is fleeting."

That was a lot of pressure. Kessa wondered if Thomas felt as if he carried the weight of the galaxy on his shoulders, because he must have shared some of it with her.

"I have not given up," she said.

Perhaps she would ask a technician to retool some tranquility meshes to enhance emotions? If there was any possibility of transforming silent penitents into emotive, humanlike friends, Kessa resolved to find the way.

# CHAPTER 10

# UNBREAKABLE

Ariock had put some thought into how to announce the conquest of a whole planet. He could say, "Umdalkdul is liberated" in a grand voice, as Garrett suggested. He could launch into a speech about valiant freedom fighters and what each battle had cost.

Or he could cast Kessa in the spotlight, as Thomas suggested. He could ask her to make the speech, even though everyone on the war council knew the Torth Empire had to be defeated by force, and Ariock was the leader of that force.

Or he could do what Kessa suggested and praise every battle leader in public, then remind everyone that penitent laborers and the civilian workforce were just as important. He ought to talk about how their victories were largely due to Thomas and the superluminal technology he had invented.

Ariock stood in the open courtyard of the war palace, facing hundreds of civilian councilors and military leaders.

He wasn't going to make a fancy speech. That just wasn't his style. Instead, he said three simple words.

"Umdalkdul is ours."

They erupted in jubilation.

Even the most reserved councilors stomped their feet and whooped with victory. Eyes shone with pride. It was one thing to hear the total-conquest announcement on the local broadcast network, and another thing to hear it straight from the battle leader who had taken the most prisoners and killed the most enemies.

Everyone felt the cost of freedom on a personal level. Every civilian was proud of the war heroes they knew, the ones who took repeated risks.

Ariock sat in his chair of polished meteorite. He wished it didn't look so much like a throne, but . . . well, the whole point was so he could stop looming over people. He had insisted that everyone have a chair.

"We are consolidating our forces on Umdalkdul," Ariock assured them. "But we need to discuss our next steps. Garrett will go over our options."

The options were preselected. Ariock did not tell the war council that he had already hashed out his next steps, in private, with Thomas and Garrett. These councilors would receive a distilled version of three strategies that Ariock had already approved of.

It was easier this way.

Ariock wanted the people under his protection to have agency and to feel empowered. Yet he could not afford endless bickering about whether Thomas was a trustworthy ally or a demonic *rekveh*. The war could not afford the strain of doubts and distrust.

Unity was what made the Torth Empire powerful. Ariock felt that sort of power whenever he rallied his troops, whenever they fought with him. Rushing into a battle solo was a far different matter than rushing in with friends and allies who had the same drive to win.

He needed unity. This war was a survival situation. There would be plenty of time for discordant fracturing and parting of ways in the aftermath of the war.

"Let's talk about the planet Parity first." Garrett used his staff to point to a holographic display.

Hundreds of semitransparent planetary holographs glowed beneath an overhang, each one rotating at a slightly different rate. Quite a few of them looked Earthlike. As Garrett spoke, one of those Earthlike planets grew until it eclipsed the others, while the rest faded to insignificant points of light. Backstage technicians were in charge of the display.

"The thing about Parity," Garrett said, "is that it's a shipping hub. Think of it like a crucial piece of an artery. If we slice it?" He drove down his staff for emphasis. "Then we can count on the Torth losing some of their nuclear weapons capabilities within that celestial sector. That renders more than two dozen planets vulnerable to our attacks. We . . ."

Ariock began to tune out, having already heard this plan in great detail.

If only he could make the Torth Empire vulnerable in the long term. They had space armadas. Ariock had a few thousand half-trained shuttle pilots.

"Can we talk?"

The voice was feminine, throaty, and intimately whispered in his ear.

For a moment, Ariock assumed Evenjos was speaking through his earpiece. But he wasn't wearing an earpiece. This was a war council, where distractions would be considered rude.

Ariock twisted around, searching for Evenjos.

He caught a faint outline of wings standing behind his chair. She was all but invisible. She must have forced a quasi voice out of dust particles.

"Follow me," Evenjos whispered.

Her voice directly inside his ear felt like an invasion of privacy. Ariock had to work to control his temper. He did not spike out his awareness. He did not cause things to float, or make the sky beyond the window cutouts grow dark with clouds.

*What do you want?* Ariock asked inside his mind.

Evenjos floated to the colonnade and beckoned with a barely there hand.

Then she breezed directly through a granite wall. She had probably sucked herself through cracks.

". . . We could disrupt their space fleets by taking over Precision Bays station," Garrett was saying. "If they can't repair their ships, they're less likely to . . ."

The war council could continue without Ariock. Most of them would have guessed that Ariock was already well-informed.

He rose out of his chair. There was no way for him to be unobtrusive, like Evenjos. All gazes turned toward him. Ariock gave Garrett a thumbs-up signal, showing that he approved of what the old man was saying.

"Ariock is aware of our options," Garrett assured everyone. "Anyway, to continue . . ."

Ariock stepped through the colonnade, rounded a corner, and went indoors.

Evenjos floated amid polished marble and mirrored walls. She solidified, her hair rippling in an intangible breeze.

"Why bother to let them vote?" she asked. "They will do whatever you decide."

Ariock glanced at the sentries on duty. Then he realized that they had not understood Evenjos's words, because she had spoken in his native language, English.

"I am not a dictator," he told Evenjos. "I want them to have a say."

She rolled her eyes. "You've been avoiding me, Emperor Ariock." She beckoned. "Come. There is a topic we ought to discuss."

Ariock hesitated. He owed Evenjos some common courtesy, since she healed warriors and soldiers during every major battle. Aliens praised the Lady of Sorrow almost as fervently as the Alashani used to do. She saved hundreds of lives every day.

And yet . . .

His burden of daily protection would only increase. He had to somehow take over more than seven hundred hub planets from the galactic Torth Empire. He needed her help as a planetary defender.

If Evenjos were to take up residence on Umdalkdul, then Ariock would no longer need to teleport there on a daily basis, making sure that the planetary population was not in danger. Evenjos could sweep her awareness through a solar system almost as fast as he could.

Maybe now was a good time to bring up his concerns about their defenses?

"Fine," Ariock said.

Evenjos glided away before he could suggest that they chat in the public garden, leaving him with little choice but to follow.

Ariock added "entitled" to his inner list of complaints about Evenjos. Really. If she had a topic worthy of discussion, she should have made an appointment. Vy was in charge of his schedule. Although the populations of Reject-20 and Umdalkdul could now talk to each other, thanks to the interstellar superluminal relays Ariock had set up—at the behest of Thomas—he still had import and export duties. He had spaceports to repair, battle leaders to get to know better, and a space armada to build.

Would Evenjos be willing to help with any of that? Did she even care?

Ariock's natural walking speed was too fast for most people, due to the length of his stride, so he usually went for a gentle amble. Otherwise Vy or council members would be unable to keep up with him. But Evenjos moved at a brisk pace. He hurried after her winged form, glad that he had built the war palace to his own scale. He didn't need to duck through doorways.

Evenjos glided onto a stone balcony and spread her wings. "Let's go for a view," she said in a giggly voice.

She leaped several stories higher.

Ariock sighed. Of course Evenjos wanted to turn a serious discussion into a pointless game.

Was he being too judgmental? If they were ever going to fight battles together, as he wanted to do, then he supposed he needed to accept her personality quirks.

Evenjos fluttered onto a clifftop behind the war palace.

Ariock suffused his body with power and leaped to join her. He reshaped wind currents to avoid their buffeting force.

Someone had landscaped the clifftop to include alien crocuses, flowery ivy along the balustrade of a scenic overlook, and hedgerows. Pretty.

Ariock landed in the garden with a bit too much force. He was used to slamming people through marble walls or shattering floors with the force of his landings. When not in battle, he tried to move only with the utmost care. He sat or knelt most of the time, to put himself closer to eye level with whomever he was speaking with.

But he did not have to contort himself downward for Evenjos.

She elongated her body, approaching his height, becoming a willowy eight-and-a-half-foot-tall giantess. Sunlight shone on her wavy hair, giving her head an electric-magenta halo. Outer strands danced on the breeze.

"Hey," Evenjos said.

Ariock stepped back, ready to fly away. Had he fallen for yet another stupid seduction attempt?

"I haven't treated you very well," Evenjos said. "And you are my rescuer. You and Thomas. You gave me your blood and lent me your power so I could be resurrected."

Ariock waited, wary.

"I'm sorry," she said.

The apology made her look vulnerable.

Ariock remembered that she had suffered, alone, for eons. Somehow, she had held on to her sanity. And some kindness. She had survived the loss of everyone she had ever known, and then she had nearly died in her efforts to revive Ariock from a depletion coma. She had done that without even knowing whether or not he was worth the risk.

Every day, Evenjos healed people in need.

People considered her to be some sort of angel, and they weren't wrong. She had freely healed Thomas, despite her fears that the boy would turn out to be some sort of combination of her worst enemies from the past.

"I'm sorry, too," Ariock admitted. "I don't think I've been judging you fairly."

Evenjos looked down in shame. "Your judgment of me was fair. I am not brave, like you."

Ariock had a hard time thinking of himself as brave. He only did what needed to be done. But he supposed he looked that way to many people. Otherwise the city wouldn't be named after him. Otherwise nussians wouldn't be carving his likeness into a cliff as a way of honoring the Son of Storms.

"I just happen to have a useful power," Ariock said. Mass-teleportation seemed to be a crucial advantage.

Evenjos gazed up at him, her lavender eyes liquid with unspoken pleas. "I want you to know that I value you. And I respect you. Even if . . ." She averted her eyes, clearly ashamed. "I understand that your heart belongs to Vy."

A tension that Ariock hadn't been aware of loosened. Was Evenjos finally letting go of her obsession?

"I am sorry that I failed to understand that," Evenjos said. "I understand, now."

Ariock felt as if storm clouds had evaporated. The sky overhead was clear, marbled with the color bands of the nearby gas giant. Could he finally stop worrying about the threat to his relationship with Vy?

He didn't have to be on guard around the deposed goddess-empress anymore.

Sighing with relief, he assessed Evenjos with fresh eyes.

She looked melancholy. But she was fundamentally a good person, and she did not need to suffer endless penance and loneliness. Someone would fall in love with her, surely.

Because, really, she was beautiful. Her skin looked silken. Pliable—yet unbreakable. Ariock could theoretically seize Evenjos and crush her without a care, and she would just laugh and toss her head back, unharmed. Not much could physically hurt her.

"I understand." Evenjos picked up his huge hand and brushed her lips against his knuckles in a slow way that sent electric tingles through his body.

Ariock refrained from reacting. He wasn't going to betray Vy's trust.

"I shall not interfere with you and Vy." Evenjos made it a noble-sounding announcement. She floated Ariock's hand away from herself on an air current. "But I feel it is my duty to warn you of the danger to your love."

"Danger?" Ariock asked, baffled.

"Mmm-hmm." Evenjos averted her eyes, looking ashamed. "You must know by now that Yeresunsa have problems with self-control. Especially in intensely emotional situations. Such as rage. Grief. Panic." She touched Ariock's chest lightly, running her slender finger down his ornamental council armor. "Lust."

Ariock's heartbeat sped up, although it was from horrified realization, not lust.

Sometimes, when Vy was being particularly cuddly—or just near him—objects floated along with his arousal. Candles. Throw pillows. Curtains might billow. Vy thought that was funny, but they were both aware of the danger.

They were in a habit of moving away from each other whenever that happened.

"Yeresunsa cannot control their powers in a fit of lust or any other strong emotion," Evenjos said in that regretful tone. "This was a well-known fact. At least, it was in my time. That is why the Yeresunsa Order nurtured a social division between ourselves and common people."

Ariock had wondered why Evenjos was such a proponent of elitism.

Now he understood. He imagined long-ago Yeresunsa accidentally tearing apart their ordinary lovers. He could see a husband electrocuting his wife during sex. Or a boyfriend causing his girlfriend to float and then plummet to her death. Or connecting to the very air and crushing her delicate body.

There would be wives with missing limbs because their husbands were too powerful.

He had to be on guard around Vy. Always gentle. Always aware of what he might do by accident.

And, apparently, there was no cure for that problem?

"But you love her." Evenjos smiled. "I am sure you are extremely cautious at all times around her because you are cognizant of how breakable she is."

Ariock swallowed. Although Vy was tall for a human woman, she was undeniably small and fragile when compared to him. Their difference in mass was like that of different species.

Maybe it was stupid to try so hard to downplay the differences?

Maybe he ought to be even more careful with Vy. Or reconsider spending so much time with her?

Even Torth Servants of All were ultracareful, weren't they? Torth military ranks owned fewer slaves and avoided civilized society.

And the Torth Empire had outlawed sharp emotions. That was an obvious way to avoid triggering Yeresunsa powers.

What about Garrett? Hadn't his human wife died when he was in his early thirties? Garrett had never remarried. He had fled from his family on Earth. Perhaps that had more to do with fear of his own power than of the Torth Empire?

"Your heart has led you in a strange direction, Ariock Dovanack." Evenjos caressed his arm with a light, sympathetic touch. "But I respect your choice." She smiled ruefully. "I only beg you to remember that—when we are saving the universe together—*I* am unbreakable."

She stole a kiss on his cheek.

Then she disintegrated into the wind that swept down off the mountains. Her sparkling particles billowed along a cliff and toward the ocean.

Ariock watched Evenjos coalesce in the sky, taking the form of the phoenix, carefree and . . . well, completely impossible to break or hurt by accident.

Clouds formed in a harsh wind overhead, reflecting his inner worries. He tried to put the conversation out of his mind.

He had to stand on the cliff for a long time before he felt ready to rejoin the war council.

# CHAPTER 11

# EARTH ABIDES

Vy was unsure what she missed most about Earth. She could have said it was safety. She definitely longed to hug her mom.

How would Mom react to the fact that she was alive?

And to the man she was dating?

A meeting like that wasn't going to happen any time soon. Vy tried to put it out of her mind. At least her mom was safe—or as safe as it was possible to be when the Torth could invade Earth at any time.

"San Diego," Vy told Ariock. "Drop us off there."

Vy and Cherise were semifamous as missing persons. Even a brief visit to their hometown might result in Torth agents learning about it, which could cause the Hollander family to be abducted. Best not to risk it.

In California, they would not run into classmates or coworkers. It was on the opposite side of the continent, and since it was still within the United States, Vy would not have to acclimate to yet another foreign culture.

Plus, the weather was pleasant, even in winter. The ocean breeze felt quite a bit like Freedomland.

Vy and Cherise walked along the downtown boardwalk. San Diego was more upscale than the northern New England coastal towns they were familiar with, with more international tourists. Luckily, they had cash. Ariock had given them each a wad of hundred-dollar bills. Apparently, Garrett had multiple stashes, and he had directed Ariock to one of many lockboxes hidden inside the now-derelict Dovanack mansion.

Vy and Cherise browsed jewelry kiosks in a place called Seaport Village.

They reacquainted themselves with the taste of ice cream.

They explored old-time ships at the Maritime Museum, including a steamboat and a submarine.

Then they rented a pedicab and found themselves in the Gaslamp Quarter. After exploring a hookah lounge and a fine art gallery—where Cherise took brochures to show her students—they wrote a list of supplies they wanted to stock up on, such as sanitary pads and other items of human civilization.

It was getting late, well after dark, when they ordered Tex-Mex food and sat at an outdoor patio where they could people watch.

"I feel like we're aliens here," Cherise said, stirring the remains of her drink with a paper umbrella. "Do you feel that way?"

"I feel less alien here," Vy confessed. "We fit in perfectly." She surreptitiously kept an eye on two college-aged men at a nearby table. One had aimed a sweet smile at Vy when she'd accidentally glanced his way. Now the other elbowed him, friendly and joking.

"I'll understand if you want to stay longer," Cherise was saying, oblivious to the guys. "But I want to call for teleportation soon. Vy?" She said the name to grab Vy's attention. "Is that all right?"

Vy put her hand on Cherise's arm, redirecting her attention. "Those guys over there"—she cut her eyes in their direction—"are into us. I'm pretty sure they're working up the nerve to come and talk to us."

Cherise looked startled. Her reaction was comical, considering how visually stunning she was, with her thick hair styled. She had added a few blue streaks, and the peacock and indigo hues were bright against the lush blackness. She looked sophisticated and sexy at the same time.

Her battered eyeglasses were gone, replaced by ocular implants. It was Torth technology modified by Thomas's biotech team. An ummin engineer had invited Cherise to sit down in a lab chair and, with her consent, had improved her vision.

Both Vy and Cherise could now see traces of ultraviolet in the right conditions. Dark alleyways held few secrets from them, because their night vision could adjust to catlike levels. Cherise's brown eyes shone with a rosy tint—a striking color. Vy knew that her own modified irises held a subtle hint of electric blue.

Cherise glanced at the guys, then hunched down defensively. "Let's escape!" she whispered.

As if attractive men were just a nuisance. Perhaps she didn't understand how much fun flirting could be?

"You sure?" Vy asked. "You don't want to make Flen jealous?"

Cherise reassessed Vy with mock envy. "I suppose Ariock's never worried, since he's the Bringer of Hope and all. You should try dating a normal man just to see what it's like."

It was good-natured teasing. Even so, Vy felt jarred, as if Cherise had accused her of cheating on Ariock. Or of being disenchanted with him.

Vy forced a smile.

Lately, though, Ariock had been more distant with her. He was as gentle as ever—even more gentle, in fact—but he seemed to be pulling away emotionally.

She told herself it was because he was ridiculously busy.

Vy managed Ariock's schedule, so she knew that he was conquering SweetNectar City on Verdantia today. Later, he would teleport superluminal relay nodes into various orbits. Then he would endure Deschuba's review of the daily mayoral reports, and he would inspect the space fleet, which was under the command of a plucky ummin named Fayfer. Ariock alone was responsible for all major imports and exports. He also conducted an ever-growing list of daily security checks and sweeps.

Overall, Vy figured it was a good thing Ariock could fly, teleport, and magically clean himself. It was amazing that he spared any time at all for her. She should be grateful for every minute.

Maybe that was why he seemed distant?

He thrived on saving people and helping people, and Vy simply didn't need to be saved. That was just who he was. It made sense that he should take his meals with battle leaders or mayors instead of going on romantic dates.

"Vy?" Cherise looked concerned. "Earth to Vy."

"Yeah, sorry." Vy tried to look content. "Maybe I miss having men look at me. Ariock is super busy." She pushed away her plate of enchiladas. She had only eaten a few bites. It wasn't as good as the sizzling street foods in the Freedom bazaar.

"I get that." Cherise gave her a look full of sympathy and warmth. "Flen isn't exactly there for me, either, with his schedule. I'm not in a big rush to go home or anything." She picked up the list of wines and specialty beverages. "Want to take another look at the drink menu?"

"No, it's all right." Vy placed folded money on the table, covering the bill. "We can get going."

Other people eyed them as they made their way toward the street. Vy stepped aside to make room for the busy waitress, and one of the young men gave her a winsome smile.

"Will you buy those guys a round of drinks?" Vy said, channeling queenly confidence. She handed cash to the laughing waitress. Then she continued past the men with an added swish to the way her hips moved, just for fun. Her prosthetic leg was hidden under leggings and a skirt. It felt almost natural after months of daily practice using it. She was young and beautiful.

Ariock should feel lucky to have her.

Heads turned as Cherise followed, letting Vy navigate the crowded street. They moved past tourists and partiers. They might need to rent a hotel room if they couldn't find a hidden space in which to vanish.

"This looks good enough." Cherise trotted into an open stairwell behind a tattoo parlor.

Two years ago, Vy would have hesitated to enter a sketchy, run-down building that stank of urine. But human beings no longer seemed all that threatening to her. She had a blaster glove folded in her pocket.

Besides, her supercom allowed her to directly call the most powerful person in the galaxy.

A shabby-looking figure sat on the derelict second-floor landing. Shadows concealed him. He watched the intruders with apprehension, unaware that their enhanced vision allowed them to see into darkness in a way that no other humans could.

Vy tapped Cherise on the shoulder and pointed him out.

"Doesn't matter," Cherise whispered. She ventured farther up the stairs. "No one will believe him."

Vy assessed the grungy-looking man, then fished out her wad of hundred-dollar bills. She tucked it between railing slats. Maybe that would be some consolation to the squatter for witnessing an event no one would believe.

Cherise had already pulled out her supercom earpiece and clipped it onto her ear. "Two to beam up," she said, knowing that Ariock was listening for their call.

It had taken Ariock hours to set up deep-space superluminal relay nodes for Earth. Other planets needed superluminal communications and ought to be much higher on his priority list. But when Vy had casually mentioned how much she wanted to visit Earth, Ariock had acted like it was the most reasonable suggestion ever. He'd roped Thomas into helping. Together, they had designed, built, and deployed the line of satellites that allowed a call from Earth to reach Reject-20.

So Vy's wish was granted.

"We're above a tattoo parlor," Cherise said, giving Ariock directions.

Ariock did not need GPS or a map. He had memorized a cosmic route to Earth, and he had learned the geography of Earth well enough to pinpoint San Diego. He remembered the hotel where he had dropped off Cherise and Vy—they had appeared in one of its unused rooms—and he knew they would be within walking distance of that hotel. Cherise's directions gave him a landmark to scan for.

Vy imagined the disembodied ghost of Ariock zooming around the streets outside, hurtling directly through hotels and nightclubs, searching for the Horton Grand Hotel. Then he would look for tattoo parlors within two blocks.

Colors barely registered to him in a ghosted state. Light didn't matter. He would recognize Vy and Cherise even in a dark building.

Nor would Torth agents guess that Ariock was showing interest on Earth. He did not need to show up in person. His massive sphere of influence remained on Verdantia or Umdalkdul or wherever his body was—except for a brief half second when he would cast his full awareness and consciousness to San Diego.

Half a second wasn't much time for local Torth to really register his overwhelming presence. It certainly wasn't enough time for them to react.

Then, once Ariock engulfed Vy and Cherise in his awareness, he would catapult them back across the galaxy—

Vy stumbled on unexpected ground and squinted in blazing daylight. Her ears popped. Her equilibrium felt wrong for a second. Different planets had different gravity.

She inhaled air that felt fresher, lighter, and that smelled like a lightning storm. Teleportation always left a scent of ozone.

Cherise tripped against Vy, then regained her balance. She laughed, apparently amused by her own discombobulation.

They stood inside the grand foyer of the Freedomland war palace.

Their shopping bags lay around them. Sunlight streamed through massive openings in the palatial edifice, allowing a sea breeze and a view of the ocean. Alien dignitaries bustled up or down the bifurcated ramp. A few shot interested looks toward Vy and Cherise, who had just appeared on the frilly balcony overhang.

Ariock was gone.

Vy sighed. It would have been nice if he had said hello, even if he didn't have time for a conversation.

She supposed they might catch up tonight. Or the night after.

Or sometime.

"This was our first visit back to Earth." Cherise regarded Vy with what looked like sympathy. "What did you think of seeing the human race carrying on, unaware of the universe?"

Vy tried to find her usual cheerfulness. It seemed deeply buried. "I guess it didn't cure my homesickness," she admitted. "But I'm really glad we went. It was fun to remember a bunch of nice things about humans."

Vy pulled out her own jeweled supercom and clipped it onto her ear. Thomas had really empowered everyone with his superluminal inventiveness.

"Don't worry." Cherise squeezed Vy's hand. "We'll be able to risk communicating with your mom soon, I'll bet."

Vy squeezed back, grateful. "I'd love that."

She didn't dare, though. A holograph would give her mother hope, which would cause her to act differently, which would cause Torth agents to take notice. A message wasn't worth the risk to her mother's life.

"I really miss her."

Cherise looked sympathetic. "Me, too."

"But you know what?" Vy said. "It could be worse. My family is here, too."

Cherise smiled. Dimples appeared in her cheeks. "Ariock?" she guessed in a teasing, speculative tone.

"I meant you, silly." Vy hugged Cherise.

Cherise hugged her back, and Vy felt as if maybe she could trust Cherise with anything. "Best sister ever," she said.

"Best sister ever," Cherise said, laughing.

# CHAPTER 12

# BETWEEN FOUR HEROES

Ariock landed on a mountain-facing balcony of one of the many towering buildings he had carved out of cliffs with so little finesse. He ducked inside.

Thomas's face scrunched with pain as he flexed his legs, using a contraption that looked like a gyroscope built for midgets. He must have included this exercise machine on one of his lists of equipment to import.

"Hey." Ariock glanced around the open-air room, checking to see if Garrett or Evenjos had arrived yet. He noticed a pile of shredded cushions and blankets that resembled a large nest. "Where's Azhdarchidae?"

Thomas rested in the gyroscope. "Winging around." Sweat glistened on his forehead. "I guess everyone knows?"

He sounded guilty, as if a pet might be against a rule book somewhere.

"Yeah." Ariock offered a smile of reassurance. "It's hard to miss a trained sky croc soaring over the academy."

The animal was probably the poorest-kept secret in the city. Lots of people commented on it, noting that the sky croc was sensible enough to avoid people. It never flew within range of shooters. Whenever it banked toward the city, fiery flares in the sky barred its path and guided it in a safer direction.

Perhaps Thomas feared that caring for a baby animal exposed some kind of vulnerability within himself. But to Ariock, the pet signaled a refreshing reminder that Thomas was human. No matter how many minds he twisted, no matter how many Dovanacks his mother had murdered, he must have inherited kindness from his unknown father.

"Has Garrett or Evenjos showed up yet?" Ariock noticed three empty armchairs. He took a seat in the extra-large chair, obviously meant for him.

Garrett's booming voice came from the doorway. "I just want to say, it's been too long since our last private council."

The old man limped into the room, leaning on his staff the way he did sometimes. "I was going to call one. But you saved me the trouble." He smiled fondly at Ariock and plopped into an armchair.

Ariock could not have explained, exactly, why he had asked for a meeting with the three of them, secret even from Vy. It was just a feeling. He kept suspecting that the mind readers on his side—Thomas, Garrett, and Evenjos—were keeping secrets from him.

He wasn't even sure why that worry had entered his mind. Maybe it was because they were no longer checking in with each other on a daily basis? The war entailed a lot of simultaneous action. They could not meet regularly anymore.

Or maybe Ariock was subconsciously worried about gossip behind his back?

According to Vy, some of the Alashani whispered that Ariock was nothing but a puppet messiah controlled by *rekvehs*. Ariock wanted to clear the air. He wanted some frank talk with his friends that did not have to be diplomatic and guarded.

"We ought to share updates with each other on a regular basis." Garrett crossed one ankle over his leg, making himself comfortable. "And chat about our trajectory."

Thomas gave him a bland look.

"Want to go first?" Garrett asked.

"It would be best if I go last," Thomas said.

Garrett raised his bushy white eyebrows. "You have news?"

"Some," Thomas said.

"I hope it's progress on immunity to the inhibitor," Garrett said. "What are you doing in that contraption, anyway? We need you for your brains, not your muscles."

Thomas resumed his exercise.

"Well," Garrett said, "I guess I'll go first. Unless— Oh. Here she is now."

Thomas looked at the rough-hewn ceiling. Ariock followed his gaze and saw dust snaking in the shadows up there.

"Hi, Evenjos," Garrett said in a friendly tone.

The dust coalesced, glittering, but it did not pour into the third armchair. Instead, it streamed toward Ariock. A woman's bottom took shape directly on his lap. More dust solidified into shapely legs, which were crossed. Her spine began to form.

Ariock shoved her off.

Or he tried to. She was not fully solid. His hand passed through her torso.

Evenjos made a trill of contentment, and then she laughed at his angry reaction and slid off his lap. She became fully solid, her wings arced high on either side, metallic pseudofeathers touching the floor.

"You're so easy to startle," she said in a teasing, singsong voice.

Ariock glared.

Evenjos sank into the waiting armchair, languid and untroubled. She bounced one leg atop the other, as if bored. "So. Do any of us have news?"

"Not much." Garrett clasped his hands. "I did catch a penitent leaking intelligence into the Megacosm."

That sounded disastrous. Ariock stared at his great-grandfather, wide-eyed.

"It wasn't anything major," Garrett hastened to assure him. "Just facts about the scarce defense network on Jerja. I added an extra contingent of warriors for the roster there starting tomorrow."

Jerja was one of the industrialized moons of Umdalkdul. It might be an airless outpost, but even so, a million people lived there. Free people. Under Ariock's protection.

"We shouldn't even have penitents there," Ariock said.

"I agree," Garrett said.

"So, what happened?" Ariock asked. "Aren't penitents kept away from anyone in charge?" A penitent should never be privy to military secrets. Everyone knew that.

"Well," Garrett said, "it turns out Choonhulm appointed a mayor who is a dumbass."

Ariock leaned back, inviting more information.

"As soon as our conquering forces withdrew," Garrett said, "the new mayor reversed one of Kessa's main edicts. Apparently, that mayor decided he needed his own former master to scrub his floors and serve him pastries."

Ariock could imagine it. The newly freed slaves of Jerja would experiment with tranquility meshes and nectar drinks. And with no one watching over their shoulders . . . the elite members of that new society would bring a few penitents into their private chambers to serve them as slaves.

Those penitents would then eagerly listen to top-secret conversations while they scrubbed floors.

"To be fair," Garrett said, "I don't think it was Choonhulm's fault. It's hard to assess someone's character at a cocktail party. We simply don't know the people of Jerja, and Choonhulm was told to appoint one of the locals to act as our military mayor. It's inevitable that mistakes like that will happen."

Ariock supposed knowledge leaks were inevitable with such a huge populace under his stewardship. "Are you sure there weren't more?"

"I checked," Garrett said. "Anyway. As soon as I detected that particular live stream in the Megacosm, I teleported directly to the source and killed him."

Ariock didn't want or need details about the execution.

"Is there a new mayor?" Thomas asked.

"Yup," Garrett said. "I made a temporary appointment, and Kessa will set up someone permanent. But I suggest we establish these free outposts with more pomp and ceremony moving forward. Make the residents of those outposts feel how important they are, and how much they matter. We don't want them falling into bad habits."

Thomas nodded. "A consul for each planet we take over would help."

Ariock figured that various dignitaries and officials could manage whatever bureaucracy was needed. Someone had to ensure that the deposed mayor of Jerja did not continue to accidentally leak military secrets to penitents.

"And thank goodness for superluminal communications," Garrett said, with a nod to Thomas. "Because the outposts need oversight."

Ariock was grateful that Garrett had not brought this incident straight to the attention of the war council. It was a gaping security hole. It could scare hundreds of councilors, which meant scaring the public. It could rile up further hatred against penitent Torth.

Best to deal with it in private and then present it to the war council as a problem that had already been solved. The councilors would only have to deal with the aftermath.

"What did the Torth Empire learn?" Thomas asked. "Did they get Ariock's mass-teleportation schedule for that moon?"

Garrett nodded.

"That means they'll have a clearer picture of his limits," Thomas said. "We'll alter his schedule."

Ariock knew he should have thought of that himself.

Perhaps he should check in with Garrett more often. What other near-threats did the old man swat away without any praise or thanks? For that matter, what about Thomas and Evenjos? What did they do, exactly, on a day-to-day basis?

Evenjos blushed when Ariock looked her way.

Ariock wondered if her pink cheeks were a conscious detail. Everything about her was so artificial. "Do you have anything to report?"

"No," Evenjos said.

"I beg to differ," Garrett said. "Evenjos has saved quite a lot of lives." He shifted his gaze to Ariock. "She's devoted all her spare time to healing. People call her the Lady of Life."

"I am working on a new face," Evenjos said in a demure tone.

Her facial features changed, subtly but unmistakably, from humanlike to Alashani. Her skin went milk white. Her head became rounder, her chin smaller, her lips like a rosebud. The magenta hue of her hair drained away, and its texture became tightly curled.

"Amazing." Ariock tried not to show how unsettled he was. He no longer recognized her face.

"That is to encourage trust." Evenjos melted her face back to her familiar sultry features. "People admire Alashani. They are not so certain about humans. Or *rekvehs*."

"But . . ." Ariock wished he could blend into crowds with her ease. "You're keeping the wings?"

Evenjos flexed her wings. "My purpose is to signal rather than to deceive. I am showing that I wish to disassociate myself from mind readers. The Alashani are my people."

That was a change.

"I owe the Alashani a great debt." Evenjos gazed out at the city, perhaps regretting the fit of destruction she had mistakenly wrought. "My people are long dead. But their descendants have survived, despite my mistakes. I wish to compensate them as much as I can. I will heal any warrior who falls in battle."

"Thank you. That's very noble." Ariock tried not to admire her goddess form. She really wasn't as self-centered as he kept assuming she was. She had an honorable sense of justice.

Evenjos looked pretty and pleased, though she tried to hide it.

Ariock looked away. He reminded himself that she was all about artifice.

"What about you?" Garrett asked him. "Anything new to report?"

Ariock studied his friends. Thomas was exercising. Evenjos and Garrett politely feigned interest, yet their curiosity had to be false.

They were mind readers. They probably soaked up every decision he made, and at least half the thoughts that went through his head.

All the same, this meeting had been a good idea. Evenjos and Garrett had shared news that they would have been justifiably reluctant to share with the whole war council.

"I think you know what I've been up to," Ariock said. Every city he conquered was public knowledge. "And I guess you know my overall concerns."

Garrett spread his hands, as if to say, *You've caught me.*

"I share your concerns," Evenjos said, her exotic accent like a caress.

"We're doing well," Garrett said gruffly. "I know we're going to hit a wall sooner or later, but the more we take from the Torth, the more they lose." He turned to Thomas. "Speaking of which, have you considered experimenting with subtle brainwashing? I get that it's unfeasible to zombify the whole Megacosm. But what about a more nuanced approach?"

Thomas stopped exercising and stared at Garrett.

Ariock stared as well. It had not occurred to him that Thomas might be capable of a gentler, more nuanced version of brainwashing.

But Evenjos had taught him about the spectrum of powers, hadn't she?

Zombification was a very high magnitude of telepathy, which meant there ought to be less powerful magnitudes below that. A gentler touch. Something that did not entail permanent brain damage.

If a gentle touch could be applied to trillions of mind readers . . .

Well. Why was Ariock risking his life every day in battles, and the lives of his troops, if Thomas could simply win the war with a thought?

"I'd have to do it to them one at a time," Thomas said. "And as soon as they figured out what I'm doing, they'd all withdraw from the Megacosm. I might theoretically be able to brainwash half a million, if I got a major power boost and worked ultrafast. But definitely not billions. Not trillions." He kicked off his gyroscope in a new direction. "We'd have to take them by surprise, and we'd only get one shot. It's definitely not worth taking that shot now."

Garrett looked vexed. He made a cigarette appear and began to smoke it.

Ariock wondered if Thomas was dismissing his own potential. He might not be able to defeat the Torth Empire with a thought, but he was certainly good at scaring them.

Was zombification the only way to keep winning? Was that approach even sustainable, long term?

Thomas seemed withdrawn lately. He stayed in his tower or in the research annex. He only ventured outside in order to zombify prisoners or to show up for war councils. He stayed quiet in meetings, lurking in a corner as if he didn't belong.

"I do have a couple of things to share," Thomas said, rotating inside his contraption. "One is something that Garrett should have mentioned. The Torth imprisoned all their supergeniuses."

Evenjos looked startled, and Ariock felt the same way. This was perplexing news. "What?" he said. "Why?"

"They didn't imprison them," Garrett said in a grouchy tone. "The boy is exaggerating." He inhaled from his cigarette. "The Torth supergeniuses have been well guarded ever since the empire declared war on us."

Thomas shook his head. "They separated the Twins."

Ariock wasn't sure if that was significant.

"They put each Twin in a battleship that can be remotely destroyed if the Majority wills it." Thomas sounded like he was gloating, but he also sounded disgusted and sad. "That tells us the Torth Empire is making panicked, stupid decisions."

"How so?" Garrett raised a bushy eyebrow. "It looks like common sense to me. You've been putting out your siren call every day. Some Torth must be secretly tempted to join you. The Majority wants to prevent another Upward Governess situation. They're just ensuring that their high-value assets don't go renegade."

"Right." Thomas smiled thinly. "Death threats work on normal people. But supergeniuses are hyper-self-aware and have high rates of unpredictable mental idiosyncrasies, plus suicidal tendencies. It's a bad idea to pressure them like this." He strained to flex, to keep his rotation going. "Especially with me offering them an alternative lifestyle."

Garrett looked unconvinced. "They're still working round the clock, according to chitchat in the Megacosm. So they're still acting loyal, at least."

He seemed oblivious to the strain in Thomas, who was also working day and night.

"If they're truly loyal," Thomas said, "they'll get burnout. And if not? They'll either figure out a way to go renegade and join me, or they'll escape by killing themselves." He looked confident. "Any way you slice it, it's a stupid move on the part of the Torth Empire. And it's a boon for us."

The topic made Ariock uncomfortable. When he thought of the empire's supergeniuses, he thought of children, such as those whom he'd seen murdered in baby farms.

"Anything else to report?" Garrett asked Thomas. "Have you finally made progress on immunity to the inhibitor?"

Evenjos clasped her hands, alert and hopeful.

Ariock leaned forward, despite his caution around mind readers. Immunity to the inhibitor would change everything. Evenjos would finally run out of excuses to fight Torth. She would smash cities.

As for Jinishta and her Alashani warriors? And Ariock himself? They would become invincible.

With immunity, they would be able to conquer multiple cities simultaneously, instead of having to concentrate all their forces in just one spot, with a trailing defense. The Torth Empire would likely go into a full-fledged panic. They'd evacuate every territory Ariock and his forces so much as looked at.

"Nothing to report on that yet," Thomas said.

Ariock sat back, disappointed.

"Um." Thomas stopped his exercises. The contraption slowed, and he looked hesitant. "I do have something to report. It's just a minor problem. Nothing to get concerned about."

"What?" Garrett scooted to the edge of his seat.

"It's no big deal." Thomas came to a complete stop. "I hope." His shoulders hunched in a defensive way. Whatever this was, it shamed him. "Do you remember, right after I got healed, you asked me to check myself for brain damage?"

They were all instantly alert.

# CHAPTER 13

# TYRANNICAL WILL

Ariock could see that whatever Thomas was about to say, it was a difficult admission. "I, um . . ." He spoke in a small, apologetic, somewhat squeaky voice. "I have a small memory leak."

The cigarette fell out of Garrett's hand and smoldered on the floor.

Thomas hurried to explain. "It's remotely possible that I had holes in my memory before and never noticed."

Clouds rolled over the mountain peaks. A chill wind blew across the tower top, with its open archways. Ariock prepared to reverse a Garrett-induced storm.

"We can't let this become public knowledge." Thomas shifted his gaze to Garrett. "The only reason I'm telling you is because you made it a command. You demanded that I report the results to you as soon as I knew."

Garrett popped out of his chair and began to pace furiously, his face apoplectic. "A memory leak!?" He punctuated each accusation by pointing. "You said you would be fine! Evenjos told us there would be no brain damage!"

Evenjos sat with her legs crossed, cool and unruffled. "I said there were likely to be changes. An intense rejuvenation like that has consequences." She glanced at Thomas and looked slightly ashamed. "I am sorry. We did our best."

"I know." Thomas gave her a fond, friendly look. "I appreciate what you did for me. I have no regrets."

"But he's damaged!" Garrett said explosively. "Don't you get it?" He flung a pointing finger at Thomas. "You made him handicapped!"

Thomas recoiled as if Garrett had struck a nerve.

Ariock assessed Thomas, who looked as healthy as any teenage boy. He kept outwitting the enemy supergeniuses. His intelligence remained extraordinary and sharp, and anyone who thought otherwise was being unfair.

"Garrett." Ariock pushed his pointing hand down. "He's fine, I'm sure. Whatever the problem is, it's minor."

"Pretty minor," Thomas assured them. "It's a few skipped moments, plus occasional gaps in my thirdhand perceptual data. I wouldn't have even noticed if not for the background subroutine you had me run. It's the sort of trivial background noise that ordinary minds filter out." He looked eager to reassure Ariock, especially. "I still have a phenomenal memory. It's just a little suboptimal compared to the other supergeniuses.'"

"Great." Garrett looked as dark as the stormy sky outside.

"It's no big deal." Ariock made his deep voice soothing, trying to calm his great-grandfather.

"Right. And it can't be fixed, in any event," Thomas said. "We just ought to make sure the Torth don't find out."

"Crap." Garrett paced. "I'll have to cut back my security sweeps in the Megacosm. I won't be able to spy on them as effectively."

Ariock felt lost. "Why not?"

"Because I'm vulnerable to mind probes!" Garrett said impatiently. "I don't have a freaky megabrain. They can get into my secrets if I stick around too long at any given time."

"I thought you were the ultimate spy?" Ariock gave him a level look. "You know plenty of military secrets the Torth shouldn't know. In fact, you know more about the future than Thomas does, since you won't let us look at your book of prophecies."

"You don't understand how mind probes work," Garrett growled. "They scan for an emotion and follow anything that seems unusual. Emotional scars often lead to secrets or traumatic memories—things that the person wants to bury. I'm not ruffled about our tactics and I've had years to develop inner peace about the prophetic paintings. But this gigantic flaw he just dumped on us? I'll need a week to calm down!" He glared at Thomas. "You shouldn't have told me, boy."

Thomas glared back. "Maybe you should think through the implications of the orders you give me."

"You'd better take over some of my security duties in the Megacosm this week," Garrett said. "I normally do a sweep right after a conquest and before we've decided on our next target."

"I don't have time—" Thomas began to say.

Garrett snorted. "What else are you doing?" He swept a gesture around the big room. "Building your own private gym? Oh. And playing with that beast." He pointed.

Outside, Azhdarchidae winged toward them, looking more like a dragon than a crocodile, with his huge leathery wings. He looked legendary.

"Do you really need a pet?" Garrett said.

Thomas glared with defiant outrage, and Ariock agreed with him. What was wrong with having someone, or something, to care about?

The Alashani warriors were smart enough to account for love. They encouraged their warriors to care about families and friends. Love was sensible. Ariock didn't know how sane he'd feel without Vy.

"I do plenty that you don't see," Thomas said coldly. "Planning battles takes time if you want to keep winning. The Torth adapt to every strategy I come up with, you know. I have to constantly reanalyze and reinvent our approaches. Oh, and outthink their supergeniuses. It's not as easy as I make it look."

"Yet you still find time to play games." Garrett was so furious, electricity snapped along his body in white jags and arcs. "I think we can cut one of your pastimes from your busy schedule. If I have to decide for you? I will."

He stalked toward the wraparound balcony.

"No!" Thomas cried. "Don't you dare!"

Ariock stood. Judging by Thomas's anguish, he must have picked up an unpleasant promise from Garrett's mind.

Would the old man actually attack Azhdarchidae? It seemed impossible to believe. The sky croc was just an innocent animal.

"If you hurt him," Thomas said, "you'll regret it."

Garrett whirled around, his mantle swinging like a cape. "Is that a threat?" Electricity crackled. "You're crossing a line, boy."

But it was Garrett who had crossed a line.

In a state of complete disbelief, Ariock rippled out his awareness and seized Garrett. He used his power to slam the armored warrior against the rough-hewn central wall, pinning him well above the ground.

Garrett flexed with his powers, trying to escape.

There was a time when a warrior as strong as Garrett could have broken free from Ariock's grip. But Ariock was no longer unpracticed. He killed Servants of All on a daily basis. He faced as many as ten Servants at once, at their peak power, all of them choreographed by some distant supergenius. He regularly walked into places where Rosy Ranks surprise attacked him. In battle, his reflexes were honed to the level of pure instinct.

"Thomas will keep his pet," Ariock said.

Garrett struggled, glaring in defiance.

"I'm done with you bullying him," Ariock said. "We're supposed to be allies. I need you to act like it. If you're going to keep threatening the supergenius who literally wins our battles, then I don't need you around."

Garrett drooped in Ariock's invisible grip. He looked shocked that his own great-grandson would dare stand against him.

"Get out of my sight." Ariock released the old man and let him drop to the floor.

He half wondered if he was overreacting. What if Thomas had provoked Garrett in some silent, mind-reader way? Had he missed some unspoken subtext?

Then he glanced at Thomas and saw grim, satisfied relief. That wasn't a smug look of triumph. Thomas had needed a friend to stand up for him.

Beyond Thomas's gyroscope, the immense beast, Azhdarchidae, landed on the edge of the tower. He crawled over the balustrade, scales rippling. Ariock prepared an air shield, but the animal seemed to understand that he was underpowered in the present company. He slunk to his nest in the shadows, folded himself, and watched them all with reptilian eyes that glinted like fiery gold.

Garrett used his powers to bring his staff into his waiting grasp. "Fine. Whatever."

He stomped out of the room. A stormy breeze made book pages flutter.

Evenjos stood with a sigh of annoyance. She had a faint goddess glow, her feathers and hair rippling. "I suppose I will go and talk to him."

She glided through the doorway and down the spiral ramp, following Garrett.

Ariock cupped a hand to his mouth and called, "Try to transform him into something other than a jerk!"

His voice echoed through the hollow center of the tower. If Garrett heard, he probably didn't care. He was probably bursting with self-righteous indignation, plotting new ways to make the war even more terrible than it had to be.

Ariock turned to Thomas. He wanted to apologize for his great-grandfather, but any apology would be inadequate. Maybe even disingenuous. Why should he be responsible for Garrett's mistakes?

He didn't want to have to manage a prickly old man who was flawless in battle yet who otherwise made all kinds of mistakes.

"Have a seat," Thomas offered. "Please."

Ariock realized he was looming like usual, blocking the light. He moved his oversize armchair closer to the gyroscope and sat. He clasped his big hands.

"I don't understand Garrett," he admitted.

He sat close enough so Thomas could soak up the truth of that admission. And once he began to talk about the problem, it was as though a dam shattered. "I don't understand what's wrong with him." Concerns, long bottled up, came pouring out. "He enjoys killing. It's not just killing. He enjoys brutality. I see how he treats you. And it's not just you. The warriors don't like him. The soldiers don't trust him." Ariock clenched his fists. "He's helpful in battles and I can't do well without him. But am I going to have to keep threatening him? Is that the only possible way to handle him?"

Thomas had a gentle look. "I can't advise you on that."

"I don't want to fight with him." Ariock thumped his fist on the armrest, frustrated. "He's my family. My only family. I just . . ." He met Thomas's gaze, wondering if his friend might provide some helpful insights. "Do you think he's a threat? To the war, I mean? Is he dangerous, to the point where I should send him away?"

Thomas seemed to consider the question carefully.

Then he spoke. "Garrett is the Will in the prophecies. He wasn't lying about that. We're going to need him in order to win this war, I think."

Ariock slumped. He wanted a better answer. An easier path.

"It may help if you get to know what drives him," Thomas said. "And his fears. He doesn't like feeling like he's not in control. We both trigger his insecurities."

Ariock mulled that over.

"He can't control either of us," Thomas said. "And that really bothers him."

The old man did seem to like controlling and manipulating others. He hoarded knowledge. He lied in order to make himself seem heroic.

"He claims that he killed his father," Ariock said. That was one claim that bothered him. Garrett tended to bluster and exaggerate his own heroic deeds, but patricide? That wasn't exactly a thing to brag about.

"Is that true?" Ariock was aware that Thomas could read the nuances and undercurrents beneath his yearning for an answer. He really wanted to learn something that would shed light on why Garrett was such an overbearing jerk. "Did he kill his father when he was six years old?"

"It's somewhat true," Thomas said. "His father did die when he was six. And the death could be attributed to Jonathan Stead."

"What happened?" Ariock leaned forward, genuinely curious. Maybe there was more to Garrett than bluster and bravado.

Thomas shook his head. "That's not my secret to tell."

"Did Garrett threaten you?" Ariock tried to stay small and tranquil. "Is he going to hurt you if you tell me?"

Thomas looked miserable with uncertainty. He seemed to be debating whether or not to reveal some fact.

"Ugh." Ariock took a deep breath, forcing his awareness to retreat out of the stormy air. "I've given him way too much leeway." If the old man wanted to threaten a child, then he did not belong on the side of the heroes. "Enough is enough. I'm going to have to give him an ultimatum."

"Wait," Thomas said, as Ariock moved to get up.

Ariock paused.

"It's not that Garrett threatened me." Thomas sounded reluctant, as if he was forcing himself to speak. "I'm just not comfortable telling other people's secrets. You'll need to ask him yourself. I think you can get real answers that satisfy you, if you ask him the right questions."

Ariock stared at Thomas in wonder. Did he actually feel sympathy for someone who bullied him without mercy?

"Garrett is a victim of the Torth, too," Thomas said. "I'm not a fan of him, obviously. But I think it's my duty to tell you that he's emotionally scarred."

"So are we all," Ariock said without sympathy. Even the progenitors of the Torth had been victims. It did not excuse their present-day atrocities.

"I think he's somewhat more scarred than you or me," Thomas said carefully.

Ariock studied the boy. Was he saying that Garrett had suffered worse than being crucified for the whims of a Torth audience?

"Ask him about his father," Thomas suggested. "But it would be a good idea to approach the subject with compassion."

# CHAPTER 14
# POWERFULLY DYSFUNCTIONAL

Ariock found Garrett sitting on a rocky outcrop in the middle of the ocean. It was beyond sight of land, utterly desolate. The frothing, crashing waves probably reflected how Garrett was feeling.

There were no other life sparks nearby. The powerful thrum of Evenjos was back in the city, where she was likely engaged in her usual healing services at the hospitals. She had clearly failed to put Garrett in a better mood.

Ariock dropped out of the sky.

Garrett jumped, then regained his composure. He gave Ariock a grouchy look. "It's nice to have the biggest sphere of influence on the planet, isn't it?"

"It makes you easy to locate," Ariock agreed, sitting on the rock next to Garrett. Yeresunsa stood out like beacons to his sixth sense. He could pinpoint the intense spark of Evenjos or Garrett whenever they were within his sphere of influence, which was roughly the size of a solar system. They could not do likewise. If Ariock was around, then his overwhelming influence washed out their ability to sense life sparks.

And Ariock teleported so often these days—multiple times per day—it had become second nature for him to scout out a location before showing up. He ghosted with ease. It was a cinch to find someone as powerful as Garrett.

"Well, I don't need a lecture." Garrett gazed at the ocean as if it angered him. "I'm sorry I lost my temper. I'll try to do better."

"Thomas is a good friend," Ariock said. "Why don't you see that?"

Garrett gave him a defiant glare full of unspoken rage. "I said I don't need a lecture."

Everything about Garrett's body language told Ariock to leave. The old man was in a deadly mood. He was the epitome of barely contained brutality.

If left alone, he would probably teleport to some faraway fringe of the Torth Empire and murder a bunch of Torth just to blow off steam. He did that sometimes. He dutifully participated in every major battle, but sometimes he created his own minibattles, going alone to dangerous dens full of Rosies or Servants. He took needless risks. The prison population was regularly refreshed with extra prisoners Garrett took. Some warriors called him a maverick, while others insinuated that he was rabid and dangerous.

"Why are you so angry?" Ariock asked.

Garrett rolled his eyes.

"I'm not going to lecture you." Ariock had no desire to act like a parent, especially not to his own great-grandfather. "But we need to understand each other."

Garrett huffed.

Ariock tapped his head. "You understand where I'm coming from. You can read minds. But I can't read your mind. And you're acting in ways I don't understand."

He stopped short of accusing Garrett of acting like a Torth. But that was what bothered him the most. Garrett claimed to despise everything the Torth did, yet he was happy to treat Thomas like a slave. He accused the Torth of being evil brutes, yet he reveled in brutal violence. He hated the way Torth hoarded knowledge, yet he was secretive and cagey.

Garrett gave him a resentful look. "You're not going to lecture me. You're just going to sit there quietly and judge me?"

"Sorry." Ariock tried to tone down his frustration.

"Go away," Garrett said.

Ariock refused to budge.

He just wanted to understand his great-grandfather. Was that so much to ask? He refused to believe that his ally—his rescuer, his surrogate father, the Will of the prophecies—was insane or stupidly evil.

There must be a story behind Garrett's simmering hatred. Thomas had implied as much.

"Will you tell me why you hate the Torth so much?" Ariock begged. "You once mentioned that your father killed your mother. Did you, uh . . ." He hesitated, wishing he knew how to approach the subject with proper sensitivity. "Did you witness it?"

Usually, other people talked a lot more than Ariock did. The silence felt awkward to him.

"I don't want to be intrusive," Ariock said. "I won't force you to tell me what happened. But you said you cared about me. You said we're family. I just wonder why our supposed family bond is so completely one-sided."

Garrett slumped.

Far below, the waves lapped at the rocks in a way that seemed mournful. The frothing rage had ebbed.

"You've seen every bad moment of my life," Ariock said. "You've witnessed this." He turned his arm over, displaying the scar of his suicide attempt. "You know exactly how I felt when I was alone in that arena. You were there when I hung, dying, from a metal cross in an alien desert." He rested his hands on his lap. "I don't know you at all. I don't understand you."

As Ariock spoke, he realized that the unequal balance of their knowledge made him uneasy.

Knowledge was power. The Torth were silent and expressionless for a reason. Their silence added to the power they held over slaves.

Garrett leaned his elbows on his knees, gazing at the vista of waves. "I don't see what good telling my story will do," he said in a weak voice. He actually sounded old. "Knowing what I went through won't change anything. I'm still the person I am."

"It will help me understand you," Ariock said.

He really wanted that, he realized. Secrets were a barrier to trust. Whatever pains Garrett wanted to keep hidden, those were points of vulnerability. Those were things that mattered to him. If he shared those things, that would signify trust, and mutual respect, which was lacking in their family bond.

"The boy told you to ask me about my father," Garrett muttered with disgust. "Didn't he?"

"I asked for his advice," Ariock admitted. "But my questions are my own."

"Fine." Garrett's shoulders hunched inward, defensive. "Yes, I had a rotten childhood. What would you expect? I had a monstrous Torth for a father."

That was vague.

"What did he do to you?" Ariock asked.

Garrett avoided eye contact. He hunched even more, and Ariock realized, with some sympathy, that whatever Garrett had suffered, it still affected him very much. It shaped who he was.

"He was abusive," Garrett said.

Ariock suspected that might be a severe understatement. Cautiously, he tried for nuance. "Every day?"

Garrett laughed in a dark way that seemed to conceal an ocean of pain.

"Did you see him kill your mother?" Ariock gently asked.

Garrett shivered. Although he was an old man with a lot of power, he curled in on himself in a childlike way.

A lot of Garrett's actions were childlike, now that Ariock thought about it. The uncontrollable rages were like that of a toddler. The need for control? That was also a quality that young children fought for.

"He smothered her," Garrett said. "With his hands. Right after I was born. I wasn't self-aware enough to remember, but he showed me when I was older. He replayed the memory and forced me to watch. Over. And over."

Ariock sat back. He almost regretted asking.

But now that he had pried open the lid on Garrett's secrecy, he wasn't going to request a therapist or offer to blow off steam in a battle together. They were talking about something meaningful. This was progress.

"How old were you, when he did that?" Ariock asked.

Garrett shrugged. "Three or four. I never knew my age. I guess I don't really know it now. It wasn't like we celebrated birthdays."

Very young.

Part of Garrett seemed to remain arrested in that stage of life. He had not had any maternal influence. Just that monster of a father. Except . . .

"Who raised you?" Ariock tried to figure it out. Surely an abusive Torth father would not nurture a baby?

Garrett gazed at the hazy horizon. "There were mothers," he said in an emotionless tone. "One poor woman after another. Mostly, they were teenagers. Runaways. Or else they were looking for a job, or a man who would support them. He coaxed them into the house with gifts and fake promises."

A coldness crept up Ariock's spine.

"We lived on a bluff," Garrett said. "There were thick woods and no one could see our backyard. He buried them there. Unmarked graves, of course. After he was done abusing each one."

A serial killer.

Ariock did not know why that surprised him. He should have expected it. He tried to shrug it off, to back away from the disturbing thought of who he was related to.

He was also related to at least two victims of that killer.

A little baby named Jonathan had been trapped in that house of terror. And before Jonathan was born, his pregnant mother had been trapped there.

Eidelwen. Ariock remembered her name. Jinishta had told him the tale, back before the Alashani underground got flooded and invaded. Eidelwen was a premier Yeresunsa warrior, impregnated by a Torth attacker. She had run away in order to protect her unborn baby. She was never seen again.

But she had survived. For a while.

She was captured, her mind was probed, and the brute who had raped her realized that her memories would get him condemned. Instead of waiting for his brethren to throw him into the Isolatorium, that rapist had stolen Eidelwen out of her dungeon cell. He had taken her away on a streamship.

On Earth, the rapist had posed as a human man with his pregnant wife.

Jonathan never saw his mother's face. She was murdered after giving birth. Maybe she had made too much noise for her fake husband to tolerate? Ariock had trouble imagining the family dynamics.

Surely Jonathan had wanted to run away as soon as he grew old enough to walk?

His very existence would have been a threat to his father. He could read minds. As an unwilling witness to criminal atrocities, surely he must have tried to stop his depraved monster of a father? He must have presented severe challenges to that rapist and serial killer.

"Why did he keep you alive?" Ariock felt a need to know.

Garrett seemed to collect his thoughts. After a while, he answered.

"I think there were two reasons. At the time, I was only aware of one. He craved an audience. Even though I disgusted him, even though he despised me . . . he kept coming up to my room in the attic to show me what he had done."

There was a peculiar sickness in that psychology, Ariock thought. Jonathan's father had been like a child, too. He had wanted to show off. He had craved attention.

And wasn't that endemic to all Torth?

They were raised to expect the presence of an audience inside their minds. That was their sole measure of self-worth. A Torth without the Megacosm—without an audience—was an exile. Hunted. Doomed. They had no status, no rank, and no hope.

Ariock saw penitent work crews, and they looked wretched. He saw Torth prisoners, dead-eyed and suicidal. Millions of exiled Torth survived within the cities he controlled, except they were no longer Torth, really. They lacked power. They could not command slaves. They were, in fact, slaves themselves.

Jonathan's father had been one like that.

Only he had been a rogue, not under anyone's control.

"He dared not confide in anyone," Garrett went on. "Except me. I was the only person in his life who had his power to read minds. So I suppose he saw me as a potential equal, in a sick sort of way. As for the other reason . . . I didn't realize it at the time, but he was trying to shape me. He wanted an heir."

Garrett cringed, saying that.

An heir to what? Ariock wondered. Had Jonathan's nameless father wanted to create a junior serial killer?

"Family is a decadence that most Torth don't get a chance to indulge in," Garrett explained. "It's against their laws. But the monster who raised me was all about indulging in illegal decadences. I was just another trophy. Like the women he enslaved and then killed."

Ariock had trouble imagining a child as a trophy.

"Most Torth donate gametes to baby farms," Garrett said. "They never get to shape the lives of their offspring. They rarely even know who their offspring are. My father must have figured that since he was in exile, he would do whatever he wanted. That included raising his very own son."

What a strange inclination, for a Torth.

Ariock wondered if Jonathan's father had been capable of a full range of emotions. Had he felt anything for his child? What about the unwilling Alashani victim who had been forced to pose as his wife?

Was she the only victim he had impregnated?

"As far as I know," Garrett said, "I'm his only child. Although I can't be sure, can I? I don't know every detail of what he was doing. His visits were infrequent. He may not have showed me everything."

Ariock imagined other unwanted children like Jonathan Stead, unaware half siblings. Had they grown up? Had they raised families of their own?

Did Ariock have a whole lot of superpowered cousins on Earth?

"Yeresunsa powers can lie dormant over a lifetime," Garrett said, responding to his thoughts. "So I suppose it's possible that we might have a bunch of human cousins descended from my father. But I judge it unlikely. Torth genetics are rife with wild-card mutations." He gently nudged Ariock. "One of them would have inherited some strangeness, like your growth disorder."

Ariock swallowed, remembering how many times he had thought himself cursed.

Maybe someone else on Earth was suffering from too much uniqueness right now, the way he had.

"And to answer your other unspoken question," Garrett said, "yes, my father had a full range of emotions, for sure. He was a Yeresunsa. We all have strong emotions. It's tied to having powers."

Ariock felt chilled, imagining how outmatched the young Jonathan had been. "He was a Yeresunsa?"

"A Servant of All," Garrett confirmed. "Yes. But I got lucky." He tapped his head. "He never imagined that I might inherit powers from *her* as well as from him. He never bothered to learn who she really was."

Jonathan, aka Garrett, had the full suite of powers, Ariock remembered. He must have had at least one or two powers that his father lacked.

"How did you . . ." Ariock paused. It seemed rude to ask how young Jonathan had survived.

Yet it was an important question. How did a very young child survive among caretakers who inevitably became victims of a serial killer? Had those victims resented the cherished son of their tormentor? Had they understood that he could read minds like their abuser?

Had they feared him, even though he was a child?

Garrett gazed at the banded planet on the horizon. He must be able to overhear Ariock's unasked questions, yet he did not volunteer any answers.

This was a sensitive subject. That made it all the more important for Ariock to hear the truth.

He took a risk and asked, "How did you survive?"

"Everything you've guessed," Garrett said, without looking at him, "is accurate. They despised me. They believed my father was a demon from hell, and I was another unholy demon. I learned to disguise my power to read minds. I learned to act harmless and helpless. But you know what? It barely made any difference. I knew they were doomed. There was nothing I could do to help them. So I . . . I couldn't get attached to them."

Ariock could hardly imagine the toxic environment that his great-grandfather had grown up in. "I'm sorry," he said.

"There was one." Garrett paused, and when he went on, there was a pained hitch in his voice. "Anna Stead."

"Stead?" Ariock wondered if he had misheard.

"Yes." Garrett shivered. "I haven't spoken her name in a long time. But she deserves to be remembered. She showed me kindness."

"I'm sorry." Ariock hoped that particular caretaker had not suffered.

"I was in love with her sister," Garrett said.

"What?"

"She had a little sister," Garrett said. "Julia. I saw her in the mind of Anna. I used to ghost to the Stead household, to see how normal people lived. The route was easy for me. They were just down the road. We were neighbors. And Julia loved books." Warmth came into his tone as he remembered. "I ghosted to Julia as often as possible. Every day. Multiple times per day. I know it sounds creepy and voyeuristic, but I was desperate to experience a happy, normal childhood, even if it was by proxy."

Julia. Ariock heard wistful love and longing in Garrett's voice. This was someone who had mattered to him.

"I grew up with Julia by proxy," Garrett said in a tone of admission. "I read books over her shoulder. That's how I learned to read."

Ariock imagined it: a lonely, abused little boy, able to escape his own body by becoming a ghost. Of course he had visited so-called normal people.

"The Stead family were everything I yearned for," Garrett said. "I would have gone through any pain, taken any risk, for a hope of being adopted by that family. I loved every one of them. Julia especially, but I loved Anna as well."

The pain of loss was in his voice. He had gotten attached to his caretaker.

"What happened to Anna?" Ariock dared to ask.

"She wanted to smuggle me out of the house." Garrett gave an indirect reply, perhaps caught up in the memories. "The trouble was, I couldn't walk at the time." He tapped his crooked leg. "This was broken in multiple places. It healed wrong, since I was never taken to a doctor."

Few Yeresunsa could mend old scars or deformities. That sort of in-depth regeneration required Evenjos's sixth-magnitude healing power, so Ariock understood why Garrett had been unable to fully straighten out his crooked leg.

But how had the leg been shattered in the first place? Ariock wasn't sure how to phrase such an intrusive question.

"My father threw me down a flight of stairs." Garrett said that as if it was no big deal. "Because I wanted to leave the attic and see what fresh air felt like. I was five or six years old. After that, I was bedridden for months. No one cared."

Ariock stared at Garrett anew. He was so used to his great-grandfather as a capable warrior, he could not imagine him as a disabled child.

"Some of my so-called mothers kept me tied to the filthy cot I slept in," Garrett said in that offhand tone. "They were afraid of me, a demon child. That's what I was. My father commanded them to keep me alive, so they fed me oatmeal and water, and they cleaned me. But mostly, they avoided the attic. They didn't want to touch me."

Unloved. Unwanted. Ariock wanted to rescue that child himself.

# CHAPTER 15

# STRENGTH OF WILL

"My father had two modes," Garrett went on, his tone uncaring. "Content or insane. He expected my approval for the nasty things he had done. If I didn't show approval, he threatened to break me in half. He would rage that I wasn't worth keeping alive."

Garrett waved in an offhand gesture of dismissal.

That offhand attitude must be a means of self-protection. Ariock had seen Thomas act the same way. And Cherise, for that matter. Garrett was doing everything possible to signal that he was beyond the pain and that his childhood no longer affected him. He was trying to convince himself.

"What was your original last name?" Ariock asked, probing to learn how much Garrett had rejected his original identity. "It wasn't Stead. Was it?"

"What does it matter?" Garrett said. "The name was fake. We didn't have birth certificates."

Ariock nodded acceptance of that bit of their family history. Names were changeable, anyway. His own name was a whim—a combination of syllables his mother had liked, plus the made-up last name created by Garrett and passed down through three generations.

Thomas, too, had a whim of a name. He had been discovered on Liberty Hill Road, by a doctor named Thomas.

Jonathan and Thomas. Both mind readers.

Both mistreated or discarded by their parents.

Both unable to walk in childhood?

"Yup." Garrett laughed without humor. "I have more in common with the boy than you thought."

"Then you should have more sympathy for him," Ariock said.

Garrett answered with a hard, flat stare. "I have sympathy for the boy's physical condition. But he is a billion times more capable than I was at that age. He isn't a victim. I was. There is a world of difference between him and me."

Ariock decided to back away from comparisons to Thomas, which might trigger Garrett's complicated feelings about mind readers. Another question troubled him. "Your father," he said, "expected you—a toddler—to approve of rape and murder?"

"He expected me to be a Torth," Garrett said.

That simple statement was enough for Ariock to piece together the motives of that long-dead renegade Servant of All. He must have missed the Megacosm. The only possible audience he had was his toddler son. Jonathan was supposed to stand in for an audience of emotionless sycophants.

Ariock pictured the helpless little kid cowering in a drafty attic, unloved and kept like a despised pet. Jonathan must have lived in dread of hearing his father's footsteps coming up the attic stairs.

Paradoxically, though, he must have felt pressure and obligation to please his father. He had been utterly reliant on that father.

Until he grew a bit older.

Until he started ghosting.

Then he had spied on other families, and he had learned that love existed and that happiness was possible.

Maybe at that point, young Jonathan had quit pretending to like his father's heinous acts. He had become rebellious.

"How did you escape your father?" Ariock wanted to know. "Was Anna Stead the one who smuggled you away?"

Garrett spoke with wounded slowness. "The problem was that my father could read minds. As soon as Anna thought up a concrete plan, the clock would be ticking. She would need to leave before he could get close enough to scan her thoughts. I told her that. She didn't fully understand what my father could do, but I told her."

There were traces of long-ago desperation in Garrett's tone.

"I helped her plan," Garrett went on. "She served him his meals, so he would read her mind if she tried to poison him. Her best chance of survival was to just run. I told her to leave me behind. I couldn't travel, even on horseback."

"Horseback?"

"My father owned a horse." Garrett saw Ariock's look of surprise and elaborated. "Automobiles weren't very widespread then. We didn't own a car. The road was dirt and mud, anyway."

Ariock remembered that his great-grandfather was quite a lot older than an ordinary geriatric human. The automobile must have been a recent invention when he was six years old.

"I told her she should take the horse, but only if she could do so without catching his attention," Garrett went on. "Otherwise she would need to run on foot through the woods. She would need to take an unplanned route. Be unpredictable. Otherwise he would track her down. He hunted down dozens of women by figuring which ways they would try to escape. It was practically a sport for him. That's part of the reason he kept a horse."

"You tried to save her," Ariock said warmly. Garrett Dovanack might have rough edges, but a good person was encased within his layers of defensiveness.

Garrett hunched his shoulders. "I wasn't very effective. I was too weak to do anything useful. I couldn't create a big enough distraction for her to get to safety."

"But you tried," Ariock realized.

"I knocked over my candle," Garrett said. "I tried to set the house on fire. In my imagination, a fire would give her enough time to get to civilization—and then maybe return with an angry mob. I wanted the town constable to arrest my father. Or better yet, kill him."

Judging by the wistful hoarseness of Garrett's voice, that wish had not come to pass.

"The candle didn't work?" Ariock asked gently.

Garrett shook his head. "The flame just flickered out."

"What happened to Anna?"

"She ran down the hill and through the woods." Garrett indicated the motion with his hand. "She got a good head start. Better than any of his other victims. My father didn't even realize she was gone until twenty or thirty minutes after she was out the door."

Ariock wondered how the monster had kept watch over his victims.

"He used to hobble his victims," Garrett answered the unasked question. "With chains. But he had grown lax about it. Mostly, he used psychological terror. He threatened torture. He threatened to murder their families. That sort of thing."

As if that sort of thing was no big deal.

"Anna was terrified that he would murder her parents and sister if she ever escaped," Garrett went on. "That worked on other women, because they thought my father was a demon. They could only guess what he was capable of."

But Anna was different, Ariock realized. Because she had dared to talk with young Jonathan instead of treating him like a detestable monster, she had learned exactly what powers his father had.

Garrett nodded in confirmation. "I told Anna that my father had never followed through on threats to families. I assured her that her parents and sister would be safe. My father kept a low profile. I didn't understand why at the time, but it's obvious now. He was living illegally on Earth. He didn't want Torth agents on Earth to suspect that a rogue Servant of All was enjoying himself in middle America." Garrett shivered. "I didn't know, at the time, that there were things even my father was terrified of."

The Torth Empire was certainly something to fear.

"So Anna took the risk," Ariock prompted. "And your father found out she was gone?"

Garrett curled inward. He looked miserable, and Ariock knew what had happened even before he responded.

"He treated Anna like a slave," Garrett said. "He trained her to respond to hand gestures. She was supposed to wait on him, hand and foot. Any time she was gone for longer than ten minutes or so, he grew suspicious. When it was a half an hour? I heard his footsteps coming up the stairs, and I knew what to expect. So I ghosted."

Young Jonathan had avoided an interrogation by abandoning his own body.

He had made himself completely vulnerable.

"But he figured it out, of course," Garrett said. "He saw my empty shell of a body and Anna nowhere in sight. He raged. But he didn't want his victim to escape, so instead of hurting me right then, he rushed downstairs and outside."

Ariock thought that it should have been impossible for the monster to track Anna, since she'd already been running for half an hour.

"I followed him in ghost form," Garrett said. "Part of the problem for Anna was that it was the tail end of the Victorian era. She tore off her long skirt, but she had to pick her way over tree branches and through underbrush. And it was night."

"She couldn't go fast enough," Ariock realized.

"Right," Garrett said. "And my father was on a horse. Anna had been too afraid of making noise, so she'd just run without trying to steal the animal."

Ariock didn't know much about horseback riding, but he figured horses needed open space, or at least a trail. "Your father rode through woods?"

"He didn't need to," Garrett said. "Mind readers can check the perceptions of any animals they pass. He could also use the perceptions of his horse, and horses see well at night. He might have been in a blind rage, but he knew those woods very well. And he kept his senses open."

"Oh," Ariock said.

"Eventually," Garrett said, "he detected her through the senses of owls or field mice or whatever."

Young Jonathan had been nothing but a spectator. A silent, helpless ghost.

"All I could do was watch." Garrett cupped his temples, hiding from long-ago trauma. "I was close to depletion, and I knew that if I spent my energy watching, I would have no way to escape my body later on. My father would be able to torture me and I would not be able to escape mentally. But I felt so anxious for Anna, I watched anyway. I didn't care if I died watching."

Ariock was familiar with the dangerous strain of clairvoyance. No matter where he went in ghost form, his mind remained tethered to his distant body. A few seconds was doable. After a minute or so, he felt like a rubber band pulled taut. If he kept at it for five or six minutes, he would feel half-crazed, as if oxygen deprived.

His limit seemed to be about eight minutes. If he pushed himself to his absolute limit, he would crash violently back into his own body, unable to stop it from happening.

Then he needed recovery time. He had to reorient his thoughts, catch his breath, regain his equilibrium.

Although Ariock ghosted many times per day—usually for no more than a minute, along memorized routes—he was aware of his own exceptional fortitude. Most Yeresunsa lacked the raw strength to ghost again and again. A half-starved, neglected child, such as Jonathan had been, would easily run the risk of depletion.

"What did you see?" Ariock asked.

Garrett hesitated. And Ariock knew that whatever had happened next, it was not something that could be stated casually. It was pivotal.

"He was going to intercept her." Garrett's voice was tense, nearly washed out by the crash of water on the rocks below. "There was a cliff where Anna would have no choice but to emerge by the road, and he could catch her there. I figured she would end up just like all the other girls and women—the mothers who were never motherly." Garrett clenched his fists, acting on long-ago fury. "He thought he was so special. For all I knew, he *was* the devil, like my other mothers had said. The dead ones. He had luck like the devil. He always won. He made cruelty look easy. He pretended it was natural. Like it was his right."

The repressed rage in Garrett made his voice stilted and thick.

"I went in front of his horse," Garrett said. "I had never teleported. Didn't know it was possible. But I was so desperate to be heard, to be seen—to put a stop to it— that reality folded, and I pulled myself into the foggy night, to that location. And I was screaming. I screamed louder than I ever had in my life."

Ariock felt the impact of that long-ago shock.

"My sudden appearance spooked his horse," Garrett said. "I teleported right in front of it, screaming like a banshee. The horse reared up. The ground was all mud and fallen leaves. And my father tumbled off, right over the cliff."

Ariock caught his breath.

Garrett had claimed that he had killed his father when he was six years old. It seemed he really had.

"He died slowly," Garrett said with savage relish. "He hit rocks on his way down, and by the time he fell into the ravine, his legs were broken. He died of exposure and thirst. No one found him in time."

Of course, young Jonathan had known where his father was the whole time. He must have felt safe with Anna Stead, or whomever she sent to rescue him.

He had probably ghosted to his dying father multiple times, just to make sure he would not recover. He might have ghosted to peer at the decomposing corpse. The skeleton. How many times?

"I visited his corpse every day." Garrett spoke without a shred of remorse. "I watched vultures pick apart his face and coyotes gnaw at his bones. I saw him disappear into the earth. Meanwhile, I gained enough strength to walk. I went to a school with other boys and girls my age."

"You got adopted?" Ariock asked.

"The Steads took me in," Garrett said with a warmth that could only be gratitude. "There wasn't much paperwork in those days. No Social Security cards, no child protective services. It was either them or an orphanage. Anna convinced her parents that I deserved a good home."

Ariock thought of Thomas, fostered by Vy's mother.

"I didn't want anyone deciding I was a demon," Garrett said. "So I begged Anna to say nothing of my weirdnesses. My powers, I mean."

That must be why Garrett had developed the habit of pretending to be a normal nontelepath. He had been doing that ever since he was old enough to comprehend things. He must have tried his best to set people at ease—and to distance himself from his father.

"I did my best," Garrett agreed. "Only Anna knew. And we eventually revealed the truth to her little sister, Julia."

Ariock folded his legs. He could fill in the rest of the story. Jonathan had taken the surname of his adoptive family. He had grown up.

He had actually married his adoptive sister Julia, which was a little weird. But times were different then.

He'd gotten her pregnant.

Gotten himself abducted by the Torth Empire.

Then he had faked his death and gone home again. He had changed his name and identity to Garrett Olmstead Dovanack. His wife had become Sarah instead of Julia.

They had moved elsewhere. To New Hampshire. Their daughter was born. The Dovanack family was established.

"Anna was murdered by a Torth agent," Garrett said.

Ariock looked at him.

"Julia and I eloped. Her family didn't approve, obviously. So we moved out. We were vagabonds, moving from city to city. At the time, I had no idea that Torth agents were hunting me." He sounded mournful. "The Torth had heard rumors of a psychic wonder child, thanks to my flamboyant public shows. I busked for a living. They suspected I might be the offspring of a renegade Torth. They just needed to meet me, to make sure. So they tracked down my family—the Stead family, I mean—and ascertained the truth about me from Anna's mind. Then they murdered her."

Ariock swallowed over an ache in his throat. Anna, he realized now, was also a part of his family. Not only was she Garrett's adoptive sister, but she would have been Ariock's great-great-aunt. She was his blood relative through Julia, aka Sarah Dovanack.

"When we heard," Garrett said, "we were shocked. But we assumed a random thug had murdered Anna. We had no idea the Torth existed."

Ariock wondered what knowledge, exactly, young Jonathan had soaked up from his Torth father. Hadn't he glimpsed otherworldly cities in his father's memories?

"I had vague notions," Garrett admitted. "I knew my father came from somewhere strange and alien—but I figured that must be hell. I assumed my father was a demon. I would be safe, I figured, as long as I stayed good and didn't commit any heinous acts of depravity."

Ariock supposed those were reasonable assumptions.

"I was a little wary, going to Anna's funeral," Garrett admitted. "I did think it was strange. Who would want to hurt her? I couldn't imagine anyone who would murder her. But by that point, I could turn ocean tides and stir up a tornado, and I was really eager to destroy her murderer. I was on the hunt."

By then, Jonathan Stead had been a teenager with secret stormbringer powers. He must have been cocky.

And utterly clueless about the rest of the galaxy.

"Exactly." Garrett's tone turned bitter with regret. "I could handle tough guys in a back alley, so I made the mistake of assuming I could handle anything."

He fell silent.

Ariock was silent with the old man. Together, they allowed the crashing waves to substitute for words, for a while.

Ariock pondered the contrasts in Garrett's family, and in Garrett himself. Strong and weak. Cruel and kind. Perpetrator and victim.

Garrett was a study in extremes. Like the weather, he blew fierce or he had a genial cheerfulness.

Ariock supposed that the same could be said about himself. He, too, was familiar with extremes. He had spent years feeling like a windblown leaf, without control over his outward appearance. He had believed that he was just a burden. He had been a plaything for the amusement of a silent audience.

And then? Immense power.

But he could never forget how it felt to be helpless.

He looked at Garrett and saw the cringing child still alive within the grizzled old warrior.

Was it any wonder Garrett was so infuriated by people who abused their power? Jonathan Stead had been subjected to abuse that few people could imagine. He had been forced to watch the tortured death of his own mother—and then all the not-quite-mothers who followed.

Young children learned by emulating people whom they spent a lot of time with. They adapted themselves to role models.

Ariock remembered his own favorite role model. Even though he had trouble remembering specifics about the way his father looked, he remembered kindnesses. He remembered feeling proud to have such a perceptive dad, with such a keen sense of fairness and so much consideration for people who were less fortunate than himself. It had seemed to him that no other adult was quite as special, kind, wise, and strong. He had wanted to be just like that man when he grew up.

What role models had Jonathan Stead had?

The adults in his life had been either utterly helpless or very powerful. There were victims. And there was the perpetrator.

Which sort of adult had he aspired to be?

It was obvious. Jonathan Stead had seized power. Instead of dying in his father's care, he had escaped that abusive household. Now he was powerful.

And merciless. And cruel.

No doubt he told himself that his cruelty was justice. He enacted violence only against Torth. Against the devil. Every time he destroyed a heartless mind reader, he was protecting Julia and Anna. He was avenging his mother. He was living his greatest childhood fantasy.

No wonder it was vital to him. No wonder he derived so much savage pleasure from destroying Torth.

Knowing helped.

Ariock could not hate a survivor of unimaginably traumatic abuse. Garrett had remade himself using the only tools available to him. He was forged in hatred, not in love. Even so, he had cobbled together a good life for himself. That was no easy feat. It required grit.

Perhaps Garrett would never dust off his grit and become kindhearted. But he was who he was.

And that was okay.

Ariock would set boundaries to protect Thomas and his other friends. Otherwise? He gave Garrett a nod of respect. He would remember the fact that his great-grandfather had been a hero once upon a time.

He would remember the family members who were no longer around to speak for themselves, or to speak in favor of the boy who had protected them.

# CHAPTER 16

# A MATTER OF SIZE

"Hello," Vy greeted a mayor who was holographically projected over her desk. "I speak for Ariock Dovanack, Bringer of Hope and conqueror of worlds."

The military mayor of Median City looked impressed. Supercoms were new to the liberated people on the planet Verdantia. Freedom was new to them.

And Vy supposed that everything about herself, and her office, looked imposing. Angled windows were scooped out of the walls. Those walls were polished meteorite, softened by tapestries and carpets.

"Ariock requests that you designate a flat area in which to assemble your voluntary soldiers," Vy went on. "Please spread word that anyone who wishes to aid in the conquest of a Torth city should assemble there."

The vast majority of liberated people were illiterate. That meant no emails, no letters, no calendars, no texting, no social media. Everything had to be a spoken conversation. Vy preferred to work while sipping a spiced drink in a café, but that was too noisy for calls.

"Have them ready by two hours after daybreak," Vy said. "Your time." According to her converter software, it was currently evening in Median City.

The govki mayor looked honored. "Thank you, Your Humanness!"

Vy didn't like that makeshift title, but she smiled and accepted it. At least the mayor had not accused her of being a Torth.

Every appointed mayor received informational videos distributed by Kessa's office. One of those videos outlined how to differentiate between Torth, penitent Torth, Alashani, and humans. People got mixed up anyway. Some called Vy an elder. Others called her a boss. Some called her an angel from paradise, or the mate of the Bringer of Hope. At least the majority of people understood that she was not a mind reader.

Vy updated the battle diagram.

She contacted more offices, making preparations for Ariock's next battle. She also added meetings for herself, determined to stay up-to-date on developments in construction, small businesses, health care, education, and the burgeoning justice system. It all worked in a helter-skelter kind of way.

She tapped her workstation to bring up a playlist of low-key music. Her office was wired with speakers.

Vy and Cherise had downloaded TV shows and other media during their jaunt to Earth. Torth devices should not be able to parse data made by humans, but Thomas had modified a few Torth gadgets. Thanks to him, Vy had gained petabytes of media simply by walking around downtown San Diego.

Now, if she or Cherise wished, they could beam movies to wall screens. They could beam music to speakers. It felt like having a superpower.

But it was a power they used sparingly, aware that they might make a cultural impact crater. The freed aliens were developing an entirely new culture—their own theater, their own music—and Vy found it all too fresh and interesting to want to hijack it or disturb its formation.

"Would you accept a gift from me?" The voice was silken and feminine.

Vy hadn't heard anyone enter. She looked up from her workstation, and sure enough, the winged Lady stood across from her granite-top desk.

Evenjos fingered one of Vy's favorite knickknacks, a quartz statuette of a thunder god ready to throw a lightning bolt, then placed the figurine back on the desk. She was expressionless, but her outward appearance was an expression itself, with luminous eyes and wings and long hair that rippled in an intangible breeze.

She was a goddess.

Vy stood. She reminded herself that she could call Ariock with a tap on her earpiece, but surely she was safe? She told herself that she was overreacting. It was embarrassing.

Evenjos offered a disarming smile. "I mean you no harm." She held out a decorative purse. "A token of my goodwill, if you wish to accept it. This purse contains longevity pills. Take one per day. When you run out, you can ask Thomas for more."

Vy studied the winged Lady, trying to ascertain if she had any ulterior motive. At least her gown was modestly cut and artfully draped. Evenjos must be in a rare, nonseductive mood.

Evenjos blushed. Had she overheard Vy's thoughts?

"I truly come in peace," Evenjos said. "I want to make that plain."

Vy accepted the purse. Inside, there were clear bags of tiny white pills.

She could have asked Thomas or Garrett for longevity pills at any time, but that had never occurred to her. Her own distant future was never at the forefront of her mind. She was so busy all the time, preoccupied with the next few days or the next week.

Decades and centuries? Those were light-years away.

"Thank you," Vy told Evenjos with warmth. It seemed sweet to think of someone else's health and future.

And was it really so out of character for Evenjos? No. It was not. Evenjos had led the healing of Thomas. She was a miracle worker in hospitals.

The former empress offered a gentle smile. "I resented you at first," she admitted. "But I no longer think it strange that Ariock chose you. How can I resent someone with as much love and compassion as you have?"

Vy blushed. Evenjos had forgiveness in her heart, and kindness. Never mind Ariock's grumblings about her selfishness. Perhaps he judged the Lady of Sorrow too harshly.

"I am letting go of the jealousy I felt toward you," Evenjos said. "I cannot bear ill will against a fellow healer."

Tension evaporated from Vy's chest. She had not consciously acknowledged the threat. But now that Evenjos herself had cleared the air . . .

Well, there was no enmity between them, after all. They did not have to be a commoner versus an empress, or Ariock's human girlfriend versus a jealous interloper.

Perhaps they could be friends?

Evenjos's smile tightened for a split second, and Vy felt a stab of fear. She didn't like being within range of a telepath. She should have guarded her thoughts.

But when Evenjos spoke, she sounded kind. "I wish I could regrow your leg for you." She indicated Vy's prosthetic. "Unfortunately, such healing is beyond my power."

It was a kind sentiment.

Vy offered a shrug in appreciation. In truth, she had begun to feel at peace with her loss of limb. These days she understood that the galaxy was big enough to offer multiple possibilities to any individual, no matter what array of abilities they had.

She was a pilot, for instance. She might not be at the level of the combat pilots, who corkscrewed through mountain valleys and slid into unlikely docks cut into cliffs. But she was also a medic. She could read and write, unlike many people in Freedomland. And she had the ear of the messiah. Few people even knew that she had a missing limb, and no one commented on it anymore.

"I really appreciate the longevity pills," Vy assured Evenjos. "That was very thoughtful."

Evenjos smiled. "It is a meager gift. But I see how much you care for Ariock. I figured you want a chance to keep pace with his nonhuman aging. You know, at least for a century, or maybe two."

Vy frowned. Nonhuman aging?

That made no sense. Ariock was mostly human, more or less.

Before she could ask, Evenjos spoke with delicate sympathy. "His nonhuman aging is a side effect of his unchecked growth mutation." She blushed, as if flustered by a sensitive topic, or as if the need to explain had caught her by surprise. "Ariock is in a perpetual state of adolescent rapid growth. His bone growth plates will never fuse and seal. His whole body regenerates cells, and replaces them, at a rapid rate, as if he is always a teenager. His cells are adolescent. He cannot age normally. And he will keep growing. Forever."

The sentences fit together, but Vy struggled to make them jell with reality. How could someone just keep growing without running into certain limits set by biology? Would he just gain a ridiculous number of cells and blood vessels to support his mass? Or would his very atoms become titanic?

Evenjos must be mistaken.

"Those of us with legendary power may bypass the limits of biology." Evenjos gestured to herself. "I cannot say how it will work for Ariock, but he may hold together by sheer force of gravity, plus his endless power to heal. He doesn't get sick."

Vy had noticed that it took quite a lot to injure Ariock. It only seemed to happen when he was on the inhibitor.

"Of course . . ." Evenjos looked even more embarrassed and flustered. "If he ever does run into trouble, whether it be injury or old age, I must give him regeneration healing. He is too vital for the universe to lose." She seemed to realize that she had left out something important, and hastily added, "And you, too."

Vy felt as if she needed air. Her lungs were empty. She wanted to be alone, to ponder the implications. It sounded as if she and Ariock might be granted a semblance of immortality. They would never age.

But Ariock would never stop growing like a teenage boy.

Vy had somehow forgotten that his growth disorder was an ongoing medical condition. It was not an immutable adult trait, but a process.

Unstoppable. Unending.

"He will keep growing," Evenjos affirmed. "For him, there is no end to puberty." She rested manicured fingers on her hips, as if her words were not devastating.

Vy attempted to persuade herself that size did not matter.

She loved Ariock. She loved the size of him, along with everything else. She loved holding on to him, the way his body seemed endless—especially if she feared enemies, or when she felt lonely.

She always knew right away if Ariock was nearby. He blocked light. He made floors or furniture creak. Whenever he was around, she slept soundly. Otherwise she was restless and suffered from nightmares. His presence alone made her stress vanish and gave her a wholesome, safe, and protected feeling.

Yet sometimes . . .

Ariock loomed. He couldn't help it, but he was like a living thunderhead, or a tsunami.

A survival-oriented part of Vy remained alert around him, aware that he could hurt her by accident. All he had to do was forget she was there.

Vy had seen Ariock kill armored Torth by smashing them into pulp against stone walls, or by stomping on them, or even by tearing them in half, armor and all. Those glimpses of him in battle were impossible to forget.

Evenjos's sympathy looked pitying. "Ariock is taller now than when you first met him." She spread her hands, as if in apology. "He will be over eleven feet within another five years."

Vy shook her head.

She had hoped to introduce her mother to her boyfriend. But even before this news, she had known it was a bad idea. A fantasy. How would Mrs. Hollander, the founder of a home for disabled children, react to a titan who slaughtered people in battle? A mutant who had accidentally killed his own mother? And who had failed to shield Vy when a Torth blasted off her leg?

Mrs. Hollander might not like Ariock.

She might consider him a brutish, thuggish freak of questionable heritage, descended from a rapist and murderer and too unapologetic to be worthy of her daughter.

"And he is yet young," Evenjos mused, apparently oblivious to Vy's thoughts. "He grows another foot taller, and adds more mass, every few years. In a hundred years? I imagine he will be a true titan, if he lives as long as I have."

Hundreds of years old. A titan. Skyscraper sized? Inhumanly large.

It would be impossible to be intimate with that.

Evenjos gave Vy a coy smile. "His relentless growth is remarkable, isn't it? Both a blessing and a curse." Her gaze flicked over the length of Vy's relatively petite body. "I suppose it is your blessing—and curse—as well."

Vy opened her mouth. She wanted to spew angry retorts. She wanted to scream defiantly that her relationship with the ever-growing storm god was shatterproof.

All traces of sympathy vanished from Evenjos's face.

"If you truly love him," Evenjos said crisply, "then consider being less selfish. You could urge him in a more caring direction. Understand that Ariock must always guard himself around you. If he caves in to raw sensation, that would be extremely danger-ous." She paused, and seemed to decide that clarification was required. "For you."

Vy barely noticed the hard shapes of the pills in the little purse she was squeezing. She felt assaulted.

By what? Facts?

Ariock admitted, often, that he had a fear of hurting Vy. That fear was in his eyes.

Vy had assumed it was leftover anxiety from early mistakes. With hard daily practice, surely he had mastery over his own power by now? He no longer killed or maimed people by accident.

Or, at least, Vy didn't think so.

Evenjos stepped back, her tone lighter. "I suppose you have both taken the risks into consideration."

Ariock probably had.

Vy felt mocked. She was so naive, so oblivious to her own fragility. So selfish. No matter how much she cared for Ariock, she was unfit for him.

She was nothing special. Just an ordinary human.

"I hope I am not being rude," Evenjos said. "Please forgive me?"

Vy was no longer certain about anything. Her feelings for Ariock were undeniable, but what if that was just an immature infatuation with a storm god? She was twenty-three. Anyone with hormones and attraction toward a strong man would want to spend time with the Bringer of Hope.

"I don't know if I believe any of this." Vy's voice was shaky, but she needed to hang on to a shred of self-respect. She was not going to quit Ariock just because a former empress told her . . .

Evenjos disintegrated into a swirl of colorful dust.

The ghostly female shape broke apart and flew through cracks around the edges of the closed door. Vy was alone.

# CHAPTER 17

# INFAMOUS

Thomas moved with the herd of traffic.

It was exhilarating to go unnoticed. He wore a brimmed hat, Alashani style, to shield his face from sunlight, and it also shielded him from being recognized. Most albinos wore mesh gloves. So did Thomas. They hid their sensitive skin from daylight, and Thomas, clad in undistinguished linens, fit right in.

The only incongruity was his hoverchair.

But the Alashani had their share of disabled people, veterans of battles or calamities. True, most disabled shani would rather be dragged in a rickshaw instead of seated in an evil hoverchair, but every population had its misfits.

Thomas felt safe.

He was so safe, in fact, he told his bodyguards and his assistants to stay home whenever he made his daily outing. He didn't need help. He was self-reliant.

This was Freedomland. There were no enemies here.

He floated up the crowded street. Hovercarts zipped past, going this way or that. He had just finished zombifying his daily quota of victims, and he was familiar with the spiritual indigestion that gave him. It was no wonder his mind was churning with taboo urges and unwanted ideas.

He saw Cherise everywhere.

Not with his eyes, but she was in a lot of people's minds. He passed a gaggle of students as he neared the academy complex, and he kept gaining accidental glimpses of her latest hairstyle, or how she looked in a new dress.

And her voice.

Her gentle way of leading students to explore fresh ideas.

Her beautiful hands.

Thomas was extra careful to avoid routes where he might encounter penitents. He didn't want to see them, even from a distance. They looked too much like humans. Like Vy.

Or like Cherise, enslaved.

The resemblance made Thomas want to rescue them. Or . . . well . . . get to know them. Especially the women. Some of them were truly beautiful, with long legs and lush lips. Some had superficial similarities to people he knew. Like Cherise. They had alluring eyes, faces full of mystery, and minds that might reveal all kinds of secrets with the right coaxing . . .

Ugh.

No.

Absolutely not.

Thomas tightened his mouth with annoyance at his own thoughts. The last thing he needed was hormones on top of everything else. He had enough to deal with. After a bout of zombifying, his thoughts were 78 percent more likely to take an unintended turn.

He doused his problematic thoughts with mathematical theorems.

Empirical research was a haven, a safe outlet for him to escape the messiness of unwanted emotions. If it was a form of emotional suppression . . . well, so what? This suppression was for the good of everyone.

Nobody wanted a lustful, cretinous supergenius around. Thomas was well aware of that.

He had multiple ongoing projects. Garrett wanted him to announce that he was whipping up immunity to the inhibitor, but Thomas had cautioned that it would take time. The Torth scientific understanding of how powers worked, on a physiological level, was full of holes.

None of the warriors would allow Thomas to run experiments on them. Only Garrett was cooperative, aware that it was a crucial project. The Twins or the Death Architect must also be researching immunity, along with whatever other nefarious projects they were working on. They probably got experimental test subjects whenever they asked for them. Whichever side of the war gained immunity first would hold a winning edge, at least for a while.

Thomas turned a corner, entering the hectic Recruitment Plaza. The vast plaza was busy at all hours of the day. Here, craftspeople and artisans and technicians found apprentices. Newcomers to Freedomland figured out whether they wanted to learn practical skills, such as agricultural techniques or weaving. Or they could learn how to hack Torth data tablets and reverse engineer Torth gadgets.

There were popular classes in folk medicine, mathematics, Alashani law, Alashani philosophy, and Alashani history. Also, mycological recipes.

Illiterate former slaves were learning to decipher Torth glyphs, and—if they took Cherise's classes—they were learning to read and write a standardized pidgin version of the slave tongue using the anglicized Roman alphabet.

Thomas floated past kiosks staffed by loud recruiters. He wove around knots of people, and he passed courtyards with fountains. He wished he'd had time to be more creative with his urban planning. He and Ariock had focused on basics: water purification, indoor plumbing, and a sewage system. But now that they had time to breathe—perhaps they should redesign some of the main plazas to be more impressive?

An Alashani maiden sat on a low stone wall, sipping a smoothie and apparently just taking in the sights. She wore a black ribbon on her floppy hat, matching her gloves and boots. So cute.

Thomas studied her from beneath the brim of his hat. She looked lonely. Usually, Alashani hung out in groups of two or more, friendly and silly with each other.

Friendly silliness would be a welcome change from the conversations Thomas tended to have.

Everyone who sought him out had something serious to discuss. It was usually about biohybrid synapses, or exocytosis, or dendrites. And it was usually Varktezo.

The cute maiden must be one of the unusually curious shani who actually wanted to learn from aliens. Maybe she was trying to decide whether or not to take classes?

She might want advice. Or friendship.

Or more.

Thomas blew out his breath, disgusted at himself. She was Alashani. If she so much as glimpsed his face, she would see that he was none other than the dreaded *rekveh*, and then she would run, screaming. Her reaction would likely spark a mass panic and interrupt the recruitment processes.

What sort of hormonal idiocy was wending through his subconscious, giving him cataclysmically stupid ideas?

It was a good thing Garrett couldn't easily probe his mind. Thomas wondered if he should quit researching the inhibitor and instead work on blocking his puberty hormones.

He needed to cement reality inside his mind. He needed to internalize the truth. No girl was ever going to willingly seek him out for fun times together.

Why should they? He was a monster.

Also, he was a disaster. Cherise was an apt reminder of that, even without being on speaking terms with him. Thomas was optimized for logic, not for emotional roller-coaster rides.

The cute albino maiden kicked her feet.

She seemed to be in a good mood all of a sudden. She tilted her head to admire one of the tall buildings, studying its windows, as if with artistic composition in mind.

A very subtle warning pinged at the bottom of Thomas's perceptions.

He was not sure what made him halt, alert for an attack. There was no overt sign of danger. He felt safe in this city. It was his home base. He had felt safe for months.

Yet he contained the battle reflexes of more than a thousand Servants of All and Rosies, as well as the Dovanacks. He knew battle. Despite his lack of firsthand experience, he had a sensation of being in danger.

He spread his Yeresunsa awareness.

Maybe he had imagined the microexpression of anxiety on the maiden's face? And the way her gaze had flitted to that window three times, as if she was trying not to look? She was not swinging her legs in a forced, fake way, was she?

He could be misreading her body language. She seemed flirtatious, so his hormone-infused brain had picked her out as being worthy of attention, which, to a supergenius, implied that she was unusual. So he was finding patterns to fit that assessment. And since his primary basis for reference was battle and Torth cruelty, he was conflating her behavior with . . .

A spear hurtled out of the window the maiden had been studying.

Then another, and a third. The short spears flew as fast as bullets, propelled by Yeresunsa powers, almost too fast to register their existence.

Thomas saw the projectiles a second before the first one could impale his torso.

He spun his hoverchair and ducked.

The spear slammed into the solid backrest and bounced off. The second and third spears whizzed past him, missing his head by inches.

People screamed. One of the spears nearly hit the foot of a nussian. Instead, it stuck in the grass, quivering from its momentum. The nussian and her mate roared in surprise and stared around wildly, looking for enemies.

Thomas straightened, aware that he had nearly been assassinated. Some crazy person—not a Torth!—was trying to murder him.

His hat had flown off. Now that he was upright again, people saw his face. And he had very Torth-like facial features.

Nearby bystanders reeled in shock.

"Torth!" someone screamed.

A panic began. Nussians, govki, and ummins stampeded for the relative cover of alleys and doorways. They ducked under tables or behind fountains. Every one of them had been rescued from a Torth-ruled city. They understood that survival during battle hinged upon fleeing and hiding. Many probably didn't even know why they were running, but they knew it was best to avoid mysterious Yeresunsa phenomena.

Taking wind conditions into account, it was easy for Thomas to backtrace the projectiles to their source, one of several open-air windows on the third floor. He saw movement inside. That must be the culprit.

Thomas mentally scanned his surroundings, collating and filing away irrelevant data. The accomplice—that maiden—had already vanished into the fleeing crowd. He absorbed glimpses of white hair. That might be her, with her distinctive hat tucked away, or it might be some other random Alashani.

He decided not to plunge into the panicked crowd like a monster chasing an innocent girl.

Instead, he would confront the shooter. That was the main threat. Warriors usually carried thirteen spears in their quivers, which meant the shooter likely had ten shots left.

Unless there was a second assassin waiting as a backup measure?

Thomas analyzed nearby facial expressions. He was unable to extrapolate any signs of guilt or murderous intentions. Even so, he kept his awareness puffed out.

Onlookers gathered at the edges of the plaza, studying Thomas with curiosity or fear. They must judge themselves to be at a safe distance. There had not been any fireballs, lightning, or thunder cracks. No blasts, either. People were unsure if this was a battle or not.

Thomas wanted to spend a few more seconds scanning for threats, but the assassin was likely already trying to escape and blend in with the crowds.

Unacceptable.

Thomas narrowed his Yeresunsa focus to the interior of the building. The narrow focus left him open to attack from the sides, but he was willing to take that risk.

He could not sense life sparks. The presence of more powerful Yeresunsa on the planet—such as Ariock, Evenjos, and Garrett—washed out Thomas's weaker sensitivity. He could, however, dimly sense thermal differences. It was a stretch, but he thought he could tell where the fleeing assassin was.

The would-be assassin was likely alone. They would not want to invite random bystanders to witness the act, since they would try to escape without notice to avoid Ariock's wrath.

Thomas ignited a horseshoe shape of wildfire around the would-be assassin, blocking their escape.

He heard a faint yell from inside the building.

Thomas shifted his wildfire, herding the would-be assassin toward the open window. He wanted to see a face.

Sure enough, a wild-eyed albino showed up, backlit by flames.

Thomas knew each and every one of the Alashani warriors. He had never met most of them, yet he strategized daily battle plans that placed warriors in various conquered cities or in battles. If he were playing a cosmic game of chess, then the warriors were bishops and knights and rooks. He moved them on a daily basis.

Besides, people idolized the warriors as heroes. Thomas knew almost everybody in Freedomland, as well as in the liberated cities. His brain was crammed with useless trivia.

"Densaava." Thomas recognized the would-be assassin as a warrior from Ellonch, one whom he had never met.

Densaava climbed onto the window ledge in desperation to escape the wildfire. Did he think Thomas was going to roast him alive?

Half the bystanders seemed to expect that. They watched, transfixed with morbid curiosity. There were whispers that the zombie maker was going to kill the war hero. Nobody was within Thomas's range, but he could guess what they expected to see. Battle. Mayhem. And death, meted out by the Wisdom of prophecies and the notorious *rekveh* with a million rumors about him.

Thomas floated closer to the building, craning his head up. "I never did anything to you. Why attack me?"

Densaava looked unconvinced.

He leaped.

A fall from that height was dangerous for anyone except a trained Yeresunsa. Densaava imbued his body with power and landed with catlike ease, whereupon he immediately drew three more spears from the quiver on his back.

He fixed on Thomas, as righteous as a priest determined to defeat the devil. There was murder in his eyes.

Thomas knew that he was in mild danger.

A thermal shield was no guarantee against telekinetic attacks. Alashani warriors were trained to win against wildfire and ice powers. On top of that, Densaava was clearly in better shape than Thomas. He was physically quicker and stronger. He would have reflexes Thomas could not counter.

Thomas let go of his wildfire, letting the flames die. He devoted more mental resources to the scenarios that played out in his mind.

He could defeat Densaava by inviting him into his telepathy range, of course. He could taunt the man, or bait him, or even fly at him unexpectedly. A mental twist would zombify the would-be assassin.

But Thomas had no desire to zombify a supposed ally.

If he caused massive brain damage to a war hero, in front of witnesses, in a public square, he would never escape rumors that he was evil. Even Jinishta would have trouble trusting him. It wouldn't matter who had started the fight. It only mattered who ended it.

"I am not your enemy," Thomas said.

He could not afford to lose public trust. That was probably why Densaava had chosen to attack him in a busy public area. Smart.

This attack had clearly been premeditated.

Densaava whipped his spears at Thomas in quick, furious succession.

The would-be assassin had nothing left to lose. Now that everyone had seen him, he would face punishment, whether or not he killed his target. Jinishta would probably condemn him to eternal guard duty in the smelliest depths of the Mirror Prison. Or perhaps she would send him to some remote outpost of civilization. She had a lot of pride. She would feel that a berserk warrior reflected badly on her leadership.

And Densaava might still succeed in his mission.

Thomas calculated the exact trajectory of the spears. He rotated his hoverchair to avoid the first two projectiles.

But Densaava was an expert marksman, and he anticipated Thomas's move.

Thomas sucked heat out of the air below the third spear. That caused it to wobble off course, enabling him to dodge it by less than an inch. Its wind ruffled his hair.

Didn't this mad warrior understand whom he was picking a fight with? What was wrong with him? Too many mind-altering mushrooms, perhaps? Really, Thomas didn't want to hurt anyone.

"Go. Run away." Thomas made a shooing gesture.

Densaava was clearly beyond caring. His purple eyes were defiant, and lightning rippled up his arms from excess fury.

Well, a spoken warning had been worth a try.

Densaava drew four more spears. He simultaneously used telekinesis to gather the previously thrown spears on the ground, raising them pointed toward Thomas.

Meanwhile, Thomas imbued the air between himself and his attacker with an ultrarealistic holographic projection.

Thomas remained seated in his hoverchair. But Densaava saw him push against the armrests . . . and stand up.

The illusion of Thomas was as tall as the Alashani warrior. Since Thomas could subitize a hundred details at once, and bend light, he could imagine scenes that were indistinguishable from reality.

His simulacrum took one majestic step.

Then another.

Thomas felt a thrill simply envisioning himself walking. As for Densaava . . . he stepped back, uncertain. Everyone knew that the *rekveh* could not walk.

The simulacrum of Thomas ran straight at Densaava with a look of smug and deadly determination.

Densaava shrieked. His spears clattered to the ground. Everyone knew that Thomas could twist minds if he got within telepathy range.

Thomas chuckled in grim satisfaction as the warrior panicked. It seemed his illusion was realistic enough, and terrifying enough, to override any small hints of reality that might seep through. Densaava did not even pause to collect his spears, as professional warriors were trained to do. He simply fled.

Thomas let his holographic illusion dissipate. He boosted his hyperawareness of other people's facial expressions, tracking Densaava through the crowd, making sure the warrior would not circle back and make another attempt.

Onlookers gawked at Thomas. Quite a few had had no idea that he had Yeresunsa powers until now.

They associated Yeresunsa with war heroes. As far as the Alashani were concerned, anyone blessed with powers had a moral obligation to fight Torth. Free aliens had picked up that attitude.

"You ought to wear a mantle!" an ummin yelled at him.

Thomas liked his unadorned clothing. A Yeresunsa mantle would mark him at a glance, since he was the only Yeresunsa who floated around in a hoverchair. If he had worn a mantle today, he'd be dead. Densaava wouldn't have needed an accomplice in the plaza. He would have hurled his spears before Thomas even became aware of a threat.

Thomas made a mental note to track down that accomplice.

And another mental note to have zombification victims brought to his tower, instead of him going to the prison every day. He didn't like the laziness of that idea. It seemed too casual, setting the wrong tone for something so severe as removing people's free will. But . . . well.

Going out in public was hazardous to his health.

All the cruel memories Thomas had absorbed from prisoners earlier that day oozed inside his depths. He was angry. He was in a dark mood. He was sick of people, and if he didn't get back to his tower soon, he might say something offensive to the next jerk who yelled a criticism his way.

Disgusted, he floated toward home. He would need a new hat.

Azhdarchidae would be a welcome presence, but he was probably hunting right now, out of sight in the nearby mountains. Thomas would absorb his memories when he returned to his nest. There was something satisfying about watching the sky croc overtake smaller pterosaurs and savage them.

"Do you need your hat?" a govki called.

Thomas paused. He had assumed the brindle-furred govki had snatched up the fallen hat only for use as a souvenir, or perhaps to sell it. Why else risk getting near the dreaded *rekveh*?

Yet the govki approached with a look of respect.

Thomas dipped into the alien's thoughts, expecting to find simmering hatred beneath the compassionate face. This might be yet another low-key assassin. A govki could conceal a blaster glove in one of those multiple hands, or beneath the hat she was so kindly offering.

Instead . . .

He learned that this govki lived with her beloved mate, and two siblings, solely because Thomas had told one of them where the others lived. She felt that she owed her happiness to the night when Thomas had freely given favors for anyone who asked.

"Thank you." Thomas took his hat.

"Some of us admire you." The govki bobbed a gesture of respect. "If you ever need anything, ask me or those of my household. We know who you are. And I think you know us."

Thomas did know them. He knew their names, their origin stories, their medical histories, their family histories.

And now he knew something else, which made all those little facts actually matter.

Gratitude felt awkward in his throat. It stuck there. All he could do was nod.

## CHAPTER 18
# ARCHITECT OF THE COLLECTIVE

Humans emanated a ripe, repulsive stench. The Death Architect used open-air cages for her experimental subjects—bars instead of reinforced glass. That way, she absorbed a fuller data set. Not only did she pick up ripples of terror—she smelled her subjects. She heard every whine and scream they made.

And they could hear her.

That added interaction, a whole other layer of fascinating data.

"Just a little more acid," the Death Architect said in a tone that approximated how an innocent human child might sound. "Try to be good. Then you can go home."

The Death Architect rather enjoyed lying to her experimental subjects. She could not lie to fellow Torth, but humans and slave species were very, very gullible. They could be tricked into believing anything.

It was a mystery to her why scientists did not use humans for experimentation on a more regular basis. Human physiology was extremely similar to that of their superior brethren. There ought to be farms of savage humans just for laboratory usage. Test every drug on them. Test everything. If nothing else, humans could be used as organ donors. They should supplement the supply of organs reaped from adolescent Torth who failed their Adulthood Exams.

The Majority was so shortsighted.

The Death Architect tapped her data tablet, causing an acid shower to rain down on the couple in the cage. They shrieked. They writhed and begged for mercy. The Death Architect accepted their noise as data, no matter how offensively loud they were to her delicate young ears.

Data was truth. Truths were always welcome in her laboratory.

Even after five days in horrendous conditions, these test subjects persisted in a foolish notion that the Death Architect was friendly to them. It was fascinating. They refused to credit the overwhelming evidence that the little girl was in charge. Ribbons and bows held back her curls, heightening the impression that she was a mere human girl.

The Death Architect dialed up the acid. She watched electroencephalography readouts on one of her overhead monitors. If mundane humans had a dormant ability to magnify active Yeresunsa powers, then this much traumatic pain should . . .

She caught a whiff of feces.

It was just another piece of data. So was the sight of their liquefying skin.

Truths made life worth living.

She might need a fresh pair of human test subjects soon, however. These two were just about used up. The Death Architect signaled her slaves. While they prepared for cleanup tasks, she ascended into the Megacosm to scoop up the latest news.

!*!*!*!*!*!

*Join Me.*

*!*!*!*!*

Replays of the Conqueror dominated the most popular news feeds. He showed up in the Megacosm every day, eroding the morale of the Torth Majority like a cancer. He had magically transformed into a supergenius in powerful health with a long future apparently ahead of him.

No one openly admitted to admiring him. That would be suicide.

Yet billions of minds flocked to his.

Every Torth in the universe should ignore him. Instead, billions orbited his massive mind every time he showed up, as if they were helpless to stop themselves. They understood the risks. They knew that the Conqueror might drill into their core and brainwash them.

And they listened to him anyway.

*I am here for you,* he thought to the masses. *If you are lonely, join Me. If you bury your sadness? Join Me. If you want love (family) (friends), then you can have that. Join Me.*

No one was quite bold enough to take his bait.

Yet.

But the Death Architect knew it was only a matter of time. Plenty of Torth did hide secret sorrows and despairs. Everyone knew it, even if no one admitted it. Those disgusting emotions streaked the galactic melodies sung by the Majority, marring their grandeur.

There were Torth who would accept a lifetime of hard labor and shame in exchange for the promises that the Conqueror offered.

They might steal a streamship and head toward that reject planet he had taken ownership of, eager to land in the makeshift spaceport of runaway slaves. Or people might go on a solo camping trip, get lost in the wilderness, and then cry out in the Megacosm that they wanted the Conqueror to send the Giant to come and rescue them.

His armies blitzed cities every day. They won every single battle. Torth civilians dropped everything and fled if they so much as suspected the Giant might invade.

The planet Umdalkdul was conquered. It no longer belonged to the Torth Empire.

And now? The Giant was conquering metropolises on the wealthy hub planet of Verdantia.

Servants and Rosies fled, unwilling to risk becoming zombified puppets.

That was bad for morale, the Death Architect knew. Civilization relied on trust. If Torth ceased to trust each other—if they stopped trusting their own military strength—then the Megacosm would lose its harmonious cohesion. It would fall into bickering fiefdoms.

That would be the end of civilization.

The Death Architect sensed the cracks.

An eruption was brewing just beneath the surface of all things. Few Torth were willing to outright surrender and kneel before the enemies—but they would be, if the Torth Empire did not start winning battles very soon.

The Majority sensed it, too. They spun in dizzying circles, begging and clamoring and silently screaming, *HOW CAN WE DEFEAT HIM???*

That was the question on everyone's mind.

Desperation reeked, but the Death Architect recognized the widespread collective emotion as a mere symptom of disease, like pus or boils. She wanted to treat the root illness.

The Majority glommed onto the largest minds in existence. One of the unripe supergeniuses hummed with pride, showing her postulations to her orbiters. She wanted to graduate off her baby farm as soon as possible.

But she was merely a six-year-old. Her orbiters were unimpressed.

High ranks led flocks of Torth minds to the elder supergeniuses. Billions orbited the Death Architect, begging for reassurance as if they were primitives rather than superior beings.

*What are You working on?*
*Give Us a hint?*
*Tell Us?*
*(Yes.) Tell Us.*
*TELL US.*

The nearly identical minds of the Twins flared with annoyance. Encrypted research had been salvaged from the lair of the Upward Governess, and now the Twins were making improvements to that project. Their work necessitated secrecy.

*We are busy.* The Twins had a distant, cold demeanor.

*We are hard at work.*

The Twins were the eldest pair of supergeniuses now that the Upward Governess was dead. Yet they had displayed an obscene amount of immaturity when the Majority voted to place them in separate ships. It wasn't as if the Twins needed proximity. They didn't need to cohabitate. Why had they wanted to do that in the first place? They were fine.

Perhaps they resented the implication that they were untrustworthy?

But really, after the treachery of the Upward Governess, the Colossal Failure, and the Conqueror himself, was it any wonder the Torth Majority no longer placed blind faith in supergeniuses?

The boy Twin had actually pitched an emotional fit when the Majority replaced all his slaves. Just how attached had he been to a few dozen ummins and govki?

Every supergenius needed to lose their old slaves. That was due to yet another clever tactic by the Conqueror that could not be easily countered. His favorite runaway minion, Kessa the Wise, had sent drawings to certain slave zones, so slaves could be on the lookout for high-value military targets—specifically the Twins and the Death Architect.

He was definitely a strategist.

As soon as the Death Architect had learned that news, she had ordered her Servant of All guardians to eject all her slaves out an airlock. No big deal. Those slaves had died on the surface of her asteroid, and her new slaves would never leave her lair and never talk to any others.

But the overwrought emotional reactions of certain supergeniuses bordered on illegal. The boy Twin would have been executed if he were anyone else. A lot of high-ranked Torth felt ashamed of having to rely on such mental deviants.

*Our projects must remain secret,* the Death Architect reminded everyone. She understood those who wished to execute the boy Twin. She wanted to do that herself. But . . . well . . . supergeniuses were vital to civilization. They were like the spiral arms of a galaxy. Without them, the Megacosm wouldn't be what it was.

*We (Torth) will prevail,* the Death Architect assured her billions of orbiters. *But if I (or the Twins) were to (stupidly) reveal Our work at this premature moment, then Our great and glorious empire would lose the enormous advantage of surprise. If We lose that advantage, the Conqueror will win. Is that what You want?*

Her orbiters echoed her message, disseminating it across the galaxy.

The Majority flattened into calmer swirls. They orbited the Death Architect like debris circling a star system.

*We (Torth) are mighty.* The Death Architect fanned out a mental display of Torth military strength. They had many battleships, swarmships, and dreadnoughts in peak condition, as well as space stations constructing comet-class warheads. The enemies had none of that. The Torth Empire still owned most of the galaxy.

What did the Conqueror have, really? A couple of planets and moons? That was nothing in comparison to tens of thousands of planets, with all the slave farms and factories that entailed.

*The fact that the Conqueror is trying (so hard) to lure individuals away from civilization,* she thought, *only proves that he is more desperate than We are.*

??? Her audience was eager to learn her reasoning.

The Death Architect thinned her lips. Ordinary minds could be so slow. *His forces are very limited,* she explained, with mental illustrations to prove each point. *He has fewer than eleven hundred Yeresunsa. He has no armadas. Once he takes over a few more cities, he will reach a critical tipping point whence he cannot defend the territory he holds. He absolutely needs Torth on his side. That is (obviously) why he keeps trying to lure Torth into joining him.*

She let her illustrations evaporate.

*He is desperate,* she concluded. *Meanwhile, We (Myself in particular, and the Twins) are inventing effective superweapons that will obliterate the Conqueror and his minions.*

The Majority buzzed with that good news. Spikes of fear and despair quieted to ripples, smoothed away.

*I will protect You,* the Death Architect assured every Torth orbiting her mind. *I will defend You.* She let that truth shine. *Our enemies will fail, just as all enemies in the past have failed. No one can defeat the Torth. I shall reveal a new (successful) war strategy when I judge the timing to be optimal.*

Her assurances were not quite as effective as they should be, unfortunately. People remembered that the Upward Governess and the Commander of All Living Things had made the exact same promise.

The Death Architect was quite a bit younger than the Conqueror. She was not considered a peak supergenius.

The Majority respected her, but not as much as they ought to.

They wanted to trust her, but they were reluctant to do so.

*For now*, the Death Architect urged her orbiters, *harry the enemies. Visit the outskirts of cities or farms the enemies have claimed and abduct random inhabitants. Reenslave them. Probe their minds. Learn what You can. Above all, make them paranoid. Make them fearful.*

The Majority silently applauded. Many Torth remained discomfited, but the Megacosm felt slightly more confident.

Good.

Or good enough for now.

The Death Architect left them to their chatter. She sank away from the Megacosm. Since she was between experiments, she sank all the way into the dreamy depths of her own mind.

There were, indeed, secrets the enemies should not gain any chance of learning.

Possibilities spun through her mental depths, as insubstantial as cobwebs. Her musings were unlike the musings of anyone else. Her ideas came not from within, but from something better than pure imagination.

Her dreams came true.

The gift of prophecy entailed execution. Toddlers who unfailingly won games of chance got destroyed. So did toddlers who saw ghostly visions of the past, because that was a sign of prophetic power.

And those who could view the future fate of any person they touched? They were executed right away, their organs ripped out and donated to medical laboratories.

The last time the Death Architect had touched a fellow mind reader, she had been a toddler on a baby farm, just beginning her journey into sentience and self-awareness.

She had immediately buried her prophetic visions beneath mundane data. Even then, at the age of three, she had surmised that her extra-special ability was illegal and must remain hidden. Not because she valued her own meager young life, but because she understood, on some level, that she was extra valuable. Civilization might someday need her uniquely powerful mind.

Privacy was overrated. But this was the sort of secret that could save civilization.

Now, in the extreme silence of her own mind, the Death Architect assessed her dreamlike visions.

She studied each vision as if they were scientific data. That was exactly what they were. Everything was data. Every piece of data was truth.

She processed the changes in her own dreams as fast as any supercomputer. Changes in the data stream were important. Those were areas that required focus or adjustment.

Many variants of the future looked bleak for the Torth Empire.

The Conqueror had a much better chance of winning this war than the Death Architect wanted to admit. He most certainly could conquer the galaxy. He might even enslave all the Torth in the known universe.

Data. Irrelevant. Revealing this data to the public would only guarantee the Conqueror's victory and ensure the loss of Torth civilization.

But the war did not have to end that way.

The Death Architect knew which future she wanted to nourish. That path was still healthy. She reexamined its length, from its roots to its terminus. She tested its vertices, or pivotal events, searching for any new pitfalls, as well as problems that still required solutions.

Somebody ingenious needed to guide the Majority out of its own brambles and into a starry victory.

That somebody was her.

Universal serendipity seemed to exist, because the Death Architect had been born in an era in which she was crucial. She understood exactly why the Torth needed to prevail. An ideal Torth had a stark, logical mentality, unclouded by slave impulses such as love or hope. Emotionless rationality was perfection.

As the Death Architect watched her slaves clean up the mess of dead human test subjects, she inhaled the stench. The cages got so bloody.

Most Torth would cope with messes like this by backing away, or by dialing up their tranquility meshes. So sad. So pathetic. Many children on baby farms would even be rude enough to vomit, or have some other disgustingly immature reaction, like tears.

The Death Architect suspected that she was as close to perfection as any living being could get.

Unlike most individuals, she was unaffected by fear. She had never felt afraid. She had never felt anything.

With such a clear head, she fully understood that torment was neither desirable nor undesirable. It was data. The Torth Majority would have to suffer in order to win this war. They would face a lower standard of living. Many would become enslaved as penitents. Many would die in battles. That was all right. Because afterward . . .

The Torth Empire would emerge stronger and leaner.

They could no longer afford to coddle mental deviants. No more mentally unbalanced individuals. Perfection would become a requirement.

That was a truth.

It was a truth that the Death Architect was wise enough not to reveal to the public.

Yet.

# PART TWO

*"Kessa used to be a slave. Now she is coming to free us all."*

—Legend among slaves

# CHAPTER 1
# IMITATION HUMAN

Kessa leaned forward, hands clasped atop a wooden table, peering into the gray eyes of her lieutenant. She wanted to feel sure this motherly ummin was telling the truth.

"Are you sure?" Kessa asked again.

"Well," the matron said, flustered. "I haven't heard any of them hold a conversation. But I swear, Jedwer would not lie. He's my son!"

Kessa leaned back in the chair, which was comfortably sized for ummins. She clicked her fingers on the armrests. She had chosen thousands of lieutenants, and most of them, like this matron, were of slave farm origin. Farm slaves had less resentment toward mind readers than city slaves, and that made them ideal for working with penitents who showed promising signs.

But farm slaves were also inexperienced with certain forms of suffering. Unlike Kessa, this lieutenant had never been ripped away from her family. She even had a child.

"Let me speak to your son," Kessa said.

Minutes later, Kessa sat in a different room of the townhouse, across from a pudgy adolescent ummin who had trouble making eye contact. Jedwer seemed overwhelmed by the visit.

"Your mother tells me," Kessa said, "that you spend a lot of time with one of the penitents on the machine shop crew?"

Jedwer stared at a poster on the adobe wall. Photography and printing were the latest fad to sweep through Freedomland, and just about everyone's private room displayed a poster or two. The apartment was festooned with photos of Jedwer and other ummins, presumably his family and friends.

One poster dominated the wall, a fanciful image Kessa had seen elsewhere throughout the city, in taverns and shops. It showed Kessa graciously extending a hand to Ariock as he stepped out of a storm cloud. There were rainbows and shining stars, and subjugated Torth in chains, bowing low.

"That artist made me look a lot younger than I am," Kessa said with a chuckle.

She was careful not to mention the artist by name. He was a talented ummin, one of the star pupils in Cherise's exclusive artists' workshop, and Kessa did not want to accidentally make him a military target.

One should always be guarded around people who worked with penitents. A bunch of penitents would likely try to scan Jedwer's private thoughts after this visit, hungry for any scrap of information about Kessa.

She gave Jedwer an encouraging smile.

The adolescent ummin twiddled his thumbs.

"It's all right," Kessa said. "You're not in trouble. I set up the lieutenant system precisely because I wanted to see former slaves and former Torth interact with each other. I am genuinely curious."

Jedwer flicked his gaze at Kessa. Then he stared out the round window, where hundreds of adobe townhouses and tenements populated the hillside.

Freedomland was growing at a rapid pace. Ariock no longer constructed every apartment, but there were multiple construction companies eager to win favors from councilors, war heroes, mercantile moguls, and anyone who had a big stake in the military economy. A system of digital war credits had replaced Alashani coins. Anyone who loved to gamble, or speculate, could win riches by investing in the right venture.

"Everyone makes fun of me," Jedwer said. "I don't have any friends."

Kessa felt like giving the child a hug. "Those who treat you with mindless cruelty are wrongheaded idiots," she said. "They are behaving like Torth."

Jedwer smiled with shy reluctance. He seemed surprised that Kessa was on his side.

"Why do they treat you that way?" Kessa asked. It was a risk to scrape at an obvious emotional wound, but she was curious. And she wanted to circle toward the topic that interested her.

Jedwer shrugged.

Kessa supplied a guess. "Is it because you and your mother work closely with penitents?"

"Maybe," Jedwer admitted. "And maybe other things. I spend a lot of time messing with data tablets. The neighborhood kids think I'm weird." He slumped, staring at his lap. "And yes. I do spend time with that one penitent. She knows a lot. She's a good tutor."

Kessa tried to mask her interest. After months of seeking penitents who might be friendly, she had gained nothing but hopes and suspicions.

It was not from lack of trying. Lieutenants, like this boy's mother, each spent many hours, one-on-one, every day, with individual mind readers. Kessa hand-selected the penitents whom she believed might be redeemed. She used an internal checklist of criteria, in terms of random acts of kindness. Tranquility meshes were rekeyed in order to test for emotions. There were therapy sessions. She suggested suitable activities.

Yet the penitents remained sullen and silent. They refused to speak unless spoken to. They did nothing that could be construed as friendly.

Kessa kept at it. She listened to a daily avalanche of reports from various lieutenants. And she utilized a secret network of informants. If she heard any hint of violence, she immediately swapped out a reportedly cruel overseer or lieutenant for a kinder one, and then she conducted follow-up interviews, wary of false reports.

Perhaps her efforts were beginning to pay off?

"She says her name is Avery," Jedwer said.

"Avery?" The word sounded somewhat English to Kessa, who was fluent in three languages. In addition to the common slave tongue, she knew the human language of English, and she had also learned the Alashani native tongue.

"Avery says it's a human name," Jedwer explained. "She says she's always wanted to be human."

Kessa hid her excitement. She publicly encouraged penitents to choose names that were not dictated to them by the Majority or anyone else, to embrace their authentic personhood. As far as she knew, none had done so. Until now.

"I would love to meet Avery," Kessa said. "Will you introduce me to her?"

Jedwer led the way.

One tricky aspect of dealing with mind readers was controlling their access to information. Kessa had purposely instructed her handpicked lieutenants to keep their penitent work crews apart from other penitents. The specialized work crews were not allowed much contact with their fellow mind readers, or with any person who was knowledgeable in military matters. That included Kessa herself.

So she did not go near Avery.

Instead, she sat on a catwalk along the ceiling of the machine shop garage, a workspace where overseers and penitents worked together in order to customize transports. She swung her legs, looking down at the female penitent who was escorted by Jedwer.

Avery was a tall mind reader with iridescent-green eyes. She must have been a Green Rank technician, someone who worked with machinery or spacecraft. Green Ranks were entrusted with jobs that Yellow Ranks were too lazy or undereducated to deal with, but they were too lowly to be permitted to govern, oversee, or architect systems. In the Torth Empire, slaves did drudge work. Green Ranks filled in for complex cognitive tasks.

"Peace, Avery." Kessa offered the typical friendly greeting of slaves. Her perch was far away from most of the workshop activity, so she should be able to hear any reply.

Avery offered a shy nod.

That was more than most penitents offered when greeted. Kessa studied the woman's condition.

As a Torth, Avery would have worn shimmery robes, perhaps a trim bodysuit. Slaves would have carried any tools she needed.

Now?

Avery wore rags. Tools were strapped to her waist, her upper arms, and also to a rack on her back. Dirt and grease smudged her face and short-cropped hair.

Most penitents went barefoot. The lieutenant had given this one sturdy work boots.

"Tell me, please," Kessa said, "what is a typical day like for you?"

Avery swallowed audibly. What would unnerve a former Torth? Was she afraid of Kessa? Or was she simply afraid of speaking out loud?

"I wake up." Avery pointed to a row of cubbies. "There."

Her voice was quiet but smooth. It seemed her vocal cords were strengthened from practice. She probably spoke out loud every day.

Avery went on. "I fetch supplies, as the overseers of this garage command. I lift heavy objects. I clean grease stains. I answer any questions they have. I help my work crew. We dine. We sleep."

No surprises there.

"What about when you work with the lieutenant?" Kessa asked. Every tenth day, Avery was required to have a brief one-on-one evaluation. The scrutiny must feel invasive—but it was less invasive than mind probes, which was what the Torth used to do to their slaves. As long as Avery and other penitents refused to openly join Thomas, they had to be treated as enemies.

"The lieutenant invites me to dine with her and Jedwer," Avery admitted. "I wash myself first. Then I prepare a meal and serve them. The lieutenant teaches me about her culture and society. Sometimes she asks me questions about Torth society. I answer."

Avery's style of speech was the usual succinct style of former Torth.

"Sometimes—" Avery interrupted herself, glancing down at the adolescent ummin.

Jedwer gave her a nod of permission.

"Sometimes I sit with Jedwer until it is time for him to attend his learning center." Avery's voice trembled. "I teach him anything he wishes to learn. Mostly, it is dynamic scripting, so he can customize control applications."

Kessa figured that must have something to do with data tablets. No wonder Avery was nervous. Penitents were supposed to be restricted to manual labor.

"She does not touch the tablet," Jedwer said with hasty assurance. "That is all me. She answers any question I ask!"

Kessa shifted her gaze to him, surprised that he had volunteered to defend the penitent.

"I can create applications on tablets that no one else can make, thanks to her," Jedwer said. "I can show you, if you'd like?"

"That is not necessary." Kessa imagined their tutoring relationship. It seemed unlikely that Avery had taught Jedwer such a niche skill without once touching a tablet. She might have bent or broken that minor rule.

Jedwer seemed to realize the implications. "I swear, I never let her touch a data tablet. She teaches me with words only. I promise!"

Kessa saw guilty defiance on his adolescent face.

It might be dangerous to allow the tutoring to continue. Tablets were ubiquitous in control centers and in scientific research labs. Avery might use her tablet skills to cause hovercarts to crash, or to spy on people, or something along those lines.

Yet she had not done so.

"I will not make you stop," Kessa decided. She was still uncomfortable with acting as an ultimate authority.

Jedwer and Avery both looked as if they might collapse from relief. This was exactly the sort of bond that Kessa wanted to study.

Unless, of course, it was false.

Some penitents pretended to be outstanding models of subservience . . . until a child got too close, or someone let their guard down. Then those penitents were eager to wreak havoc. They were showered with glory in the Megacosm even as overseers shot them to death.

"How long has Avery lived in your family's garage, Jedwer?" Kessa asked.

"Two lunar cycles."

That was quite a while. The fakers tended to be short term. They did not keep up the act for multiple months.

There were other types of fakers, though. Some penitents ascended into the Megacosm against the law. Garrett usually rooted out the spies, but every once in a while, he was too late. They leaked information to the Torth Empire.

Kessa tapped her fingers on the catwalk, musing. How would Avery react to a disruption between herself and Jedwer?

"With such good tutoring skills," Kessa said, "perhaps I will consider taking Avery away from manual labor. She might teach classes instead."

Jedwer looked shaken.

Avery squeaked and fell to her knees, as if struck by a great invisible weight. "No! I am not suited to teach like that!"

Kessa studied the penitent, astonished. Perhaps she lacked confidence in her voice?

"We would keep you away from the academy, of course," Kessa said. That was common sense. Penitents were not permitted near the uptown campus, where cutting-edge military concepts might be discussed. "You could teach at a satellite office, close to your home here."

Avery remained bowed on her knees, trembling. "Please, Wise One," she said in a small voice. "I get overwhelmed in crowds."

Kessa supposed that crowds might be hard for telepaths to cope with, when they were not busily repressing their emotions.

"And I would be in danger," Avery added. "Please, I beg you. I want to stay here!"

"All right." Kessa would never force a benign penitent into a deadly situation, as her own Torth owner used to do to her. Perhaps this particular penitent had never mistreated her own slaves. Her reaction looked like a genuine bond of friendship—with an ummin!

Avery's trembling subsided.

"Jedwer says you wish to be a human." Kessa studied every detail of the penitent's reaction. "Is that so?"

Avery bowed in a groveling way, exactly like a slave to a Torth master. "Yes, great Wise One."

Kessa hid her excitement. If this penitent was truly ready to ally herself with Thomas and Kessa . . . "How did you pass your Adulthood Exam?"

Avery looked alarmed, perhaps not anticipating such an incisive question. "I thought I would fail," she answered in her quiet voice. "Those that tested me must have been lenient."

Kessa examined that answer.

Avery seemed to realize how unsatisfactory it was. Her gaze up toward Kessa was defiant. "Not all Torth are monsters."

That was what Kessa needed to prove—against popular opinion.

"Hmm." Kessa chose her approach with deliberate care. She wanted to tease out any hint of buried cruelty, so she switched to a topic that should elicit emotion. "I would have liked to meet Torth children who never underwent the Adulthood Exam. I am deeply regretful about the baby farms ended by the Torth Empire."

It was common knowledge in the city by now, but Avery was distraught enough to show it on her face. Jedwer looked troubled and thoughtful, possibly just now realizing why there were no underage Torth penitents.

"Do you think some of them would have acted like human children?" Kessa asked, genuinely curious about a Torth perspective.

Avery stammered. "I . . . I do not know." She looked ashamed, hands clasped and head bowed. "What the Torth Empire did was wrong. It was terrible."

Avery seemed genuine. Kessa swallowed. If she could get Avery to admit her new allegiance out loud, she could become the first renegade Torth citizen of Freedomland—not counting Thomas and Garrett.

One renegade would open the way for others. Avery's new allegiance could open floodgates and usher in a new era of victories, with Torth renegades fighting alongside ummin pilots.

"Avery," Kessa said. "Will you fight the Torth Empire?"

The penitent looked taken aback.

"Will you join Thomas in this war?" Kessa leaned forward. "And me?"

Avery looked anguished, and Kessa's hope dimmed. This potential renegade was going to refuse.

"I cannot," Avery said in a mournful tone.

"Why not?" Kessa demanded.

Silence.

Even Jedwer looked disappointed as a minute passed and Avery only shook her head.

"Do you remain loyal to the Torth Empire, Avery?" Kessa asked.

She hoped for an emphatic rejection of the Torth. Instead . . .

"I am a Torth," Avery said quietly.

That answer would not satisfy freed slaves who were suspicious of penitents. It would not satisfy the war council.

And it did not satisfy Kessa.

She wanted to build friendships across the species, but there could be no friendship without mutual trust and some understanding. How could anyone trust the penitents, or understand them, if they remained secretive?

There was only one workaround to that problem: A trustworthy mind reader—Thomas—could tell why Avery remained allied to the Torth Empire. At the very least, he would know for certain whether Avery was a faker or a genuinely remorseful and kindhearted penitent.

Not everyone would trust Thomas's word, but as far as Kessa was concerned, it was better than her own assessment. It was foolproof.

"Avery, I would like for you to meet Thomas," Kessa said. "How would you feel about that?"

Avery reacted as if Kessa had stomped on a raw nerve. She threw herself to the ground. "Please, no! Please, no!"

Kessa had to interrupt the begging. "Why not?" After all, Thomas was the original person who had pleaded for mercy for captured Torth. He was the reason why penitents were relatively safe instead of getting executed or worked to death.

Avery gazed up at her with haunted green eyes. "Please, do not make me meet him!"

Kessa clicked her beak, unwilling to drop her unanswered question. This job would be so much easier if she had the powers of a mind reader.

Which was exactly why she wanted Thomas to assess Avery.

"Why not?" Kessa insisted.

Avery seemed at a loss for words. She moved her hands, clearly frustrated by an inability to translate her mentality into the slave tongue.

Finally, she choked out a reply. "When the first Torth invaders set foot on Umdalkdul, twenty-four thousand years ago, would you have agreed to meet that era's Commander of All Living Things?"

Kessa shook her head at the non sequitur. "Thomas only zombifies enemy combatants. You are not an enemy combatant. You are under my protection, and I promise, he will not harm you."

Unless Avery turned out to be a treacherous Torth. But that did not need to be stated.

"He is the Conqueror!" Avery said.

"He is not the monster that the Torth Empire imagines him to be," Kessa said, marveling at the power of Torth propaganda. "He is actually quite kind."

"He contains worlds," Avery said. "Hundreds of thousands of lives exist simultaneously inside his mind! There is no universal truth in a multifaceted cosmos such as that. He presents one face to you. He will present something different to one such as me."

Kessa found that hard to believe.

And yet she wondered. Why did Thomas avoid penitents so assiduously?

Thomas was friendly with his lab assistants. He was affectionate toward his sky croc. He was polite to councilors. He dined with Kessa every week or two. Was it possible that he would treat Torth allies like filth, even though he claimed to need them?

Kessa needed to find out.

"Thank you for meeting with me." She stood, holding on to the catwalk railing. "Please do not brag about your tablet lessons."

"Thank you!" Jedwer seemed ecstatic. "Can I show you a game I designed on the tablet? It's really cool. It's like a maze, except it's—"

"Some other time, sorry." Kessa gave a gentle smile to soften her refusal. Her mind brimmed with questions. If Torth penitents were going to go renegade and fully join this side of the war, they would have to publicly let go of their loyalties to the empire.

And they would have to work with Thomas.

Thomas, too, should take on some of that responsibility. He insisted that the only way they could win the war was with friendly Torth allies. Well, if that was true, then assuaging the fears of promising penitents ought to be near the top of his priority list.

Kessa planned her next dinner with Thomas. He needed to stop avoiding the penitents.

# CHAPTER 2
# STORMBRINGER

Ariock basked in the quietude of an alien prairie. The air was searingly hot and the gravity was heavy, but his powered suit of armor kept him at a comfortable temperature.

He studied the floating city he was about to conquer.

CloudShadow MetroHub was one of the grandest megalopolises in the galaxy according to both Thomas and Garrett. It looked the part. Buildings piled atop buildings, and they all defied gravity like towering thunderheads. Vast districts rotated, letting rays of sunlight play over the croplands below. Gauzy veils of artificial rain swept over other crops.

There was even more urbanization underground. When Ariock expanded his awareness, he sensed countless millions of life sparks crowded, unseen, in what must be a warren of bunk rooms and factories.

Cables ferried slaves between the upper, middle, and lower portions of the megalopolis, up to work or down to sleep.

"Are they alarmed?" Ariock asked. His local regiment was nowhere in sight—and the bulk of his army was standing by on a faraway planet—but his own huge sphere of influence was detectable to anyone with Yeresunsa powers.

"Nope. They have no clue about the coming storm." Garrett seemed pleased. "They're not expecting us at all." He sat next to Ariock in the grass. "I guess the boy was right. The empire can't imagine we'll interrupt our conquest of Verdantia to strike a city on Nuss." He shook his head in mock consternation. "This is going to be fun."

Verdantia was a wealthy, beautiful planet, habitable for humanoids. The Torth Empire assumed Ariock planned to take over that entire world, so they had mostly evacuated. That made conquests easy.

*"It's dangerous for us to fall into a routine pattern,"* Thomas had said during a recent private council. *"The Torth Empire studies our every move. We should target an unsuspecting city on a different planet and try a new battle tactic."*

So here they were.

Ariock worried about his cities on Verdantia and Umdalkdul. How would the Torth react when news of this invasion on Nuss hit the Megacosm?

*"The Torth Empire will go into panic mode,"* Thomas had predicted. *"They'll throw all their resources into evacuating Nuss rather than make a concerted effort to reclaim the territory they've lost elsewhere."*

That panic would subside, eventually. The Torth Empire would rally. But Ariock figured his military arms on other planets could stave off whatever meager raids the few remaining local Torth could muster.

If worse came to worse, he would mass-teleport millions of people to the safety of Reject-20. It shouldn't be a problem.

Garrett grinned. "I sense upward of a thousand Rosies in that city." He rubbed his armored hands together, and his grin turned savage. "That will translate to a lot of zombies for us."

"Not what we're here for," Ariock said.

"I know, I know." Garrett stood and began ratcheting his armor, tightening the seals. "Don't worry, they won't all survive long enough to be zombie fodder. I'm sure a lot of the morons will die pitting themselves against me."

Ariock sighed. It was useless to warn Garrett not to be reckless, but he tried anyway. "Please remember that some of them approach your level of raw power. If they team up, especially ten or more—"

"Yeah, whatever." Garrett rolled his eyes. "Look, I may be a little bit decrepit"— he tapped his bad leg—"but the Rosies are called Recruits for a reason. They're a bunch of amateurs."

"They've had months of practice," Ariock reminded Garrett. "I'm not sure we can keep calling them amateurs."

He said it without rancor. After learning about Garrett's childhood, he felt protective of his great-grandfather. He understood now that Garrett was insecure, constantly striving to prove himself a hero rather than an abusive tyrant like his biological father.

"You can go on thinking of me as flawed." Garrett clapped Ariock on the back. "Especially when you're within range of Torth. Make sure to think of me as extra slow and stupid."

Ariock winced with shame. "I don't . . . agh." He reconsidered his thoughts. "I just think you're too valuable to lose."

That was nothing but the truth. Garrett's skills and abilities were unmatched by anyone except Ariock himself. The old man made the winning difference in battles whenever Ariock wasn't around.

"So are you." Garrett clipped on his earpiece. "We'll look out for each other. As usual. Right?"

"Right." Ariock had to stop himself from giving his great-grandfather a reassuring pat on the shoulder. That would be too paternalistic.

Standing, Ariock cast a shadow like an inverted obelisk. He must be visible even from the floating city.

But that was all right.

The battle was about to begin.

Ariock activated his armor, causing it to tighten within a second. His helmet faceplate came down and sealed.

Garrett's voice was gritty in his earpiece. "Let's go kill some Torth."

Ariock infused his body with extra strength and leaped high into the air. He soared upward nearly fast enough to create a sonic boom.

That was so he could gather a lot of momentum in free fall.

As he plummeted toward the ground, he went into a clairvoyant trance. He and Garrett had studied wireframe maps of this city. With Thomas's help, they had memorized critical locations. Ariock ghosted through skyscraper walls. His target, the spaceport mall, bustled with activity.

It was strange to see Torth conducting business as usual. Ariock was used to conquering mostly empty cities. Here, people browsed high-end clothing or trinket shops, followed by personal slaves who carried their shopping bags or who pushed hoverbaskets. There was a luxury gymnasium, where Torth did aerobic exercises amid holographs. Others lay on massage beds.

Ariock grinned, disembodied.

He chose a place near the glass ceiling. It was important that he appear beyond the easy range of blaster gloves. The first half second after he teleported was always a critical, dangerous moment of vulnerability.

No time to waste. The longer Ariock ghosted, the greater the mental strain and the more drained he would feel.

He snapped his plummeting body to the location of his mind.

Ariock had teleported in midaction so often, he was growing used to free fall. He was aware of pointing fingers and upturned faces, many eyes wide with shock. Slaves dropped their burdens. A hovercart careened off course and slammed into a crowd. People screamed in pain.

Quite a few Torth hurried to don their blaster gloves.

Ariock puffed his awareness outward to seize doors and furniture. He quickly blocked and sealed every exit. He slowed his fall to a stop at the same time.

He hovered in the central atrium. Fiery explosions slammed against his shield. Flames engulfed his fireproof armor until he seized the surrounding air and channeled the flames away. Excess electricity snapped off his arms and fists.

He gazed down at the crowd.

They ran.

Torth tripped over their robes or over each other. They shoved slaves off balconies or mowed them down in hovervehicles in their blind panic to get away. Many Torth attempted to cower in shops, commanding their nussian bodyguards to serve them as living shields.

The smarter mind readers realized there was no viable escape. Those knelt in surrender.

Ariock encompassed everyone on the ground floor within his awareness.

It was a flat disk of living mayhem. People trampled each other. The Torth didn't want to become corpses or slaves, and the slaves just wanted to survive the next few minutes.

Ariock had already predesignated a flat prairie outside the city limits for the purpose of winnowing prisoners, penitents, and former slaves. He ghosted to the winnowing area. Then he yanked his extended awareness to that location—and everyone and everything he encompassed came along with him.

Ariock caught himself high up in midair.

Meanwhile, the people below him stumbled or fell. Thunder rolled as teleported air dissipated. Hovervehicles and other debris, released from Ariock's awareness, hit the prairie ground.

Ariock had stationed an army regiment nearby, protected from the sun beneath a series of canopies. Armored ummins, govki, and nussians rushed toward the mass of disoriented mall shoppers. A few of his soldiers struggled, unused to the heavy gravity of Nuss, but their powered armor helped.

They shot inhibitor serum at any Torth they saw. A squad of shani warriors, protected by powered armor and commanded by Guradjur, one of Jinishta's no-non-sense peers, would take care of any unanticipated problems.

Ariock left them to do their jobs.

He shot upward above puffy white clouds. Then he dipped into a clairvoyant trance, uncaring that it left his body in free fall, albeit well beyond the range of blaster gloves. He only needed half a second to ghost across the galaxy.

He followed a cosmic route from Nuss to Reject-20 that he had repeatedly practiced and memorized.

The rain was letting up over the teleportation flats of Freedomland. Scattered clouds revealed the neighboring planet's rings, enormous streaks of color in the afternoon sky.

Ariock appeared above fifteen thousand eager and ready soldiers. Thomas had already advised the battle leaders on how best to prearrange each unit for this con-quest, so Ariock did not need to make estimates or deal with stragglers.

The primary regiments were obvious. They included ragged-looking zombies on the outer fringe, ready to serve as living shields for the shani warriors.

Ariock tried not to think too hard about the zombie factor. His warriors and soldiers could conquer a city without such help, but Jinishta insisted that the presence of zombies boosted morale. They saved lives. They were like an extra layer of armor.

The zombies were doomed, anyway. No one could reverse their brain damage. No one could save them.

Ariock encompassed the first regiment within his awareness. He ghosted across the galaxy, back to CloudShadow MetroHub on Nuss, and deposited this regiment onto the now-empty spaceport mall floor.

Thunder rolled, causing pillars to shake. That was a side effect of mass-teleport-ing so many people.

There were differences in gravity and air pressure between Reject-20 and Nuss, and the regiment sprawled. The soldiers would need a few seconds to regain their equilibrium. Ariock, floating in midair and used to teleportation, needed less time.

Soon the soldiers would recover and hike away in well-trained units. They had all participated in conquests before. Ariock had surreptitiously set up data relays on buildings within the city at Thomas's behest in order to create a local communi-cations network. His soldiers all wore earpieces. They obeyed orders about which major boulevards and intersections they needed to secure.

Ariock ghosted to the next location on his mental list: a transport bay.

Just as Thomas had predicted, it was overcrowded. The Torth were now in panic mode and trying to escape. Some of them vomited in sheer terror upon seeing Ariock.

He almost felt sorry for them.

Almost.

Ariock seized thousands of people within his awareness. It would be all too easy to drop them into outer space or to kill them in some other near-accidental way . . . but fortunately for them, he was not in murder mode.

He deposited them onto the winnowing prairie.

It was a good thing it was such a large prairie. The first load was mostly sorted and collared, and the winnowing regiment moved in to deal with the fresh arrivals.

Ariock went back to Reject-20 to import more of his army.

Thomas called this particular tactic the turbine method. Ariock churned blades of mass-teleportation, an ability no one else in the known universe had enough raw strength to pull off. One blade of the turbine removed Torth from the target city and deposited them to a winnowing ground. Less than ten seconds later, the other blade replaced the absent Torth with friendly soldiers.

Ariock repeated his mass-teleportation turbine routine twenty more times. He mentally crossed off each location on his memorized checklist. Within a matter of minutes, he had cleared away the densest populations of the upper city, replacing them with his own people.

Fifteen thousand of his soldiers marauded through boulevards and intersections. They invaded gardens, lounges, and even private suites. They liberated slaves. They shot inhibitor serum at any Torth they found, then collared them. If they ran into problems? They could switch their blaster gloves into deadly mode.

Liberated slaves threw themselves prostrate on the ground when they saw Ariock, mistaking him for some sort of demigod.

Not that he did anything miraculous. Once the invasion was underway, Ariock merely walked down a boulevard, listening to battle updates in his earpiece. In past battles, he would quell the most violent hot spots, but now . . . ? Well, Garrett was more than enough in the brutality department.

The final body count was grim for the Torth.

None of Jinishta's warriors died.

None of Weptolyso's soldiers died.

It was a total victory. Again.

Ariock mass-teleported more than five hundred inhibited Rosies and Servants to his Mirror Prison on Reject-20 to await zombification.

And then he brought in the finishing stroke of any conquest: Kessa.

The floating gladiatorial stadium of CloudShadow MetroHub had very steep tiers, each tier wide enough to accommodate hoverchairs and bodyguards. Now those tiers were filled with nussians and other freshly liberated slaves. Huge, airy cutouts in the crowning wall let in plenty of fresh air and sunlight.

Ariock teleported Kessa directly to the center of the stadium.

He did not show himself. Instead, he hid behind one of the cutout pillars of the miles-high stadium. Garrett and any Alashani troops would stay out of sight as well. Most of the Alashani were securing newly collared penitents anyway, herding them into the filthy tunnels of the lower city.

This stage was for former slaves.

Weptolyso and Nethroko loomed behind Kessa. Since this planet had a lot of nussians, Kessa had insisted that her favorite nussians speak to the crowd. They had already introduced themselves and primed the audience.

"You are free." Kessa's amplified voice filled the stadium.

A huge cheer went up.

Kessa went on, speaking to the newly liberated city, with interjections by Weptolyso and Nethroko. Their speech was live-streamed to holographic displays and monitors. There was a makeshift audio system, jury-rigged by former slaves and designed by Thomas.

". . . And we also owe our freedom to the Son of Storms!" Weptolyso said.

"It is true!" Nethroko boomed. "You may have seen him. He looks like a Torth. Except he is the size of a nussian!"

The audience stomped their feet with pride. Thousands of jubilant nussians looked and sounded more intimidating than an army of Red Ranks.

"Perhaps he may be good enough to show himself?" Nethroko queried the air.

*"It's in everyone's best interest for you to be visible,"* Thomas had told Ariock during one of their private councils. *"It makes our troops feel more connected to you and more honored to fight for you."*

*"Also,"* Garrett had added, *"the imagery gets back to Megacosm. You should always do your best to come across as godlike and unstoppable. It helps to scare the Torth."*

The two nussians onstage searched the sky with exaggerated hope while the vast audience of newly liberated slaves hushed in anticipation.

Ariock would rather stay hidden. His powers were impressive, but he didn't like the way he looked so much like a gigantic Torth.

Then again, this conquest had been the best one yet.

Perhaps . . . well, perhaps it wasn't such a bad idea for him to take a tiny bit of credit for it?

He couldn't have done it without help from Thomas and from so many thousands of soldiers and warriors. But that was implied, wasn't it? Anyone who celebrated him would also be celebrating those who had helped make this victory possible.

Ariock stretched his awareness and squeezed vapor from the clouds.

A vibrant triple rainbow shimmered into existence, framed by the huge cutouts in the stadium. The rainbow arced above the shining skyscrapers of the floating city. Ariock had practiced rare weather phenomena for Vy, to make her throw her arms around him with delight. It impressed this audience, too.

Ariock zeroed in on the staging area where Kessa and the two nussians stood. Instead of landing gently, he threw himself down with enough excess force to make the whole stadium tremble. Sparks of energy rippled up his body.

Let them see a conqueror.

Skeins of lightning crackled off him. He straightened, tall and gigantic in his spiky black and purple armor, impossible to ignore.

"ARIOCK!!!" More than fifty thousand freed nussians shouted, lifting the syllables of his name in a thunderous chorus.

"Son of Storms!" Weptolyso pumped his fist in the air.

"He is fearless!" Nethroko roared.

"ARIOCK!!!"

His name sounded like a storm, bellowed by thousands of gravelly nussian voices.

A younger version of Ariock would have assumed that the praise was unwarranted.

But not today.

Ariock pumped both fists like a gladiator winning a fight. The audience screamed and stamped so hard, the stadium shook.

Every one of these nussians would likely be eager to fight in future battles. They understood that no Torth would behave like Ariock was acting, or wear armor that gave him an artificially nussian appearance.

They saw him. They knew he was a former gladiator, a former prisoner, just like them.

*This is where I belong*, Ariock thought. *This is what I am meant to do.*

And why shouldn't he and his people celebrate? Why shouldn't Ariock be proud? He was doing what he was best at, amid people who appreciated that.

"This is your home." Ariock amplified his voice so he could be heard even over the praise. "From now on, it will be governed by nussians!"

The crowd went wild with cheers.

CHAPTER 3

# ALL THE RAGE

The baryonic halo beyond the galaxy's outermost arm was probably the loneliest stretch of space accessible by living beings. If not for the ever-present bustle of the Megacosm, a Torth might go stir-crazy this far from civilized life.

But rough living did not bother the Red Rank known as the Steadfast Aplomb.

He lounged on a recliner, sipping a smoothie, with a govki slave massaging his feet. His job was supposedly undesirable. But these days, babysitting a supergenius seemed a lot more pleasant than, say, living in a megalopolis on some hub planet.

During the past few months, the Torth Empire had lost nearly half a billion citizens on Umdalkdul and Verdantia. While those former citizens labored as penitents, the Steadfast Aplomb had gotten a lot of rest.

One of the Green Ranks lounging nearby mentally poked him. *Aren't You late with doing Your duty?*

Oh. Right.

The Steadfast Aplomb dropped out of the Megacosm. He wasn't supposed to do his duty with any sort of an inner audience. That was protocol.

Losing the Megacosm was tough even when the loss only lasted for a few seconds. He missed his orbiters so much. How were those so-called penitent Torth able to survive without mental feedback? They must feel so . . .

Well, he didn't know how emotions felt.

They must feel sick every day. It probably felt akin to severe arthritis or something.

Sipping his tranquility smoothie, the Steadfast Aplomb paged through cargo bay records that were streamed to his private data tablet. He accepted supply packages. His underlings would go through the supplies later and their slaves would repackage any items that needed to be sent to the scientific vessel his military ship guarded.

He checked his inbox for the latest top-secret military research update. It was his duty to obfuscate the location stamp and then send each update to a relay station, which would then distribute it to other military scientists. That way, supergeniuses could disseminate their research to lesser scientists without accidentally sharing their locations.

His inbox was empty.

The Steadfast Aplomb was annoyed, yet rather unsurprised. The supergeniuses all claimed to be hard at work. But . . . Well, the Steadfast Aplomb had private access to the surveillance feeds that came directly from that scientific vessel. He could spy on the boy Twin any time he wanted to.

And that chunky kid was not sweating every second.

Oh, sure, most of the time the boy Twin was busy calculating data at a workstation or monitoring mysterious experiments in test tubes or beakers. He did look studious.

But every once in a while, the Steadfast Aplomb caught the boy Twin gazing off into space with a decidedly slave-like expression. Perhaps that was just the way he looked when processing complex equations? But more likely, the boy Twin was still pining away for his erstwhile roommate, the girl Twin.

They had mentally screamed when torn apart from each other.

How melodramatic! The Twins were pubescent, so some immaturity was excusable, but they had both passed their Adulthood Exams. Why couldn't they put aside childish tantrums and behave with adult dignity?

Really. Most citizens would revel in the perks the boy Twin received. His own private ship! Luxury accommodations! Twenty fresh new personal slaves!

How spoiled did one have to be, to want private companionship on demand? The Twins could easily converse with each other in the Megacosm, the way everybody else in the galaxy chatted.

Ah well.

The Steadfast Aplomb sent a ping to the boy's on-location guardian. She was a Servant of All who resided on that scientific vessel with him. Since the boy was late with his daily report, it was her duty to make sure he uploaded his research.

No response.

Five seconds passed.

Ten seconds.

The Steadfast Aplomb thought this was odd. The boy Twin might be irresponsible enough to neglect to upload his top-secret military research, but his guardian was reliable. She was better than a typical, average Servant of All. The ones chosen to guard supergeniuses were exceptionally loyal to the Torth Majority. They were elected by their peers based on that quality.

He pinged her again. And again. She wouldn't be asleep at this hour.

He toggled to the surveillance camera feeds. He paged through views of various laboratories and other rooms aboard the scientific vessel, searching. Part of his duty was to make sure the boy Twin and his Servant of All guardian were all right. If they were in trouble, he would have to save them.

And if the boy Twin turned into a problem?

Well, there were the nuclear warheads with preprogrammed trajectories permanently locked onto the relative coordinates of the scientific vessel.

The Steadfast Aplomb had memorized the unlock-and-send code for those warheads. In a worst-case emergency, he would do his duty for the empire and destroy that scientific vessel with its valuable occupant trapped inside. The Torth Majority was not going to allow another supergenius to turn renegade.

*Superior officer?* A Green Rank mentally intruded on his private thoughts, seeking his attention.

That was rude. The Steadfast Aplomb glared at her, hardly able to believe such uncharacteristic rudeness. Private thoughts were . . . well, private. He wasn't in the Megacosm. That fact should be enough to ward off any—

*We may have a problem.* The Green Rank radiated fear. It leaked off her in a repulsive mental stench.

Everyone in the control room looked alert and fearful. They sat on the edges of their lounge chairs.

The Steadfast Aplomb smelled something odd in the air, like chlorine mixed with fermented ale.

*What is it?* The Steadfast Aplomb gave up on his duty for the moment. *What is that scent in the air?*

The Green Rank radiated *(?)* uncertainty. She didn't know.

The Megacosm would surely provide answers.

The Steadfast Aplomb ascended into the gloriousness of the collective, gathering bits of news as he went. CloudShadow MetroHub on Nuss had been conquered. Its captured citizens were still crying for help, but so what? That had nothing to do with him.

Other than that? It was the usual. Neighbors watched each other for aberrant behavior. Many Torth were jittery or using tranquility meshes. Anyone might secretly attempt to become a minion of the enemies. Anyone might be capable of mind control and secretly hiding it. The Giant and his army might pop up anywhere and wreak havoc.

Ugh. The news.

*Something is wrong (something is wrong) something is wrong.* The Green Rank foamed at the mouth. *Maybe wrong with You, maybe wrong with Me. I don't know but I have to protect Myself!*

The Steadfast Aplomb jumped back to get out of her range. Really, she ought to be considerate enough to self-isolate until her strange mood passed. Nobody sane wanted to share a mood like that.

She swiped at him.

Her fingernails tore at his cheek, drawing blood.

The Steadfast Aplomb did not scream. Like any Red Rank, he was trained to endure more pain and more surprise than an average Torth. He had been in combat situations.

But this was not a slave. This was a peer! A fellow citizen! What in the galaxy was wrong with her? Had she consumed an illegally caffeinated substance?

*DEATH!* Another of the crew members leaped at him. This one was a man with a potbelly, and he was normally quite tranquil.

The Steadfast Aplomb reflexively shielded himself with one elbow. He whirled in a combat kick, knocking away the out-of-shape crew member.

This time, he did not hesitate to don his blaster glove.

*!!!*

When the female Green Rank leaped at him again, he thumbed his trigger. Her head exploded in a fountain of gore.

The headless body thumped down. The Steadfast Aplomb sensed her mind blink out of existence. All that remained of her personality were floating after-images, like the visual blotches that could occur after a bright light went out.

The potbellied man lunged at the Steadfast Aplomb with bloodstained hands, knocking over smoothie cups in the close quarters. *DIE YOU NEED TO DIE!*

Green Ranks were supposed to be levelheaded technicians. This was insane. Greens never attacked Reds!

The Steadfast Aplomb cured the potbellied Green Rank of his insanity by shooting him. What else could he do? There was no protocol for dealing with such wild, unpredictable behavior.

Everyone else in the control room was either dead or gone. The slaves had quietly sneaked out.

Blood spattered the walls.

*Close the air vents*, his orbiters suggested.

*There might be a neurotoxin in your ship's air supply.*

*Your heart rate is elevated.*

*Careful. You are being affected.*

The Steadfast Aplomb was grateful for the advice from cool, rational listeners. His mood was already curdling in strange, unfamiliar ways.

He dragged a chair so he could reach the nearest vent.

*Were slaves affected?* some Torth wondered.

*If it is a neurotoxin, could it have been custom-tailored for Torth physiology?*

*We need to track down WHY and HOW.*

His orbiters replayed scenes of violence from elsewhere aboard his military vessel. The whole ship had somehow been poisoned. Everyone was acting paranoid and violently killing each other.

The Steadfast Aplomb closed one air vent, then dragged the chair to close the next one. He was shaking with unfamiliar rage. He had never felt any emotion this intense in his life. He wanted to rip the eyes out of someone's sockets. Whoever had done this would pay.

It was almost certainly that fat little supergenius.

But how had the boy Twin contaminated the military vessel? He was on a separate ship. Besides, there were safeguards. Protocols. The boy had a guardian. If she had failed in her duty . . . ? The Steadfast Aplomb would beat her with her own—

*Grab a tranquility mesh*, his inner audience advised.

*Dial it to the maximum setting.*

*Drink more of that tranquility smoothie.*

*That smoothie is probably why you fended it off for longer than the others.*

The Steadfast Aplomb dived toward a table where one of his now-dead crewmates had left her mesh. He fitted it around his temples, then dialed it to maximum tranquility.

He did not feel calm.

Maybe it helped, a little.

The Steadfast Aplomb sipped the last dregs of his smoothie and opened himself to more advice. Sane commands might help him fend off the chasm of rage that now occupied his mind. *Help Me. Tell Me what to do, you lazy idiots!*

Eight hundred billion Torth mobbed his brain.

They lounged on beds, or trained on exercise machines, or shopped in forums, or sunbathed, or picnicked in wildernesses, or flew transports above bustling metropolises. How nice. None of them were having rage seizures.

*Release the nukes.*

They sounded rational, but the Steadfast Aplomb hesitated. Was he imagining this command?

*Release the nuclear warheads*, billions of distant Torth chorused.

*Kill the boy Twin.*

*This attack must have been his doing.*

*We cannot imagine why or how, but—*

*—just to be safe—*
*—DESTROY THE BOY!*

The Steadfast Aplomb hurried to his data tablet. There were many, many voices inside his head. They were legion, they were infinity, they controlled the cosmos. He had no choice. He was honored to serve the Majority.

*DO NOT.*

A singular, godlike mental voice thundered through his brain.

The girl Twin was buoyed by her own immense audience. Billions of admirers orbited her. She was, after all, the eldest living supergenius. That counted for a lot. She might not be the elected leader of the Torth Empire—the Torth had no Majority-elected leader, currently—but she was very close to that position just by default.

Of all the empire's supergeniuses, the girl Twin was voted to be the most knowledgeable, the most intelligent, and the most trustworthy. She had clout.

*DO NOT MURDER THE BOY TWIN.* The girl Twin used her vast influence to dampen the Majority's thunder. *Check on him,* she urged. *He would never betray the empire. He is as loyal as I am.*

The Majority reeked of doubt.

*Kill him,* many insisted.

The Steadfast Aplomb picked up his data tablet, ready to obey. He was eager to make a ship explode.

*DO NOT,* the girl Twin insisted.

Her towering mind bristled. It was not rage, precisely, but she did emit a thorny feeling. She was irked.

The Steadfast Aplomb did not think he had ever personally experienced an irked supergenius mind. It was intimidating, like standing beneath ominous clouds, unsure whether to expect rainy drizzle or a deadly tornado.

Another supergenius entered the fray. Minds rippled in her wake like stars orbiting a black hole. The Death Architect whispered to the Steadfast Aplomb, *Send Me the boy Twin's latest research.*

So many sycophants echoed her command, it was inescapable. The Steadfast Aplomb shuddered.

He checked his inbox again. But it was still empty.

*Let Me guide You.* The Death Architect's mind became a mirror of his hands. She showed him exactly what back-end protocols he needed in order to access data packets on the scientific vessel.

The Steadfast Aplomb followed her mental lead. He opened files and tapped in codes he had never known existed.

*This. This. And this.* The Death Architect selected whatever top-secret military data updates she wanted. *Now let's send it.*

She did not seem interested in stripping away any location data. She did not seem concerned about the safety of the boy Twin or anyone else.

Once the top-secret military update was on its way, bouncing from relay station to relay station, the Death Architect withdrew from the Megacosm. Presumably she wanted to get back to work.

*NOW DESTROY HIM,* the Majority commanded.

The Steadfast Aplomb was shaking. Saliva dripped onto the tablet screen. His mouth was foaming, he was so furious. And so thirsty.

*DESTROY THAT SCIENTIFIC SHIP.*
   *DESTROY.*
      *DESTROY.*

He tapped a military access code onto his tablet.

The girl Twin twisted taller in the Megacosm. Her gigantic mind seemed to spit hailstones at random orbiters. *If You (the Majority) are so quick to accuse and execute loyal supergeniuses, then We have already lost the war.*

Her mind was as certain as death. There was no halo of doubt, no room for questions.

*If We (the Twins) were traitors,* the girl Twin went on, *then I would not be so stupid as to remain vulnerable in my floating lab with nuclear missiles aimed at Me and ready to fire. I would have called for help from the Conqueror long ago.*

That made sense. Maybe.

The iciness that swept off the girl Twin's mind caused teeth to chatter throughout the empire. *If You (Majority) (in Your moronic impulsivity) murder a supergenius without any investigation into His guilt or innocence, then You will lose all Your remaining supergeniuses. Not just Me. You will lose the Geodesic Flux, the Rind Topographer, the Spin Overture, the Mechanized Meeter, the Stemmer Linguist, the Neurobioticist, the Death Architect. Why would any of Us work for stupid, greedy, shortsighted murderers of Our kind?*

The Majority spun in shock.

   . . .

The Steadfast Aplomb hesitated. None of the supergeniuses who had tuned in were disputing the girl Twin's assertions.

*We are loyal,* the Stemmer Linguist thought.

*We are doing Our best,* the Spin Overture thought.

Both of the younger supergeniuses emanated weariness. They were overworked and tired of exceeding deadlines. Small promotions did not seem like enough of a reward for the innovations they were making. They opined that supergeniuses deserved greater respect.

And they wanted to be sure that the boy Twin was all right.

The girl Twin went on. *I want to serve You (the Torth Majority). But You seem to purposely want to lose My respect. I serve stoic minds ruled by logic and rationality. Not small minds ruled by fear. Please explain: If You turn into paranoid, trigger-happy murderers, then how are You any better than a bunch of slaves? I am not a so-called penitent. I will not serve idiotic, terrified inferiors who murder their betters on a whim.*

The Majority fractured into a cacophony of suspicions and doubts and uncertainties and certainties.

*Without supergeniuses,* the girl Twin thought, *the Conqueror will go unopposed.* She imagined the mass enslavement of cities and the conquest of worlds. *Is that what You want?*

The Steadfast Aplomb choked on his own homicidal mania. Electric shocks of fury kept slicing his thoughts into incoherence. His face was wet with saliva, and that was worse than pathetic.

He didn't want to die like a clueless slave writhing on the floor. That was so undignified. So unworthy of his rank and his title.

Amazingly, he still had a mental audience, despite his bestial mood.

Billions of Torth urged him to calm down. They wanted him to toggle through surveillance feeds. Find the boy Twin.

A minority harmonized within that thunder, urging him to unlock the warheads.

He could not remember why his job mattered more than his own survival. Every one of his crewmates was dead. He was the only one left.

His thirst was crippling. He wanted to demand water, but the slaves had fled.

He would go find them. Tear open a throat. Drink its gushing blood.

*Do your duty,* his waning audience urged. *Fire the nukes.*

He could hardly remember what duty was. He had trouble remembering his own name-title or why there were dead Torth on the floor. He himself was writhing on the floor. Salivating.

Even so, he found enough wherewithal to enter his secret trigger code on the data tablet.

*Do NOT.* A hailstorm of righteous dismay radiated from the girl Twin. *STOP.*

Her outsize influence no longer mattered to him. Rage thundered through his skull, making long-term consequences impossible to think about. His vision was clouded with irrationality. He was losing consciousness, fading as if reality was at the far side of a tunnel. But he was eager to see the big kaboom.

Which never came.

The nuclear warheads sailed through space, charged and ready to detonate upon impact, but they went straight through the emptiness where the scientific vessel was supposed to be.

# CHAPTER 4

# A SLAVE QUEEN

"I want you to know," one of the ummin pilots said, "I appreciate all the time you spend with us, Lady Vy."

Vy smiled. A medic was an important part of a fleet. That was why she felt needed.

But she was also learning, to her chagrin, that certain species had advantages as pilots. Ummins could adjust their vision to an almost telescopic focus, and they were also quick at processing dangerous obstacles. She doubted that even the best Torth pilots could escape a determined ummin fleet.

At least she was getting to know which ones were mavericks. It was useful to learn who took daring risks, who asked for instructions, and who was good at cheering others up.

They would soon see combat. Vy knew that Thomas was getting ready to use this fleet, probably for some inventive new strategy. He had asked for regular updates from Fayfer, the little ummin who served the war council as admiral of the aerial militia.

"Have a wonderful night," Vy told her fellow pilots.

They offered cheerful goodbyes. Many would continue to hang out, visiting all-night cafés, but Vy was never in the mood to join them. Not while Ariock was busy conquering yet another metropolis on Nuss. Was it Lava City today? Or Playland Arena?

She walked toward a lamplit street with her hands shoved in the pockets of her bomber jacket, wondering when—or if—she would get to hang out with Ariock again.

There were always more cities for him to invade and conquer. Considering how enormous the galaxy-spanning Torth Empire was, this war would drag on for centuries.

More than a human life span.

All the while, Ariock would keep growing like a teenage boy. If Evenjos had told the truth, Ariock was destined to become a literal titan. He might forget Vy entirely within a few decades, or think of her like she was a childhood doll he used to play with.

And he wouldn't think twice about causing violent deaths if he did it every day for centuries. All that guilt that humanized him . . . it would ebb away.

He might become worse than Garrett.

A breeze stirred some wooden marionettes on display outside a shop, knocking them together like wind chimes. Vy studied the wood-carved ummins and kneeling penitent Torth. The latter looked uncomfortably like human figurines. Like praying children.

Like the abused children her mom sheltered and raised.

Vy wondered how her mom was handling the Hollander home without help. She must be struggling, and also mourning the loss of her only biological child.

She might even blame herself for the disappearance of Vy, Cherise, and Thomas. It hurt.

Vy moved on, past unique little shops that were all closed for the night. The air had a salty freshness out here. She tried to appreciate it. She kept trying to make her peace with being an alien among aliens.

The banded planet in the sky ensured colorful days and nights, so the mountain peaks each seemed to have a glowing corona even in the depths of nighttime. The city was perfectly laid out, designed by a supergenius. It was easy enough to find one's way to major boulevards.

Yet she kept remembering her small hometown on Earth.

"Good evening," a feminine voice said. "May I join you?"

Vy turned around.

There stood Evenjos, resplendent in a gown made of clingy fabric. Her purple hair was loose and flowing in the breeze. Her angelic wings arced behind her, framing her in that extra-imperious way.

And she was roughly eight feet tall.

Vy did not bother to force a friendly look. Evenjos might be the best healer in the universe, and she might have earned the worship of many folks, but she had a lot of personality flaws. Like, why had she made herself eight feet tall? Did she really find it necessary to tower over Vy in an intimidating way?

"Let's have a little chat," Evenjos said in a perky tone.

"Not interested." Vy began to turn away.

Evenjos whipped toward her faster than a snake. Before Vy even registered what was happening, her feet left the ground. She was wrapped in an iron embrace with wind roaring around them.

Evenjos was flying. With Vy.

Vy tried to scream. But a hand clasped her mouth, silencing her. All she could do was hyperventilate through her nose.

She had flown in this helpless way before, with Ariock, but he made it fun. He took her to beautiful, private destinations, known only to him and no one else. They had hiked on the rim of a volcano. They had swum in a tropical sea.

Evenjos seemed to be taking her straight up.

The wind grew cold and thin as they passed through a wreath of clouds. Vy quit struggling and gripped Evenjos's arm with both of her hands. *Don't drop me,* she pleaded in her mind, too frightened to speak out loud. *Please let me live.*

"Have no fear, Violet." Evenjos spoke with lazy assurance. "I have no desire to hurt you."

She plucked the jeweled supercom off Vy's ear and tossed it into the shadowy canyons below.

So much for communication.

Vy swallowed the lump of terror in her throat. Terror, and shame.

This helpless feeling was slavery.

Anything she tried would backfire. If she bit the woman's hand, Evenjos would just laugh and instantly heal.

Vy had been foolish enough to feel safe. All the enemies on this beautiful planet were either in cages or wearing collars, and she slept in a room near the ruler of the city. Everyone knew who she was. She had even refused bodyguards whenever Weptolyso, Jinishta, or Ariock offered them.

Not that bodyguards would protect her from Evenjos.

Now she realized that her blithe queenliness was wrong. And stupid. She was just a girl from Afton, New Hampshire, not a queen, no matter how nicely people treated her. And she was dating far, far outside her league.

"I have learned a few things from you," Evenjos said. "For that, you have my gratitude. So I am giving you a chance."

*A chance for what?* Vy asked in her mind.

"It will be obvious." Evenjos sounded amused.

They were flying away from the city, into a wilderness where twelve ton predators roamed. Beyond these mountains, herds of even more massive beasts caused the ground to tremble. Their migrations squashed the grasslands into a soupy bog.

Evenjos took her hand off Vy's mouth. They were too far away from people for a scream to be heard.

"Where are you taking me?" Vy was ashamed of the wheedling sound of her own voice. When Evenjos ignored her, she did not ask again. She merely held on tight and tried to imagine what Ariock would do once he found out about this. He would probably yell at Evenjos. Storm clouds would appear.

And then dissipate.

There wasn't much anyone could do against Evenjos.

Ariock would not physically attack her. Not near a city full of innocent people. And although he could banish her . . . would he?

Probably not. If he did, he would blame himself for all the people who died from the lack of an expert healer.

He should blame Vy.

Evenjos was one of the four heroes of prophecy. If Ariock lost the war because he decided to banish Evenjos, it would really be Vy's fault. She would know that truth even if no one accused her out loud.

She was such a useless burden.

Evenjos angled toward a cliff that was as toothy as a jawbone. As they drew closer, Vy saw a shack, like a hermit's cottage. It looked ramshackle rather than cozy. It was all loose slabs and planks.

Who would be insane enough to live out here?

"I built it this morning," Evenjos said, perhaps answering Vy's thoughts.

They landed on the promontory.

Vy stumbled on the uneven ground. At least she managed to keep from falling.

"It's to protect you from predators." Evenjos gestured to the shanty. "You should be safe inside. You'll find torches just in case. And you have your blaster glove. I left you an igniter and a jug of water. There's even some blankets for bedding."

"Why . . ." Vy stared from Evenjos to the shanty hut.

"This is one of the regular pilot training routes." Evenjos gestured at the canyon. "I'm sure a pilot is likely to spot you tomorrow. Or the day after." She sounded sympathetic. "You will be fine, I am sure."

With that, Evenjos took a few jogging steps and leaped off the cliff.

"WAIT!" Vy yelled.

The Lady of Sorrow soared away. If she heard Vy's lonely, echoing shouts, she ignored them. She banked toward the distant glow on the horizon, heading back toward the bustling city.

Vy reached for her earpiece. But the damnable Lady of Sorrow had thrown it away.

The wind blew. It was cold and lonely.

Vy kicked a rock off the edge of the cliff, cursing. She felt like a discarded piece of junk. Or a child locked up in a playpen so her mother could get some "me" time. She just couldn't guess why Evenjos wanted her out of the way.

On second thought, she could imagine it.

All too well.

Vy made fists. She kicked gravel off the cliff, then hurled rocks, one after another. But she could not stay furious at a canyon wilderness. Soon her rage curled inward, toward herself.

And tears came.

# CHAPTER 5

# WITH HER ON TOP

Ariock leaned against the polished meteorite wall in the antechamber of his suite and leafed through a tiny little photo album.

Actually, it was a normally sized album for humans. He just had to be extra careful when turning the plastic sleeves with his large fingers.

Mostly, he saw kids he did not recognize. The stout woman in many of the photos was obviously Vy's mother. She looked good-natured and kind. Vy herself was in some of the photos as a kid, and it was strange to realize that he had only known a sliver of her life, just the last year or two.

He got to the end and paged through the photo album one more time. There were a couple of group photos that included Thomas and Cherise, younger and more innocent than the friends he knew now.

Cherise had given him this gift idea. Ariock had surreptitiously gone to the academy and asked for the human teacher, accidentally interrupting one of her classes.

He had just wanted to get a better sense of what would please Vy. Rainbows and vacations were nice but fleeting. The prosthetic leg was as much a gift from Thomas as from Ariock. Surely there was something unique and valuable that Ariock alone could give her?

Cherise had gone to a chalkboard and sketched a cutaway view of a large house. She had pointed to the attic and said, *"There should be a bunch of photo albums in a cabinet there. I think Vy might love to see pictures of our mom."*

Ariock did not need to physically show up in a place to take things. So he had ghosted to Earth, to the Hollander house attic, wrapped his awareness around this photo album, and snapped back to his waiting body with the item in tow.

He wished he could reunite Vy with her family, without the consequence of reminding the Torth Empire that they would make good hostages. This album was the next best thing, he supposed. Maybe it would bridge some of the distance that had opened up between Vy and himself? They could go over each photo together. Ariock would ask who these people were.

It was worth a try.

He tucked the album in his hand, hiding it completely. Then he left his suite and crossed the hall. He gently knocked on Vy's door.

"Vy?" he said.

No answer.

Maybe she was having a late-night hangout with friends. That wouldn't surprise him. Vy was spending less and less time in the war palace.

Dejected, Ariock headed to his own suite. He had just won a third metropolis on Nuss, and he really wished he could share that happy news with someone who cared. Someone who remembered how powerless he used to be.

He spread his awareness out of habit, just to gain a rough idea of where the chambermaids were. He didn't like to be surprised by walking into his bedroom only to find strangers changing his bedsheets.

And—if he was honest with himself—he also wanted confirmation that Vy was not actually in her room, avoiding him on purpose.

The whole neighborhood was filled with the powerful, indistinct thrum of Evenjos. She tended to wash out all life sparks in the immediate vicinity.

Ah well. Ariock figured Evenjos must be visiting the war palace in order to hold some kind of meeting with Garrett or Jinishta. She was working more closely with them in her capacity as a military medic. Ariock no longer needed to worry about her attempts to seduce him. She had finally quit that behavior, and what a huge relief that was.

He opened the door of his bedroom, prepared for another lonely night. He would try to see Vy tomorrow. Or the day after. He would figure out some casual way to surprise her with the gift of her family photo album.

A scent of fragrant oils filled his room.

Ariock paused.

Glowing spheres illuminated every marble surface, reflecting colors in a cozy way. Someone must have spent hours arranging this extravagant display.

Vy lounged on the gigantic bed amid plush blankets.

A semitransparent black negligee stretched across her full breasts and emphasized the curves of her body. She was nude underneath. At least, nudity was strongly implied.

Something clunked on the floor. Ariock realized that he'd dropped the photo album.

Vy offered a shy, sweet smile. "Sorry if I surprised you." She leaned up on one elbow. "I just missed hanging out with you. I'm tired of this . . . distance . . . that's happening between us."

The love and relief that washed through Ariock were more powerful than a million aliens praising his name.

He picked up the photo album, closed the bedroom door, and went to her.

Vy did not scoot away to make room the way she normally would. She seemed to approve of every move he made, even when he came close enough to tower over her. Even when he carefully sat, which made the mattress compress. She slid closer.

"I've been afraid for far too long," Vy said. "I don't want that to stop me anymore."

She trailed her hand across his huge forearm, past the iron spike, and up his bicep. She had to kneel in order to reach that far up. This close, their size difference was obvious and disconcerting.

Ariock did not dare touch her. Vy had been in sexy moods before. Any second now, she was likely to remember her fears and change her mind.

"Uh." He presented her with the photo album. "I wanted to give this to you."

Vy seemed slightly annoyed, as if Ariock had distracted her from an important task. "What is it?" She cuddled next to him and took the album.

"Your family photos," Ariock announced.

He watched Vy's face as she turned pages. He could hardly wait to see her delight. When Vy was delighted, her whole face became almost too beautiful for him to handle.

Vy absorbed the sight of each photo with a fixed smile of fondness. But her smile did not change from page to page. She spent the same amount of time gazing at her foster siblings as she did gazing at her mom.

Maybe the losses were too painful?

She was probably just pretending to like this gift.

Ariock wished he could take it back. Why had he thought that an album full of her past happiness was a good idea? He was an idiot. Cherise might not have any clue what Vy wanted. He should have—

"Oh, it's amazing!" Vy threw her arms around his broad neck. "I love that you got this for me."

Her reaction seemed genuine. Ariock laughed, relieved that he must have misread her smile as forced.

Vy climbed onto his lap. The photo album seemed forgotten. She smelled freshly perfumed with cinnamon and spice, as if she had added aromatic oils to her skin. It masked her familiar scent, which Ariock would have preferred.

She kissed him hungrily on the mouth, in a way she never had kissed him before.

"My sweetheart," she whispered. "I'm sorry I made you wait so long."

Ariock tried to gently push her off. Vy wasn't acting quite like herself. He wanted to know why she had decided to discard all her well-warranted anxiety. Was she forcing herself to get sexual for some reason?

Also, he wanted—he needed—for her to slow down.

His awareness kept snapping out, snagging ornamental spheres. One part of him strained against clothing that was too tight, demanding access to Vy.

Her fiery kisses were delicate to him. Each cute kiss sent a ripple of electricity through him, until he worried that he might cause an earthquake.

"Can we slow down?" he managed to say.

Vy straddled his lap, causing her negligee to ride up. "I want you."

Ariock began to protest, but Vy was a lot more determined than usual. She ripped open his jacket and ran her hands beneath his shirt, touching skin. She pressured Ariock to lie back, full length, on the huge bed.

That was a commonsense position. It seemed Vy had premeditated this encounter.

She crawled onto his chest. She kissed him again and again, all the while undressing him, her blue eyes hungry in a way that made her look ageless and bestial.

Ariock used every ounce of his willpower to restrain himself from moving aggressively. A gentleman rather than a giant. He touched her, encompassing her waist with his hands. His awareness expanded. He tried to stay small and calm, but every part of him yearned for the pliant woman on top of him who was clearly eager for his touch.

If Vy was ready . . . Well. How could he not be?

# CHAPTER 6

# NOT QUITE A FIT

Maintaining the deception was far more difficult than Evenjos had anticipated.

She had studied Vy from every angle. She had sculpted Vy and sketched drawings of her. She had practiced her voice, her gait, and her mannerisms for several hours per day. She thought that she had mastered the look and feel of Violet Hollander.

But.

Focus was paramount for any newly mastered form. Ariock was a taut, hot, hard mass of epic distraction.

"Wait." Ariock gently pushed at her. His purple eyes seemed almost to glow with lust from beneath the shadow of his brow. "This is dangerous."

Vy would not roll her eyes. Vy would react in a cute and harmless way, like re-arranging her loose hair into a curtain on one side. So that was what Evenjos-as-Vy did. She wiggled a little bit, pretending it was accidental, just to make Ariock even more hot for her.

"I'm ready." She made herself sound like Vy, with just the right note of hesitancy and nervousness. "I've thought about this, Ariock. I want to be with you."

Ariock emanated concern.

Evenjos scanned his surface thoughts, searching for just the right way to soothe his worries. "I . . ." She bit at her lower lip, as if trying to look brave, despite human shyness. "I just don't want to live my life in fear."

She leaned down and kissed him. She let her lips linger on his, and she sensed the tingles of pleasure that gave him.

In fact, she sensed that Ariock was quite close to losing control and ripping off her negligee.

The worst thing about impersonating Vy was the fact that it actually worked. It worked on Ariock like magic. He loved that human ragamuffin.

Evenjos-as-Vy stretched atop his body and wondered when it might be safe to reveal who she really was. She wanted to teach Ariock yet another power lesson: that it was possible for him to fall in love with an ancient immortal.

He had too many wrong ideas about Evenjos.

For one thing, he was under the wrong impression that Vy was braver than Evenjos. That was ridiculous. Which one of them shuddered in fear at the mere concept of sex with a giant? Which one of them was afraid to bring Ariock home to meet her mother?

Sex did not have to be a big scary deal. It could be wonderful. Evenjos was going to prove that to Ariock. And once he finally let loose and enjoyed himself, he would be so relieved that no one was damaged, he would probably choose the woman who could give him that pleasure.

Not Vy.

Evenjos-as-Vy yanked at his pants until he pulled them down for her. She teased him, pretending to have some shy, virginal ignorance. It was hard to maintain the illusion of being a virgin, but she dared not lose herself in passion the way Ariock was doing. Not yet. She needed him in a receptive mood for when she revealed herself.

Skeins of electricity snapped across Ariock's body. Objects around the bedroom floated, caught in ripples of his lust. Something rumbled far away. Had Ariock accidentally connected to one of the distant volcanoes?

Evenjos-as-Vy kissed Ariock, trying to prevent him from noticing how poor his control was.

All stormbringers had poor control during sex. It was a known hazard. That was why, in her day, the most powerful stormbringers often took vows of celibacy.

Ariock stopped kissing her. He studied her, troubled by her carefree passion. This was not the Vy he knew. Although he enjoyed her desire . . .

Evenjos sensed a stir of suspicion in the depths of his mind.

Great.

She caressed his massive shoulders, trying to make him aware of her dainty size. "It's okay," she said in a light, soft Vy voice. "Sometimes it's worth it, to take risks."

She nearly suggested that they fly to a remote location away from the city. That would be responsible. It was definitely something Vy would suggest.

Except it was risky in a way that Ariock was unaware of.

Away from other people, Ariock might detect Evenjos's powerful life spark and realize that she could not possibly be in a meeting nearby. The ruse would be given away.

The idea of leaving the city began to occur to him.

Quickly, Evenjos kissed him, as if overcome by steamy passion. She worked her body down his.

"Stop." Ariock held her trapped.

Evenjos had to force herself to give him a patient Vy look, instead of the scathing glare that his obstinance warranted. Why was he turning the simple act of sex into an obstacle course?

"Sorry." Ariock pushed to a sitting position, one-handed. "It would be better to do this when I can take a few days off from the war, so I can inject myself with inhibitor. I don't want to risk this while I'm powerful."

Evenjos wanted to scream in frustration.

She swallowed her feelings, reminding herself to act sweet. "No, no." She leaned up and pecked his chest with a kiss. "Can't we just both put aside our fears?"

He held her gently and gazed at her with worry. "I might hurt you. I won't risk that."

Argh.

Evenjos trailed her hand up his inner thigh. She was on his lap. Let him think about what her hands could do. "I'm really past the fear. I promise. I just want to enjoy you."

Something seemed off to him.

Ariock was not consciously suspicious—not yet—but he was getting close to it. He looked troubled.

Evenjos-as-Vy sat back, giving him space. She should have spent more time practicing her Vy impersonation. It seemed she had not mastered it as perfectly as she had thought.

In the face of her genuine hesitancy, some of Ariock's self-reflection melted away, and he was all sympathy again. "I'm not sure now is the right time," he said, apologetic. "I thought we would talk a bit first? We haven't really been talking lately."

"I guess that's true," Evenjos said, pretending to be Vy. "But a lot of that was my own stupid fear of being with you. It makes me ashamed."

As she tried to figure out how to get back to kissing, Ariock leaned on his side. Orb lights reflected on his skin, lending extra definition to his muscular body. He was clearly unaware of how good he looked.

"I conquered a city of ten million today," he said. "Do you know what I kept thinking, while thousands of freed slaves shouted praise for me?"

She looked at him, frustrated beyond words. Who wanted sappy chitchat? Couldn't they get back to their crazed make-out session?

"I wanted you there." Ariock was solemn. "I know my life is full of danger. But there are wonderful moments, too. And I don't want to go through those alone." He caressed her. "We have time. Sex doesn't have to be a milestone. We can work our way up to when we both feel safe." He gave her a gentle, frank look. "If we ever get there."

If?

Evenjos struggled to mask her appalled disgust. She knew for a fact that Ariock craved good sex. Just a few minutes ago, she had straddled this giant and sensed his nearly uncontrollable lust. He craved carnal pleasures, and if he denied himself those pleasures, then he would always feel a dissatisfaction in the back of his mind.

What a fool.

What a shortsighted, immature idiot.

Oh, and also? He was a stupid coward. He was a literal force of nature—did he really believe he could suppress his own innate violence? He was far too respectful of Vy's delicate nature.

He should kick that human aside and let himself be magnificent.

"So." Ariock studied her, and she quickly forced her face back into a pleasant Vy expression. "I thought you could tell me about your family." He used his powers to retrieve the book he had dropped earlier. "I'd like to know the people you're missing."

Evenjos gazed at the photo album as if in contemplation. She had not, and could not, absorb Vy's memories. As a second-magnitude telepath, she could only scan surface thoughts and emotions.

She caressed Ariock's scruffy cheek, trying to figure out how she might salvage this situation.

Might it be prudent to make an excuse to leave the bedroom? She could try again some other time—perhaps when Ariock was fresh from a violent battle, splattered with blood and still steaming and looking for a way to release his leftover passions. That would have been better timing.

But she would need to figure out how to keep the real Vy quiet.

Threats?

The problem was that Vy had powerful friends. Even if Vy agreed to keep her mouth shut, she was close with her foster brother. Thomas would likely figure out what had happened.

And it might be an exceedingly dangerous move to anger Thomas.

Evenjos was beginning to regret her entire approach. Maybe the prize of winning over Ariock was not worth the effort and cost.

"I'm not in the right mood." Evenjos-as-Vy pushed the photo album away, trying to seem shy despite being playful. She tried to look sexy. Inwardly, she urged Ariock to cave in to his carnal desires. He just needed to choose her. And then? After some amazing sex? Evenjos would morph to her default form and show him what a great choice he had made.

He was supposed to choose her: Evenjos.

"Let's get out of the city, at least," Ariock said. "I don't want to risk anyone getting hurt."

"No. I like your room." Evenjos-as-Vy picked up his gigantic hand and used it to touch both her breasts. "We can go slow, okay? I trust you."

His gaze explored her body, which was still packaged in the negligee. He gave a self-deprecating laugh. "I wouldn't trust me."

It was increasingly hard for Evenjos-as-Vy to hide her impatience and frustration. The Yeresunsa of her day had not been this overly considerate. Had they? A few stormbringers had avoided sex, but otherwise . . .

Prince Jace used to host wild orgies at his hereditary palaces.

Prince Mokrul charmed every noble lady he ever met.

And Prince Elome? He used to kiss Evenjos on her neck and shoulders in a way that made her lose her wings and her clothing. Now, *that* was princely behavior.

Perhaps it required certain training? Or certain life experiences?

Ariock gave her a very boring, very chaste kiss. "I know a place where I can take you."

Evenjos absorbed a representation of the place he had in mind. A secluded lagoon with a waterfall. It was hundreds of miles away.

He would probably bring the photo album.

Ariock sat up and used his powers to float a human-size blanket into his waiting hands. He began to wrap it around her shoulders.

Even if Evenjos successfully managed to trick him into sex, he would be cringing every inch of the way. He would be terrified of accidentally hurting his fragile little human lover. Any mature relationship with Ariock was going to take forever.

Beyond forever.

Evenjos wasn't sure she had that kind of patience.

On top of that, away from the city, there was a significant risk that Ariock would figure out that Evenjos was impersonating Vy. It was hard enough to keep up the fakery without the added stress of trying to reassure the giant every time he touched her.

He would figure it out before they could do anything enjoyable.

"No." She pulled off the blanket.

He gave her a gentle look of concern. "You've changed your mind?"

She wanted to yell bitter words in his face. She wanted to poison his glowing love for Vy. Maybe she would shout that she had never loved him! That she thought he was a monster! Really, Evenjos-as-Vy could regurgitate every hurtful phrase that Ariock had ever imagined Vy might think about him. That should put an end to their loving tenderness.

But such poison would only backfire on Evenjos if she ever wanted to impersonate Vy again.

Besides, she thought it was unlikely to work. Vy was not the sort of person to spew hateful phrases or scream at Ariock. He would get suspicious.

Even if he believed every word, he would mope around until somebody else—like Thomas—got suspicious.

It just would not work.

Nothing worked.

This seduction had seemed like a brilliant plan, but Evenjos now realized that she had failed to account for Ariock's fumbling, immature, sweet-hearted nature. She supposed it was a side of him she rarely saw. Mostly, she followed him in the wake of his conquests, all glorious and victorious.

It would be easy to walk away. But she absolutely needed to figure out how to handle Vy. Beg her forgiveness? Threaten her? Murder would have been a permissible answer in the era when commoners were expendable, but that was no longer socially acceptable.

Or desirable. Evenjos did not wish to kill her competition. That seemed so petty. It was despicable, even. Ariock would not forgive her if she did such a thing.

None of her options were good.

"Let's talk later, all right?" Evenjos told Ariock, focusing on her Vy disguise. "I'd rather be alone for a while."

Ariock's sympathetic concern deepened. "I didn't mean to offend you."

"You didn't." She slipped off the bed and headed toward the door. "I'm just in a weird mood." She searched for a credible excuse. "You know, hormones. It's that time of the month."

She paused in the doorway to blow him a kiss.

Ariock looked confused and forlorn.

Evenjos gently closed the door, leaving him with that expression.

She looked around, making sure there were no chambermaids or anyone else watching. Then she dashed across the drafty stone corridor, uncaring that she was barefoot and in a negligee. Her innards were dust. She never got too cold or hot.

As she ran, she hollowed out her density, shifting her weight into wings. She hurried onto the veranda. Hopefully Ariock would assume that Vy had gone out with friends.

At last, she allowed herself to drop her mental guards and to shift her mentality. The Vy skin melted into Evenjos's default goddess-empress form. Not breakable. Not fragile.

Much better.

She spread her wings and circled downward through cold drizzle. She needed to find a plausible reason to have been in the vicinity—something Ariock would believe. She also needed solid advice on how to keep the real Vy quiet. And how to appease Thomas, if he needed appeasing.

If anyone was likely to understand her frustrated failure, she knew it would be Garrett.

# CHAPTER 7
# LEFT IN THE RAIN

Night was never truly dark on Reject-20, thanks to the sunlike gas giant planet it orbited. So Vy could see the canyon below her, illuminated by the diffuse glow of nighttime clouds.

She knew it was dangerous to sit outside. Sky crocs were a lot like dragons, and one might devour her before she even saw it coming. She had noticed one earlier.

But she was not going to sleep in the hovel Evenjos had so charitably made for her. The roof was full of holes and a misty drizzle kept falling, off and on. It was damp and disgusting in there.

So Vy hunkered in the doorway, protected by the lintel. She kept a flashlight in one hand and a blaster glove ready on the other.

Without her data tablet, without her supercom, without people around . . . all she could do was think. Did she belong in Freedomland? Did she deserve Ariock?

She had allowed her foster brother to suffer much worse than this, letting him rot blindfolded in a dungeon pit. Did she have any right to complain?

Was she imagining the distant light flying toward her?

Some pilot must be out for a random predawn practice session. Vy flicked her flashlight on and off, signaling.

To her immense relief, the transport banked toward her. It hummed over the cliff and alighted near the shack, gentle as a dragonfly. The passenger door slid open invitingly.

Vy bundled herself into the dry warmth. "Varktezo?" She was astonished. The adolescent lab assistant was not officially part of the fleet. "How did you know to find me out here?"

"Thomas told me."

Oh.

Vy huddled closer to the heater vents. The blush in her cheeks had nothing to do with the temperature. Thomas must have absorbed this whole situation from somebody.

"Who else knows?" Vy dared ask. Was she going to have to endure people snickering behind her back?

"I don't know what you're referring to." Varktezo sounded irked, piloting the transport toward the distant glow of the city. "Nor do I know what you were doing way out here." He gave her a curious look. "Can I ask?"

Vy warmed her hands, trying to study his expression without being obvious. Varktezo looked genuinely curious.

"I'll tell you later," she said.

Varktezo made a clucking growl of frustration.

The drizzle was becoming a downpour. Varktezo banked toward the main part of the city, where the largest buildings had rooftop docking zones. "I assume you want to go to the war palace?"

That was where Vy's bedroom was located. She pictured herself slinking past Ariock's bedchamber and trying to curl up under her blankets.

And hearing moaning sounds of pleasure from his suite.

She imagined barging in without knocking, interrupting whatever Evenjos was doing with Ariock. Shouting. Maybe she would throw something heavy at them?

They would probably just shove Vy out of the room with a bubble of air or a tendril of dust.

*That's not fair to Ariock*, Vy told her cynical imagination. *He cares about me.*

But why?

Why should Ariock constantly have to worry about Vy? Why did he have to protect her all the time? Wasn't that a drag on him? Didn't Ariock have enough to worry about, what with saving the universe?

Vy was tired of being his burden.

She realized that she did not want to confront Ariock with Evenjos. She might as well be a mouse yelling at two titans. And she was so tired of feeling that way. Small. Inadequate. Inconsequential.

"Not the war palace," Vy said.

If Ariock truly preferred the power of Evenjos? Then he should be allowed to make that choice. Let him decide entirely on his own, without any pressure or outside influence.

It hurt. It was agony. But Vy was done trying to compete with a goddess-empress. She was done struggling to prove herself worthy. She was human and fragile and underpowered, and if that wasn't good enough for Ariock, then Vy needed to move on and give her heart time to heal.

She could not handle a devastating conversation after a sleepless night. She needed to cry first. Or scream.

Or gather some solid advice from someone who knew her well.

"Do you think Thomas is still awake?" Vy asked.

"I'm sure," Varktezo said. "He doesn't sleep enough."

"Do you think he would mind if I visit him?"

"He said you are welcome to visit." Varktezo banked the transport toward the complex of cliffside buildings that comprised the academy with its many annexes.

They landed on the rooftop lot. Varktezo led her inside, through a myriad of laboratories.

There were gadgets, there were beakers, there were test tubes and clean rooms and mysterious readouts on monitors. It was like visiting another world after sitting outside in the rain.

As Vy limped through lab after lab—her prosthetic joints had missed their regular oiling—she contrasted the bustling alien scientists and technicians with the dull-eyed laziness of every Torth she had ever known.

The Torth Empire claimed to value science. Torth scientists were supposedly light-years ahead of these trainees . . . but according to Thomas and Garrett, a lot of the empire's technology was quite old. And it was all stolen.

The Torth conquered civilizations and appropriated their technology. Why innovate? The Torth owned everything in the galaxy. They had near-infinite resources and quadrillions of expendable slaves. The Torth Majority seemed content to entrust supergeniuses with all the hard mental labor.

Maybe that was a mistake on the part of the Torth.

Varktezo led Vy through a scientific labyrinth that he was obviously familiar with. He waved to cheerful aliens who wore goggles and lab coats, and they waved back.

Thomas wore a lab coat as well. He floated in his smoky-translucent hoverchair, engrossed in adjusting a complexity of circuits. The room was a chaotic mess of robotics equipment. Every surface, even the walls and ceiling, were layered with displays and shelves of gadgetry. Technicians worked at various workstations.

"Hi, Thomas." Vy hesitated in the doorway. She didn't want to interrupt important work.

"Hey." Thomas switched to English, a language no one else in the room could understand. "Are you all right?"

Vy leaned against a cluttered counter, trying not to cry. She was so tired of being an object of everyone's concern.

"Who stranded you out there?" Thomas's gaze was intense.

"You mean you don't know?" Vy could hardly believe it. She had assumed that Thomas knew every humiliating detail.

"Well, I have a guess." He sounded darkly certain.

"Then how did you find me?" Vy felt unnerved. Was she microchipped or something?

"Azhdarchidae," Thomas said.

Vy recalled the juvenile sky croc she had seen a few hours ago. Was it possible . . . ?

She stared at Thomas as implications took shape in her mind.

"I like to absorb his memories after he gets back from hunting." Thomas sounded embarrassed to admit that. "I wasn't tracking you. I promise. I just happened to absorb his visual memory. Azhdarchidae thought it was weird to see a person way out there." Thomas shrugged. "I tried to reach you on your com. No answer. So I figured you might be in need of a lift."

"I was. Thank you." Vy leaned against a counter, studying her foster brother. Had anyone considered training sky crocs as military scouts?

"Will you let me, uh, see what happened?" Thomas asked.

For a moment, Vy resisted. But she had come here with a vague notion that she might gain advice. So she shrugged and stepped into Thomas's range of telepathy.

His curious expression swiftly changed to one of grim purpose.

"I don't want anyone hurt," Vy said. "I just . . ." She slumped. "I just want to feel safe."

"You should feel safe." Thomas made that sound like a threat.

Vy felt like crying. Should she break up with Ariock so she could cease competing against a magical goddess-empress? Should she return home to Earth?

"I have a gift for you," Thomas said. "It's timely."

"A gift?" Vy struggled to keep up with the change of topic.

"Over here." Thomas floated to another part of the room and opened a well-lit drawer.

Vy followed him, peering over his shoulder. The drawer contained a prosthetic leg.

"Oh," she said, marveling that Thomas had spent some of his work hours on a prosthetic that looked more high-tech than her current leg. "Thanks."

Thomas lifted the upper end of the prosthetic. "It's an upgrade."

His movements were so natural, it was jarring compared to how underdeveloped he used to be. He pressed the upper leg, and a previously disguised compartment opened up. "Storage," he said. "For extra coms and data marbles and whatnot, so no one can easily steal them from you. I'll give you trackers, if you'd like, so I can find you anywhere."

Vy picked up the leg, examining it. A hidden compartment would be useful. She rarely had pockets.

"It's also a weapon." Thomas tapped the knee.

A strip glowed on the false skin. It looked like the display of a blaster glove.

Vy raised her eyebrow.

"Knee someone, or kick outward," Thomas said. "When it's in blaster mode, the action will cause it to shoot a blast from the knee or the foot to a living target. Few people will anticipate that."

"Wait a second." Vy rotated the prosthetic, searching for signs of weaponization. "It's not like I'm capable of kicking."

"You will be," Thomas said, "with this upgrade."

Vy examined the top of the prosthetic more closely. A metallic mesh crowned the prosthetic, with sensors that looked like they were meant to touch her skin.

"It can read impulses from your nerves," Thomas said. "It should work and react exactly like your natural leg. Only it's stronger and more durable. And also fireproof. Mostly blasterproof, as well. It will give you extra speed and strength when it's in the right mode."

Vy's eyes widened. This prosthetic sounded like an improvement over a natural limb.

She had not imagined that such a thing was possible. She had been certain she would never be able to run again.

She stared at the sleek new prosthetic. The upgrades sounded impossible to believe.

"It's got a few other neat features," Thomas said. "I figured I might as well see what I could build for you."

He was trying to downplay the gift, but anyone could see that a lot of craft and artistry had gone into this prosthetic. Vy blinked away tears.

She threw her arms around Thomas. "Thank you," she managed to say.

Thomas awkwardly reached around her, giving her a cautious hug.

"You're a saint," Vy said. "I got too lucky with you as my brother."

"It wasn't luck," Thomas said. "It was your mom." He seemed to reconsider that phrase. "Our mom."

That made Vy smile.

"We'll need to do a noninvasive procedure to your amputated thigh," Thomas said, "to tune the prosthetic to your body. It won't take long." He spoke to an assistant, asking him to arrange a medical appointment for Vy. That done, he floated back to the robotic chaos on his worktable. "Once you've tested it out for a few days, you should make a list of fixes and improvements. I'll perfect it when I have time." His tone darkened. "I'll also add inhibitor microdarts to its blaster capabilities. That will make Evenjos think twice about messing with you."

Vy bit her lower lip. She might scare any Yeresunsa, even Ariock, yet she liked the idea. Not the idea of power-tripping, but the protection. She *would* be harder to mess with.

Thomas picked up a tool and manipulated tiny pistons.

"What is that?" Vy asked.

"Just a side project," Thomas said.

Vy went back to leaning on the counter, since every chair and table in the room was piled with robotics clutter. She didn't want to go to the war palace, where she might accidentally overhear Evenjos and Ariock together. So she tried to think of a safe topic of conversation.

It occurred to her that Thomas had similar problems. Not only did he have to obey Garrett on a regular basis and zombify prisoners, but he must miss Cherise.

And hadn't someone attempted to murder him a few weeks ago?

"What happened to that rogue warrior?" Vy asked. "The one who tried to murder you?"

"Oh, he got sentenced to extra patrol duty on Jerja." Thomas continued working.

As if that was an acceptable form of justice.

"What, really? No imprisonment? No one punished him?" Vy wondered if she needed to get involved with the justice system. Thomas shouldn't have to spend every day looking over his shoulder.

"Our elite warriors are above the law." Thomas tamped a bundle of thin wires into a shell designed to hold them. "They're too valuable to waste away in prison. We need every one of them."

He did not sound cynical. He sounded factual.

"You agree with that?" Vy asked.

"We're not in the best position against the Torth Empire, despite our victories," Thomas said. "We're going to need a miracle. So I won't get rid of any powerful ally, even if I can't stand them. We need allies."

Vy recalled that Thomas wanted Torth allies. None had materialized.

Had he been wrong about that?

As she watched him tighten wires, she wondered if he was inventing power armor. That would be something.

"We need Evenjos, too," Thomas said. "Unfortunately. But . . ." He manipulated delicate forceps, pinching at a wire. "I'm going to have a little chat with her."

Vy remembered his "little chats" with bullies back home. There was a reason why most of the Hollander kids had been afraid of Thomas. Even Vy's mother had been cautious around him.

"That's not necessary," Vy said.

"You're not a victim she gets to mess with," Thomas said fiercely.

Vy swallowed a mixture of feelings. She loved Thomas for his loyalty to her, especially when she had not been the best caretaker or foster sister. But she did not want him to fight someone as powerful as Evenjos. One or both of them might end up dead.

Actually, Vy realized, she knew who would win that fight. One drop of the inhibitor could kill Evenjos.

And Thomas was sneaky, fast, and far too smart. Evenjos would never see him coming at her if he decided to end her life.

"Really," Vy protested. "Don't talk to her. I can—"

"You've been dealing with her crap for long enough," Thomas said in a tone of finality. "If she's unwilling to stop, then someone needs to clarify the boundaries for her."

There seemed no way to argue with that tone.

"Although," Thomas said, adjusting a wire, "it's possible her plan didn't go the way she expected. This rainstorm suggests Ariock is in a mood."

Vy gazed out the window at the city. She had completely overlooked the significance of the weather. The rainstorm had come out of nowhere, and it was only raining over the city, not the mountains. That was generally a sign that at least one of the Dovanacks was in a bad mood.

"You're welcome to stay here tonight," Thomas said. "But you may want to check on Ariock."

Vy felt like collapsing into a puddle of relief. Laughter bubbled up, uncontrollable. Maybe she should check on Ariock, after all.

As long as they were conversing in relative privacy . . .

"Um." Vy looked around. Varktezo had left, probably eager to get back to whatever project he was in charge of.

As she considered what her foster brother might infer from the question she wanted to ask, she blushed. This wasn't a topic for a child, no matter how mature he was.

But it was already too late. Thomas was close enough to read Vy's mind.

"I wouldn't trust Evenjos's word," Thomas said. "But yeah, it's possible Ariock will keep growing. The Torth Empire put limits on hard-core mutations via their baby farm pedigree system, but the Dovanack family went outside that system. Ariock seems to have inherited some heavy-G adaptation that got enhanced by his demigod power level. He's been subconsciously incorporating extra energy all his life. He's got extra vigor."

Vy tried to distract herself from that problem. She studied the prosthetic package, trying to cling to her good feelings. She didn't want to feel crushed.

But if Ariock was going to grow into a titan, then crushed was a likely outcome.

Thomas put aside his tiny forceps and gave Vy an exasperated look of compassion. "What are you worried about, specifically?"

She knew her blush was embarrassingly visible. That was part of the curse of being a redhead.

"Let's say, fifty years from now," Thomas said, "Ariock is taller than a two-story house. And you're the same size. So what?" He emphasized that. "We're not in the future. We're living right now."

Vy gazed at him, surprised. Maybe he had a point. She was fretting a lot over a distant future that might never happen.

"You can't predict who you'll be in fifty years." Thomas floated to his mysterious project and fiddled with wires. "I mean, unless you meet an oracle. But I don't think any are alive in this era."

He went back to work.

His arms used to look like withered twigs. Vy thought about all the doctors who had predicted Thomas would die young.

That guaranteed doom had not happened.

And perhaps no one—not supergeniuses, not prophets—had predicted the twists Thomas's life had taken. He had turned everything around.

"If I had worried realistically about my future," Thomas said, "I never would have befriended Cherise. I would have been too aware that I would never grow up, so there was no chance of growing old with a partner." He gestured at his skinny body. "I would have thought of myself as a burden, holding back good people like Cherise. So I wouldn't have let myself get close to anyone. And when the Torth inducted me into their society? I would have stayed among them, because I would have had no one to rescue and no one I cared about." He gestured around. "And none of this would have happened."

Vy straightened.

The root cause for billions of slaves being liberated was Thomas. The only reason he had challenged the Torth Empire was because he had taken a chance on Cherise. It was because he cared about someone.

Even if Thomas and Cherise never resolved their differences . . . this was the future. The past still mattered. That original friendship was what had changed the course of galactic history.

As Vy considered giving up on Ariock, she realized that to do so would denigrate not only herself, but all disadvantaged and disabled people. She feared that equality with someone as powerful as Ariock was impossible? What if she was wrong?

She kept obsessing over all the differences between herself and Ariock.

Maybe it was time to focus on the similarities, instead.

# CHAPTER 8

# OF AN AGE

Evenjos was forced to guess where, exactly, Garrett Dovanack slept.

His rotating choice of bedchambers stymied potential assassins. Evenjos found his craftiness annoying, since she could not sense life sparks as long as Ariock's sphere of influence washed out all others. She could not read minds while disincorporated, so she was obliged to physically walk through drafty corridors to scan the surface thoughts of passersby, searching for any hint of the old man.

Finally, she noticed a pair of zombified Torth standing guard on either side of an ornate pair of double doors. They blinked in unison every so often. Gross. Even with brain damage, they were still telepaths.

But zombies might as well be an advertising sign that someone important slept within.

Evenjos turned to dust in order to bypass the zombified sentries. She rematerialized on the far side of the door.

His taste in decor was . . . different.

There were no appropriated Torth gadgets, no monitors aglow with informational displays. Garrett's furniture was iron and stone. Heavy drapes added a secretive atmosphere, barely lit by gas-lamp wall sconces. Evenjos had glimpsed the Dovanack mansion in a few people's memories. This was similar.

Garrett sat at a desk with his back to Evenjos. Pipe smoke made the air fragrant. A large, ancient-looking book lay open on his desk, illuminated by the colorfully pebbled glow of stained glass lanterns.

That must be the book of prophecies.

Evenjos relaxed her bodily coherence. She transformed to dust, eager to peek over his shoulder.

Garrett flipped the book closed. "Evenjos." He straightened out of his slump. "Didn't anyone tell you it's rude to enter without knocking first?"

Well, it had been worth a try.

Evenjos coalesced to her default shape, wearing a simple white dress. White should help her look more innocent. "Good evening, Garrett." She perched on a corner of his agate-topped desk so he would not have to rotate his armchair to face her.

Garrett made the book vanish with a gesture. Then he leaned back in his chair, smoking his pipe and otherwise giving Evenjos his full attention.

"I am afraid that I . . ." Evenjos abandoned that line of explanation. She took a deep breath, wondering how best to broach the subject. "I am in need of some friendly advice."

"All right." Garrett smoked and gave her an inviting look.

It seemed he was actively resisting the urge to scan her memories.

Evenjos aimed some chagrin at herself. She had expected Garrett to behave like a professional telepathic counselor. In her time, such counselors were expensive, so they usually went straight to business. But Garrett was downplaying his telepathy, as usual. He wasn't going to probe her mind as if she was a paying client. He was treating her like a friend.

Evenjos opened her mouth to explain. Outside, wind gusted and rain pattered against the windowpanes.

Garrett gestured at the window with his pipe. "Is that Ariock weather?"

"Maybe." Evenjos clasped her hands together.

"What did you do to him?" Garrett asked.

Evenjos felt Garrett rooting around in her memories, now that she had triggered his concern for his great-grandson. She forced herself to remain seated and let it happen.

Garrett genuinely understood the vast gulf between royalty and commoners. He wanted a dynastic lineage for Ariock. He wanted the very best for his great-grandson. He had explicitly approved of a union between Evenjos and Ariock. Surely he would forgive her methodology? After all—

*!!!*

Garrett jerked to his feet, leaving his pipe smoldering on the desk. "You *tricked* Ariock?"

Evenjos had expected a more prosaic reaction. She stood, making herself titanic and imperious, to remind Garrett of whom he was speaking to.

The old man stormed at her and seized her upper arms. "I gave you my blessing to pursue Ariock, yes, but I didn't expect you to toy with his feelings. Or to outright deceive him! Agh!" He absorbed more from Evenjos's mind, and he actually dared to shake her. "You stranded Vy in the mountains? What were you *thinking*?"

Disdain rolled off him.

Evenjos could have ripped his hands off her. She could have ripped his arms out of their sockets. She had quite a bit more raw strength than Garrett. She could have reminded him that she was a greater Yeresunsa and he the lesser.

Instead, she hung her head and let him shake her.

She wished she had not impersonated Vy. She was beginning to regret all of it . . . not just her mistake tonight, but almost every moment of her consciousness since she had been resurrected in the prison of mirrors.

It was all a mistake.

She was older than any sapient in the known universe, except for a few uncommon alien species bound to their homeworlds. She dared not fall asleep. She did not require food. She rarely remembered to eat except when she was in the company of someone she admired.

She was actually more alien than any alien.

And she truly understood, now, that no one in this era was ever going to love her unnatural nature. She was unlike any of them. She was ancient. Her true form was dust.

Ariock didn't deserve her, after all. She could not turn back time and make herself young and pure and innocent, like him. She was unsuitable for him.

Nor could she bear children with her womb made of dust. There would be no dynastic lineage—no family—in her future.

She was extraneous. All she could do was imitate things. She would never have true blood or organs.

Why was she bothering?

"Stop that." Garrett glared at her. "Stop feeling sorry for yourself."

Evenjos pulled free from his arthritic grasp. She was done with this farce of a therapy session. Garrett was not a professional counselor.

Anyhow, not even the best counselor in the universe could fix all the things broken inside her.

Evenjos gazed over Garrett's shoulder and confronted her own reflection in the mirror-paneled wall. False beauty. What if Evenjos decided to stop caring about what anyone else thought of her?

She would reveal the truth and face it. She was a horror.

Why not?

Evenjos allowed the illusion of youthful beauty to melt away. Her mouth was toothless from starvation. Bags under her eyes symbolized her complete inability to sleep. Patchy white hair crowned a head that had seen too much suffering.

Really, she had no right to be alive, no right to have any form whatsoever. Her true form was the dust of corpses.

Evenjos clawed bony fingers through her ugly old face, ripping it apart, breaking it into dust. She was a wretch. Even a corpselike form was too good for her. It was just an illusion to humanize the vile reality that was her unnatural existence.

"What are you doing?" Garrett snapped. "Stop!"

She was nothing.

She was a headless blight amid beauty . . .

Garrett's grip tightened, infused with supernatural strength. His fingers dug into her bony, hag-like arms. If she were an ordinary mortal, he would have broken her bones.

"Don't you dare disincorporate," Garrett said. "Stay."

Evenjos hesitated, on the verge of losing bodily cohesion. Was he threatening to lecture her?

Ugh.

Maybe she deserved a lecture, but she couldn't bear it right now. She had let Garrett down, too. He loved his great-grandson, and she had stupidly ruined any chance for a civil relationship, never mind marriage or romance or—

"You're a broken mess," Garrett said, interrupting her thought stream. "So am I."

He kissed her corpse mouth roughly.

Evenjos developed eyelids and blinked.

Everything about Garrett was rough. His bearded mouth, his gnarled hands, his angry mind. He was a brute.

She liked his utter lack of consideration.

Garrett wasn't brooding over the idea of accidentally hurting her. He knew all the ways in which she was irreparably hurt and broken, and he was well aware that her body was impervious to harm.

There was a definite brokenness inside him, as well.

Evenjos sensed a raging chasm of pain and loneliness inside his mind. Garrett did not want to care about anybody except for his great-grandson. Garrett was unwilling to put effort into a relationship. He would not emotionally forsake the wife he had lost, and perhaps he could not cobble together all the bits of his soul that had shattered when his wife died. He was probably incapable of love.

Fine.

Evenjos slammed Garrett against a wall, forcing him to accept her body wrapped around his. She reverted to her illusion of being lush and young and fertile. It was all lies.

Garrett was not deceived in the slightest.

He seized Evenjos and shoved her against the wall, uncaring and brutal. When he ripped off her dress for better access, and pushed inside her, she moaned with a satisfaction she had not known it was possible to feel.

# CHAPTER 9

# TRANSFORMATION

Ariock tossed and turned on his huge bed, unable to sleep. The downpour outside reflected his relentless worries.

Was he losing Vy?

She had behaved so strangely. She hadn't even asked about Ariock's clairvoyant visit to her family home. Instead, she had been physically needy, even desperate. She'd acted like a maiden trying to seduce a king for her own survival.

Ariock rolled over, clutching his pillow. He might have believed that a year ago. He would have feared that Vy felt pressured into seducing the ultrapowerful gigantic freak and that their whole relationship was a ruse. But now he understood how wrong that fear was. It was an insult to Vy.

They had shared so many wonderful moments together. They made each other laugh. They talked in private about their most tender hopes. He knew Vy would never fake the way she cared about him.

So why had she tried to seduce him only to hurry away?

Where was she now?

Ariock didn't want to be an overbearing boyfriend, or a stalker, but he couldn't help but expand his awareness in lieu of sleep. He'd sensed that her suite was empty. No life spark within. Vy had not gone to bed.

Had she gone to Cherise, or some other sympathetic friend, to complain about Ariock?

Was she pacing the palace halls, full of pent-up frustration?

The sky began to lighten. Dawn was arriving, cloaked by rain.

Ariock gave up on sleep. He used his powers to wash and dress himself. Then he walked out of his suite, unsure where to go. Maybe he would visit Thomas. If anyone could guess where Vy had spent the night, or why she was acting so weirdly, it would be her supergenius foster brother.

Vy was in the hallway.

Ariock stopped in surprise.

Why was her hair so damp and tangled? Why were her clothes stained? She must have been outside in the rain.

Vy looked equally surprised to encounter Ariock in the hallway. "Uh, hi?" she said. "I was just coming to see you."

"Are you all right?" Ariock crouched so they could face each other at eye level. Her tremulous smile conveyed that she was not all right.

Ariock gently wrapped her in his arms. Vy leaned against him, chilly and shivering a little bit. It felt good to just hold her. He wanted to keep her warm and safe. Vy had let him derail her entire life. He didn't want to lose the one and only person who cared about him to that significant degree. He couldn't imagine what had caused the problem last night, but he would do anything to heal whatever had happened.

Vy stepped back and tugged Ariock toward his suite. "Can we talk?"

"Of course." Ariock held the door open for her, then followed her inside.

In the light of glass lamps, Vy looked angelic, like a dream painted by some Renaissance master.

"I'm so sorry," Ariock said. "I was trying to be protective and safe, but I guess I was being overprotective? I didn't mean to offend you. I . . ."

He trailed off, seeing her sickened expression. His words didn't matter.

"So," Vy said in a tone that was the opposite of casual. "You think the person who visited you in the night was me? You didn't notice anything weird? Or out of character?"

Why did she look so upset?

"What did she say to you?" Vy said. "What did she *do* with you?"

A second later, an explanation clicked into place in Ariock's mind.

Vy nodded, seeing realization dawn on Ariock. "Yeah," she confirmed. "That wasn't me."

Ariock wanted to smack himself for missing so many obvious clues. Evenjos was a shapeshifter who could imitate anyone if she studied them for long enough. How had he forgotten that?

That resurrected hag must have done something to get Vy out of the way.

She could have killed Vy by accident, playing her sick game.

"Are you injured?" Ariock knelt in front of Vy and held his hands out, inundating her with healing energy. He sensed minor bruises fading to healthiness. "I should have checked right away," he said. "I should have realized. I'm so sorry. What did she do to you?"

A second later, he realized that might be a rude question.

But Vy didn't seem offended. "She made a leaky shack for me. In megabeast country. I thought I might have to hike back and try not to get eaten, but it turns out Azhdarchidae is a good scout." She laughed. "He showed Thomas where I was. And then Thomas sent Varktezo to rescue me."

Vy had been stranded in the rain-drenched nighttime wilderness.

Where massive predators might have eaten her.

She was safe now, but that was thanks to Thomas, not to Ariock. While Evenjos had laid hands on his girlfriend and then on him, Ariock had been utterly clueless.

Evenjos had role-played as Vy.

She had gotten Ariock naked. Kissed him. Climbed all over him. Pretended to love him! While Vy was trapped and alone, Ariock had missed every hint that something was off with his supposed girlfriend. He had nearly . . .

"EVENJOS."

It was not just a word.

The war palace rumbled, shaken on its foundation. Fury erupted out of him, and his enemy's name came through the wrenching and groaning of bedrock. People throughout the city woke, swearing. Ariock heard distant shouts.

He didn't care.

He was already on his feet, coasting outward, in search of the ultrapowerful thrum of Evenjos's life spark. If she'd had a bedroom, he would have smashed through it. But Evenjos wasn't mortal enough to need sleep.

He expected her to flee. She was such a coward. If she flew into the wilderness beyond the city? Well, then she'd better stay gone.

Instead, Ariock sensed her power inside the palace. It felt intensified due to an overlap. Evenjos plus Garrett?

"I'll be back," Ariock told Vy.

Vy jumped to her feet, and Ariock hoped she wouldn't ask to come with him. He needed to banish Evenjos, or punish her in some public way, but he didn't want Vy to see him as a tyrant.

"Take me with you?" Vy pleaded.

Well.

Ariock wasn't going to argue.

He embraced Vy within his awareness and ghosted to the approximate location of the powerful thrum.

Much of the war palace was shielded with plates of burnished meteorite or sea glass. That messed with clairvoyance. Ariock could not teleport directly to where he wanted to go, so he deposited Vy in the airy atrium of the hallway, then flickered to a reinforced door.

He seized the door with his powers and wrenched its titanium-alloy thickness into twisted scrap metal.

Garrett and Evenjos looked surprised in some sort of parlor.

But not entirely surprised. They had felt the earthquake. Evenjos had prepared for a confrontation by defaulting to her immaculate form: a hag masquerading as a goddess. What a sham.

Garrett wore stately council garments with a Yeresunsa mantle. He stepped in front of Evenjos, shielding her with his arms. "She's sorry, Ariock. She didn't—"

Ariock wrapped both Evenjos and Garrett in his awareness and teleported them to the atrium where Vy waited. It was a public hallway. Onlookers were gathering.

Ariock didn't care. Let everyone learn what a monster Evenjos was. She deserved public humiliation.

"You attacked Vy." Ariock pointed an accusing finger at the former goddess-empress. "You imprisoned her. And then you tricked me, so you could play stupid, selfish mind games."

Evenjos opened her mouth.

"You don't get to speak." Ariock cut her off. "You did enough speaking last night, although it wasn't in your real voice."

The onlookers looked ready to run if anyone lost their tempers, but they were also enthralled.

"Ariock." Garrett sounded like someone placating an overwrought child. "Let's take this down a notch."

Ariock turned on his great-grandfather. "Was this your idea?"

"What? No!" Garrett sounded affronted. "Of course not. I would never—"

"But you knew." Ariock was seething. A storm rumbled outside, and there were dust motes suspended in his widened awareness, yet the shaken barrier between himself and his limits seemed unimportant. He wanted to prove that Evenjos and Garrett had limits. They were not gods. Not in his city. Here, he was the one in charge.

"I just found out," Garrett said. "I promise, I would never mess with you like that."

Ariock narrowed his eyes at Garrett, trying to read his face. How could he tell whether the old man was lying?

He needed an ally who could outsmart Garrett and Evenjos. Thomas was probably asleep, but he might bring him here anyway.

Evenjos drew a ragged breath. "I'm sorry. I regret what I did."

As if this was some trivial offense.

"Our lives are not a game." Ariock glared at her. "I can't trust you around the people I care about." He pointed to Vy. "That's someone I love. You hurt her. You could have killed her."

Evenjos looked stricken. "I wouldn't—"

"I don't believe you," Ariock said. "Get out of my city. I don't want to see you again."

Garrett's eyes went wide. "Now, now," he said in that placating tone. "That's not necessary. Ariock, she's truly sorry. I guarantee it."

Ariock glared from one mind reader to the next. These were supposed to be his advisers? His friends?

"Let me make this clear," Ariock said, his quiet tone belying his rage. "I will not work with people who threaten the people I love."

Evenjos opened her mouth, as if to protest.

Then she seemed to see his determination and she slumped.

"We are two of the four heroes of prophecy," Garrett said. "You can't just throw us away."

Ariock imagined asking one of the onlookers to shoot Garrett with the inhibitor serum. Then Ariock would scoop Garrett and Evenjos up and deposit them in some miserable outpost on Umdalkdul. They would have no way to return to Reject-20 and Freedomland. At least, not for a few days.

Let Evenjos think about what she'd done.

Ariock clenched his fists and willed his awareness to remain human-scale. He really needed to remember that Garrett was a vital asset in battles. And Evenjos did heal thousands of injured soldiers on a daily basis. The troops couldn't afford to lose that.

These two were supposed to be his friends.

His imperfect, self-absorbed, telepathic friends.

"Ariock?" Vy spoke up from behind him.

He turned. Beyond the atrium window, the clouds had parted to let in a small amount of dawn light, giving Vy an aura. It was impossible to stay furious when he was gazing at her.

"Thomas gave me a means to protect myself." Vy tapped her prosthetic leg. "An upgrade."

Ariock tried to work through the implications.

"I can shoot inhibitor serum," Vy said.

Well. That would give Evenjos pause if she decided to attack Vy again. Maybe that would be enough.

Ariock knew he couldn't win the war and defeat the galactic Torth Empire without his powerful allies. But what could he do about them?

He felt constrained, the way he felt in caves. Even here, in this airy palace of his own making, the ceiling seemed too close. The thick pillars might as well be twigs, easy to snap.

"You will never approach Vy again," Ariock told Evenjos. "Unless you have my permission."

She nodded.

"You're never going into my bedroom again," Ariock said. "Not even as dust. And you won't ever pretend to be someone else. If I catch you doing any of those things? You don't get another chance. I will kick you out."

Evenjos shrank with every ultimatum. Her wings drew close, as if to protect herself.

"I don't want to talk to you," Ariock said. "Or see you. Unless it's for strategic purposes in battle."

"Ariock? There's no need to be so punitive." Garrett limped closer, looking small despite his large frame. "She's genuinely remorseful."

Ariock glared at his great-grandfather. Why was he so assiduously defending Evenjos?

"She isn't your enemy," Garrett said in a pleading tone.

That was easy to say. But how was Ariock supposed to go into battle while constantly worrying about Vy and Evenjos on the same planet together?

"Please." Garrett gripped Ariock's sleeve. "You can trust her from now on. She really is sorry."

"Why are you speaking for her?" Vy asked Garrett.

Evenjos walked toward Vy. Ariock tensed, ready to intervene.

But the winged Lady knelt smoothly, facing Vy. She bowed like a supplicant. "I am truly sorry, Lady Vy. I allowed jealousy to overcome my sensibilities."

That was a start.

Ariock wondered how repentant Evenjos actually was. He ought to drag her to Thomas's so-called Dragon Tower. Let Thomas read her mind. Let him decide how far Evenjos could be trusted.

"I have not earned forgiveness," Evenjos said to Vy. "But I will never inflict such an insult upon you again." She bowed lower. "If a time ever comes where you need my services, I will serve you as needed. I promise."

As if Evenjos could offer anything superior to what Ariock could provide.

"That includes regeneration healing," Evenjos said. "I cannot regrow your leg, but I can fix scars and blindness and other maladies. As long as I live, you and Ariock will both retain the vigor of youth instead of suffering the frailties of old age."

Ariock thought of Torth longevity pills. Was Evenjos offering the magical equivalent of those?

"I am sorry." Evenjos stood, disincorporated, broke into dust, and flew down the ramp and out of sight.

Ariock almost wondered if he had been too harsh.

Nah.

Garrett blew out a breath as if ridding himself of tension. "I need to show you the book of prophecies." He put a gnarled hand on Ariock's arm. "There's compelling proof that she's important. I'm telling you. You need her."

Ariock stared down at his great-grandfather, sure this was manipulation. Why had the old man waited to mention the prophecies? Unless . . .

Maybe there was some future event that Evenjos shouldn't learn about?

"The fewer people who know the future," Garrett said, "the better." He gave Vy an apologetic look. "Would you mind excusing yourself?"

"I don't keep secrets from Vy," Ariock stated firmly.

"She spends more time with the boy than you do." Garrett sounded frustrated. "I'm trying to prevent our supergenius friend from learning too much. When you visit him, he isn't usually trying to suck up every secret in your mind. But if he's hanging out with Vy? He might glean something he shouldn't. And for someone with a mind like his . . . ? Well, it wouldn't take much for him to become a problem."

People made all kinds of wrong assumptions about Thomas.

Ariock wondered, not for the first time, if the oracle Ah Jun had made the same mistake and painted something misleading about Thomas. "What sort of a problem do you imagine Thomas presenting?"

"Agh. Never mind. This one won't matter." Garrett tugged Ariock. "Come on, let me show you the book."

Vy fell into step beside them. Garrett looked disgruntled, but Ariock said, "I'd just tell her anyway."

"Have you showed it to Evenjos?" Vy asked pointedly.

"No." Garrett led them through the door Ariock had mangled, stepping over broken metal scraps. He cleared off an ornate desk, then gestured. A thick tome fell out of thin air and landed on the polished agate of the desktop.

Pages turned in rapid succession, too fast for Ariock to get a glimpse of what was on them. Garrett was using his powers. Then the book settled open.

"Here. Have a look at the next prophetic pivot," Garrett said.

A painting spread across two pages, illuminated in a dusty beam of dawn light. One of the figures in the painting had to be Ariock. The painted version was a colossus dressed in spiky black armor, but limp and weak, possibly unconscious.

And his helmet looked wrong. It was more like a crude, medieval helm than space armor.

A winged angel with flowing hair carried the giant through clouds. The painted version of Evenjos clutched Ariock, looking terrified and determined. Her wings spread rays of light. The painted giant seemed to drag darkness and chaos behind him.

"The Transformation of Strength," Garrett said. "That's the title of this painting." He stabbed it with his gnarled finger. "I don't know what's happening here, but I think we can assume you need her."

Ariock didn't like the implications. Was he going to fail badly in some future battle?

Was there any way to avoid it?

"Are those missiles?" Vy pointed to dots and dashes in the painted clouds.

"They could be," Garrett said. "Or Torth military transports. They don't look friendly, whatever they are."

Prophecies were generally inscrutable until they happened. Ariock reminded himself of that. The last pivot had shown Thomas naked and screaming, as if tortured, by Evenjos. It had looked bad, but it had turned out to be good. Regeneration healing had saved Thomas's life.

The Transformation of Wisdom. That had been the title of the last pivot.

Now the upcoming pivot was the Transformation of Strength.

Ariock stepped back, trying to quell his inner disquiet.

"Well, it looks pretty straightforward," Vy said. "Is that normal for these prophecies?"

"Not at all," Garrett said dryly. "I've found the paintings to be exceedingly hard to interpret. All this really tells us is that Evenjos and Ariock are going to play a vital role in some upcoming pivotal event. And the event has to happen, or else we're bound to be defeated by the Torth Empire."

Ariock searched his great-grandfather's face. "Do you have any estimates as to when?"

"I don't know." Garrett shook his head sadly. "Soonish?"

Ariock tried to accept that.

"But I know that we need each other," Garrett said. "We can't lose sight of who our real enemies are: the Torth Empire." He touched Ariock's arm. "Evenjos does feel remorse. I promise. Please remember, Ariock, she has baggage. She was tortured. She isn't healthy in a lot of ways, despite her sixth-magnitude healing power."

That was probably true.

"I'll look after her," Garrett said. "So you won't have to worry anymore. All right?"

That sounded so paternalistic and responsible, Ariock wasn't sure if Garrett was serious.

Vy scrutinized the old man. "You and Evenjos," she said. "You're in on things together. Are you . . ." She paused. "A couple?"

Garrett looked shocked and affronted.

"Are you lovers?" Vy asked.

Garrett grumbled defensively. "All right, all right. You don't have to make a big deal about it."

Ariock's jaw fell open. He had assumed Vy was just teasing Garrett, trying to embarrass him.

His imagination tried to reassemble Evenjos and Garrett into a romantic paradigm. Maybe it could work, if they managed to treat each other with whatever tiny scraps of respect they could scrounge up. After all, they were both . . . well . . .

Old.

Really old.

"You're going to heckle us about our ages?" Garrett shot Ariock a nonplussed look. "Really?"

Vy giggled.

"Try to keep a lid on this," Garrett said with dignity. "I happen to think Evenjos has some admirable qualities that you keep overlooking. That doesn't mean we're a couple of teenagers pining away for each other. It's a friendship. Nothing more significant than that."

He was protesting an awful lot.

Ariock chuckled and hugged Vy. She was laughing, too.

# CHAPTER 10

# CLASS OVER

Cherise gawked at the tablet Vy had just handed to her. She was looking at a media browser.

Movies.

TV shows.

A lot of premium subscription services from her homeworld, plus apps, including a web browser. She was holding a magical iPad.

"How . . . ?" Cherise struggled to form a coherent question.

"Thomas set it up," Vy said with pride. "He mirrored a lot of content from Earth—like, practically the whole internet—and he has it hosted here in the academy. You can press a button and it translates everything to the slave tongue." She demonstrated.

Cherise began to hand the tablet back.

"No, this one's yours." Vy pushed it into Cherise's hands. "It's a gift."

Cherise felt speechless. She hadn't spoken to Thomas since his near suicide-by-cannibals in the dead city. Was he rewarding her for ignoring him?

"Thomas wanted me to tell you there's no strings attached." Vy sat across from Cherise in the teachers' lounge, legs crossed. "He figured you can use it as a teaching tool."

It probably wasn't a bribe. Maybe it was a lazy afterthought? Vy's new prosthetic shone with a metallic meshwork surface that matched her coppery hair, and it was a clear upgrade. Thomas was showering gifts upon his favorite foster sister. Perhaps Cherise had received this Earth tablet by extension, by accident?

"It works like any data sleeve or tablet," Vy explained. "You can beam it to display screens."

"This is thoughtful," Cherise had to admit.

It was more than thoughtful. It was magical.

And it was not the only miracle Thomas had introduced to Freedomland. Everyone in the city was buzzing about the latest generation of supercoms. People were able to see regular news broadcasts from liberated cities on foreign planets. Kessa even had undercover spies in Torth cities, reporting in real time from slave tunnels.

And this tablet was just for Cherise. This was special.

"Can you tell him thank you from me?" she asked.

"You could tell Thomas yourself." Vy's tone was full of hints. "He specifically wanted you to have this."

Cherise sighed. Vy clearly believed that a visit to Thomas would be no big deal.

But Freedomland was full of gossipers. If anybody spotted Cherise near the research annex, Flen would hear the rumors, and he would . . .

She was going to need to hide this tablet.

Certain forms of human entertainment seemed like wicked *rekveh* magic to Flen. He'd be all kinds of offended by sinful, flirty behavior from American culture. Cherise could imagine the accusations he would hurl at her. Was she in love with power? Was she a Torth sympathizer?

Was she brainwashed?

"I'm not ready to visit Thomas," Cherise said.

Mostly, she wanted to avoid a bunch of arguments with Flen. But there was apprehension mixed up in her feelings toward Thomas. He was a miracle worker, but he was also . . . well.

Few people knew how cruelly the zombified Torth were treated. Vy might hear rumors, but she never visited the Alashani quarter. She never went to active battlefields. So she never witnessed those shambling messes who used to be sapient beings.

Even if Vy saw the abuse, she would just blame the hotheaded Alashani warriors.

Vy, like Ariock, would entirely skip the inconvenient truth that her foster brother was the source of the whole abominable system. Alashani rage toward Torth was justified. They feared extinction, and they were right to be afraid. What excuse did Thomas have? Why was he doing it?

"Thank him for me, please." Cherise brandished her new tablet. "I'll definitely use this for my classes."

Vy had learned not to pressure Cherise. So she smiled and changed the subject.

Cherise used the tablet in her humanities class later that same day.

She purposely wanted to delay the introduction of movies and animation. She would not inundate her students with torrents of alien images, thereby reducing art to mere noise. Instead, she would guide them, in measured steps, into realms of expression that went beyond anything they had ever known.

Creativity often meant a death sentence in the Torth-ruled galaxy. Slaves had never gained opportunities to refine their musical or artistic talents over continuous generations. Their stories were whispered, their songs quiet, their artwork mostly hidden.

So movies were inconceivable to her students. Under Torth rule, slaves could never unite as a team working toward a creative vision.

Cherise started with music.

Week by week, she introduced her students to genres and styles of music. During the fourth week, she cautiously began to show them still images of paintings.

"Yes, Rhyow?" Cherise pointed to a govki who had raised one of his quartet of hands.

"Teacher." The student seemed to gather his thoughts. "Would you say these masterpieces are analogous to what the Torth see when they speak to each other in their minds?"

Other students continued to gawk at the ceiling as if feasting upon a portal into heaven. A dramatic fresco of Olympian gods, painted by Giulio Romano, glowed up there. It was the last entry in the slideshow Cherise had put together.

"I don't know what Torth see." Cherise leaned on her desk. "I am not a mind reader."

A few students chuckled. Her denials of being a mind reader had become a running joke, since she was obliged to remind people so often. Her classes were so popular that the auditorium was overcrowded, with people standing between the seated students.

"But they repress their emotions," Cherise reminded her class. "So I don't think they see things like this." She gestured at the dramatic fresco.

There were more questions. Cherise answered, explaining what she knew of the mythologies or emotional ideas conveyed by each fresco.

Many of her students had seen artistic relics from conquered civilizations, as well as Torth versions of fashion and architecture, and gardens, and advertisements. Slave farms had their own art: pictograms and statuettes. It was enlightening to discuss comparisons that resonated with the experiences of former slaves.

When the questions began to wind down, Cherise used her tablet to cue a music playlist that she thought fit the mood.

"On my homeworld," Cherise said, "it is said that artwork is how we decorate space, but music is how we decorate time."

The music played, light and sweet. Aliens looked at each other, enchanted by what they were hearing.

Cherise sat back in her chair. She knew that some of her students experimented with their own makeshift musical instruments after school. Digital recordings were being sold in shops around the city. Former slaves would pioneer new forms of music. And a few of her visionary students were already practicing art, working toward becoming masterful painters or sculptors.

Every day brought something new.

The future stretched out, unknown yet exciting. There could be ummin film directors, nussian architects, govki game designers. Today's generation of former slaves had a lot to learn, but tomorrow's generation would be born into freedom. They would inherit all the technology and science of the Torth Empire—assuming the Torth got conquered.

They would have the wisdom of many civilizations.

They would change the universe.

Humanity would be left behind, in the dust.

Cherise let the music wash over her, sweet and nostalgic. She told herself not to worry about weighty matters such as the fate of humankind. That wasn't her job. It shouldn't be her concern.

But what about Flen, and the fate of the Alashani?

She suppressed a groan. The faces of her students were gray, red, yellow, furry, or beaked, but none were albino. Cherise taught multiple classes, many hundreds of students, and not a single one of them was shani.

She didn't think Flen had gone around telling people to avoid her classes.

But the Alashani, as a people, saw no value in learning about foreign cultures. As far as Flen was concerned, humans were fat and weak versions of Alashani. He thought humankind had been preserved like zoo animals. So why bother to learn from them? It should be the other way around.

That was what most Alashani believed.

Cherise gazed at a pile of cherished picture books on her desk. Those came from Earth, imported by Ariock. She used them to teach aliens how to read and write. Flen refused to look at them.

She had asked, *"Do you think I'm just a fat and weak version of an Alashani?"*

Flen had hugged her, and said, *"No! Of course not. You've been honed and sharpened by your experiences."*

He meant her Alashani experiences. He thought of her as something like an adopted Alashani.

Cherise wondered if she was being too judgmental of Flen's judgmentalism. He was open-minded enough to date her, to call her an angel. And who else would be thoughtful enough to buy jars for her that were embossed with her artistic designs?

Flen surprised her with gifts every week. A decorative scarf. A beautifully crafted kitchen set.

It wasn't like he had free time to go shopping between battles. He must gain special favors for being a war hero. Cherise understood how many people admired him, because some of that admiration scattered onto her. People invited her to parties. Every door in the Alashani quarter was open to her.

Anyhow. His efforts to please Cherise showed how much he cared.

And she cared as well. How could she not? Flen wept in the middle of the night, woken from nightmares. He clung to Cherise as if she was the mother he had lost.

To Flen, family was everything. All he had left was an elderly chambermaid who treated him as if he was a knight in shining armor. And Cherise.

That was probably why he kept bringing up the topic of babies.

He wanted Cherise to stop using the birth control pills she had gotten through Vy. He considered birth control to be a self-imposed curse peddled by soulless *rekvehs*. He would lay a hand on Cherise's stomach and tease her about how good she would look, pregnant. He held her hand and speculated about how they would be wonderful together as parents.

Cherise tried to laugh off those uncomfortable conversations.

*"I'm too young,"* she had said. *"On Earth, I'm not even legally an adult. I'm not ready to look after a baby."*

Flen had said, *"Underground, it is a blessing to have children young. Children are always a blessing."*

He looked forlorn, perhaps remembering loved ones who had died in the flood or in Torth raids. He did not have to say Cherise was now his family. It was plain by the way he treated her.

The next song in the playlist came on, whimsical and playful. Class was over, but few students moved to leave. They often stayed for the music.

Perhaps Flen was right. Cherise did not feel at all motherly, but she did not need a mind reader to explain why the idea scared her so much. She was terrified of becoming her ma.

Was she letting fear rule her?

After all, she used to feel terrified of speaking in front of people—only to learn that teaching was the most fulfilling thing she had ever done. She loved her students. She knew their names and their stories, and she loved helping them grow into different people, from meekness to confidence. She could not imagine giving that up.

She used to fear wearing fashion-conscious clothes, until she learned how to pull it off in ways that turned heads.

She was beginning to enjoy facing her fears. There was exhilaration in meeting a challenge and coming out victorious.

So maybe she ought to remember that she had a lion within herself? She was not the mousy girl her ma used to scream at. She was loved. She was safe. Why not challenge herself to do something braver than she would have believed possible?

To raise a child.

It might be worth every moment of fear and pain. She could be light-years better than the selfish beast who had been incapable of raising her.

While Cherise imagined bouncing a child on her knee, the door at the top of the auditorium banged open. A panicked mob of students poured into her classroom.

Cherise jumped up. She was not the only one.

"Torth!"

"They're in the building!"

"We need to hide!"

Cherise felt frozen with disbelief. This was Freedomland. This was a college campus in the safest city in the known universe. It was impossible for Torth to invade without warning.

Had the Mirror Prison failed somehow?

The prisoners were kept under surveillance and on the inhibitor serum. Zombified victims were used in battlefields far away, on foreign planets, and they had no free will. Thomas ensured that they could never be used against his own allies.

Maybe this was a penitent riot? Had a bunch of penitents broken free and gone on a rampage?

That seemed equally impossible. Penitent work crews were chained together. Some penitents did earn the privilege of serving a family without being chained up, but they were never allowed to touch a weapon.

An attack on the academy didn't make any sense. Penitents and prisoners were never allowed uptown. Even if they somehow went on a rampage, they would have to fight through miles of crowded streets to get into the academy. There were always trained soldiers in the city.

Freedomland was fortified with blaster cannons and military transports, and everyone owned a blaster glove. Rampaging Torth would be easy targets for speeding hovercarts or snipers shooting at them from windows.

Plus Thomas.

Even if Ariock and his military forces were on another planet, Thomas was always here. He lived and worked in the research annex of the academy. And he was powerful.

. . . and he was a definite military target.

"Crap." Cherise decided that she could determine the how and why of this attack later. Students were panicking and stampeding. The lighthearted music made for an obscene auditory contrast. She shut off the playlist.

"Quiryeskul!" Cherise made her voice a commanding whip.

Her favorite amateur engraver gave a start. Quiryeskul was a bronze nussian who had a friendly manner. She also happened to be a soldier. Most of the students were wild-eyed, but those who had trained as soldiers remained stoic.

"Will you please get some fellow soldiers to block the doors?" Cherise asked. "I'll alert Ariock." She activated her supercom.

Her surety had an effect. The jostling students calmed slightly, making room for students with blaster gloves.

Like the various military mayors and battle leaders, Cherise was entrusted with access to the emergency broadcast channel. Everyone with that privilege knew better than to abuse it. Ariock could be in the middle of a conquest. Some of his tasks required his full focus, so he should never be interrupted. Not unless there was a life-or-death emergency that needed immediate attention.

Mostly, the emergency channel was used to report random, unexpected raids by Torth aggressors.

But it was on fire now.

"—under attack!"

"We're being invaded!"

"—TriSolstice City, also!"

"And us! Amass MetroHub!"

"—where—"

"A thousand warships, at least!"

"We need—"

"Where is Ariock?"

The babble of panic made Cherise realize that this was a real emergency. Cities were being raided. Not small raids, either. Something major was happening.

In the midst of so much mayhem across multiple planets, would Ariock even notice if the academy was under attack?

He wouldn't expect it. Nobody expected Torth to be able to invade the heart of Freedomland.

Cherise selected Ariock's icon in an attempt to reach him directly. But, as she had feared, there was no answer. Ariock was busy.

She tried Vy as well.

No answer.

Cherise sank behind her desk and considered reaching out to Thomas on the emergency channel.

But he was Thomas. He likely knew already. He probably knew more than anyone in existence. And he wouldn't prioritize protecting a random classroom. He had to protect himself.

Cherise searched the auditorium for anything that might be used as a makeshift weapon. Orb lights might be heavy enough to throw if she turned off their hover technology.

Students crowded next to her on all sides.

"We're in trouble," one of the govki moaned. "Aren't we?"

All Cherise could do was nod.

# CHAPTER 11

# MIND MASTER

"Done with titration?" Thomas asked in a friendly tone.

The lab technician scooted her chair aside so Thomas could view her workstation. She emanated fear, unwilling to be so close to a mind reader.

"Oh," Thomas said, reading her mind. "I guess Varktezo already checked in with you. I trust his judgment, so there's no need to go over it with me."

The lab tech smiled nervously. Thomas moved on. He didn't want to pretend to be friendly, especially toward someone who was terrified of mind readers.

It was a sunny day. Lab equipment gleamed. Outside the windows, the steep terrain of Freedomland plunged to the beach.

Thomas passed people in lab coats, practicing hydrolysis and saponification techniques. At least a few of the technicians had begun to adopt Varktezo's scientific curiosity toward mind readers. One of them dared to bob her head to Thomas. He nodded back.

If only he could spend all his time in the research annex. He would have slept here if it wouldn't make the technicians nervous. Machinery and chemical smells meant that innovation was happening. Everything in sight had a scientific purpose. It was beautiful.

"Teacher?" Varktezo called from a table in the robotics room. "Are these sensors elastoresistive?"

Thomas floated over to inspect the nanofibrous mesh that his chief assistant was working on. "Correct."

Varktezo seemed happy.

Thomas picked up a stylus, wanting to nudge sensors into a more precise configuration.

"Oh, I can do that," Varktezo said, solicitous.

"I like doing things myself." Thomas worked on the mesh, proud that he could do so unaided. He could lift lab tools, pick up data tablets, and push his goggles up or down. His limbs were no longer skeletal. Physical therapy was paying off. Soon—really soon, he thought—he should be able to walk.

He spoke as he worked. "I'm sure you can guess why it was important to coat the sensors in that plasmic colloid?"

"I get it!" Varktezo said, always appreciative of how Thomas prodded him to reason out the answers on his own. "It's fireproof, but also permeable and semi-conductive. That's perfect for biowear."

"Exactly." Thomas set the stylus aside and used a magnifying lens for a better view of his handiwork. "You might be able to layer on a couple more strips."

"Thank you." Varktezo sighed. "I thought creating an exoskeleton would be a lot easier than this."

"For most scientists," Thomas said, "breakthroughs like this happen once in a lifetime. And they often take a lifetime."

Varktezo looked disbelieving though his goggles.

To former slaves, Thomas knew, self-edification and the process of scientific discovery seemed decadent and nonessential. On top of that, patience was hard for many fifteen-year-olds to master. Varktezo was a teenager. He had to deal with the ummin equivalent of hormonal surges, much like Thomas.

"I worked on NAI-12 for multiple years," Thomas said, "before I had a version that was efficacious."

The implication was obvious. Varktezo ought to temper his expectations and align them with reality. This exoskeleton project would take time. The big, important projects in their lab, such as inventing immunity to the inhibitor serum, might require years of hard work, even with a large team plus a supergenius at the head of the endeavor.

"Then how are we supposed to beat the Torth?" Varktezo blew out a breath in frustration. "They have thousands of labs like this one." He gestured. "They have more than we do."

"Uh-huh." Thomas used an eyedropper to add a chemating agent to one of the ongoing experiments nearby. "Those are excellent points. Which I've brought up to Garrett."

Varktezo considered that.

"All we can do is our best." Thomas carefully put the chemating liquid back on its rack. "Who knows? Maybe we'll have a surprise breakthrough. It wouldn't be the first time. And meanwhile, the Torth have lost a few of their eldest supergeniuses."

The Upward Governess had embraced the possibility that the Torth Majority would be deprived of her brilliance. The Colossal Failure had gone willingly into death.

But what about the boy Twin?

Thomas wondered if that one had legitimately gone rogue. He did not know the empire's remaining supergeniuses well enough to properly theorize on what threats they posed. He wished he had spent more time orbiting their minds back when he was a Yellow Rank citizen of the empire.

Varktezo checked the results of a nearby autoclave machine. "Are you still doing those standing exercises?"

"Every day." Thomas's latest piece of gym equipment looked like a toddler's bouncy seat. Vy or Nror had to help him get in and out of the thing. It was humiliating. And yet . . .

"I can stand up now," Thomas said. "For up to three minutes. I can walk a little bit." Well, he could lurch around, anyway.

"That is wonderful!" Varktezo put down his tablet to marvel at Thomas with pride. "Soon you'll be rushing around the lab like the rest of us."

The prospect made Thomas smile. "I'll need a lot more practice before I can build up to running." He tapped his thigh, which had enough muscle for normal activities. What he lacked was muscle memory.

Varktezo paged through a tutorial on his tablet, storing formulas in his memory for later use. Thomas sensed that his chief lab assistant felt impatient about rote memorization, finding it tedious and repetitive. Thomas was amused that he felt the same way about the process of daily exercise. It was so repetitive. But he needed to stimulate his muscles for nerve integration.

An emergency klaxon shrieked. "TORTH!"

The alert was loud enough to startle everyone, causing lab assistants to drop beakers or spill chemicals. Someone cursed.

"What in the sand sea?" Varktezo jabbed his wristwatch, seeking a news broadcast.

Thomas considered using his control sleeve to call Ariock or Garrett. His armband was a wearable data tablet, complete with holographic projection capabilities and a supercom.

But he had a more accurate, more direct way of finding out what the Torth Empire was up to, if they were up to anything.

He ascended.

It was almost a reflex. The Megacosm was where one went to gain knowledge, and Thomas figured he only needed a millisecond to soak up the latest news from the Torth side of the war. It was a worthwhile risk. Other supergeniuses might attempt to glean his scientific research in that brief time window, but they were likely bogged down with their own work.

Torrents of information made Thomas shudder from bliss. Ah. It had been fifteen hours, five minutes, and seventeen seconds since he had last ascended to offer amnesty to any secret Torth renegades.

*Freedomland.*

Torth shouldn't be here, in the academy.

*Grab slaves.*

 *Scan their minds.*

  *Locate the Conqueror.*

Thomas's good mood soured as he peered through hundreds of faraway eyes. Torth military ranks were wreaking havoc in his cities. And not just Red Ranks.

Servants of All and Rosy Ranks—they had drilled enough to get past the recruit stage—stomped through deserted corridors that were normally crowded with students.

They wore space armor, complete with slim air tanks. They seemed to be setting up mysterious devices at intervals.

*Remember, don't confront him directly.*

 *Lure him.*

  *Whosoever defeats the Conqueror shall be revered for all eternity.*

If the Torth were here, in Freedomland, then why hadn't they dropped a nuclear bomb? The lack of devastating bombs implied certain limitations. They didn't have shuttles. They must have teleported here.

Like Garrett, the Torth teleporters probably could not bring anything large. No armies. No transports. No nuclear bombs. They could show up by themselves, and maybe armed with individual weapons. That was it.

But they did have devices that hissed.

Gas emitters? None of the Torth lingered in place, so Thomas couldn't study the devices. He would have to probe one of their minds if he wanted to learn—

*!!!!!!!!!!!*

Exclamations sliced his thoughts.

*The Conqueror!*
   *He's watching Us!*
      *He knows!*

Billions of Torth, newly alerted, piled into Thomas's perceptions in an overwhelming flood that made him accidentally bite his own tongue.

*Found him.*

The mental invaders focused on his sense of location and collaborated on mocking up a map.

*Kill him*
   *Get him*
      *Here he is . . .*

Thomas ripped himself out of the Megacosm.

He and Varktezo stared at each other, sharing a horrified realization as emergency klaxons blared. Militant Torth were marauding through the safest cities in the galaxy.

Torth had actually teleported into Freedomland.

Thomas knew, from the intelligences he had just absorbed, that the Torth had not teleported from any astronomical distance. They had sneaked individual jumper shuttles into the local solar system of Reject-20, dispersed enough so Ariock failed to detect them in his sweeps. That was smart. It was also alarming, since it represented a leveling-up in Torth capabilities.

They could leap across a parsec.

This attack was alarming on a strategic level as well. The Torth were sending valuable champions into Thomas's stronghold—and they didn't seem to care about alerting him. What made them so confident? Was it related to those mysterious gas emitters?

Had they invented some new weapon?

Something that could defeat Thomas?

He tapped his control sleeve, unleashing a distress signal. That would alert his own military. Ariock would get the alert and know that Thomas probably needed to be rescued.

But should he really invite Ariock into an unknown melee that might involve an unidentified gas?

The Torth had a million advantages over Ariock in terms of knowledge. Mind readers would locate Thomas far faster than Ariock could. The reflective surfaces of his laboratory were probably the only reason why none of the Torth had teleported here already.

"Everybody?" Thomas raised his voice. "Get out of sight. Torth are in the building. You need to hide!"

Lab assistants scampered through the exits, no doubt seeking workstations to dive under.

Only Varktezo remained. "Where are you—"

Thomas interrupted him. "I'm their target. You need to get away from me."

Everyone knew where Thomas lived and worked. Maybe he should have listened to Garrett and set himself up in a secret off-world lair instead of making himself publicly available. He had just wanted to set an example. He'd wanted to be able to welcome any mind readers who defected from the Torth Empire.

So the Torth were raiding his research annex. They would likely invade his Dragon Tower as well.

Unfortunately, Azhdarchidae was fiercely loyal. If the juvenile sky croc saw his parent's turf being invaded . . . he might do something brave and get himself killed.

Cherise was also a military target.

That was Thomas's fault. He had proven that he cared about her in front of the Torth.

"I have a blaster glove!" Varktezo pulled out his weapon. "I can protect you, Teacher!"

"No. I need you to protect Cherise." Thomas ignored Varktezo's hurt feelings. He couldn't guarantee anyone's safety if they stayed near him. His fireballs were sub-par. He had no hope of matching the gravity-defying gymnastics that Torth military ranks were capable of.

"Please," he begged Varktezo. "Cherise is in the artisan building, ground floor." He had absorbed her class schedule. Not to be creepy—well, maybe it was a little bit creepy—but because he hadn't wanted to risk an awkward chance encounter with her. "You can get there quickly if you—"

The far doors slammed open.

A trio of Torth fanned into the room, moving with predatory coordination. Their helmet faceplates were activated, as if they were in outer space or some kind of toxic environment. The lack of faces made them look insectile.

Gas began to pipe through the open door. It was ominously pink.

Thomas knew he was trapped. The only exit was through the pink gas and the three Torth combatants. Secret passageways riddled the academy, but the emergency klaxons had started too late. He'd had no time to flee and hide.

His mind was a weapon. But the Torth knew that. They would not be so stupid as to enter his range of telepathy. Indeed, they hung back.

Thomas considered rushing at them. His hoverchair was faster than a person at top speed, although he would have to maneuver around counters and lab equipment.

Anyway, the combatants would not stand around and wait for him to twist their minds.

Thomas figured he had only one option left, one slim possibility for survival. He ascended into the Megacosm.

*DEFEATED!*

   *HA!*

      *THE CONQUEROR IS CORNERED!*

       *HE WILL SOON BE POWERLESS!*

         *WHAT A LOSER!*

Frenzied victory choruses poured over Thomas. He ignored jeers and insults, filing them away for later processing. He sought the minds of the particular combatants who had him cornered.

They were eager to gloat.

*We are superior to you, Conqueror.*

  *So much superior!*

    *You have lost the war!*

      *Inhale the inhibitor gas!*

*As soon as you lose your powers,*
*We will take you into custody,*
*and bring you to the Death Architect—*
*—who will break your precious mind!*

Supergeniuses hardly ever gave someone their entire attention. Never with invasive, in-depth probing. It was beyond rude. Thomas didn't care. He burrowed deep into the core of one Servant of All, the Trepidatious Blaze. He tore past that man's varied hopes and dreams and arrowed straight to his primal depths.

*!!!!!!!!!*

The Trepidatious Blaze understood, a second too late, that he should have dropped out of the Megacosm.

He tried to do so now. His triumph morphed into a snarl of horror.

It was a good thing Thomas had gotten a lot of practice at twisting minds. He zombified dozens of victims per day in an ongoing effort to keep the Mirror Prison clear and clean. He zombified the Trepidatious Blaze with practiced ease.

It was trivial.

The only difference between doing it up close and doing it at a distance was the type of connection. Up close, Thomas could forcibly twist any mind. From a distance? It had to be consensual. The victim had to literally invite him in.

Which the Trepidatious Blaze had done.

That was what being a Torth in the Megacosm was all about. Torth normally swung in and out of each other's surface thoughts and perceptions with the casual ease of monkeys swinging from trees.

*!!! Uh-oh !!!*

Thomas sensed shocked dismay from his mental audience. Orbiters flung themselves away in a panic, rejecting him. Thomas's full-focus attack had already ruined his own tenuous connection to his orbiters. He lost access to the Megacosm.

That was all right.

He doubted that any more Torth would allow themselves to be victimized. This was a onetime, single-use trick. He had been saving it for a battle such as this.

"Come into my range!" Thomas commanded.

Fortunately, the space armor suits seemed to include auditory processing. The zombie formerly known as the Trepidatious Blaze heard him and obediently sprang into action. He backflipped over a chair and sprang over a counter, shattering beakers. He landed within Thomas's range of telepathy by a hair.

Thomas slipped into the broken mind of his zombie.

He wore its body as if he was stretching a new glove. The zombie's sensations were now his. The zombie's limbs were his limbs. The zombie's eyes were his eyes. Thomas had gained a second body, and it was enhanced with superstrength, superagility, and powered armor.

In his multifaceted peripheral vision, he saw the remaining two Servants of All raise their bulky blaster gloves, ready to end the threat to their galactic empire.

Time stretched out for Thomas as he kicked his mental processing into high gear.

He imbued his proxy body with martial arts knowledge as well as his will and sent it forth. The zombie leaped across the table and seized one Servant's gloved arm. He wrenched it hard enough to crack an armored joint, then used that momentum to swing that Torth toward the other. She lost her balance and Thomas's zombie swept a roundhouse kick, enhanced by powered armor, at that one's helmet. The faceplate dented.

The zombie finished his move by throwing the broken-armed Servant toward Thomas.

She tried to scramble to her feet, but she wasn't fast enough.

Thomas wrenched her mind. He then settled into her body, wearing it, testing it out, fitting his mind to her athletic contours.

Tendrils of pink gas snaked closer.

A gaseous inhibitor? Thomas could only guess at whose brilliant idea this was. He took a deep breath and held it.

He used his two proxy bodies to seize the third invader. He-she wrapped strong arms around the fighting Servant of All, dragging him closer to Thomas's central-ized hub of a body. Never mind that his lungs burned with a need to breathe. He didn't dare risk inhaling any trace of the pink gas.

*Noooo!* the third Servant of All gibbered in silent panic. *You tyrant!* He flailed, trying to escape, but he must know that he was doomed.

Thomas dived deep into his core mind.

Within a microsecond, it was over. Thomas wore a third heavily armored body.

He knew the Megacosm must be roaring with dismay. He could guess what they were thinking.

A grenade rolled through the open doorway. Its countdown display was al-ready morphing from yellow to orange.

Thomas hadn't dared draw a breath. He was going to black out soon. Nevertheless, he used a proxy body to leap toward that grenade and hurl it back the way it had come.

The explosion boomed in the adjacent lab.

Walls rattled. Glass equipment broke and dust sifted down. A lab technician screamed in fear.

Thomas directed his proxy bodies to knock over the gas emitters. He sped through the broken doors, seeking fresh air. He had to skirt past the mangled victim of the grenade—a Torth in the white armor of a Servant or a Rosy.

His home was under attack. He could really use more than three proxy bodies.

"Teacher?"

Varktezo cringed when the three proxy bodies plus his Teacher swiveled their heads in unison.

Thomas took a breath. "I ' m  f i n e," he said with multiple voices. "T h e s e  b o d i e s  a r e  u n d e r  m y  c o n t r o l." His other mouths rasped, their vocal cords underused. "S t a y  p u t."

He collected his three extra selves and sped away, hunting threats to conquer.

# CHAPTER 12

# PINK BLITZ

Ariock's supercom was blowing up with cries on the command channel.

"They're taking prisoners!"

"I'm inhibited!"

"Me, too!"

"Run!"

"Warrior down!"

"Torth are teleporting!"

The faraway panic was incongruous in a landscape of untouched sand and patient beach waves. The ocean around his private island was pink, reflecting sunrise-tinged clouds that had been serene moments ago.

Ariock held his arm away, as if his supercom was a venomous leech wrapped around his wrist.

Vy touched him. "You need to go."

No excuses were necessary. Vy wore her own supercom, and she was also receiving a deluge of personal calls.

Jinishta's icon popped up on Ariock's display. He answered her call. Jinishta was garrisoned in a hub metropolis on Umdalkdul today, and she should be nominally in charge of all his armies and fleets on that planet.

"Ariock?" Jinishta's voice blared, tinny through the speaker. "I hope you can hear me. Garrett is injured and powerless. The Torth are netting him right now, and they also have more than two dozen Alashani warriors. We're in TriSolstice City. I'm afraid we cannot hold this land."

Ariock swore.

"I cannot rescue them." Jinishta sounded anguished.

She kept speaking, describing the battle's location, but her voice was interrupted by an emergency buzz. Ariock recognized that unique buzz pattern. It superseded all other distress signals.

It meant Thomas needed to be rescued.

Ariock stared at his wristband.

Thomas never left Freedomland. If he was in a crisis, then everyone in their cradle city was under threat. Kessa was in danger, too.

Everyone was in danger.

Ariock went calm. His people needed him.

He entered a clairvoyant trance, sending himself across hundreds of miles of ocean to the distant shore of his favorite city. Freedomland looked secure as Ariock ghosted through its stone buildings. But the streets were devoid of people.

His citizens must be hiding, perhaps in the underground passageways and bomb shelters that Thomas had instructed Ariock to build. Neighborhood leaders knew where to guide people in an emergency.

Ariock decided to explore later. For now, he needed to exchange his beachwear for armor.

He ghosted into his suite. He had two sets of galaxy armor, inspired by nussian physiology, and he item-teleported one set onto his core self standing on the beach.

He was battle-ready within a second.

The armor added even more bulk to his size, which he regretted when he was standing so close to Vy. He was more tank than person. But it was awesome for battles. Microdarts, blasts, bullets, lasers, and even ionic blades could not cut through the hyperdense layers of plates. Wildfire could not burn him. Ice could not freeze him. If the Torth dropped a nuclear bomb or otherwise ruined the air, he could raise the faceplate with a twist of his wrist or his neck, and the backup air supply would kick in. He could fight in space if necessary.

He was pretty much invincible.

Now he just had to decide where Vy would be safest, and then he would—

"Go!" Vy shoved him.

Her shove was as ineffectual as the ocean breeze. Ariock didn't budge.

"I don't need a rescue," Thomas said in his ear.

"What?" Ariock tuned in to the command channel, ignoring other panicked reports. Thomas was no match, physically or powerwise, for a single Servant of All. When he linked with someone stronger, gaining a raw power boost, he might be able to zombify a thousand Torth, but that required planning and a controlled conquest. There was no way the boy could defend an entire city by himself.

"I have things under control," Thomas said. "Never mind my emergency signal. Go rescue Garrett, but be extra cautious. The Torth have a gaseous weapon. I'm not sure what it does—they kicked me out of the Megacosm—but be extra wary of pink gas."

"Help Garrett." Evenjos's throaty plea came through his helmet speaker. Was she actually willing to defend Freedomland?

"Please," she said.

"Go and save people!" Vy held up her wristband. "I'll call for help if anything happens."

The Torth didn't know about this island of cute kiwi-like critters. They couldn't use Vy as a hostage if they couldn't find her.

Ariock tuned out of the command channel and inhaled the salt air one last time. Did the Torth believe they could freely reconquer and take his territory?

Let them try.

Ariock would rip their fragile little bodies in half with the power of his mind.

He ghosted to war-torn Umdalkdul. Once he located the city on a desert plateau above an inland sea, he yanked his body to that location. He appeared in the fiery sky with a clap of thunder and a spray of lightning.

Torth transports veered. Two flying vehicles crashed into each other. Debris rained down, along with flailing Red Ranks.

Ariock could normally find Garrett by his life spark. He sensed only ordinary combatants, and he remembered that the inhibitor was in effect. He would need to find Garrett visually.

That might be tough, since the old man was the approximate size and shape of a Torth.

Ariock sent his core self down into the thick of an intense battle.

The indoor plaza Jinishta had described was a confusing mass of speeding hoverbikes and blaster explosions. Soldiers of different species hunted or confronted Red Ranks. A strange pink miasma hung in the air, exacerbated by smoke from wildfires and emissions from blasters.

It must be the weapon Thomas had warned him about.

Why hadn't Garrett mentioned any hint of a new weapon in development? Would Servants of All and Rosy Ranks tolerate a threat to their own powers? Probably not. So how dangerous could it be?

People on the command channel were shouting Ariock's name, demanding his attention. Their chatter faded to meaningless noise as Ariock expanded.

His shoulders widened to become storm-heavy clouds, unfurling into arms of rainfall and electrical energy. He encased his core self in a bolt of lightning huge enough to cause blindness. As lightning, he slammed through the glass dome of the plaza, uncaring where shattered glass flew.

His landing caused an earthquake.

The impact ripped golden plates off the ground and shattered crystal casings. Skyscrapers rocked and groaned with a sound more ominous than thunder.

Ariock straightened to his full height, bristling with lightning and spiked armor.

Torth Red Ranks shot at him like mindless beasts, as if they had any chance of hurting him. Ariock strode past the idiots. The pink miasma floated well below his height, so he left his faceplate open, breathing in the scents of violence. He wanted to hear if anyone shouted for his help.

Civilians cowered and hid. Torth on hoverbikes sped into the ruined plaza, as if eager to meet Ariock in battle and die.

This was the opposite of a battle planned by Thomas. This was chaos.

What was the overarching plan of the Torth Empire? Even if they retook a few cities, they were likely to lose them again. They probably didn't care about temporary and minor victories. So what was this really about? Was it all to capture Garrett and a few Alashani warriors?

Or was that merely a way to distract Ariock from their true goal?

The Torth would value Thomas as their top target, not the old man. Not some random city. Was Ariock being a blind fool? Was he allowing the Torth to sidetrack him—

"*Aonswa!*"

Ariock turned toward the desperate cry. A woman reached out to him, her albino face stark against her black armor. She was half encased in a net. Two Torth Red Ranks dragged her toward a prison hovercart.

Dozens of netted prisoners lay on the floor of that hovercart.

More prison hovercarts sped away, laden with netted warriors. One of those prisoners wore Garrett's unmistakable black and purple armor. The old man looked unconscious.

Ariock used his powers to clear everything else out of his way. He knocked Torth aside and brought the prison hovercarts toward himself. The prisoners aboard seemed badly injured. Some moaned from pain, but more alarmingly, their life sparks guttered, impotent and powerless.

Ariock couldn't guess how so many warriors had allowed Torth to beat them.

Their armor should fend off microdarts of the inhibitor. And didn't they train daily to avoid Torth trickery? Weren't they professionals?

He would ask later. For now, he had to act. Some of the warriors would die without immediate triage.

He used his powers to clear the air. He knelt beside Garrett.

His great-grandfather looked like an abused geriatric patient, suffering from all the weaknesses of being more than a century old. He only looked strong when he had access to his superhuman powers. His strength was gone.

Old Garrett didn't belong in a war zone right now. He was going to die unless Ariock healed him and teleported him elsewhere.

"Watch out for the miasma!" One of the defeated warriors rocked in her net, trying to warn Ariock about something.

"Get out of here!" another warrior begged. "You're in danger!"

Ariock needed all his focus for healing. He couldn't allow himself to get distracted.

He let go of his titanic stature, withdrawing his expanded awareness from the sky. Slaughtering Torth could wait. In his galaxy armor, he was more or less invincible. He needed to—

Something heavy barreled into him from an unexpected direction.

The force of a nussian tackle would crush anybody less substantial. Ariock rolled with it. He didn't need his powers to throw off the one-ton beast, but he infused his body with extra strength. The bronze nussian went flying.

Ariock sat up and glared at his attacker. Nussians were supposed to be on his side.

"Son of Storms!" The bronze nussian cringed upon seeing Ariock stand up, the storm overhead crackling with his fury. Even so, the nussian kept talking. "If you breathe the inhibitor gas, you will lose your magnificent powers."

Inhibitor gas.

Ariock hoped this nussian was playing a prank. The inhibitor was one of the worst dangers in battle, but Ariock had gotten so good at shielding himself, it no longer seemed like much of a threat. Microdarts could not pierce his armor.

"It's all around here!" The nussian gestured.

Ariock became aware that the unnatural pink tendrils of fog were spreading toward him. He was tall enough so the miasma was normally below his face, but that wasn't the case when he knelt. He had only avoided it by pure luck.

No. It wasn't luck. The nussian had purposely shoved him out of harm's way.

"It's true." That was Jinishta's voice on the command channel. "The Torth have a gaseous inhibitor. That's what I was trying to tell you."

"They're setting traps," Weptolyso's gravelly voice added.

Traps?

To capture unwary Yeresunsa. Such as Garrett.

Ariock swore and sealed his faceplate. He used his powers to send a cleansing wind through the plaza, but still, he dared not breathe the outside air.

Implications barreled through his mind.

The Torth had bided their time.

They must have prepared for this multipronged attack, training their military units, positioning troops to deploy at the right time, perhaps burying caches of weapons. They were swarming Ariock's territories en masse.

Now that they'd rendered his warriors useless.

Unlike Ariock, the Alashani had modest spheres of influence. They were the size of a room, or a city block at the most. They could hurl spears with superhuman speed, but they needed to be close enough to see their targets. With inhibitor gas lurking in every city, his Alashani Yeresunsa could no longer afford to run fearlessly through urban areas, where anything might lurk around a corner. They might run into a tendril of inhibitor gas.

*This changes everything*, Ariock realized.

Even major Yeresunsa such as Ariock would have to tread carefully when they were in enemy territory. As for Evenjos . . . ?

"Get the warriors off the field," Ariock said hopelessly. "All warriors, retreat."

In full armor, it was difficult to perform healing magic. It required proximity and usually touch. But Ariock managed to close Garrett's wounds and give him enough energy to awaken.

The old man immediately spoke into his com. "Evenjos, get out of the city. The Torth have a gaseous form of the inhibitor."

A whiff of inhibitor gas could unmake Evenjos. She would certainly quit healing soldiers in battle zones.

And things would get worse. No doubt the Torth Majority wanted the inhibitor gas to be totally invisible and undetectable. It was only a matter of time before the Torth supergeniuses ironed out the pink kink.

All Ariock's future battles would require space armor. He dared not breathe on battlefields.

He swept a sharp wall of lightning at the Torth combatants, frying them where they stood. The survivors began to flee.

Ariock let them go. He had bigger concerns.

When he was certain he'd cleansed the air, at least for now, he retracted his faceplate and looked at the bronze nussian who had saved him. Judging by the soldier's many scars, he was a former gladiator.

"What's your name, soldier?" Ariock asked.

The nussian seemed honored. "I am Hathmalarskel."

Ariock repeated the name. "Hathmalarskel." Saying it out loud implied respect in nussian culture. "I'm going to leave and take all the Yeresunsa warriors with me."

The nussian soldier snorted in acceptance. He seemed to think that was a sensible decision.

"Can you tell me who's in charge of the garrison here?" Ariock asked. "Beneath Jinishta and her warriors?"

Hathmalarskel named a name. Judging by the brevity and cadence, it was probably an ummin.

"Great." Ariock made a mental note to visit the ummin leader. "Hathmalarskel, you proved brave and capable in saving me today. Are you a battle captain?"

"No, I am not." The nussian's small eyes were round with wonder.

"I would like to appoint you in charge of a garrison." Ariock wished he could offer more than a few words of gratitude. He would likely never be able to repay the debt he owed to this nussian. "For now, will you help to defend this city against Torth?"

"It would be my honor, Son of Storms." Hathmalarskel looked like he might burst with pride. "May I offer rewards to anyone who helps me?"

That was a battle captain's prerogative. Captains could hand out war credits or neighborhood turf as rewards to exceptionally heroic soldiers.

"Of course. Use your best judgment." Ariock clapped the newly raised captain on his pebbly back. "And thank you."

As Hathmalarskel loped away, Ariock thought of all the people who would be relying on such captains from now on.

And on scientists—especially the one supergenius on their side.

Immunity to the inhibitor was going to be crucial in saving the galaxy. Everyone needed Thomas, whether they knew it or not.

# CHAPTER 13

# AS MANY

Thomas was no longer afraid. He saw all possible threats.

If his mind had been limited in capacity, with normal processing speed, he would have been unable to puppeteer even one extra body. Instead, he utilized a flood of extra perceptual data as only a supergenius could. He was seven bodies at once, including his own.

He issued unspoken lists of instructions while speeding through corridors. Mental commands were much faster than spoken words. He gave his zombified proxies enough nonconflicting priorities to keep them self-sufficient in case he got distracted.

His extra bodies moved like Olympic athletes. He had imbued each proxy with his absorbed database of gymnastics, martial arts, and combat training. They wielded weapons: blaster gloves, rifles, and a scimitar.

No powers, though. Yeresunsa powers required self-actualization, and their minds were too broken to even process their own emotions and basic survival needs.

He made do. The proxy bodies fanned out around his hoverchair, protective. Thomas compelled only one zombie to lope within his range. The rest were satellites, within telepathy range of that first one or each other. That way, Thomas could control all his proxies without needing to be within four yards of every single one. He leapfrogged commands from mind to mind to mind while remaining in centralized control.

Halfway to the artisan building, Thomas slowed, using his extra ears to listen for distant sounds and analyzing everything he heard. He detected an ambush from his own side. This could turn into a friendly-fire incident.

He muted the command channel and switched to the local city military dispatch. "This is Thomas," he said in a low voice. "I'm between the research annex and the artisan building with six zombified Torth at my command."

He waited for an acknowledgment.

"Ah! Uh, Thomas, got it." The dispatcher sounded surprised.

"Tell the squad in the research courtyard to stand down," Thomas said. "These six Torth belong to me."

A mer nerctan cocked its bony head to peer around the corner. It assessed Thomas's literal orbiters, one eye visible and narrowed with suspicion.

"Don't shoot." Thomas did his best to sound nonthreatening. It was difficult to dredge up any emotion while so much of his mind was occupied with directing zombies. He was still processing their brutal life experiences in the background of his consciousness.

"You are the Teacher?" the mer nerctan asked. "Thomas?"

"Correct," he said.

The mer nerctan muttered with disgusted fear. Thomas did not have to read its mind to understand why. There were rumors that Thomas had bluffed and brain-washed his way onto the war council. Not everyone believed Thomas was a super-genius, but plenty of soldiers believed he was a conceited and overly entitled *rekveh*.

This was why he rarely left his annex.

The mer nerctan spoke to its squad leader through its earpiece, and Thomas sensed the soldiers begin to withdraw. He floated forward.

A distant scream claimed his attention.

"Shots fired in the artisan building," the dispatcher said.

"Thomas here. I'm heading to the artisan building with my zombies to deal with the threat." Thomas floated in that direction, not waiting for the local squad to make a decision.

Instead of diving into the building, Thomas skimmed alongside its stone wall. He moved as close to the wall as possible, his senses open and listening.

—*Conqueror. Where is—!*

*!*

  *!*

Thomas twisted one mind, then another, then another. He sent mental instructions to the newly zombified Torth.

Those fresh zombies did their best to seize the remaining Torth raiders in the vicinity. A few zombies got killed by Rosies with powers, their armor twisted or their necks wrung with telekinesis. Even so, most of the Rosies fled rather than stick around to face Thomas.

Except for one.

A chunk of archway exploded just as Thomas entered the building. Rubble rained down. Zombies protected their central body, as instructed, and yanked Thomas's hoverchair back, using their own bodies to shield him. They caught a stone chunk and hurled it aside before it could crush Thomas.

He sent several of his fearless zombies rushing toward the hidden sniper. One zombie went down, ankle twisted and broken by an invisible force. Others kept going.

Maybe the sniper was exhausted? If all these Rosies had teleported to Freedomland, then they might all be near depletion. Not even Garrett could take teleportation lightly. He would deplete himself after five interstellar teleports.

Thomas silently instructed two more zombies to circle around and cut off any possible escape route the sniper might take.

Next, he floated to the one with the broken ankle and ordered it to sever itself from the chain. He didn't need a defunct body. He left it with instructions to kill any nonzombified Torth raiders, and to obey commands from any former slave soldiers.

With that, he made his way inside the artisan building, in full control of three proxy bodies and with six more acting semi-independently. That should be enough to take down a squad of Servants of All.

Thomas proceeded with caution anyway. This attack had been well executed and preplanned, and not by the Majority. He was dealing with an enemy supergenius.

He was actually grateful that Garrett and Jinishta had talked him into keeping the Mirror Prison clear and mostly empty of prisoners. If he had left it chock-full of Rosies and Servants of All, he might face a lot worse than a few dozen invaders. They would have recruited local help.

Thomas traversed a lobby full of sculptures and other artisan displays. The classrooms were interconnected, and he took a winding path through emptied rooms, past students hiding behind seats and workshop tables. He scouted ahead with his proxy bodies. He listened. He stuck close to walls.

And deep down, he fumed.

The Torth Empire was a corpse. The Majority was just a shambling horde of proxy bodies for some supergenius or two. She—it must be either the girl Twin or the Death Architect, or perhaps the two of them working in a secret concerted effort—had lashed out at his home. His sanctuary. This was where he collected his favorite people.

And if his best people couldn't feel safe? Then no one was safe.

The important work they were doing would grind to a halt. Thomas would lose—not just the war, but everything and everyone he cared about.

*You dare come into My home?* Thomas ascended into the Megacosm as rudely as possible. *You dare threaten Me?*

Amazingly, the Torth Majority did not ban him.

Too many Torth wanted to learn what was going through his mind. More than a few Torth went into orbit around his angry mood, and although they cringed, they also fed upon Thomas's knowledge.

Thomas likewise gained an overview of multiple battles from the Torth perspective.

The Torth Empire had regained Lava City, Straddler City, and Tempest Arena.

They had made a point of going after albino warriors and assassinating them. They had successfully killed more than two dozen, and they had captured many dozens more. In fact, the Imposter himself had blundered into one of their inhibitor-gas traps. A trio of Torth champions had captured him with ease, and they would have killed him if not for the infernal Giant and those infernal supercoms the Conqueror had invented. The Giant had whisked the crippled old man and a bunch of albinos away to safety.

The Majority was seething with disappointment.

So far, they had failed to kill or capture any of the four enemy heroes. A lot of Red Ranks and Rosies were dead.

*But it is not over,* millions of minds chorused.

*Right,* many others agreed. *(Also) This is a costly battle for the enemies.*

We (the great and glorious Torth Empire) will give the enemies many more costly battles.

Thomas dropped out of the Megacosm with his lips compressed. His side truly could not afford to lose so many Yeresunsa. The Torth Empire had a near-infinite supply of Rosy Ranks. In contrast, Thomas's side now had fewer than nine hundred and fifty warriors with Yeresunsa powers.

He was dangerously outmatched.

If this war was a game of chess, then Thomas was the king piece for his side, weak yet crucial to victory. And a few minutes ago, he had almost been checkmated.

But not quite.

Was she disappointed? Whether his nemesis was the Death Architect or the girl Twin, she must realize, as Thomas realized, that their mutual stalemate was unsustainable. She would plot more nastiness.

Thomas did not want to be taken by surprise again. He needed to reconsider his entire approach.

Heck, maybe he ought to become a warrior? If he fought alongside people like Flen, maybe the Alashani squads would learn to respect him. Was he being fool-hardy? Was that even possible for a supergenius?

Microdarts hit his scouting proxy bodies.

Thomas shielded himself with heat and the invisible projectiles burned before sticking into his skin. He needed to avoid the inhibitor.

Egg-shaped objects hurtled toward him. Grenades. Their timers morphed from orange to red.

As fast as thought, Thomas directed proxy bodies to jump up and intercept the grenades. They acted as living shields for Thomas's core body, and they died. Limbs and gore exploded outward.

Blood spattered across Thomas's lab coat and face and hoverchair. Oh well.

He used his other proxy bodies to leap around the corner and seize any armored Torth they encountered.

There were blasts. There were fireballs. Thomas's proxy bodies each combined the expertise of multiple Servants of All. In many ways, they were better than their brethren who still had free will. They walked through wildfire and did not care if their hair burned off. They dodged using borrowed supergenius mental reflexes. They sprayed inhibitor microdarts, they forced arms into deadlocks, and they dragged new victims toward Thomas in his hoverchair.

Thomas won.

He won again.

Each new proxy body added to his processing burden. Once he gained more than fifteen bodies, his thoughts lagged by a few milliseconds. It didn't matter. He was still more clever than an average Torth. He outmatched every combatant in terms of skill, strategy, methodology, and sheer number of bodies. He seized another combatant, and another.

He surged forward, speeding through the building with a phalanx of appro-priated bodies. Extra bodies scouted ahead or behind, relaying visual data to the central command brain who sat in the hoverchair.

The next batch of Servants of All he encountered did not attempt to murder him. They simply fled.

Thomas chased them with proxy bodies. He threw obstacles in their paths. He attacked them. Once they were apparently depleted? Thomas used proxy bodies to drag them, writhing and kicking, into his telepathic range.

He zombified one after another after another.

One Servant of All escaped. She was in the grasp of one of his proxy bodies when she vanished with startling suddenness. Air rushed into the vacant space, causing a thunderclap that smelled of ozone.

Thomas sent proxy bodies to search adjacent rooms and hallways, just in case she had teleported to someplace nearby. He didn't find her.

The fact that none of the other victims escaped told Thomas how weak they were, on average. Each one of these invaders had teleported from streamships that were less than a parsec away. A return trip would require rest and recovery time. Only one had been able to get away within an hour of showing up.

They definitely weren't as powerful as Garrett.

The Torth Empire might be conserving its best champions for a later attack. Either that, or the Torth Empire didn't have such great assets to begin with. Thomas hoped for the latter.

One of his proxy scouts observed a few Servants of All hurrying toward Cherise's classroom. The Servants were as single-minded as sharks, intent on winning eternal praise in the Megacosm.

Too bad for them.

Thomas commanded nine of his proxy bodies to surround the invaders, block them, and then shoot them in the head. Brains splashed across the walls. Armored Torth bodies fell into the gore that used to be their own heads.

Silence from the classroom.

Thomas cautiously floated forward, commanding his many proxy bodies to stand aside in sentry mode. He bypassed corpses. When he reached the door, he overrode the low-security setting that kept it closed.

"I t ' s  m e," he said.

Dozens of simultaneous voices whispered his words with him. Thomas winced and suppressed his other mouths.

"Thomas," he said alone.

He dared to use the door control to slide it partway open so he could peek inside.

Hundreds of alien faces stared at him with fright.

"It's all right." Cherise made her way up the aisle. Her attitude toward Thomas was wary and mistrustful, just like the soldier students who stood with their blaster gloves ready, but there was hope in her face as well.

That was a look Thomas had waited a long time to see from Cherise.

"You're safe," he said, answering the question no one had quite dared to ask out loud. It didn't matter. He heard it anyway.

Cherise stopped well short of him. She knew his range of telepathy, and she stayed outside of it. Her gaze flicked across Thomas's lab coat, taking in the spatters of blood. She must have heard the blasts.

And she must notice that Thomas wasn't wearing a blaster glove.

"The Torth who invaded here are no longer a problem." Thomas's voice did an embarrassing puberty thing. It dropped an octave.

Cherise still looked worried, so Thomas decided to clarify. "I zombified most of them." He cleared his throat. "And killed the rest."

Just to be on the safe side, he said that in English so her students could not understand his words.

"Oh." Cherise hesitated.

Normally, it was easy for Thomas to think of how to guide a conversation. But nothing he thought of seemed adequate here.

He gave Cherise a nod of acknowledgment. That was the best he could do.

They gazed at each other. The space between them seemed so huge, it might as well be a solid wall.

Cherise looked as if she wanted to speak, but she kept changing her mind.

Thomas's proxy bodies relayed a problem to his attention. Someone was hurling spears at bullet-fast speeds and slaughtering them. The bodies did not defend themselves, of course. Self-defense was not one of the basic batches of commands Thomas had installed in their minds.

With a sigh, Thomas sent commands down the chain.

Soon the proxy bodies seized their attacker. Torth military ranks wore white or red armor, but this one wore all black.

Flen?

Ugh. Thomas recalled the complex roster of warrior duties, and sure enough, Flen would have been home when the invasion hit. He must have hurriedly put on his armor and then run all the way from the Alashani quarter to the academy to rescue the love of his life.

How noble.

Thomas used his extra bodies to hustle the warrior into the classroom. Released, Flen stumbled and caught his balance.

"Sorry," Thomas said to Cherise. "I need Flen to stop attacking my zombies."

Flen flipped up his visor, revealing a face that was flushed red with outrage and humiliation. He saw Cherise. Enraged, he turned toward Thomas.

"*Rekveh.*" Flen bared his teeth and drew two spears. He looked ready to kill.

"No, Flen!" Cherise jumped between him and Thomas. "He's protecting us!"

Thomas prepared to send proxy bodies to disarm Flen. He wasn't going to allow the hothead to accidentally spear Cherise.

Flen gripped his spears but stopped short of throwing them. A muscle in his jaw flexed. He must be gnashing his teeth.

Thomas attempted to give Flen a respectful smile. He hoped it looked friendly rather than mocking. "You got this?" He made sure that his other mouths stayed quiet and forced himself to sound like a human. "If so, I'm going to go get rid of any other Torth on campus."

Cherise looked nearly as flushed as Flen. That couldn't be anger, could it? She was too far away for Thomas to sense her mood. Why was she so red-cheeked? Was she embarrassed?

"Thank you." Cherise nodded to Flen and then to Thomas. Her eyelashes were longer than Thomas remembered. Pretty.

He rotated his hoverchair and exited the classroom, shielded by extra bodies.

Sure, he had words he wanted to say to Cherise. Although he had apologized to her in the dead city, she hadn't heard him, and he wanted to tell her again. But, then again . . .

Did she really need to hear it?

Thomas respected the space Cherise maintained between herself and him. That space was significant. It was where Cherise wanted Flen, not the boy everyone hated and feared.

Perhaps she had made a wise choice. Thomas figured he was unsuitable as boyfriend material. He had the body and hormones of a teenager, but he was mentally something very different.

A sovereign.

A Conqueror.

He floated down the corridor, where thirty zombified Torth awaited his commands.

# CHAPTER 14
# CRACKS IN CIVILIZATION

Some people still treated the Former Commander with respect. She wondered why.

She chewed an antacid tablet while the Megacosm wailed and writhed around her. None of today's battles had gone as well as they were supposed to. Perhaps there would have been a decisive victory if she had been in charge?

Instead, she sat in a luxury suite like a fat, useless Blue Rank.

*We should have won,* the Majority moaned.

*Instead, We have lost.*

*It is as if We are led by idiots—*

*—instead of supergeniuses!*

This latest round of defeats could not be blamed on the Former Commander. Everyone was clear on that, at least. Torth champions who could teleport were in limited supply. She never would have wasted champions on a flimsy, throwaway strategy.

The raids had actually given sneaky skeptics an opportunity to pack camping supplies and flee from civilization. They'd vanished while the Torth Majority was focused on multiple battlefronts.

The Former Commander did not approve of draft dodgers. Sure, she understood why her fellow champions wished to avoid military duty. The Giant might as well be invincible when he wore space armor. Any battlefield that included him was a death sentence.

And the Conqueror, now . . .

It was impossible to think of the enemy mastermind as the Betrayer anymore. No one wanted to face that monster in person. Not even in battle. Not even the champions.

*None of Our rogues will actually join the Conqueror,* millions of Torth tried to assure each other.

*Surely not.*

*Even Our renegade champions (Rosies and Servants) wouldn't dare—*

*—to go near the mind-twisting Conqueror.*

The Former Commander silently agreed with that sentiment. No one sane would join the enemies. Spies existed among the so-called penitent populations in enemy strongholds, and they would report any rogue traitors and attempt to assassinate them.

Exiting the Torth Empire was harder than ever.

And it was more illegal than ever. The Majority had ratified new laws when the boy Twin *(escaped)* disappeared: No one was permitted to travel from one star system to another without military approval. Spaceports were locked down. Any nonmilitary streamships or starships must follow preapproved routes. Everyone was under surveillance.

That ought to prevent rogue and renegade breakaways.

Even so, no one could fully control the most elite military ranks. The Former Commander supposed that she could ghost to Earth right now if she wished. She could teleport from planet to planet.

She was just wise enough to remain loyal to the greatest civilization that had ever existed.

Perhaps some of her traitorous colleagues were cavorting on the playground of Earth right now? If so, they would need to stay secretive and hope the Giant never found out about their illegal activities. She hoped they were miserable, having to put up with disgusting human cultures.

*Why???*

Hundreds of millions, and then billions, of Torth hurled that question at the empire's remaining supergeniuses.

*Why (why) why are We losing???*

*What can We do to stop hemorrhaging champions and supergeniuses?*

*How can We hold on to Our glorious cities and planets?*

Junior supergeniuses emanated shame, although they were not at fault. Not really. They were mere cogs in the machinery of the empire. The Majority wanted them to obey the Lone Twin and the Death Architect, and so they had.

*I have a suggestion,* the Geodesic Flux tentatively announced.

His inner audience sharpened with interest. The Geodesic Flux was eleven years old and had mentally ripened. Perhaps he ought to be promoted to replace the two underperforming girls at the top?

*Reflective surfaces confuse clairvoyance,* he pointed out. *We ought to establish rotating crystal-chrome surfaces in deep space, along obvious routes to Reject-20 (the planet the Conqueror has established as his home base). That should aid Us in deterring and regulating interstellar teleportation.*

Another supergenius, the Rind Topographer, endorsed that idea. *Yes,* she thought. *Let's set cosmic traps. Lace them with inhibitor cannons. That might even stop the Giant and the Imposter from flitting around.*

*At least it could slow them down for a while,* the Geodesic Flux agreed. *And it should help to prevent more of Our own champions from going renegade.*

The Majority roared in approval. At least some of the mutant brains were thinking, unlike the failures at the top.

*FAILURES!* the masses screamed at the eldest supergeniuses.

*YOU FAILED!*

The Lone Twin's response seemed to hold an emptiness. She cared not a whit for other people's uncontrolled anger and disillusionment. *You asked for a new weapon. I gave You a new weapon.*

An echo was missing. Her counterpart was absent.

The boy Twin's continued absence was . . . well, it was improbable.

Military dreadnoughts and cargo carriers patrolled the outer rims of every hub solar system, thanks to the war. They would notice any lone scientific vessel. The boy Twin was alone in space, without any supporters or allies. His ship had limited supplies. If he was traveling slowly, avoiding temporal jumps—and he must be—then he was bound to starve.

So where was he?

Conjectures eddied within the quieter pools of the Megacosm. What unconventional routes might he take?

But the roaring Majority had no interest in unproven theories about a wayward supergenius. They figured he would be found and executed. Their focus was all on the untrustworthy leaders of the Torth Empire.

*WE WANT SMART LEADERSHIP!*

*WE WANT IT NOW!*

*BETTER LEADER BETTER LEADER BETTER LEADER!*

*WE NEED A REAL COMMANDER OF ALL LIVING THINGS!*

The Former Commander surveyed the masses. Her political detractors had dragged the horned shroud from her bony shoulders.

If only she could see a worthy successor to her former office.

Apparently the Majority felt the same way, because the mantle remained stashed in a chest. Everyone ignored the contenders who dared to claim it.

Accusations of incompetence pummeled the Death Architect. She could not invoke any more authority than the Majority had already vested in her. When the enormous audience began to reach peak froth, like a cresting tidal wave, the little girl delivered a simple response.

*We won.*

She was so smug. So confident.

*???????????????* Her orbiters twisted into uncontrolled spins, contorting with questions and discussions.

The Former Commander inwardly admitted that the Death Architect might have a flair for dramatic messaging. Perhaps the child was as socially savvy as the Upward Governess used to be.

*You (Majority) are not thinking long term, like I am.* The Death Architect mentally folded her babylike hands. *The enemies barely skated through this attack. They lost more warriors today than We lost champions. And they did not have nearly so many to start with.*

There was merit to that assertion. The Torth Empire, indeed, still had tens of thousands of champions who were capable of teleportation.

Even so . . .

*Shouldn't We have held off on this attack?* the Rind Topographer wondered. *Shouldn't We have waited until We could surprise the enemies with a more perfected version of the gaseous inhibitor?*

*Right,* the Geodesic Flux agreed. *Surely it wouldn't take long to refine the current version, to make it wholly invisible and undetectable?*

The Lone Twin was so uninterested in the conversation, she exited the Megacosm.

Perhaps she was hiding humiliation? After all, she and her boy Twin counterpart had invented the pink gas. It was their responsibility. Clearly, they had failed to work hard enough at making it undetectable.

The Former Commander found that she didn't care. She did not particularly relish the idea of an improved inhibitor gas.

Battles were going to entail full spacesuits, thanks to the Twins. Air tanks. Helmets. What a pain. That much armor was uncomfortable even for superior beings with musculoskeletal enhancements.

The Former Commander surreptitiously took a low-grade painkiller.

Her aged body seemed to be wearing down. Nothing worked the way it should anymore. Her spine, her joints, her bowels . . . she had begun to carry pills at all times, plagued by digestive problems. The ailments seemed physical, but she had learned enough about humans to suspect that her symptoms were indicative of a psychological condition that was common among lower species.

Stress.

How embarrassing.

The Death Architect seemed untroubled by such maladies. She must be enjoying the stash of NAI-13 the Former Commander had privately delivered to her. She remained tranquil.

And she milked the impression she had made, waiting for the Majority discussions to peak and fall off.

Then she went on. *The Conqueror has foolishly bitten off more than he can chew. He cannot defend the amount of territory he purports to have conquered. Our inhibitor gas has effectively removed some of his greatest (allies) weapons: His albino warriors. And also: The Shapeshifter.*

That was true. The Majority swirled with relief.

Except . . .

*What about his zombified hordes?* a champion demanded to know.

*Exactly!* another piped up. *The Conqueror is unbeatable! He makes his own armies out of Our military ranks!*

The protests piled into another crescendo.

*It is too late to stop the Conqueror!*

*He isn't going to fall for an inhibitor trap now that he knows what the damnable pink gas looks like!*

*What can We do?*

*WHAT CAN WE DO?*

Certainty dominated the Death Architect's mind, as blatant as a volcano looming out of a tranquil sea. *I am not worried.*

She was so influential, her certainty dragged everyone else along.

Trillions of Torth yearned for someone to put their faith in. They wanted someone smart to solve their problems. And why not? The Megacosm was a storm-tossed disaster these days. No one had yet volunteered to join the Conqueror, no matter how many times he extended his horrid invitation . . . yet whenever the Giant conquered a city, hundreds or even thousands of Torth refused to flee.

They knelt instead.

They knelt to the Conqueror.

The kneelers assured everyone in the Megacosm that it was only a pretense to fool the enemies. They wished to serve the Majority as spies. Never mind the fact that the enemies did not permit penitents to work near anyone of importance, so spying was all but futile. And there were far more voluntary "spies" than could ever be needed.

The kneelers seemed earnest. How could they lie to fellow mind readers?

It was enough to make one wonder if a lot of Torth were somehow deceiving themselves.

The Former Commander chewed another antacid tablet.

*The inhibitor gas is only the first in a series of new weapon rollouts*, the Death Architect assured the masses. *The Conqueror can no longer utilize his warriors or the Shapeshifter in battle. Next, We shall remove the Giant. And then I shall remove the Conqueror himself.*

Many Torth had to admit that sounded promising.

Was it possible to get so specific with targeting?

*Yes*, the Death Architect assured the skeptics. *I shall release these (future) weapons when the timing is right. Timing is crucial.*

No one could argue with that.

And the Majority knew better than to dig for details. Secrecy was important these days. The Imposter might be listening.

*You are All doing well*, the Death Architect thought with rock-solid confidence. *For now, it is imperative that You follow My simple strategies. I want the enemies to get used to a new paradigm. I want to change Our approach from defensive to offensive.*

She threw that suggestion into the galactic population like someone casting a fishing line. It made ripples.

??? The Majority was listening.

*Instead of ceding territory*, the Death Architect thought, *We will attack. Even when it costs Us. Even when We lose champions. Let's not keep gifting the Conqueror with enough leisure time to create whatever he feels like creating.*

The Former Commander stiffened.

But the Majority ate up the directive like fools. It was easy for them to cheer, since only military ranks were obligated to go into battle. Most telepaths would remain safe in outposts that were unlikely to be targeted. Even high ranks, such as governors, would avoid combat. They did not have to worry about facing the Giant in battle, or being zombified by the Conqueror.

*Our civilians can help*, the Death Architect suggested, perhaps because she sensed silence from the military segment of the population. *We should make a habit of sabotage. Destroy transports, streamships, factories. Destroy enemy-held facilities the enemies fail to guard well enough.*

The masses cheered.

*Force the enemies to huddle in the cities they have stolen from Us*, the Death Architect went on. *Make them afraid to leave safety. Just make it a habit. No big goals. Simply harry their outskirts.*

Torth agreed. *Let's sow fear*, they told each other.

The Majority buzzed with renewed faith in their child leader. They didn't exactly trust the little girl, but they trusted her more than, say, the lone Twin. Or the Unsung Spur. Or the Prying Point, or any of the pundits who were constantly vying to win over the Majority.

*We will win*. The Death Architect radiated certainty. *It is impossible for My plans to fail.*

That much confidence from a galactic leader was extremely reassuring. Throughout the galaxy, Torth resumed their workouts at private gymnasiums, or they again sipped nectar smoothies, or whatever else they normally did.

*Just place all Your trust and faith in Me*, the Death Architect reiterated, her mood unchanging.

Many Torth found her steady tranquility to be soothing. Perhaps the serene supergenius was truly a once-in-an-eon hero? She had, after all, bested the Upward Governess.

*She is smart*, many Torth assured each other.

*Yes. Perhaps We are fortunate to live in such a memorable era?*

*Yes. This is quite a time to be alive.*

*Life will (easily) return to normal routines, once We win.*

*Yes*, the Death Architect assured everyone. *It will all be over soon.*

# PART THREE

*"I turned to find my shadow grown long, the ground scorched by my footsteps. Death pooled in my wake. I was the devil."*

—Thomas the Conqueror

# CHAPTER 1
# UPRIGHT AND TRUSTWORTHY

Kessa waited in a dark lobby that was paneled in a quasi-crystalline coating polished to a reflective sheen. That warded off teleporters. Tall windows revealed the night sky, which was starless and eerie, striated by bands of dull colors. It enhanced the mysterious feeling of the Dragon Tower.

She clicked her pointy fingertips. She had not expected Thomas to be late.

Might he be feeding his sky croc? Or did he no longer value the ummin elder he had put in charge of all penitent Torth?

He seemed to want to forget about Kessa and her job. He never checked in with her. He never called. It seemed entirely Kessa's prerogative to contact him, and her liaison clerk had only wrangled this meeting with difficulty, ten days in advance, after a series of cancellations and reschedules.

Her clerk had specifically said Thomas would greet Kessa in his lobby. They would dine alone, without interference from waiters—

A door clanged.

A slightly built person entered the room, making whirring sounds. For a moment, Kessa assumed it must be a random albino. It couldn't be Thomas. Thomas could not walk.

He approached her. Every step was stilted.

Kessa's beak fell open. There was no mistaking his sand-colored hair and his general Torth-like appearance.

"You're walking?!" Kessa jumped to her feet, unsure if she could trust her eyes.

Thomas halted. Or rather, his legs halted in an unnaturally robotic way, and his upper body wobbled, overbalanced by a tiny bit. He had to maneuver to redistribute his weight.

"I got tired of how long it was taking." Thomas patted his thigh, and something made a hollow sound. "So I built braces to speed my progress along."

Now that Kessa's attention was directed toward his legs, she saw that a subtle, lightweight exoskeleton supported his legs and lower body. The framework blended in with his dark clothes. It was a minimalist arrangement of braces, wired with sensors and tiny hydraulic pistons.

Thomas gave her a searching look. "What do you think?" He was far away enough to respect Kessa's mental privacy.

"It is . . ." Kessa fished for the right word. "Incredible?" She wanted time to process the notion of Thomas walking around. It was good, but it was strange.

"It's a temporary measure." Thomas seemed anxious to explain. "I'm working on training my core muscles, but this exosuit helps my body to get familiarized with balance and other processes involved with walking."

He squeezed a small device that snaked out of his sleeve. The exosuit performed the complicated motion of turning around.

"It looks like a big help," Kessa observed.

"Yeah." Thomas whir-stepped to the door. "I use a remote to operate it since my brain doesn't send the right impulses yet."

The brass door looked enormously heavy. It must have hydraulic hinges, because Thomas held it open with ease. "Dinner is this way," he said in an awkward invitation.

Kessa followed him down a glossy, dark corridor. Thomas's exosuit lifted and planted each of his feet in a precise, mechanical way, so he plodded rather than walked.

She stayed out of his telepathy range, because she could not help but wonder how many hours Thomas had devoted to his custom built exosuit. She didn't want him to catch any whiff of her consternation. But shouldn't he prioritize other things? Such as inventing better space armor for warriors? Or immunity to the inhibitor?

Or converting penitents into loyal allies?

The free cities were under a dire strain. The Alashani warriors were no longer used in garrisons abroad, so the Torth Empire had stepped up their raids. Thomas was zombifying more captive Torth than ever. He had even begun to twist the minds of the lowest military ranks. Red Ranks lacked powers and were therefore much more disposable than Rosies and Servants of All.

They all became equal with massive brain damage, though.

The extra zombies were useful for softening up Torth garrisons. They fought to the death. Inhibitor had no effect on them.

But they were useless for general defense. Pilot training required a lot of practice, and there was a shortage of experienced pilots. Ariock and Garrett could kill Torth raiders from a safe distance using storms and earthquakes. But it was difficult for them to target only enemies rather than cowering allies.

And they had to sleep.

People died every time Ariock took a break to catch up on sleep. The Torth Empire grew aggressive during those periods. The Torth were even daring to re-enslave liberated people.

"Did you show your new legs to Vy?" Kessa doubted that Thomas ever opened up to anyone, but if he did, it would probably be to his former caretaker and foster sister.

"No," Thomas said. "So far it's only you who's seen them, plus Varktezo and the team that helped with creation. In case you were wondering, I spent less than an hour on the design and development. It was just a quick brainstorm on my end, and I thought it out before the pink gas showed up. Then I handed it off to Varktezo. The engineering team is using it as a proof of concept for an upgrade to our powered armor."

"Oh." Kessa felt relieved and a little chagrined. "That's great."

It was difficult to gauge Thomas these days, unless one actually talked directly with him. There were so many unkind rumors. People claimed Thomas had mind-controlled fifty Servants of All during the raid on the academy. People said he was a demon. Some said he held dominion over millions of penitents and that he would soon begin to use them as his own personal militia. He supposedly controlled animals. People speculated that he used vermin and roaches to spy on innocent civilians, and that was how he knew so much. And so forth.

Nobody had even whispered that he could secretly stand up and walk.

Kessa supposed that news would eventually circulate, depending on how discreet Varktezo's team was. She imagined goggle-eyed reactions. "What did Varktezo say about it?"

"He said the exosuit is brilliant," Thomas said dryly. "A wonderful miracle, of course. He says similar things about everything we work on."

Judging by Thomas's ironic humor, Kessa figured there must be depths to Varktezo's exuberance. She didn't ask. The secrets of Thomas's work colleagues were none of her business.

"Here we are." Thomas led the way onto a cozy outdoor balcony.

Nearby cliffs kept the area private. Bell-shaped lids kept their dinners fresh and waiting, lit by a crackling brazier.

The table was too cozy.

Thomas must be used to lab assistants who trusted him. But Kessa worked with penitent Torth, and they were a different matter. Out in the fields and the factories, everyone knew to avoid their telepathy ranges.

Not that Thomas was a penitent. Still . . .

"I do not wish to sit within your telepathy range." Kessa picked up her dinner and carried it to the stone balustrade, which had a surface flat enough to serve as a countertop. She pulled the chair over as well.

"Sorry." Thomas looked ashamed of his own presumptuousness.

"I am sorry for my rudeness," Kessa said. "I may sit closer later." She just wanted to make a point. Thomas should not presume that it was his natural right to read her mind and wield that advantage.

"No need to apologize." Thomas braced himself, then used his remote to manipulate his legs into a sitting position at the table. "It was wrong of me to cross that boundary."

Kessa sat. When she pulled the lid off her meal, the aroma of grilled herbs and vegetables made her lick her beak in anticipation. "Coastal silver?" she guessed. It was a type of local fish.

Thomas nodded. "It's prepared in a way that is common among humans. Simple, but I figured an uncomplicated meal will allow us greater focus for discussion."

Kessa gave him a warm look. "Good idea." She used the provided utensils to cut a slice of grilled fish.

Soon they were eating.

It seemed Thomas did have something to say, even though he had declined to meet with her several times. "Kessa, I have a favor to ask."

She raised her brow ridges, inviting him to go ahead.

"Will you please remind the spaceport commissioner to treat solo ships as friendly?" Thomas asked. "I told him, but the message will seem more imperative if it comes from you."

That was accurate. Too many people muttered that the *rekveh* was dangerous.

"I will do so." Kessa enjoyed another bite of fish. "Why? Do you expect renegade Torth to show up here?"

She kept her tone polite, hiding her skepticism. Thomas telepathically asked Torth to join him daily. He had done so for many months. Closeted renegades, if they existed, had had plenty of time to honor his offer.

"I keep hoping," Thomas admitted.

"Why are you so hopeful?" Kessa knew she was prying, but that was her prerogative. She was curious. The Torth Empire had collectively outlawed interstellar travel unless it was for military purposes. With that blockade, she guessed the chances of Torth allies showing up were slimmer than ever.

"There were a few high ranks that went rogue." Thomas sounded noncommittal. "No one knows where they are."

"Really?" Kessa put aside her next bite of alien fish.

Thomas nodded. "They're probably not on Earth due to the risks of me or Ariock finding out. I suspect they're camped out in wildernesses, hoping to wait out the war."

Kessa shrugged. That was welcome news, but it didn't make much difference.

"I take it as a sign that the Majority is dangerously out of touch with the sentiment of their military champions." Thomas forked a bite of fish. "Because those were who deserted. A few starship navigators also went rogue. They fled in their personal streamships and cut themselves off from the Megacosm." He swallowed his food. "And the boy Twin went rogue a few weeks before the rest."

Kessa almost leaped out of her seat. This was major news! Such an ally might be like gaining the Upward Governess.

"The boy Twin delivered some kind of new neurotoxin to his guardian ship," Thomas went on. "He must have killed his minder, who was a very capable Servant of All. Either that, or he somehow persuaded her to collude with him. I assume he reprogrammed his scientific vessel, and now he's gone. No one knows where."

Kessa closed her beak. She imagined how helpful a second version of Thomas would be.

"I'm not sure why he hasn't showed up here yet," Thomas said. "It could be because he has to sneak around Torth military surveillance."

That made sense to Kessa.

"Or," Thomas said, "for all I know, he's setting up a degenerate cult on some reject planet, with his slaves as worshippers."

Kessa tried not to react to that.

"Or he might be heading into deep space in order to die," Thomas said. "Or he's aiming to start his own spin-off empire. All I can do is guess. Except . . ." Thomas lowered his voice. "I caught a hint from Garrett's mind that the Twins are in the prophecies."

Kessa leaped up, too excited to sit still. "Both of them?"

"Don't get too excited," Thomas warned. "The Torth Empire has a metaphorical gun to the head of the girl Twin, retitled by the Majority as the Lone Twin. We need to keep any news about the Twins a secret, whether or not the boy Twin shows up here. Okay? We can't let rumors leak out. If we do, penitents will pick up on the news, and it will get to the Torth Majority, and they'll take murderous action against his partner."

"I understand." Kessa knew that penitents had a lot of trouble abstaining from the Megacosm. She suspected most of them flickered into the Megacosm every few hours, despite their pleading assurances that they would be good.

Everyone at the spaceport needed to comprehend the vital importance of welcoming a refugee supergenius or two.

"I will see that it is a top priority." Kessa made a mental note to hold an in-person meeting with Commissioner Gojal. This was too important for a supercom call.

"Thank you." Thomas ate another bite, as if he had delivered minor news of little significance. He looked strange to Kessa, seated in a normal chair instead of floating in his customary hoverchair. "I'm concerned about the neurotoxin the boy Twin released," he said. "It appears to induce rage. That could be a side effect, but who knows?"

Kessa considered the implications. What would rage do to a Torth?

Or to a Yeresunsa?

"I would assume that whatever scientific knowledge the boy Twin has," Thomas said, "the girl Twin also has it. And she would have been pressured to share it all with the Death Architect."

Kessa acknowledged the danger with a click of her beak. "Do you have any particular guesses about Torth plans?"

"No," Thomas said. "But I can imagine a few terrifying possibilities."

Guesswork must be so much easier for Thomas, with his baseline knowledge. Kessa had never forgotten her long-standing wish to know everything. To be a mind reader. That silly, impossible dream still burned within her.

"All I have are clues," Thomas said. "I know that the Upward Governess was an accomplished chemical materials engineer, and these weapons originated from her research notes. The Death Architect specializes in psychological and physical torture. The girl Twin is an expert neurobiologist. And the boy Twin has—or had—a creative flair. He's innovative."

"And you?" Kessa knew he was a conquering strategist or a philosopher king, but she wanted to know how he classified himself.

"I'm a neuroscientist," Thomas said with a dismissive wave of his hand. "I do other things—we're all generalists—but that's where my greatest interest lies."

Kessa wondered if a neuroscientist could figure out a way for an ummin such as herself to telepathically process knowledge like a supergenius.

"Anyway," Thomas said, "my point is, I take their special interests into account as I hypothesize what their next moves will be."

"And what are your ideas?" Kessa asked with interest.

"There are a lot of gaps in my knowledge." Thomas sounded miserable. "But I'm sure the Death Architect is preparing something nasty, possibly with this rage-inducing neurotoxin. It could be meant to target Ariock. I'm worried about him."

"He fights from afar," Kessa pointed out. "And he wears a lot of armor. How could they get him to breathe toxic air?"

"I don't know," Thomas confessed. "I just want him to be extra careful."

They ate in companionable silence for a few minutes. Kessa expected Thomas to continue guiding the meeting, but it seemed he had said everything that was on his mind.

She was the one who had asked to meet. She supposed the next risk was hers.

"Thomas," she said when the meal was mostly done. "Do you have a good reason for avoiding the penitents?"

He grimaced.

Kessa put down her utensils. She wanted to signify the importance of what she had to say, so she turned her full focus on him.

"I have identified more than one hundred individual penitents who I am reasonably sure have emotions," she said. "They are able to hold a conversation. A friendly conversation," she clarified. "Like humans. When asked, they claim they felt like frauds when they were Torth. They are everything we could want."

Thomas put aside his utensils. "Kessa, that's wonderful. That's real progress!"

"It is!" Kessa agreed. "But I find myself at an impasse." She held up her hands, as if pressed against an unwelcome barrier. "I wish to integrate these exceptional penitents into our society, but they refuse to swear allegiance to me or to you, or to anyone on our side. They refuse to renounce their ties to the Torth Empire."

Thomas seemed to deflate.

"I cannot search their souls." Kessa locked her gaze on him. "I believe that a guarantee from you is of the utmost importance. We need to be able to judge if we can put weapons in their hands and expect them to fight for us."

Thomas looked down at his plate. He shook his head.

"I have done all I can." Kessa gave him a severe look, trying to convey the power he had. "I beg you to meet twenty of the most solid candidates I can find. Just twenty."

Thomas looked like he was under attack.

"If you care about building a bridge between former slaves and former Torth," Kessa said, "and I know you do, then a brief visit from you will mean a galaxy of significance."

"You want me to face people I've conquered?" Thomas's purple eyes gleamed in the firelight. "The ones whose civilization I'm wrecking? They despise me."

Kessa heard fear in the voices of penitents whenever they spoke of the Conqueror. Not hatred.

"I already endure hatred from zombification victims," Thomas went on. "Not to mention every albino I pass in the street. Oh, and half the population of Freedomland." He threw up his hands.

Kessa supposed this explained why he avoided the general population.

"Do you know how many Torth I zombify every day?" Thomas demanded. "I keep the Mirror Prison *empty*. I am destroying hundreds of lives on a daily basis. I am a *monster*." He emphasized that. "People are right to hate and fear me. The penitents see more truly than most. They know what I am!"

The fire flickered.

Kessa felt a thread of fear herself. Her query had scratched a wound, something that Thomas kept bottled up and hidden.

He called himself a monster.

And he believed it.

He was one of the smartest people in the galaxy, if not the smartest. And he believed he was rotten on the inside, or wrong in some intrinsic way, or simply a terrible person. That was heartbreaking.

It also seemed rather . . . well, it might become problematic.

Kessa understood now. His low opinion of himself wasn't the sort of thing that should be allowed to leak into the Megacosm. Even so, she gave him a direct question he could not dodge. "Why do you refuse to go near the penitents?"

"Because . . ." He slumped. "Isn't it obvious?" He gestured helplessly at himself. "Because I'm one of them."

Kessa gawked. Did he actually believe that?

It was ridiculous. Thomas was many things, but defeated? Enslaved? Not even close.

"You are not," Kessa said fiercely. "You are a courageous renegade, not a penitent. There is a difference."

"It's not a difference that matters." Thomas nudged a saltshaker closer to his water glass, as if trying to instill order. "I'm the same as they are. I'm even enslaved, like them."

He was serious.

Kessa rolled her eyes. Garrett's supposed ownership of Thomas was a sham, as far as she was concerned. It was a mockery of true slavery. "You and Garrett play-act," she said, trying to be gentle instead of scornful. "It is silly."

He looked troubled.

She could not believe that Thomas, the all-knowing supergenius, mistook a game of pretend for actual slavery. That was the sort of naive outlook a child would have.

Or, perhaps, someone with underdeveloped emotions?

"You have powers and privileges no slave or penitent has ever had," Kessa pointed out. "Slaves are powerless. And slaves are uncertain. They lack knowledge." She took a small bite of grilled vegetable before going on. "The penitents understand that."

Thomas looked off balance, as if trying, and failing, to figure something out.

"It's all right," Kessa said. "You do not need to be a slave in order for us to be friends." She gave him a fond look. "Even if you were subjugated, I would not consider you to be the equivalent of the penitents."

He looked suspicious. Did he think she was exaggerating?

"You are not like them," Kessa emphasized. "You have human characteristics that shine through."

Thomas looked amazed, as if that was the highest compliment he could possibly receive. "I do?"

She nodded. In truth, she was not sure what those characteristics were. But she was sure that Thomas had them.

"Of course," she said. "You are half human." His heritage alone should be enough to quell doubts.

Thomas studied her, no doubt thwarted by the distance. "I just think nothing good can come of me mixing with penitents. We're too much alike. Up close, side by side, the similarities are inescapable."

He did look like a penitent, seated in that ordinary chair, dressed in drab clothes.

"The similarities are only superficial," Kessa countered. "You are not one of them."

Thomas looked unconvinced. "Who would trust my word that a bunch of penitents are trustworthy?"

"I will trust your word," Kessa said firmly. "So will Ariock. Trust has to start somewhere. We lead by example." She gestured toward the research annex. "People see ummins working alongside a renegade mind reader, and they reconsider everything they thought they knew. And us?" She indicated herself and Thomas. "We are showing them that a friendship between former slaves and former Torth is possible."

Thomas looked thoughtful.

"Twenty is a small number," Kessa said. "But it is enough for a start."

"Once I vouch for your twenty," Thomas said, "you won't need me anymore?"

"I may need you again," Kessa admitted.

He looked dismayed.

"I could not trust an evaluation by a mind reader with ordinary mental capacity," Kessa explained. "Nor could Ariock. The ordinary ones cannot soak up lifetimes. I am sorry, but if we are ever going to trust reborn penitents to pick up weapons and fight alongside our soldiers? Then we do need absolute guarantees." Kessa folded her hands and waited. "It has to be you."

If Thomas truly wanted the penitents to have a path toward redemption and freedom, then he must see the value in evaluating the first few himself.

Besides, his help with redeeming penitents might be a moral counterbalance to all the Torth lives he was destroying.

If his goal was as important as he claimed it to be, then he would prioritize it above his personal comfort. He would make time for it.

"All right." Thomas dropped his napkin, as if to signify defeat. "Fine. Every point you've made makes sense. I'll evaluate your promising penitents. We'll see how it goes."

Kessa had not been playing any sort of game. Even so, she knew that she had won.

# CHAPTER 2

# ABOVE ALL

The penitents of Freedomland dwelled in a ghetto of barracks amid mud and trash. Scavenger crawdads scrabbled over the junk.

Thomas wrinkled his nose at the stench. At least he wasn't robot-walking through the muddy pathways cleared by the slum residents. He floated in his translucent hoverchair.

"Don't look at him." A motherly nussian hid her child behind her thorny bulk. "That's not a penitent," she said in a hushed tone.

The motherly nussian had apparently hauled a trash wagon here. Her neighborhood must be using this place as their dump. Not a surprise. A citywide police force prevented liberated people from outright murdering penitents, yet many citizens dumped broken items and rotting leftovers between the ramshackle barracks. It was a clear insult to former Torth.

Indeed, a lot of former slaves wanted to chop penitents into meaty chunks for feeding livestock. They wanted to work the penitents to death. They said that would be justice.

Thomas caught glimpses of the penitent residents peering at him from behind heaps of trash, or from the rough-hewn windows of barracks. They kept their distance. They knew who he was.

Did they hope he would intervene and grant them better living conditions?

Ha.

Thomas tightened his lips. Penitents were prison labor, not honored guests. There was a cost for refusing to willingly join him.

He was sick of dealing with sullen, uncooperative mind readers. He wasn't sure why he even bothered to keep inviting Torth to join him. None ever did. His life consisted of zombifying unrepentant prisoners. Later today, Ariock would teleport Thomas to some recently defended outpost so he could twist more minds.

And more. And more.

"Thank you for coming." Kessa greeted him in a pre–agreed-upon meeting square, with a communal fountain and a soup kitchen. An entourage of soldiers and clerks backed her up. That was standard for anyone who oversaw penitents.

Thomas gave a nod. Why had Kessa insisted that he visit the slums, rather than bringing the hand-selected penitents to his Dragon Tower, where the ocean breeze erased urban odors? His tower was more secure. Black mirrored surfaces prevented enemy Torth from ghosting or teleporting into his stronghold—if any were nearby. Ariock swept the solar system every morning.

Did Kessa wish for Thomas to feel sorry for the penitents?

Thomas resisted his urge to accidentally veer into her personal space. He would let Kessa keep her secrets. He just wanted to get this unpleasant task over with.

Kessa led him inside a large, drafty building, constructed from imported corrugated metal and canvas. It probably served as an assembly hall. Spaciousness was always a consideration when dealing with mind readers. Penitents had to be kept apart from overseers, soldiers, and each other. They were not permitted to congregate in groups larger than ten.

The soldiers gave Thomas a wide berth. These were not his lab assistants.

Well, he took no offense. He welcomed a break from catching whiffs of fear or hatred aimed his way.

Anyhow, average people ought to be in the habit of avoiding mind readers. That was prudent.

The twenty penitents awaited him in a row.

They were chained to stakes, collared, dressed in clean garments, and under guard. Except for the cleanliness, they were not much different from zombification victims. They seemed just as terrified.

"Do you need us to bring them to you one at a time?" Kessa was solicitous.

"No." Thomas floated toward one end of the row. "I can work through these on my own."

He entered the range of a middle-aged former Brown Rank who could have passed for human. She watched him with alert amber eyes that gleamed in the dimness.

*Please have mercy, Great Conqueror*, the penitent silently begged. *I am no threat to You or Yours.*

Thomas knew that self-deception was an integral part of being a Torth. They lied to themselves constantly. One could not bow to the Majority without willful ignorance. His own firsthand experience told him that.

So Kessa was correct. The only way to certify that these penitents were trustworthy was to have a supergenius dig into their souls.

Thomas braced himself . . . and absorbed the woman's entire life history.

It took roughly half a minute. He examined childhood memories that she herself had forgotten. The process was like dredging stones from the bottom of a well, then turning them over to look at their mossy undersides.

One particularly haunting memory caught his attention. When this woman was eight years old, she had found a govki slave crying in the corner of an unused room. She had touched the slave in order to give her comfort. Then she had struggled to hide her moment of kindness from examiners. She had managed to forget the incident during every exam. It never came up during her Adulthood Exam.

So she had passed. She had earned Torth citizenship instead of being slaughtered to serve as an organ donor.

Still, that childhood memory scorched her like a secret shame. Tears rolled down her cheeks as she relived the moment.

Thomas sought her reaction to the assassination of the Upward Governess. Had she jeered at the only renegade who had willingly joined Thomas?

No.

This middle-aged woman had secretly yearned to follow the Upward Governess's lead. When the Swift Killer murdered the Upward Governess? Shock. Sorrow. This woman had been quietly devastated.

Thomas incorporated that into his whole image of her. He weighed her moments of cruelty against her secret kindnesses.

At last, he backed away, out of range, reeling with freshly absorbed memories. For a half a minute, he had not been Thomas Hill. He had been a Brown Rank formerly known as the Reclining Cloud, now known as Jakka.

Thomas shook himself and regained control of his identity.

"Jakka is trustworthy," he told Kessa and her people, since they were waiting for his verdict.

Kessa gave him a searching look, as if to make sure. "Is there a reason why Jakka will not forsake her allegiance to the Torth Empire?"

Thomas gave the woman a pointed look.

When she refused to answer, Thomas offered the explanation he had cobbled together. "Our side is outmatched. She doesn't trust us to win."

"Ah." Kessa's beak had a wry twist. She did not state the truth Thomas had so often shared with her in private: the heroes needed penitents on their side in order to win.

Thomas considered ways he might pressure Jakka to publicly swear allegiance to Kessa. Enticements? Promises? Perhaps a proclamation that she was officially human?

But he didn't want to set a precedent.

If he was correct about how many penitents were capable of redemption—most of them—then Jakka would only be the first of millions. Kessa needed to architect a system by which any and all penitents could earn redemption and equal rights with the rest of free society. Thomas would not steal Kessa's autonomy or authority by dictating how it got done. That wasn't his role. He and Kessa were the prime example of a former Torth and a former slave as partners. Their mutual respect for each other was crucial.

So Thomas backed away and let his ummin partner decide what to do.

"This penitent has earned trustworthy status," Kessa said. "But not equality. She will earn redemption when she lets go of her distant desire to be rescued by Torth and to become an owner again."

That satisfied most of the guards and onlookers.

"If Jakka wishes to train with weapons, she may do so," Kessa said. "The Megacosm is still off-limits to her."

At a nod from Kessa, guards led Jakka away. The penitent woman wept with quiet gratitude. It seemed she was glad to remain in bondage.

Well, Thomas understood that. Atonement needed to be more difficult than a pass-or-fail exam. Jakka wanted to atone for a lifetime as a plantation overseer. Her orders had gotten slave families torn apart on a regular basis. Her casual whims had led to people's deaths.

Thomas himself was still atoning for his three months as a Yellow Rank.

He had no idea when he would be forgiven. It might be when Cherise decided to risk talking to him again.

And if that turned out to be never?

Hadn't he already made amends for his misdeeds? And was Cherise entirely blameless, having left him to die in that Alashani dungeon pit?

Thomas shut down that line of thought. He was one of the most powerful individuals in the known universe. If he let himself feel victimized, that would make him angry and vengeful. That volatile mixture usually led to self-deception. For someone with Thomas's power, that was an easy slide to evil.

The Conqueror absolutely needed to hold himself accountable and avoid blaming others. He needed self-critique the same way Ariock did—and for the same reasons. Otherwise he might well become the monster feared by Evenjos and Migyatel and anyone sane.

If Cherise figured out her own reasons to do penance, well, good. It had nothing to do with him. Penance was a personal thing.

Thomas refocused on the present. He had nineteen more life histories to absorb, assimilate, and judge. He braced himself and dived into the next one.

And the next.

The worst was the thirteenth. By the time Thomas worked his way that far along the row, he had full confidence in Kessa's selection process, so he expected a softhearted person who was full of regrets for her Torth deeds.

But she was different.

The thirteenth was a teenage girl roughly the same age as Cherise. She had long, lush black hair. Somehow, her dark beauty augmented her glare of defiance.

*Is it not enough that you conquer Us?* the girl thought when he entered her range. *Must you also defile (rape) Our minds?*

Thomas hesitated. He wanted to get this job over with and move onto the next penitent in line. But after that accusation . . . how could he blithely sift through her deepest secrets and forbidden desires?

The girl was correct. Whenever he absorbed somebody's life history, he was violating them in a grossly intimate way.

It was easy to justify. It was easy to do. But still. He knew it was wrong.

The girl watched him, emanating defiance and vulnerability and . . .

Ugh. Sex appeal.

Thomas turned away. His arousal was wrong on every level: morally, ethically, socially. He absolutely could not be turned on.

Math equations. He forced himself to focus on mathematics.

The girl offered her identity. *I am the Pink Screwdriver.* Her salutation glowed on the periphery of his awareness, too appealing to ignore.

Thomas wondered if she had just made up that identity. Did she think it might hook his interest?

No, that was unlikely. A former Torth, unfamiliar with emotions or sex, could not have much idea about methods of seduction.

*The Majority named Me.* The Pink Screwdriver shared her Adulthood ceremony with Thomas.

Pink, because she was as bubbly and light as the sugary, fizzy pink beverages that children liked. And her method of digging for information was akin to turning screws, pestering adults with questions from every angle until they finally yielded the answers she sought.

The Pink Screwdriver had not yet chosen a spoken name. She didn't want a slave name.

*I know why I am here.* The Pink Screwdriver stood defiant in her chains, at eye level with Thomas in his hoverchair. *Kessa the Wise selected Me as a penitent with potential for conversion to your (loser) side of the war.*

Her attitude implied that Kessa's endeavor was stupid.

The Pink Screwdriver glared at Thomas with iridescent-yellow eyes, silently blaming him for her predicament and for the sorry state of galactic civilization. She blamed him for the war.

*So you think the Torth Empire should have been left to continue its course?* Thomas silently inquired.

The Pink Screwdriver broke eye contact. She radiated uncertainty.

Thomas gleaned that this young woman had begun to reevaluate her core convictions ever since she was forced to endure degradations. She now understood—on a subconscious level, at least—that slavery was problematic. She could no longer embrace the Torth way of life without question.

*I am not sure*, she silently admitted. *I cannot determine which side is right and which side is wrong.*

Thomas accepted that. It was a step in the right direction, away from the Torth.

*But . . .* Her resolve solidified. *I am sure of what I can withstand, and I absolutely cannot be a slave. Not long term.* She bared her neck, showing the slave collar that glowed with dim white light. *Kill Me.*

Thomas recoiled.

*I want you to kill Me*, the Pink Screwdriver invited. It was partially a plea, and partially a stab of rage. *Come on, Conqueror. It is very easy for you. Give Me a pain seizure. Or tell your minions to shoot Me.*

She fanned out scenarios, showing Thomas how he might oblige her. He could burn her alive. He could twist her mind and turn her into a brain-damaged zombie. He could kill her any number of ways.

*Kill Me (kill Me) kill Me*, she demanded in an agony of anticipation.

Thomas nearly fled out of her range.

Instead, he firmed up his own resolve and met her challenging stare. He certainly wasn't going to commit murder on demand.

If this teenager, this Pink Screwdriver, truly wished to die, then she could have gotten herself killed in any number of ways. Penitents died all the time. Some of them died in work accidents. If a penitent tried to harm someone—even another penitent—they would be shot and killed. All they had to do was disobey one of Kessa's laws.

So why had she waited?

Why had she acted docile, working her way into the good graces of Kessa's lieutenants, until she was hand-selected to meet the Conqueror up close?

Was she a spy?

*I am not acting at the behest of the Majority.* The Pink Screwdriver curled her upper lip in disgust at his misguided guess. *I want you (Conqueror) to face what you have wrought. I want you to see Me.*

She gestured at her body, which he really wanted to avoid looking at. Gaps in her rag-like clothing revealed tantalizing feminine curves. She was frustratingly beautiful.

*Behold*, she thought. *Behold a slave that you have made!*

It seemed her rags were the point.

*If you believe slavery is wrong*, the Pink Screwdriver went on, *then why do you tolerate shackles around My ankles and a collar around My neck? I would rather die!*

Ah. This was a protest.

Thomas acknowledged her complaint. The Pink Screwdriver thought she was entitled to freedom.

But had she learned the value of freedom? Did she wonder if all the slaves owned by Torth were entitled to freedom as much as she was?

Did she consider freedom to be a universal cause worth fighting for?

*You can earn freedom,* Thomas reminded the Pink Screwdriver. *That was, after all, why she was here.* Anyone who legitimately joins Me (in fighting for universal freedom) will have their collars and shackles removed. That could be you.

He did not delve into her childhood memories or her dearest values. Instead, he held her gaze.

And he wondered if he could trust her without ripping open her core self.

The Pink Screwdriver looked away, blinking back tears. Thomas sensed that she did, indeed, want to earn freedom rather than be given it. But she grappled with doubts that she, or any former Torth, could truly earn it.

She wanted to trust the gigantic, towering mind who held her and half a billion other mind readers in captivity. She wanted someone so competent to be right.

She wanted the Upward Governess to have sided with him because that was the smartest and wisest and right choice—not only on a personal level, but for the entire Torth Empire.

She wanted to get to know *(Thomas)* the Conqueror up close.

She eyed Thomas's straightened limbs, no longer frail or underdeveloped. Thomas sensed how much she wanted to touch his skin, to see how that sort of touching felt.

"Trustworthy," Thomas announced, struggling to hide the hoarse edge in his voice. "She hasn't chosen a name yet, but she's trustworthy."

Kessa raised her brow ridges, implying that she wanted an explanation for the lack of a spoken name.

"I vouch for her," Thomas said.

Kessa nodded to the nearby soldiers, and they ushered the Pink Screwdriver out of the assembly hall.

As the teenager left, she cast one more anxious look over her shoulder. Thomas sensed her departing thoughts. She wondered if she would see him again.

Thomas swallowed an odd tightness in his throat.

He made a mental note to learn who oversaw the Pink Screwdriver and where she slept at night.

Not that he needed to find her again. Why should he care where she got assigned? It wasn't like he intended to compel a penitent to visit his bedchamber. Of course not! That would negate all the good things he was trying to accomplish. It would be sexual exploitation. That sort of power-tripping relationship would throw all his motives and schemes into question.

Thomas firmly banished the Pink Screwdriver from his thoughts.

And never mind his dreams. He had lurid dreams about Cherise, and he suspected the Pink Screwdriver might make an appearance tonight, but so what?

Whatever.

Thomas threw his focus into absorbing the next bunch of penitents' life histories. He would absolutely not give Garrett, or Kessa, or anyone any excuse to doubt his moral rectitude.

# CHAPTER 3

# FOR ALL HUMANKIND

"Do you still hate Thomas?" Vy struggled to pick her words with sensitivity.

Cherise's voice was quiet as they walked past alien dignitaries in the war palace. "Not really."

"Not really?" Vy shot her foster sister an annoyed look. No one wanted to talk about the fact that Thomas was a war hero. He had taken over forty minds in a dangerous situation. He was as good as any warrior. Better, really. And he couldn't even walk. "Didn't he save your classroom full of students?"

"Yeah," Cherise admitted. "He's powerful. He does good deeds. But also . . ." She shivered. "I can't ignore what he does to people's minds."

Vy rolled her eyes. It wasn't like Thomas zombified innocent children. He only did it to the worst Torth military ranks.

All the same, she did wonder if Cherise had a point.

*"The zombies are gruesome,"* Ariock had admitted to Vy when he was in private with her. *"And we're too reliant on them. Thomas is going to hit a limit at some point. I'm already having to give him power boosts."*

Thomas mind-twisted hundreds of prisoners every day now, boosted by Ariock's power. The zombies softened up entire cities for conquest.

And yes, Vy did wonder what that was doing to his psychology.

But what better options were there? The Torth Empire needed to stay wary. Otherwise they would attack on multiple fronts. They would attack Earth.

Vy led Cherise around a corner, toward the meeting chamber that was their destination. She was shocked to see zombies in the hallway.

Cherise jerked to a halt.

"What the hell?" Vy said.

A dozen zombies stood in front of the double doors. They smelled foul.

"Come in!" Garrett's gruff voice called from the chamber. "The zombies are mine. I figured, why not?"

As if living beings were toys.

The zombies shuffled aside at a silent command. They failed to blink enough. Those blank white ocular implants only enhanced their unnerving stares.

Vy knew, from conversations with Ariock, that Garrett hadn't taken well to being defeated and inhibited for three days. He was more insecure than ever. Now that the pink gas was an obstacle, Jinishta had finally granted Garrett permission to protect himself in whatever ways he saw fit.

"They won't hurt you," Garrett called. "They're just a precaution. We have a lot of military targets sitting in this room."

Vy sneaked past the zombies. Deep down, she admitted that they were creepy. There wasn't much difference between a brainless stare and a holier-than-thou

Torth stare. These creatures looked like Servants of All dressed in shabby uniforms instead of gleaming white armor.

"Is this really a meeting about Earth?" Cherise hurried to catch up.

Ariock's deep voice rumbled. "It is."

Vy and Cherise entered a large, airy chamber. Daylight streamed through tall, angular windows. Sea glass was reflective enough to deter ghosting clairvoyants. The war palace now featured a lot of reflective glass, as well as burnished bronze and granite or marble polished to a sheen. No one could teleport directly inside. Ariock tended to enter from his balcony.

He sat at the head of the conference table, dominating it. To his left sat Garrett. Thomas floated on his right.

The chamber was otherwise empty.

"This concerns you." Thomas gazed at Cherise. "I promise."

Judging by Cherise's face, she was on the verge of striding away. Her fiery amber eyes made for a striking contrast with the peacock-blue ends of her hair.

"Come on." Vy gently touched Cherise's arm. She had no idea what this meeting was about, either, but Ariock was the one who had scheduled it. She trusted that he had good intentions. "If it's about Earth, we need to be here."

Cherise looked reluctant, but she walked to the huge conference table and sat at the far end with stiff dignity. She was apparently not going to risk having her mind read.

Vy took a seat between her foster siblings.

Sometimes she wanted to kick out her prosthetic leg and yell at Cherise, *"See? He's not a bad person!"* Thanks to Thomas, she could walk and run with more athleticism than ever. It was almost as if her leg had never been amputated.

"Thank you for coming to this meeting." Ariock offered Vy and Cherise each a kind look.

"All right." Garrett gestured to the double doors, which obligingly swung shut and clicked into place, sealing them in privacy. "We've tabled this matter long enough."

Ariock held up one huge hand. "I'll lead this."

That stopped Garrett from saying whatever he had been about to say. Vy was glad. The old man had a way of stirring up animosity. He just wasn't the leader Ariock was.

Ariock let his hand fall on the table. "I've asked the five of us here," he said, "so we can decide the fate of humankind."

Well. That was dramatic.

"We want to decide whether or not to involve humankind in the war," Thomas clarified.

Cherise's eyebrows shot up.

"You mean, like . . ." Vy tried to imagine it. "You want to add human fighter pilots to our fleets?"

"That would be one benefit," Thomas said. "I envision the benefits going both ways."

Cherise stared around the table. She took in Garrett, Ariock, Thomas, and Vy.

After a moment, she spoke. "You're saying that you want us . . . me included . . . to make a huge, future-altering decision for billions of people?"

Ariock looked guilty. "Yup. Pretty much."

Vy supposed he was getting used to making such decisions himself. He was the de facto ruler of three planets and more than ten billion people. He had enormous decisions to make every day, from appointing military mayors to prioritizing garrisons. Earth might just be one more concern upon a heap of concerns to him.

"Shouldn't this be a decision for only humans to make?" Cherise shot a pointed glare toward the mind readers.

"I know I'm not qualified." Ariock hunched, looking ashamed. "If you don't think I deserve input into this decision, I'll completely understand. I can stay out of it."

Cherise's accusing attitude turned quizzical.

Vy knew all about Ariock's hidden insecurities. "Of course you're human!" she assured him.

Ariock looked unconvinced. "Genetically, sort of. But most of what I know about humanity comes from TV." He indicated the mind readers. "Thomas and Garrett have had human families, and they've soaked up human minds. I trust them to know humanity better than me."

Cherise looked like she wanted to argue.

"We all have reasons to care about the fate of humankind." Garrett's gesture included everyone at the table. "All five of us. That's why we're making the decision together."

"The definition of human should be for people who biologically originate from the planet Earth," Cherise dared to say.

Garrett folded his arms and raised one finger, like a flag. "Born and raised."

"Same," Thomas said.

Cherise pushed back her chair and stood.

"Humans," she said, as clearly as if she was teaching a classroom full of students, "don't automatically assume that their species is superior or inferior to everyone else in the universe." She gave Thomas a defiant glare. "To a human, Earth isn't a piece on a chessboard." Her gaze shifted from Thomas to Ariock to Garrett. "A human won't treat this decision like a checklist item that needs to be checked off."

They all stared at her. Inwardly, Vy applauded. Cherise had made some good points.

"Look here." Garrett unfolded his arms and planted his fists on the table. He stared defiantly at Cherise. "I am painfully aware of my heritage. But I spent most of my life on Earth, and I have a lot of fond memories of my family. My *human* family," he emphasized. "And my *human* wife. You don't think I care about the fate of Earth? That's your mistake."

He sounded so passionately offended, Cherise looked away.

Her accusing gaze landed on Thomas.

"Earth saved my life." Thomas said it with casual simplicity.

Vy wondered if he felt grateful for getting bounced through numerous group homes. His early experiences in foster care were enough to turn anyone cynical.

"And," Thomas relented, "I'm trying to get more in touch with the human side of my genetics."

Cherise looked pained by her own suspicions.

Vy understood the doubt. Thomas had never shown much interest in acting human. He had been emotionally distant even when they'd lived together in the Hollander home.

But maybe that was the old Thomas? He was so different in a myriad of ways.

He even looked different. On top of his healthy physique, he was a bit lankier. Taller? He was definitely beginning to look more like a teenager than a child.

"I value knowledge," Thomas said. "And Earth has a lot of it."

"Okay." Cherise took her seat at the table. "You can justify your presence here any way you want. I'll stay and vote." She glared at the mind readers. "I'm not going to let their input go unchallenged."

"This is just a discussion," Ariock said with forbearance.

This sounded more momentous than a mere discussion, Vy thought. It was a decision.

A terrifyingly huge decision.

"I guess I'll start." Vy wondered if she could appease everyone at the table. "On the one hand, I'm really worried for my mom and everyone back home. I hate that Earth is under this constant threat."

Everyone was nodding.

"But on the other hand . . ." Vy grimaced, imagining human-alien conflicts. "I think that, in general, adding humans to the mix would cause more problems than it solves."

"Yup," Garrett said.

Thomas and Cherise both stared at Vy as if she had gone insane.

Vy stared back. Didn't they remember what humanity was like? Tribalism. Bigotry. Racially motivated genocides. Surely they must understand what she was talking about?

"Our species doesn't have the best track record," Vy explained, urging everyone to take reality into account. "Even if a lot of ummins and nussians are welcoming"— and she had her doubts about that—"our species is bound to focus on the fact that everyone in Freedomland looks like weird aliens."

"Exactly," Garrett said. "Humans have all kinds of nutty ideas, and plus, they look like Torth. That's just a bad combination."

"Right." Vy huddled inward, somewhat ashamed of her species. "I just don't think humans are ready for the rest of the universe."

Ariock gave her a gracious nod.

Cherise, to Vy's surprise, gave her a critical head shake. "Do you think all of humanity is like the worst bullies in high school?"

"I mean . . ." Vy wanted time to reconsider.

"Humanity," Cherise said, "values artwork that captures emotional beauty and nuance. Humans make music and movies and things that express emotion." She stood, planting her hands on the table. "They're not Torth. Some humans are awful, yes, but on the whole, they're like ummins or govki. They're not useless leeches who create nothing and who pretend to be benevolent rulers while their uncaring greed kills those they rule."

Vy was speechless. She had not considered the way humanity looked from Cherise's point of view.

"When I escaped my mother," Cherise said, "I had no voice. But I found other ways to communicate." She made sketching motions. "It will take time for humans to learn the slave language and to learn how to integrate with the rest of the universe. But we can connect instantly through the arts."

"Exactly." Thomas sounded excited. That was so unusual, everyone looked at him.

Thomas went on in a more restrained tone. "You've all seen what an outsized influence the Alashani have on the culture here. Imagine what an impact humankind would make?"

Former slaves did tend to emulate Alashani culture. Vy had figured it was because they wanted to learn what freedom entailed. Maybe they were starving for new knowledge and new ways of doing things?

The Alashani, on the other hand, tended to cling to the past. They wanted to preserve the fragments of their civilization that had survived.

Cherise was staring across the table at Thomas. Not with enmity or exasperation, but something new. She searched his face.

"People are curious about humans," Thomas said. "Thanks to Cherise and her classes."

True. Vy sometimes overheard aliens talking about art or music she recognized.

"They see humans in leadership positions." Thomas indicated Ariock. "So they want to learn more about those people. They're primed to welcome humans."

Vy felt strangely off-kilter, as if Thomas and Cherise were unexpectedly attacking reality.

Did people really want humans around? Vy didn't think so. Some people believed Earth was a heavenly paradise full of angels, sure. But lots of people suspected that humans were just an offshoot of the Torth species.

Vy heard all kinds of wacky misconceptions about humans. Some people believed Earth was another version of the Alashani underground, except with evil technology and a nascent version of the Megacosm.

"I agree that it would be nice to help humanity prepare to defend itself." Vy folded her arms, shielding herself. "But you're talking about a really volatile situation. We might end up with a civil war on top of everything else."

"We've already got the makings of that," Thomas said.

Vy gave him a sharp, questioning look.

"Just . . ." Thomas spread his hands. "Former Torth and former slaves don't like each other."

Everyone knew that. Vy nodded and said, "Then let's not add a bunch of cocksure humans to the mix."

Cherise remained standing. She gave Vy a pained look. "Can you look at this from humankind's point of view instead of just from Ariock's perspective?"

Vy gaped, offended.

"If we leave Earth out of this war," Cherise said, "we put humankind at a huge disadvantage. Forever."

"That's exactly it." Thomas sat up straighter. "The free people on our side are learning the latest in Torth technology. They've already had millennia in which to learn how to speak a universal language, the slave tongue. Humanity is excluded from those advantages."

Cherise nodded in agreement. "People move forward with a shared culture. You'll be relegating humankind to the dustbin of history. They'll be permanently backward, culturally and socially."

"Eh." Garrett tipped his chair back, so he could thump his boots on the tabletop, one on top of the other. "We have enough to deal with without adding blundering human bumpkins to the mix."

Vy felt like a traitor to Cherise and Thomas, but she inwardly agreed with Garrett. Earth was a Pandora's box. It was best to leave that box locked for as long as possible.

"If we're having a vote," Thomas said, "then I say that humans deserve to be informed." He rapped his knuckles lightly on the tabletop. "I vote for integration."

Cherise looked as if she had swallowed something bitter. She stared at Thomas, but she nodded in solidarity. "I vote for integration."

"I'm against it," Garrett said.

"What do you think, Vy?" Ariock gave her an encouraging look.

Vy hated to betray her foster siblings, but she was worried about the safety of her mother and friends on Earth. "No," she said. "Let's protect Earth from afar, like we've been doing."

Ariock had to be the tiebreaker.

Everyone looked toward him, expectant.

"If we bring Earth into this war," Ariock said with heavy reluctance, "then we would be obligated to defend it. And I'm struggling to defend three planets as it is."

"Your thinking is too small-scale," Thomas said. "We want to win the whole galaxy, not just a handful of planets."

"Eventually," Ariock agreed. "But for right now? Our people have enough to police without the added strain of human-alien relationships."

He looked across the table toward Vy, and she saw that he understood her misgivings. Of course he did. They used to watch the same TV shows.

"I hate to bring this up," Thomas said. "But I personally believe Earth is fated to become a battlefront whether we like it or not, whether they know about us or not."

Everyone looked at him, questioning.

"Humankind," Thomas said, "has a monopoly over a precious natural resource that no other population has."

Vy tried to imagine what he was talking about. She was pretty sure that her home planet was a worthless backwater.

"No one else has figured it out yet." Thomas directed his explanation toward Ariock, almost as if challenging him. "Although the Alashani are starting to put two and two together. They're talking about hybrids."

Cherise gasped.

Vy wondered if she had heard Thomas correctly. "What do you mean? Hybrid Torth?"

"Hybrid Yeresunsa." Thomas turned to her. "Some of the more astute Alashani are whispering that human genetics are a power augmenter. And they are correct." He gestured toward Ariock. "There's proof right there."

Ariock turned red. He avoided looking at Vy.

He might as well have ravished her with his purple gaze. Neither of them had spoken of the possibility of raising a family, but this was an unspoken wrench.

Or a catalyst.

Or something.

"Yeah, yeah," Garrett said in a bland tone. "There have been human hybrids among the Torth, as well." Including his family. "A lot of Torth suspect human genes are an augmentation factor. After the war, if they win, they'll probably sanction any Rosy or Servant who wants to try crossbreeding with humans."

The implications made Vy want to shrivel up and hide.

Servants of All and Rosy Recruits were going to want to use her, and other humans, as breeding stock.

And they could teleport.

Some might already be self-exiled on Earth, trying to impregnate humans.

"Anyway." Thomas cleared his throat. "I'm just saying, Earth is more than a wilderness preserve the way Torth leadership always pretended it was. Humankind may become a vitally important asset."

Trust Thomas to sound clinical about the possibility of human-hybrid breeding farms all over the place.

"Well." Cherise slumped down in her chair. "That's just great."

"As far as I'm concerned," Garrett said, "this is a solid point *against* integration. Remember, we have an Alashani population who fear extinction."

Albino matchmakers were everywhere, scheming to bring certain families together in order to raise a new generation of war heroes. The Alashani were desperate to rebuild their numbers. If they learned that human genetics could augment their warrior population . . .

Vy nodded fiercely. "Don't tell anyone."

"Why not allow them to mingle?" Thomas asked.

"Oh, come on," Garrett said. "Human genetics are, like, a golden ticket. Can you imagine all the rape and coercion that will go on?"

Garrett made that cruel assumption, but Vy recalled that he had not coerced his human wife. He had loved her.

She tried not to be obvious about reassessing Ariock. If he impregnated her—and was sex even physically possible for them? She had yet to find out—any children they had together were likely to be ludicrously powerful. They would be legit demigods.

Was Vy prepared to mother a demigod?

She reminded herself that her window of physical compatibility with Ariock might be very limited or nonexistent. Surely children were beyond the realm of possibility for them.

The other day, she had measured Ariock for new custom-tailored clothes. She had climbed a stepladder so she could reach his outstretched arms while he was standing. It was a good thing he had not shown the slightest curiosity about his measurements, because then she would have felt obligated to inform him that he had grown quite a lot since the last time he had been measured.

He was nearly ten feet tall.

*It doesn't matter*, Vy had kept telling herself. *It's just a number. It's meaningless.*

"It might go the other way," Thomas said, beyond Vy's range and oblivious to her thoughts. "Humans might just attempt to seduce Alashani warriors. The warriors are in much shorter supply."

Garrett huffed. "Can't we just leave the whole issue alone? Let's allow Earth to remain the idyllic paradise it's been for the last twenty thousand years. It's a beautiful place. I'd rather not corrupt it."

"That's wishful thinking," Thomas said with an edge to his tone. "You and Ariock have proven to the galaxy at large that hybrids are a force to be reckoned with."

"You're a counterpoint to that," Garrett said. "You only have the raw strength of an average Rosy or Servant, despite being a human hybrid."

"But he has powers no Torth has," Ariock said.

"Powers no Torth has awakened," Garrett corrected. "Yet."

Cherise stood again. "Regardless, everyone is getting interested in humans. We have a moral obligation to tell humanity what's coming."

Vy gazed at her hands, so like her mother's hands.

Her mother was blissfully unaware of the Torth Empire. Ignorance was, perhaps, the only thing keeping her safe. Didn't Cherise comprehend that?

"If we show interest," Vy said, "aren't we just inviting the Torth to get interested?"

"Knowledge is always better than ignorance." Cherise's amber eyes were intense. "Knowledge is worth pain."

Everyone knew that slave proverb. Vy swallowed. She felt small.

"I was left in the dark for most of my childhood." Cherise sounded passionate. "I wasn't allowed to speak and no one spoke to me. So I didn't know that freedom was even possible. But if I had known I had a choice? I would have taken it."

Vy could hardly meet Cherise's eyes. Maybe she should reconsider her vote.

"Please?" Cherise's voice trembled. "Let's give humans the freedom, and the dignity, of having a choice?"

Thomas nodded.

Even Garrett looked as if he was reconsidering.

Everyone turned to the big guy.

Ariock looked as if the weight of a galaxy was draped over his shoulders. He leaned on the table, huge hands clasped, brow furrowed.

He clearly did not want to be the deciding vote. He had arranged this meeting, but he had tried to outsource the decision to trusted friends. Ariock made gigantic life-or-death decisions every day. Did he have to take this on as well?

"Why don't we postpone it?" Vy asked everyone at the table. "We can decide at a later date."

"Postponing this decision *is* a decision," Thomas said testily.

Ariock offered Thomas and Cherise both a look of apology. "It doesn't seem like a crucial emergency right now." He glanced at his supercom wristwatch and showed them a scrolling list of alerts. "In the time we've been talking, two cities were raided. I have places I need to be."

Thomas and Cherise wore nearly identical looks of crushed disappointment.

"If someone had told me about my powers when I was a child," Ariock said gently, speaking to Cherise, "I could have saved my father's life. And my mother. Knowledge is always worth pain. I understand that."

Garrett hid a look of guilt. He had purposely kept his family in the dark. That had led to their deaths.

"So I agree that Earth needs to be told," Ariock said. "Eventually."

But not yet.

"So you vote no?" Garrett sounded relieved.

"For now." Ariock looked anguished about it. "Only because I don't feel like I can do justice to defending them, and I don't want to draw too much attention their way. If the Torth start attacking them? Then of course we'll reveal ourselves and give humankind every means to defend themselves."

Cherise stood, ready to leave. She did not look entirely dissatisfied.

"I want human representatives on the war council, though," Ariock said. "We should have made that official a long time ago. Cherise?"

Cherise looked at him, startled.

"And Vy," Ariock said. "Would you be willing to take on that duty?"

The responsibility sounded so enormous as to be mythical. It seemed unreal. Vy sat there, stunned.

"I guess we're the only possible candidates," Cherise said. But she sounded thoughtful rather than bitter.

"Yes." Vy tried to imagine herself being addressed with the honorific of "Councilor."

"Thank you." Cherise seemed to appreciate being included.

After the others had left, Vy remained in the meeting chamber with Ariock. She put her arms around his huge shoulders, leaning into his thick neck.

Her mother seemed so far away.

Elaine Hollander must believe her daughter was dead. Meanwhile, Ariock had just casually entrusted that daughter with acting as a voice for billions of strangers on Earth.

An alert chimed. Ariock sat up, preparing to teleport away.

"I'll see you tonight." Vy stood on tiptoes and kissed him.

She felt the burden of this responsibility. But she also understood that it was a sliver of what he coped with all the time.

# CHAPTER 4
# BLACK AND WHITE

Flen hated his job.

For him, the worst part wasn't the blood-soaked gore. He rather enjoyed monster slaying—when he got to slay them. That was almost never.

He missed the days before everyone had to wear airtight armor into battle zones. He had been good at identifying Torth who acted a little too confident or a little too ruthless. It had been fun to sneak up behind a busy Torth and use his telekinetic powers to hurl spears ultrafast, impaling the monster.

Now?

Flen waited in a square formation with other exhausted war heroes who were near depletion, like himself. A few of his companions joked and chatted, but their chitchat sounded stale. What was there to talk about? Every day was the same routine. They used their powers to drag corpses and torn limbs into garbage chutes. They scrubbed blood off floors.

They were garbage haulers.

Healers were the only Yeresunsa who did anything useful anymore. There were more injuries than ever as Torth raiders grew bolder. But Flen and his fellow warriors were no longer risked in battle. Nor were they permitted to retire, or to do as they pleased. No. Premier Jinishta wanted them to work like common laborers.

"You all right, Flen?" A stout warrior cheerfully patted Flen's armored back.

"Sure." Flen tried to inflate that word with empty-headed agreeableness.

He hated work that had nothing to do with combat. He hated propaganda and lies. He hated clouds and weather.

The armored figure of Ariock appeared in the overcast sky with a crack of thunder, and the warriors stopped jostling and went still.

Flen braced himself. He especially hated the magic of teleportation, which he had no control over. It made him feel so helpless.

*Buh-buh-BOOM.*

His ears popped. The scent of ozone filled the air. His sense of gravity and balance shifted, and thunder rolled, spreading away from the teleportation flats.

The sky and the scents were different. The air was more humid. If Flen hadn't been ready for this twice-daily procedure, he would have fallen to his knees.

"I love how easily the messiah teleports us every day." The stout warrior beamed. "We are so blessed to be part of his army."

Right.

Flen regained his balance, although he kept his face downturned. The last thing he needed was for a messiah worshipper to glimpse his seething resentment.

He found it incredible that anyone could still believe in the messiah. Really. Whose fault was the apocalypse in the first place?

The alleged messiah had caused it.

That same messiah had ruthlessly picked Flen up and slammed him against a pillar, causing him to lose control of his bladder in front of everyone. Why? For the sake of that despicable little *rekveh*. Flen had refused to deliver a case full of dubious medicine to the *rekveh*, and apparently, that was enough for the supposed messiah to lose his temper and act like a brute.

The square formation broke apart, and Flen followed his fellow garbage-hauler warriors toward the various gates of Freedomland.

Ariock was already gone. The alleged messiah hardly ever spoke to the lowly war heroes who did most of his cleanup work. No doubt he was running yet another errand for the mastermind *rekveh* who was really in charge.

Anyone who believed in freedom was a fool.

Wide streets funneled through the upper city, lined with merchants' displays that were meant to catch the attention of soldiers on their way home to loved ones. Flen paused at a kiosk of decorative pottery. He recognized Cherise's stylistic templates painted on bowls and plates. Vines. Flowers. Winged animals, which she called birds. And, when she was in the right mood, mushrooms and other forms of fungi.

She was amazing.

Other artists tried to imitate her style, but they never got it quite right. Flen received compliments meant for her all the time. Warriors received a decent income of war credits, but Cherise's commissions actually earned a lot more than Flen's income. He didn't understand why she gave so much to charities. She could have bought a palace.

At least she really seemed to value Flen's courtship gifts.

Might she appreciate that little decanter, painted with human runes? Maybe it spelled a word in her native language?

As Flen considered the gift, he wondered why he was bothering. His shoulders slumped. Cherise had a lot of wonderful qualities, but she was also frustratingly inscrutable. And she resisted making good choices.

Why wasn't she eager to become a mother?

Why did she want to put off their marriage ceremony?

Could she be persuaded to care about raising children with Alashani values, in an Alashani way?

Flen had made his peace with the concept of fathering children who looked like humans. If their skin was the color of hearth-warmed sandstones? That was okay. They would thrive in daylight better than he could. They would look ethereal, like Cherise. That was good. But . . .

Would other free people mistake them for *rekvehs* and treat them like penitent slaves?

Would they be at the mercy of anyone who wished to hurt them?

Flen kicked at a pebble.

For all he knew, Cherise was unfit to be a mother anyway. She seemed far too obsessed with teaching pointless things to aliens.

For all he knew, Torth might invade Freedomland again and slaughter everyone.

How could he protect a wife, or a family, when he was restricted from combat? Not even the alleged messiah could defend all the territory they had liberated. No one dared enter zones where inhibitor gas might be lurking. It had been weeks since their last victory over a Torth-ruled city.

"Flen, my man!"

He turned at the familiar voice. He could hardly believe it. "Haz?"

"Indeed!" Haz hurried over, outfitted in the same black armor as Flen. "They finally gave me a reprieve from garrison duty in Tempest Arena. It's too unsafe for warriors on Nuss these days."

Haz looked as depleted as Flen felt.

"I'm sorry about Koresh," Haz said. "I heard that he died during the pink blitz."

Koresh had been among their cadre from Hufti, a peer with whom they had grown up sparring. He had entered a pink gas zone, lost his powers, and then a Rosy Torth had used her powers from afar to slam him against a wall.

Just like that, Koresh no longer existed. He would never have children. His future was gone.

"I saw it happen," Flen said.

Haz winced. "Sorry. Were you able to attend his funeral procession?"

"I would have," Flen said stiffly. "But I was on garbage duty in AllLogic MetroHub at the time."

"Ah." Haz looked embarrassed, perhaps on behalf of Jinishta. He must remember the way she used to be. She had once been a fearless leader instead of a pushover who obeyed commands from the war council.

"Well," Haz said, "I lit extra candles in his memory. I know you would have done so."

Flen wondered how many close friends and family members Haz had lost. Didn't he still have his parents?

As for Jinishta, her parents and siblings were all alive and well. Was it any wonder she acted invincible? Some people had all the luck.

"Well, hey." Haz gave Flen a playful punch, making their armor thunk. "I heard you're in line for a promotion, my good friend. A whole bunch of councilors are urging Jinishta to make you a junior premier on the war council."

Flen would have felt proud and honored, if this were the lamplit underground.

But this was the sunny aboveground. Flen was unsure whom to trust, or who wanted him elected. They might be his compatriots. Then again . . . if Flen had to attend council sessions, he would need to take pains to avoid both of the *rekvehs*, Thomas and Garrett. This might be a machination by Thomas. He might want Flen under close surveillance.

"I am honored," Flen lied.

"Let me buy you a meal." Haz pointed to a rooftop restaurant. "It's been too long since we've seen each other. Who knows what the future will be?"

Warriors died far too often.

Flen was gratified to see that the restaurant featured a sign framed by stalactites and stalagmites. That implied an Alashani business.

"That sounds nice," Flen said.

They took the stairs, and a beaming albino woman gave them a private balcony where they could take in the breeze with a view of the street below. She served them slow-cooked meats thickened with mushroom milk. All Alashani knew what purple mantles on black armor meant, and the waitress seemed overawed, giggling shyly at Haz and Flen in turn.

Neither of them spoke until the flustered waitress had disappeared inside, leaving them in peace.

"So." Haz asked as they enjoyed their meals. "Were you shopping for Cherise?"

"Guilty," Flen admitted.

"I am a little envious." Haz sounded lighthearted, as always, but then he reconsidered his words and said, "No. I am a lot envious."

Flen laughed, grateful for his friend's good-natured honesty. "You'll find someone," he assured Haz. "I am sure."

"Oh, I already have." Haz sounded surprised. "I wasn't talking about romance. Romance is easy." He scooped up the last of his stew. "I am talking about *who* you have. Of course."

Flen raised an eyebrow, inviting more commentary.

"I mean," Haz said, "she gives you a head start on everyone else."

Haz's mind seemed to be wandering through a mysterious place where Flen could not follow. "What do you mean?" he asked.

Haz gazed outward at the street, but his bitter look seemed directed inward. "We're changing, Flen. And it will get worse. Our people are going to become humans."

Haz seemed to expect an understanding, but Flen shook his head, mystified.

Was Haz hinting that he disapproved of the war? Perhaps he had finally gained the same perspective as Flen. Perhaps he, too, did not like seeing Alashani culture watered down and devalued.

"Every warrior is soon going to want a human wife or husband." Haz raised his mug, as if to give Flen a bitter toast. "They'll all want what you have. Including me."

All Flen could do was stare, perplexed. Haz seemed to be referencing a conversation Flen had missed out on.

"Oh. Oh no." Haz saw his confusion. "You don't know about hybrid strength?"

Flen wondered if he had misheard.

"I would have thought Cherise would know, at least." Haz looked embarrassed. "Sorry. I assumed everyone knew."

Flen's bafflement became annoyance. "What are you talking about?"

Cherise probably *did* know whatever it was. She had a data tablet that she kept hidden from Flen. Sometimes she played music from Earth, and she tried to hide that from him as well.

And now she sat on the war council, supposedly to represent her entire homeworld. She had been reluctant to tell Flen about that.

What other secrets was she hiding? Didn't she realize how disrespectful her constant secrecy was?

She had trust issues. It seemed to be a human flaw.

"Please, explain what you are talking about." Flen tried to make his expression inviting. "Cherise has not told me, but I haven't had much chance to catch up with her lately. She's always teaching or drawing. And I'm always . . . well." He didn't need to explain how often he depleted his powers in service to the alleged messiah. Haz also had to clean up bodies after the zombies took their toll.

"All right." Haz held his steaming mug. He hesitated, but he saw what the anticipation was doing to Flen, and he relented. "Humans augment powers."

Flen tried to process that. He wasn't sure it made any sense.

"Orla figured it out," Haz went on. "It's about lineage and families, as you would expect. I'm surprised no one figured it out sooner. It's obvious. Ariock has so much raw power because he has a lot of human lineage, mixed in with ours."

Flen had supposed that Ariock was a freak of nature, just a random fluke.

"Garrett is a mind reader," Haz went on, "powered up by Alashani heritage, then further amplified by humans. That is what created the messiah." Haz moved his mug, as if to demonstrate something. "A Yeresunsa." He threaded a linen napkin through the handle of the mug. "Plus a human." He opened his palms. "Equals a super-powerful Yeresunsa baby."

Flen stared at the implications.

"Humans are augmenters," Haz said. "Orla isn't sure about it, but she says it makes sense, if one accepts the premise that all humanoid species are cousins to each other. Alashani and Torth have Yeresunsa among their populations. So humans must have something, as well."

Flen narrowed his eyes. He had doubts about Alashani and Torth deriving from the same common ancestor. It sounded like propaganda. The war's leadership wanted Alashani to be kind to penitents, so they spouted whatever lies would accomplish that.

"And I think Earth will enter this war sooner or later," Haz went on. "Imagine how humans will change the Alashani population. There are a lot more of them than us."

"Wait." Flen felt as if his mind was running to catch up with the conclusion. "Are you saying that if I have children with Cherise . . . ?"

Haz nodded. "They will not be like you or me." His tone emphasized the conclusion. "They will be powerful."

Powerful.

Like Ariock.

"At least, that's Orla's theory." Haz sipped his brew, perhaps hiding his own doubts.

"Hmm." Flen sipped from his mug as well.

Could this be an elaborate piece of propaganda? Something meant to trick Alashani and humans into interbreeding?

After all, the *rekveh* Thomas required power boosts in order to zombify more than a hundred Torth in a row. His alleged human lineage had not made him super powerful. He was super smart, yes, and probably super evil, but he relied on minions to do the heavy lifting and the fighting for him.

But Thomas did not have the benefits of superior shani genetics. That was an indisputable fact.

And perhaps he was lying about being half human?

Flen turned the idea of hybrid strength over in his mind some more. What if Orla's theory was true? What if Cherise could bear Flen a child that was as powerful as the alleged messiah? In fact . . .

What if Flen's future child was the actual, real messiah?

Not a fraud, but the genuine savior?

Flen mentally reviewed the messianic prophecy, which he and all Alashani children were taught to memorize. "*He will leave with an army at his heels . . . You will know him by his great height and the wound on his shoulder . . . Mind readers shall grovel for his mercy . . ."*

As a whole, the prophecy seemed to be undeniably about Ariock.

But wasn't there room for doubt?

Most humans would seem to have great height compared to Alashani. And penitent Torth groveled for mercy from anyone, not just from Ariock.

*"Only he can lead you into light and restore you to your former glory . . ."*

A lot of idiots figured that was a reference to Freedomland. They said this city, and the other liberated cities, represented a return to the soaring glories of their ancestral past. After all, they walked in daylight now.

Flen figured they were making a colossal mistake.

*"Follow him or perish."*

The Alashani seemed to be perishing quite a lot, despite having obeyed the prophecy.

"Well," Haz said. "I wish you and Cherise much happiness." He bounced his eyebrows. "And may you be fruitful with children."

After they parted ways, Flen wandered the streets for a long time. His head churned with musings, misgivings, worries, and—for the first time since before the deaths of his family—hope.

The *rekveh* Thomas should not be in charge of the destiny of the Alashani civilization. That should be obvious to anyone.

A true messiah needed to be born.

An Alashani messiah.

Flen bought a golden hair net for Cherise. Maybe he would buy her extra gifts and offer to massage her shoulders every night.

She would look beautiful in bridal ornaments, reflecting the warm glow of wedding lanterns.

# CHAPTER 5

# DEALING WITH BEASTS

Unsuspecting zombies milled about the exercise yard. They might as well be livestock, although this bunch was in worse shape than the usual herds of sauropods and cave sheep. Thomas leaned on the fence and watched them.

A quiet, inner part of him felt guilty. He always instructed his zombified victims to take care of their own basic survival necessities, but that kept them usable for only a week. After that? They were likely to drop dead from pure exhaustion.

Constant alertness for commands took a toll. Zombies could not sleep and did not dream or even hallucinate. So after a week or so, they could not survive without intense care. Nobody was willing to donate a lot of care to brain-damaged enemies who had no chance of recovery or redemption.

One zombie ambled close.

Thomas sent overriding mental instructions to that one, silently ordering it to spread the instructions to the other penned-in zombies. He wanted them to emulate a fight-or-flight response to danger.

In other words, he wanted them to temporarily act like people.

Once Thomas was sure his mental instructions had made their way to most of the zombies, he sealed his mouth around two fingers in order to make a loud, piercing whistle.

Azhdarchidae came roaring out of the clouds.

The sky croc was much larger than when Thomas had first rescued him. His wingspan was the width of an ultralight aircraft. As he plummeted toward the zombies, he opened his huge crocodilian maw.

The zombies scattered. They were as empty-headed as scarecrows, but they ran as if they had free will.

If this was a real combat situation, Thomas would target the enemy commander. So in this training session, he hurled a fireball at a fast-moving male zombie. His fiery flare lasted only a few seconds, but it was enough.

Azhdarchidae ignored all the other targets, whether they were running or crawling or standing still. He rammed into Thomas's target at missile speed. Jaws meant for snatching alien fish out of the ocean broke the zombie's spine with a thick crunch.

Impressive.

But instead of swallowing the zombie, or dropping it from a high elevation, Azhdarchidae decided that a pen full of zombies was a good place to land. He alighted on a hill, spat the still-living zombie to the ground, and eyed Thomas with reptilian orange eyes. Apparently he was accustomed to tastier meat.

If that barely chewed victim was a functional Torth, he would still be able to send mental commands to other Torth. Not ideal.

"Kill." Thomas said it in a warm, approving tone.

His commands to Azhdarchidae were always in English. Very few people in Freedomland used that language, so the animal was unlikely to respond to someone's casual conversation by accident.

Azhdarchidae eviscerated the zombie.

Thomas watched the carnage with perverse pride. He knew he shouldn't derive satisfaction from watching a humanoid die in a violently gruesome way. But his sky croc needed combat training, and anyway, if Thomas did not use expired zombies for target practice, someone else would.

His sky croc knew better than to eat clothing and undigestible materials. He spat the remains out in a glistening, bloody lump.

The Earth version of Thomas might have vomited upon witnessing such visceral brutality.

But the Earth version of Thomas was buried inside a Torth version.

And that was buried inside a Yeresunsa version.

And that was encapsulated inside an able-bodied version who stood in an exosuit.

Over all of that? A nearly endless patchwork of life experiences cloaked Thomas, serving as a constant reminder that he was an amalgamation.

Thomas used to be a child. But that might as well be ancient history. It no longer seemed relevant. Or real.

Azhdarchidae raised his head, saw-toothed grin dripping blood. How could Thomas ignore that look of innocent expectation? The sky croc had obediently tracked Thomas on command, and then he had obeyed Thomas's ultraloud whistle summon. He sure deserved a treat.

"All right, you big turkey." Thomas used his powers to toast the edible innards of the corpse.

Azhdarchidae waited impatiently for the flames to die and the smoke to dissipate. Then he tore into the charred meat with savage delight.

Thomas hobbled to his hoverchair and sat, eager to rest. He was glad Azhdarchidae was enjoying his meal. He was such a good boy.

The remaining zombies cowered along the fence. Such was Thomas's army.

He needed Rosy Ranks and Servants of All on his side—not as disposable mind-controlled bodies. He needed their minds, and especially their powers, intact.

He needed real allies.

Every night, he ascended into the Megacosm and begged Torth to join him. The Majority had instated new laws to make exile next to impossible, but anyone determined enough could escape. Thomas was sure of that. A renegade Torth could whisper the tale of Kessa the Wise to their slaves in order to create a distraction. And then? They could sever themselves from the Megacosm and flee into the wilderness.

A renegade Torth didn't even necessarily need to steal a spaceship. They could self-isolate in a forest or a canyon or a cave and then ascend for a few seconds, just long enough to send a message that they wanted to join the Conqueror. Ariock would need to teleport and pick up the renegade before the Torth Empire could get to them.

It should be doable. Dangerous, but doable.

So where were the renegades?

Where was the boy Twin? Where were the other high ranks who had gone rogue and exiled themselves from the Megacosm?

Ariock had publicly praised Thomas after his defense of the academy. "Quick thinking" and "decisive actions in combat." That was how Ariock had characterized his zombification of a few dozen Torth. Ariock didn't like zombification, but even so, he'd loudly proclaimed that Thomas had saved a lot of lives. He had even said that Thomas would make a fine warrior.

Thomas had forced a laugh at that, trying to dismiss the praise as a joke. He belonged in scientific laboratories, not on battlefields.

Yet in the secret depths of his mind, Thomas had felt a warm glow at Ariock's esteem.

That was why he was here, training Azhdarchidae for combat.

He had even begun to wonder if, perhaps, he ought to make time in his schedule for martial arts practice? Once he could walk without an exosuit, he might seek a sparring partner—someone comparable to his own modest size and strength, not a Dovanack—so he could instill enough muscle memory to match a Servant of All. With his absorbed knowledge database, he should be able to ramp up at an inhumanly rapid pace.

As if any of that could make up for his strategic failure.

Migyatel had seen Thomas conquer cities with endless numbers of unhappy Torth in rags. She had foreseen his zombie hordes. Thomas would have done anything to avoid it, but . . .

Well.

He dared not give the Death Architect and the Lone Twin endless time to scheme and invent new superweapons. He had to press ahead.

Azhdarchidae stilt-walked on his wings over to Thomas. The sky croc was far too big for cuddles, but he nuzzled his long neck over Thomas's lap. Thomas stroked the massive animal's reptilian plate-armor skin and inhaled the familiar scents of carnage and charred meat. He absorbed all the bestial pleasures Azhdarchidae enjoyed. Gorging. Flying. Being petted.

Those simple pleasures were a welcome escape from Thomas's daily routines. Zombification. Dead-end military research. Failing to gain Torth allies. Dealing with people who despised *rekvehs*.

Thomas might turn into an evil mastermind, but at least he had a sky croc who adored him. Azhdarchidae was on his side no matter what.

*?!*

Alarm spiked through Azhdarchidae. The beast cocked his head, eyeing the overcast sky, and Thomas absorbed his animal perceptions. Another sky croc was soaring just beneath the thick clouds.

An interloper.

Azhdarchidae roared a warning and took off in a great whoosh of flapping. The other sky croc screeched and then plummeted, angling toward Thomas.

Most people would have fled upon seeing a deadly predator speeding toward them. Thomas merely folded his arms and tightened his mouth in disapproval.

He didn't flinch when the seemingly wild beast landed directly in front of him, close enough to swallow him in one bite.

"You got the wing claws wrong," Thomas said. "And the proportions are unrealistic."

The false sky croc uttered a throaty laugh. "I didn't spend enough time studying your beast."

She shrank, becoming recognizable as the winged Lady in a reptilian headdress and a gown of black scales. Her wings matched, shiny and metallic black.

Thomas was disinclined to be friendly to the former goddess-empress. "Do you mind not imitating people I care about?"

She pouted. "I was just having fun."

Fun.

How nice that she could afford playtime.

Was she purposely trying to sabotage his reputation? At least one-third of the city already believed Thomas was something like the devil. If they saw a wild predator acting unnaturally sapient, they would assume Thomas was puppeteering a dragon-like beast.

"I don't want you to mimic Azhdarchidae," he told her.

Evenjos danced back, well out of telepathy range, apparently unnerved. "I'm sorry. I meant no offense."

"Why are you bothering me?" Thomas let himself sound as dead as he felt inside.

Her cheeks pinkened. "Can this be a friendly visit? I did not intend . . ." She seemed to force herself to go on. "I never meant to hurt your family." She folded her wings tight. "I am sorry."

Thomas considered asking her to take one step closer so he could know whether her apology was sincere.

He reminded himself to be grateful for the regeneration healing Evenjos had given him. She had opened up his future with endless possibilities. He owed her for that.

And he did feel affinity for Evenjos. He felt empathy for anyone who was unusually exceptional or exceptionally unusual.

But if she thought he would meekly tolerate bullying . . . well. Thomas could reeducate her.

"I don't like pranks," he said. "Especially pranks that put my sister in danger."

Evenjos clasped her hands over her scaly black dress. "It was never my intention to make you and Ariock hate me. I wish to make amends."

Thomas said nothing. He was aware of the vast differential in raw power between them. Evenjos could literally eat him.

But he would twist her mind if she dared lunge close enough to take a bite.

"Uh . . ." Evenjos seemed less and less certain of herself. "I am here partially on behalf of Garrett. He wants to open some inquiries with you."

"Why would he send you?" Thomas searched Evenjos's face for hints. Why would the former goddess-empress agree to act as a mere messenger?

Secretive warmth flashed across her face in a microexpression. That was enough of a clue.

"Oh," Thomas said.

Evenjos seemed defensive. "I'll have you know, he is a very generous lovemaker," she said in response to Thomas's knowing look. "He fulfills me. And—"

"All right," Thomas ruthlessly cut her off. "I don't need details."

Evenjos and Garrett. Woo-hoo. Lucky them.

Everyone in Thomas's social circles seemed capable of stumbling into romance. Why was it so impossible for him? Thomas wondered if he would ever get to experience the fun kind of intimacy.

"One thing Garrett wants to know," Evenjos said, "is whether you have learned how to brainwash gently."

"I've given it some thought," Thomas said noncommittally. Gentle brainwashing might be more useful than zombification—except that it had many troubling ethical implications. In some ways, it seemed even more invasive and evil than zombification.

"Hmm." Evenjos glanced toward Azhdarchidae, distracted. The sky croc had landed nearby and was eyeing her with extreme prejudice.

"Are you training your animal to devour Torth?" Evenjos asked.

"It's prudent," Thomas said. "Since you're no longer in the Torth-eating habit."

Evenjos fiddled with her scaly dress. She looked genuinely ashamed. "I would be brave if not for the gaseous inhibitor."

"I know," Thomas said. His side of the war was on the verge of losing ground to the Torth Empire, but as much as he wanted someone to blame, he knew that Evenjos was not the reason for their losses. She was just one factor.

"Garrett and I could both really use immunity," Evenjos said. "That's another thing he wants to ask you about. Are you making any progress whatsoever?"

Thomas rolled his eyes. Garrett asked about immunity every day. His near death due to the pink inhibitor gas had humiliated him.

"It's dead ends so far." Thomas wondered how he was supposed to make progress on anything scientific while zombifying thousands of Torth per day.

Evenjos seemed to wilt. "Without immunity, I am utterly useless in battle." She sounded disgusted with herself. "With it? I could make a real difference."

"Our research is stymied in a few ways," Thomas explained. "Not least of which is a lack of test subjects. We would make faster progress if our warriors would subject themselves to brain scans and other noninvasive experiments."

Jinishta had tried to persuade her people. No one was willing.

"The Torth have plenty of Rosy Ranks who would rather hang out in labs, undergoing tests, than face Ariock in battle," Thomas said. "That's why the Torth scientists are pulling ahead of us."

"They are?"

Thomas spread his hands. Wasn't it obvious? "They invented that inhibitor gas. I couldn't have done that. I don't have the faintest clue how they did it. All the reverse engineering I've done isn't enough."

"Oh." Evenjos gave him a shy look. "Is there anything I can do? To help your research?"

Thomas eyed her. This was unexpected.

"Can I volunteer as a test subject?" Evenjos clarified.

Thomas sized her up, wondering if this yet another prank.

Garrett had volunteered a few times, and Ariock had also allowed the lab technicians to scan his brain, but Thomas had yet to find any clues about the biogenesis of powers. If only Unyat's scientific notes could have outlasted the eons. That long-dead scientist must have known all the secrets.

Thomas cleared his throat, making himself sound businesslike and not inviting in any way. "Would you be willing to lend me some of your dust? For experimentation purposes?"

He expected a refusal.

Evenjos held up one slender hand. Her flesh evaporated in the breeze, becoming dust particles. "Would it be useful to you? My body is unlike that of any other Yeresunsa."

Her dust might lead Thomas and his team toward new lines of thought. After all, the new version of the inhibitor, a phase-shifting substance invented by Torth supergeniuses, seemed just as mysterious as Evenjos's dust. In fact . . .

What if its purpose was specifically to target Evenjos?

Thomas shifted in his seat. All his research was based on an underlying assumption that Yeresunsa powers were rooted in brain chemistry, and that that was what the inhibitor targeted. After all, powers were tied to moods. His team kept analyzing neurotransmitters and brain waves.

What if he was wrong?

Maybe the biogenesis of powers was rooted in a phase shift in the realm of histones and nucleosomes, a basic alteration of substance, rather than the mechanics of neurochemistry. Evenjos's dust might hold the key to figuring it out.

"I'll need an uncontaminated sample." Thomas's thoughts leaped ahead to experimental possibilities. He would need to upgrade his excimer laser.

Evenjos reconstituted her hand except for her pinkie finger. She blew it toward Thomas as a ribbon of dust. "How much do you need?"

"I'll tell Varktezo." Thomas couldn't mask his excitement. "Will you please visit my lab? Varktezo will have glass vials and vacuum chambers ready, and he'll walk you through how to donate your sample."

Evenjos re-formed her pinkie finger. She gave him a saucy look. "Let me know if you ever want a sample you can contaminate."

Thomas ignored her innuendo. He understood Evenjos well enough to know she was insecure. She wanted men fighting over her. And she was trying to see if she could provoke that sort of competition between Garrett and Thomas.

Yikes.

He definitely wasn't going to insert himself into that sort of drama.

But her sauciness, and her suppressed hope, reminded Thomas of why he liked her, despite her flaws. How could he not? They had both suffered in a pit of despair. They both understood hopelessness. He had saved her, and she had saved him.

Azhdarchidae walked closer, seeing Thomas's ease with Evenjos. The sky croc towered over both of them. He tentatively nuzzled Evenjos with his gigantic head, which was larger than she was.

Evenjos petted him. That was a kind, fearless reaction.

"Please don't mimic him again," Thomas said.

"I won't," Evenjos said.

"And don't pretend to be anyone else," Thomas said. "I want you to stop fooling people. Especially people I care about."

His own sternness made him inwardly annoyed with himself. He was actually glad she had stopped by. It was nice that someone on his side cared enough to check in with him, just to see how he was doing.

"I will respect your boundaries, Thomas," Evenjos said. "And I will visit Varktezo as you have asked." She spread her wings. "Thank you."

Thomas struggled to think of how he might reopen a friendship with her.

He just could not think of anything that would convey his sympathy and re-spect. Every sentence that ran through his mind seemed inadequate.

Before he could speak, Evenjos launched herself skyward. She was gone.

# CHAPTER 6

# UNIVERSAL FREEDOM

"Do you realize that more than a thousand people have been reenslaved?"

"Are we safe even in Freedomland?"

Kessa felt smaller than usual. She was the only ummin on the dais. Everyone else who faced this aggressive audience—Ariock, Garrett, Jinishta, and Thomas—had impressive powers.

"Will we ever get an antidote to the inhibitor? Or is that just an empty promise?"

"Why can't the Lady of Sorrow help us?"

"Are you planning to zombify the entire Torth population?"

Open air and the distant ocean formed a backdrop behind the councilors and correspondents. Most of them were nussians, govki, and ummins, although a few exotic species had sent emissaries to this public assembly. A sluglike sapient clung to one of the marble columns. Kessa also identified a yoftian gnome and two feathery kemkorcans.

There were rarer peoples. The galaxy had extremophile sapients, but military units required a few basic commonalities, so for now, they mostly ignored populations who were unsuited for a normal range of gravity or air breathing.

"My lab is working around the clock." Thomas's voice echoed from speakers around the outdoor atrium.

The whole assembly quieted down, paying attention. They had come for answers.

"We are making progress toward immunity against the inhibitor." Thomas floated in front of Ariock's colossal chair, rough-hewn from a silvery meteorite. "Both the microdart kind and the gaseous kind."

"How much longer will it take?" someone shouted.

"I won't speculate on a timeline," Thomas said. "We're working hard on the problem, but we have research hurdles to overcome."

Kessa had spoken with Varktezo about the obstacles. According to the chief lab assistant, no one understood what caused powers, let alone how to block them. The fact that the Twins had invented a gaseous version of the inhibitor implied that they were quite a few research steps ahead of Thomas. It was a cause for concern.

"We have discovered some good news," Thomas said. "The gaseous inhibitor is too unstable to store. The Torth have to generate it on location."

Ariock nodded. No doubt he had already been informed.

"That will inform our strategies going forward," Thomas said. "And give us a chance to recoup some of our losses."

He paused for more audience questions. An overhead causeway sheltered the dais from the brightness of the striated sky, and an officiant stood up there. She used a spotlight to select one of the many people with raised microphones.

"The Torth can't store the gaseous inhibitor?" the chosen correspondent shouted. "Why not?"

"Because it's a phase-shifting substance," Thomas answered. "It is both a radio-active wave and a gas." He projected a holographic demonstration. "In wave form, it has no effect on us. The Torth set up wave-generating devices in a configuration that will cause a phase-shift buildup. Like so." His holograph glowed with pyramidal points. "When it reaches a critical buildup? It phase shifts to the pink gas." His holograph morphed accordingly. "But the gas itself is unstable. After thirty minutes or a few hours, depending on accumulation, it will collapse back into waves and dissipate."

Garrett's mouth was a thin line. Kessa figured that he did not know enough science to comprehend the explanation.

The rest of the assembly looked just as stymied. A few of them had scrunched-up faces, trying to translate Thomas's explanation into concepts they were familiar with.

"The bottom line," Thomas said, "is that, for now, the gas is only a threat when the Torth choose the battleground. If we pick the fight? Then we should be able to send in a few Alashani warriors."

Jinishta's frown deepened.

"But Torth combatants can teleport across the galaxy now?" someone shouted out of turn. "How can we stop them?"

That riled up the assembly. Everybody hated the new paradigm.

"Galactic teleportation is costly for Torth champions." Thomas raised his voice to be heard over the rising hubbub. "Even more than it is for Garrett. They get depleted after one jump."

The assembly was not reassured.

"But they can show up in Freedomland!" An albino councilor gestured at the vista of the city. "We aren't safe!"

Voices overlapped, adding emphasis. There were far more Torth champions than Alashani warriors. What if a Torth teleported into a busy intersection and began shooting? What if a Torth teleported into the midst of a penitent work crew and led the penitents on a rampage? Did everybody need to carry a blaster glove at all times? If so, how long could freedom last?

What if the Torth Empire could not be overthrown?

In fact, what if a serious challenge to the Torth Empire was upsetting some mysterious universal karmic balance?

Thomas touched his fingers to his forehead, as if he had a headache.

"Any Torth who shows up in Freedomland will be trapped." Ariock's deep voice had a boom that no one else could match.

Kessa tapped the microphone clipped to her headdress, indicating that she wanted to speak. The others paused as she stood.

"If there is an invasion," Kessa said, "your supercoms will direct you to the nearest shelter."

"That's right," Ariock said, backing her up. "Our shelters are mirror protected, meaning no one, not even me, can teleport into them."

"The Torth won't even be able to find them," Garrett added.

"Most Torth champions are too weak to ghost to our out-of-the-way planet," Thomas added. "They would have to enter our solar system first."

"And believe me," Ariock said, "I am keeping watch."

The assembly looked slightly mollified.

In private, Kessa knew that Ariock had promised to allow lone streamships to get close to Reject-20, because the Freedomland spaceport must remain open to renegade Torth. Victory might depend on gaining an influential ally such as the boy Twin.

But there was no reason to publicly announce that random Torth could show up.

People were afraid. Kessa was proud of both Thomas and Ariock for clearing time in their schedules for this broadcast session. People deserved solid reassurances from the top leaders, not just empty platitudes from a clueless spokesperson.

"I know we're stretched thin," Ariock said to the assembly, his tone apologetic. "I'm well aware that we need more of everything. We need more soldiers. More equipment. And more allies."

Heartfelt agreement rippled through the assembly.

"That's what we're going to address here. We do have some good news to share." Ariock gestured for Thomas to go on.

Thomas told the assembly that his technicians had developed a new kind of radar that could detect fast-flying transports. He named a few technicians who deserved special recognition for their creative thinking. His laboratories were making drastic improvements to the space armor that warriors and pilots wore in battle zones, and they had other military innovations in the works.

"Overall," Thomas said, "I'm hopeful. But I think our technological innovations are only a humble part of the larger picture." He gestured toward Kessa.

This moment was inevitable. Kessa had known that she would need to address the liberated galaxy, yet she felt frail and inadequate. Surely she did not belong at the head of anything?

Sometimes she wondered if Thomas had made an actual mistake in appointing her as the face of the war.

"Kessa has an excellent plan," Thomas said, "to help us gain allies in our fight against the Torth Empire."

A lifter swept onto the dais. The little platform stopped in front of Kessa, offering a silent invitation. A technician was controlling it from the causeway overhead.

"Thank you, Thomas." The microphone amplified Kessa's meager voice.

She hopped aboard the lifter, and it boosted her higher. Now everybody in the outdoor assembly could see her. Hundreds of dignitaries lifted their gazes to study the elderly ummin.

They looked unimpressed. Or so Kessa imagined.

"Friends," she said. "You know we have a large population of penitent Torth. They work our fields. They build our apartment homes. They weave our clothes, maintain our transports, and generally serve us as slave labor."

Silence. She was stating the obvious.

"But," Kessa went on, "permanent enslavement was never the long-term plan for them. We are not going to fuel a new empire with slaves." She gave a nod toward Thomas, who floated in a corner, unobtrusive. "We are not going to transform ourselves into Torth. If we do that . . . then what is the point of victory over the Torth?"

Most of the assembly watched her with arms folded or tightened lips. Only a few people nodded in agreement.

"So let's just get rid of the penitents!" a premier warrior shouted. "Kill them!"

Ariock aimed a stern look in that direction. Kessa was glad he had not been raised Alashani. At least their superpowered military leader was not eager to turn all the penitents into corpses.

"My lieutenants have verified several thousand penitents who want to earn redemption." Kessa's amplified voice overrode the whispers. "I asked Thomas to personally guarantee a subset of those. He did. He telepathically soaked up twenty life histories, and he is certain that every one of the penitents we chose are unequivocally on our side. Those penitents will aid us. They will do whatever is necessary to help us defeat the Torth Empire."

That stirred up dark mutterings.

"She trusts that *rekveh*?" someone said.

"Yes." Kessa stared at the accuser. "I trust my *friend*." She emphasized that. "Thomas personally removed my slave collar. And I think you know he is responsible for the freedom of everyone here. This is his war against the Torth as much as it is ours."

She was never sure why so many people hated Thomas. He did have vocal supporters among the alien population, but they seemed more timid than the loudmouths who opined that all mind readers were evil.

"We need allies," Kessa said. "It is imperative that we give willing penitents a path toward becoming our allies and friends."

They listened. Deep down, she thought, they knew this was the right path.

"It is likely the only way we will win this war," Kessa dared to say.

The spotlight went to a nussian councilor. She bellowed, "You want to let thousands of penitents near families? With children?"

"Yes." Kessa offered a gracious nod for the relevant question. "I choose lieutenant overseers based on their capacity for empathy. These are people who inspire kindness and mutual understanding. I trust their judgment. If they trust a penitent around their own children, then that is for the good of all of us. And I do have a long list of volunteer families."

A lot of former slaves wanted to own their former owners, or to own a Torth in general. Kessa had ruled out any who showed a propensity for cruelty.

"Household penitents must obey the same laws as any citizen," Kessa said. "But we trust them in society. That is the whole point. We trust them with weapons if they volunteer for the army. We trust them as fighter pilots if they—"

"You can't just let Torth loose in Freedomland!" the nussian roared.

"I'll kill any Torth that aims a weapon at me or my family," an albino warrior shouted.

Kessa sighed. The whole point of her program was to grant penitents the same rights as anyone else. It seemed simple to her.

"Freedom is for everybody." Ariock stood, adding his towering size to Kessa's conviction. "I have friends who used to be Torth. I've seen them do heroic things. They've saved my life." He gestured toward Thomas and Garrett. "We could use more like them."

His deep voice made an impression. People exchanged glances of speculation.

"Are you going to take penitents into your own household, Kessa?" someone challenged. "What about you, Ariock?"

Kessa hesitated. She knew she ought to lead by example. But the idea of owning people . . . it filled her with disgust.

"So you don't trust them near yourself," someone shouted.

"I do trust them." Kessa searched for a way to alleviate popular concerns. She hesitated to admit that she knew too many military secrets. Every penitent promised to avoid the Megacosm, but military leaks were always possible when mind readers interacted with each other.

"When I see penitent soldiers," Ariock said, "or penitent pilots? I'll bring them into battle. I'll treat them like any troop or fleet."

Kessa wanted to study his face. Ariock secretly had the same concerns as any warrior. One traitorous penitent could end his life. One mistake on whom to trust would end any possibility of universal freedom.

Garrett stood. "We forbade the penitents from contacting the Torth Empire, and from congregating on their own. They cannot summon help. Whenever I catch one breaking the no-Megacosm rule?" He hammered his fist into his open palm. "I get to kill them."

A few people looked reassured.

"What if they pretend for a long time?" someone shouted.

"Right!" an Alashani councilor yelled. "They're expert manipulators."

Shouts of agreement spread throughout the assembled councilors and battle leaders. "They're used to gullible slaves!"

"Perhaps a runaway slave is not the best judge of *rekvehs*?" An elderly Alashani councilor gave Kessa a challenging stare. "She was trained from birth to obey and please them."

Someone laughed with contempt.

When Kessa swallowed, she felt a phantom constriction around her throat, as if from the grip of a slave collar.

Was it possible the Alashani were right about her? Was she unaware of her own flaws?

"Kessa has proved, a thousand times over, that she isn't a slave," Garrett said.

Of course, no one quite trusted Garrett. He was a *rekveh*.

Thomas looked as if he also wanted to speak up on Kessa's behalf, but he knew it was futile.

Kessa surveyed the upturned faces of the assembly. Now that winning was no longer easy, it seemed people were losing faith in the war. They didn't trust Thomas. But more saliently, they were losing faith in Ariock. And in Kessa.

That was a problem.

The last thing their side of the war needed was to break apart into rival factions. A bunch of bickering gangs could not defeat the Torth Empire.

Kessa was just an ummin, but she had the stage for now. She was going to use it.

She used her toes to lift her hoverplatform higher. "I suppose to an Alashani, the only trustworthy person is another Alashani?"

A few of them paid attention.

"Let us suppose that the shani have more value than any other sapients in the universe," Kessa said. "Unfortunately, there are very few shani. Freed slaves and penitent Torth greatly outnumber them. So they rely on allies."

No one could argue that fact. Albinos were overrepresented here, but in ordinary society, they only had a handful of neighborhoods. Everyone knew the exact number of surviving warriors. There were fewer than nine hundred of them left.

"Do you know what the greatest flaw among mind readers is?" Kessa asked.

A few people began to shout replies.

Kessa ruthlessly cut them off. "Any slave, former or otherwise, will tell you, it is their inflated sense of superiority. Even the penitents suffer from that wrongheaded superiority complex. Every mind reader has it."

She paused, so that her next words would make an impact.

"And I observe the same in their albino kin." She swept the assembly with her gaze. "The Alashani are just another type of *rekveh* to me. And to many former slaves like myself."

Her accusation hit the assembly like a meteor strike. Everyone, particularly the shani, gaped in shock.

"That's right." Kessa did not care if her words cut them. She glared at the albinos, because she felt offended.

Did they really believe she was forever a slave?

She was the face of the rebellion. She was the main reason why newly liberated slaves were so ready and willing to trust their liberators. Her speeches, custom tailored for every population, urged people to abandon their Torth loyalties and embrace a new paradigm. Her loyalists risked their lives to spread underground rumors and prepare slaves for freedom. Her lieutenants risked their families in order to rehabilitate former Torth.

Without those former slaves? There would be no space fleet. No transport armadas. No soldiers. No technicians. No scientists.

No possibility of success against the Torth Empire.

If Kessa and her ilk were just slaves to the brave, smug warriors? Then there was no hope. There was no future for her people or theirs.

"I have as much reason to hate the Torth as you do." Kessa indicated the scarred ring around her neck. "Do you think I blithely trust every penitent I meet? I am not a fool. I don't go near them without soldiers and blaster gloves. Do you think I love mind readers?" She gestured toward Thomas. "You don't know what it took for me to consider that one my friend. We saved each other's lives more than once."

Thomas gave her a respectful look that she would never forget.

"Trusting penitents is not something I consider easy," Kessa said. "I don't expect anyone to trust them casually."

The assembly listened.

"There is a great chasm between our species." Kessa rotated the lifter so she could address everyone equally. "Bridging that chasm may take multiple generations. I understand that many former slaves are too scarred to ever trust a mind reader. But some of you are willing and able, and you are the path forward. Compassion is vital. It is the core of what separates our society from the sick toxicity of the Torth Empire."

A flood of fresh opinions poured forth.

"Are we really going to end slavery?"

Could Freedomland become a place where no one was inherently inferior or superior to anyone else? What if slave collars and ownership culture no longer existed? What if penitents and free people actually started to get along?

A well-respected govki councilor gained the spotlight, and she shouted over the hubbub. "I would personally like to foster a penitent whom Kessa guarantees as friendly." She folded her upper pair of arms. "In fact, I am quite curious to meet a reformed Torth."

"Yes." Jinishta looked enthused. "We trust Thomas to plan our battles and zombify our prisoners. Why shouldn't we trust his guarantees on this? We really do need more soldiers."

Conversations became more lively, and Kessa recognized ideas that she had never dared make public because they seemed too far-fetched to take seriously. Battle leaders talked about converted enemies. Even now, it was hard to believe that a future full of trustworthy penitents would actually happen.

"Yes."

"Why not?"

Kessa kept her back straight. She had just won a battle.

# CHAPTER 7
# REAPING REMORSE

Thomas floated down each aisle of staked penitents, then up the next.

He absorbed moods, ideas, experiences. He spent less than ten seconds on each individual's mind. He might pluck one salient experience, maybe two, and ignore the rest of a person's life history.

Sure, that was sloppy. It might be considered dangerously sloppy, but so far, the penitents he'd vetted were benign. Jinishta had pressured him into evaluating hundreds per day, so he was leaning into expedience.

*I am Yours forever.* A woman fell to her knees, weeping, desperate to be noticed as the Conqueror hovered past her. *Give Me any command.*

A man knelt with the same desperate fervor. *I will obey. Let Me be your slave (I'll do anything) just let Me continue to exist (oh please) . . .*

Another. *I will follow anywhere You lead, Great One. If You start a new empire? I am there.*

Another. *I will serve You however You want.*

Each penitent bowed to Thomas as he floated past, judging them. Their praise was silent, of course. Chains and fence posts kept them spaced at equidistant intervals in the field. They could not run. They could not hide, or read each other's minds, or cheat. They were immobile, like a crop.

*Can I serve You, mighty Conqueror?*

*How may I please You?*

*I worship You.*

*I adore You.*

These wretches had had weeks or months to ponder how they would confront the Conqueror, should they ever meet him. This was their chance of a lifetime. Each penitent knew they would have only a few precious seconds in which to seize the undivided attention of the mental titan who had conquered them.

At least they understood that the Conqueror was more than a traitorous child. Penitents could not deny the evidence all around them: Thomas had established a new civilization. He kept doing things nobody had ever done before, and nobody could predict what he would do next.

Their worship was genuine.

*Would you like to use me as a sex slave? I will pleasure You, Great One!*

Thomas floated at a quicker pace. He figured he didn't really need an in-depth analysis of every life. All he needed was a gestalt.

When Jinishta and others had pressured him into making these regular evaluations, he had complained. *"Drilling into lives is intensive. We have half a billion penitents. Are you asking me to vet them all? Personally? Because I can't spare that kind of time."*

*"You'll ramp up,"* Garrett had said. *"You'll get faster at it."*

*"I don't have time,"* Thomas had insisted. And when they pushed back: *"You're asking me to soak up too much. Even my mind has limits."*

But his friends had limits, too.

They needed Torth allies, and they were too afraid of mind readers to have them any other way. They wanted guarantees. So here Thomas was, meeting a daily quota.

He sped between heads that bowed to him in reverence. He tore through haunted pasts while ignoring secret invitations.

Like:

No, he did not want an orgy. That penitent's notion of a lurid orgy was childish at best. What a bunch of stupid fantasies.

No, he did not need a private militia.

No, he did not want aid in assassinating the secret society of Alashani undergrounders. He didn't want to lose any of his allies, even the ones who hated him.

No, he would not set himself up in a pleasure palace with penitents serving him as chambermaids.

No, he was not going to start a fresh offshoot of the Torth Empire. Ugh. What a perverse notion.

What? No! He was absolutely not interested in *that* offer.

No, he was not having fun at all. He did not enjoy being worshipped. He would rather not spend another minute in the company of . . .

One of them lacked emotions.

She was one of the many youthful adults. Unlike the others in this big assessment field, she had no secret offers for the Conqueror. No imaginative favors. No worship.

Thomas stopped his hoverchair and threw it into reverse.

The emotionally deadened penitent realized, too late, that she had gained unwanted attention. She hurriedly offered a few memories.

Thomas tore past her meager offerings. Never mind what she'd eaten for breakfast. Never mind her baby-farm playpen. He didn't care about her Adulthood Exam, or her career path, or where she used to live. He sought threads of strong emotional value. Sympathy. Empathy. Kindness. Compassion. Or just passion.

He found none of those things in the Becalmed Dipole.

Instead, he sensed a buried, half-hearted hope. The Becalmed Dipole had bided her time. She believed that the Death Architect would *(win)* prevail, and she wanted to sabotage some of the Conqueror's accomplishments in order to impress the Torth Majority. Thusly she had pretended—for more than eight weeks—to be an obedient penitent. She had gone unnoticed.

Until now.

Thomas pointed to the deep-cover agent. "Kill her."

Soldiers rode speeding hoverbikes into the field, outfitted with long-range blaster cannons.

Thomas forged on ahead while the Becalmed Dipole croaked, "Pleeeeease—"

Her plea was torn apart in wet, meaty thuds.

Thomas did not watch. The staked-out penitents likewise ignored the barbarous execution. They were too focused on striving to prove their loyalty to the mind reader who could have them killed on a whim.

*I will obey any command You or Your minions give!*

*How can I help You?*

*I am Yours!*

A strange feeling, suspiciously like self-hatred, twisted just below the level of Thomas's conscious mind.

Some warriors whispered about assassinating him, although he pretended not to know that. What if the undergrounders were right about him on some fundamental level?

He didn't want to act as judge, jury, and executioner for so many people. Wasn't he behaving like a tyrant? What if he accidentally ordered the execution of someone who didn't deserve it?

Thomas really hated his job.

When his daily ordeal was finished, he didn't bother to visit with Kessa or anyone else who was standing at the edge of the field. Life experiences churned within his head, assimilating into the amalgamation that was his personality. He could not muster enough warmth for pleasantries or small talk. He could barely tolerate the bright colors of the sky or the sounds of distant foot traffic.

He navigated a winding footpath that led back toward civilization and uptown. He had absorbed memories of enough routes to know every inch of every trail around Freedomland.

"Thomas?"

It was Kessa.

Thomas glided to a halt, letting her catch up, but he clutched the armrests of his hoverchair in impotent annoyance. Couldn't she read his body language? Did she even care that he was not in the mood for chitchat?

"Are you all right?" she asked.

Thomas stared balefully and let her draw her own conclusion.

"I am completely willing to reduce the quota." Kessa stood at her usual respectful distance, not quite within range. "If Jinishta or anyone has a problem with that, send them to me."

The offer was kind. Thomas knew that he ought to feel something. Gratitude, maybe.

He felt nothing but a churning of many lives.

"It's fine," he said, and moved onward.

Even after all this time, the penitent population stubbornly refused to forswear the Megacosm and the Torth Empire. They would do anything else. Worship the Conqueror. Clean latrines. Talk out loud.

But pick up a weapon and agree to shoot Torth? No. They wouldn't do that.

So perhaps his vetting process was the only road toward gaining legitimate Torth allies. This could soften up the penitents until they became soldiers and pilots.

It had to work.

Kessa strolled alongside Thomas's hoverchair. "When I have lieutenants who look how you are looking, I tell them to take a vacation."

As if he could do that.

"I hope you do not feel guilty over the one we had to kill today." Kessa's tone was gentle. "Everyone is grateful that you uncovered her before she could cause damage or hurt somebody."

"I'm glad she's dead," Thomas said.

Kessa assessed him from the corner of one gray eye. She looked almost wary, like she didn't quite trust him.

"Let me ask you something." Thomas stopped. He was in a dangerous mood, but he ignored the warnings in the depths of his mind and gave Kessa his full attention. "Does it make any difference?"

Kessa looked inquiring.

"I give them my stamp of approval," Thomas said, "and you place them into households. And supposedly some of them will volunteer as soldiers or military pilots someday. Is that going to happen? Tell me. Because I don't see it."

Kessa regarded him for a moment. She looked frustrated.

At last, she spoke. "Trust takes time."

Thomas wanted to pound his fist against his armrest, but he dared not reveal his hopelessness. Kessa and others would lose morale if they knew.

No one on his side seemed to be asking certain strategic questions. Questions such as: What would the Torth Empire do once it discovered its hidden reserves of brainwashers and mind controllers?

Statistically, there had to be a lot of fourth- and fifth-magnitude telepaths hidden among the Torth population.

The brainwashers were likely unaware of their dark power. In a culture with so much repressed emotion, it would be exceptionally hard to trigger that power. But they existed. Thomas had no doubt. His ability to brainwash people was not a lucky fluke. It must be common, or somewhat common.

And the enemy supergeniuses must be aware of that potentially enormous advantage on their side.

With mind-controlling champions, the Torth Empire could easily win. All they had to do was mind-twist Ariock. Heck, they could ruin any free city.

The penitent population wasn't stupid. Thomas figured this was why they were not jumping to join his military. Gossip spread among them like wildfire. If one penitent thought of an idea, that idea wended its way through their barracks and work crews within a matter of hours.

Many penitents believed that a Torth Empire victory was inevitable. That terrified them into inaction. They worshipped the Conqueror, but they also suspected that he was bereft of any way to counteract enemy brainwashers.

That was probably why his outreach efforts were failing. That was why his invitations in the Megacosm went ignored. The boy Twin hadn't shown up yet—perhaps he, too, doubted that Thomas could win.

"We need a lot of penitents integrated on our side," Thomas said. "That's why I'm spending time here every day. We *need* them. We cannot win without them." He figured he could be frank here, on an open path where no one was within earshot. "We're in a precarious stalemate with the Torth Empire. When it breaks, I think we will be the ones losing ground. And people."

Thomas could juggle facts. But social variables? Emotions? Solving these sorts of problems might forever be beyond his capabilities.

If only he could brainwash himself into not losing morale.

Kessa gave him a soft look. "Let me ask you something. Why did you order that spy killed, rather than twisting her mind so she can be of use?"

It was an insightful question. Kessa had correctly perceived his mercy.

"If I start casually punishing penitent transgressors with a fate worse than death," Thomas said, "then I become the tyrant everyone fears. I would be encouraging our side to see the penitents as potential tools rather than as people." He shook his head. "I'm not aiming for genocide. I want the penitents to become equals among us."

Few people would care.

Kessa's gray eyes held a deep understanding. "You go to great lengths to show mercy to the Torth as a people. Why? What do you see in them that is worth saving?"

Thomas began a tedious reply.

"I don't mean your military reasons," Kessa said. "I mean your emotional reasons."

Thomas thought his reason was obvious. "Knowledge," he said.

Kessa invited him to go on with a raised brow ridge.

"I want to save their knowledge," Thomas said. "The Torth collectively have an enormous amount of preserved knowledge. A thousand generations multiplied by thirty trillion people."

Such a loss would be exponentially worse than the loss of ancient prophecies, the destruction of the buried city beneath the Stratower, or the burning of the library at Alexandria in Earth's antiquity. The very idea of destroying the Megacosm made him ill.

"I can't imagine any worse crime than to let their collective knowledge die," Thomas said, unable to hide the raw despair in his voice.

Then he realized that his priorities must seem screwed up to a former slave of the Torth Empire. Thomas cringed in preparation of being judged.

But Kessa looked as if a key had clicked into a lock and opened a new door. She understood.

Very few people valued knowledge as much as Thomas did, and she just might be one of them.

"I might have an idea," Kessa said.

Thomas looked at her. He felt hopeless, but he would listen.

"I am not sure you will welcome it." Kessa looked embarrassed. "And I cannot guarantee anything. It is just a meager idea."

No matter how many people called her Kessa the Wise, she did not believe it herself. Perhaps someday she would.

"What is it?" Thomas gave her an inviting look. "I value your advice, very much."

Kessa looked as if she doubted that, but she played along, straightening her back. "I believe that most former slaves are doing all they possibly can to welcome the Torth. They are treating the penitents better than they were treated as slaves." She included herself in her gesture. "We have invited them into our homes and our families."

Thomas nodded, acknowledging those truths.

"A bridge is being built," Kessa said. "But construction must come from both sides."

"You don't think the penitents are trying hard enough?" Thomas realized that she was correct. Of course Kessa had noticed that even the nicest of penitents refused to fully cast off their Torth loyalties, even if she didn't know why.

"It is not a matter of what they do," Kessa said with delicate caution. "It is a matter of acknowledgment. In many ways, the penitent Torth have not suffered the worst degradations of slavery. None have been forced to murder their own children. Or their own parents. None of them understand how it feels to hold in screams while Red Ranks drag away the love of their life to be tortured to death."

That had happened to Kessa.

Thomas was painfully aware that she had loved her mate, Cozu, as well as the family who had raised her. Those loved ones were gone. The Torth had stolen them from Kessa, and the pain of those losses would never go away entirely.

It could never be repaid.

A comparatively small number of Torth had tortured, humiliated, and ruined countless generations of multiple sapient species. The injustices perpetuated against slaves, in general, were far too much to be repaid in kind. That would lead to the genocide Thomas and Kessa both want to sidestep.

"I think back to how I learned to trust you," Kessa said. "At first, I dismissed you as just another self-serving, greedy Torth. Even after you severed yourself from the Megacosm, you acted superior and condescending. I could not consider you a friend."

Thomas began to wish he had acted more human. Perhaps behavior mattered more than he thought?

"But you showed remorse," Kessa assured him. "You acknowledged the pain you caused, and you risked your life to save ours. You did it so often, no one could deny that you cared. It is a continuous act of atonement. And it matters."

Thomas swallowed. He had assumed that he was destroying the Torth Empire based on rational reasons with a side helping of vengeance. But it was more than that. Kessa had seen a motive in his actions that he had hidden from himself.

His nameless mother had set him on the path to atonement.

There were other Torth who wanted to atone. Thomas felt sure of it, knowing about his birth mother, and also from the many Torth lives he had absorbed.

Most of the penitents didn't realize it consciously, though. They were in denial, clinging to the peer pressures of their past.

"A bridge can be built." Kessa clasped her hands behind her back. "But it is the penitent Torth who must take the next step."

She was right. Thomas saw it clearly, now that she had pointed it out.

"They need to join our military," Thomas said. "But you have something else in mind."

He knew what was needed. In every way that mattered, he, too, was a penitent.

"They must show remorse," Kessa said. "If they are ever to earn the dignity of respect from those of us who used to be slaves, that is necessary. They must prove that they regret injustice."

# CHAPTER 8

# EXPENDABLE ASSETS

The Former Commander had traveled all the way to Gnar in semisecrecy for an in-person meeting . . . inside a derelict factory?

Six of her fellow elite military ranks sat around a defunct boiler vat. There were no cushy recliners, no massage chairs, not even any attendant slaves, just a grated metal floor.

One of them had arranged this meeting. Whoever it was had poor taste in location.

With a sigh, the Former Commander joined her cohort. Few individuals could be trusted to make wise decisions. That was a fact. It was no mystery why the Majority had elected supergeniuses to serve as the truest champions of civilization, even though several of those had proven to be disloyal and self-serving.

Four of these so-called elites had pink eyes. Rosies. They used to be ordinary civilians, and not the stellar kind who got promoted fast. Their power was significant—she could sense it—but if not for the Giant's hammer blow, they would have lived and died as mundane middling ranks. They were not leadership material.

*Ooh, the Former Commander!* The greeting came from a gangly mutant with a bad haircut and buck teeth. *I didn't know You were invited. I (the Unsung Spur) am honored.*

So he clearly wasn't the organizer.

The Former Commander already missed her inner audience. Meeting in secret seemed downright uncivilized. Some of her orbiters had followed her since before she had been elected the Commander of All Living Things. Didn't they deserve access to her every thought? Wasn't this a betrayal of the implicit trust between herself and them?

Another attendee agreed with her. *It is stupid (and pointless) to meet in person.* Her pink eyes glowed bright against her dark skin. *Why are We doing this?*

Another Rosy agreed. *The Giant and the Imposter probably scan for gatherings of power like this one. We are making Ourselves into targets.*

That seemed paranoid. Two individuals could not scan the whole galaxy, no matter how much raw power they had. There were over ninety million inhabited planets and planetoids.

*This planet (Gnar) is safely beneath enemy notice,* the Somehow Nexus silently pointed out. *It's a commonplace tidally locked world. Even if the Conqueror keeps winning, he will target richer (and more populous) worlds before he turns his attention to places like this.*

The Somehow Nexus was a bland-looking man with a bland attitude. Yet the Former Commander recognized him as among the most capable Servants of All.

He was a veteran of slave revolts and other dangerous assignments, his blond hair graying, his face beginning to show his age.

*Did you arrange this meeting?* she wondered, picturing the secret invitation that had been slipped into a data packet on her tablet.

The Somehow Nexus shrugged and neither confirmed nor denied the accusation.

*Well, I, for one, am glad to have been invited.* The Forcer Burn stared around the circle with his rosy-pink eyes. *A secret meeting (of extra-capable champions) ought to yield valuable ideas.*

The Former Commander gave the Forcer Burn a level look. She had commanded all living things back when he was still playing with logic toys on a baby farm. She did not need a lecture from a youthful Rosy.

*Well, We (elite military ranks) are being treated as disposable garbage.* The Forcer Burn laced his gloved hands over one muscular leg. *I cannot be the only one who balks at the Death Architect's ongoing offense.*

The other attendees exchanged looks, radiating a gladness that the super-geniuses were not permitted to travel.

*I don't like the way she (the Death Architect) is provoking the Giant,* the Null Distraint admitted. *Why mount the severed heads of slaves on display outside Our garrisons? Isn't that barbaric? Why are We (the Torth Empire) doing such garish things?*

*It makes no sense,* the Snap Analogy concurred. *What is the purpose?*

*It needlessly enrages the enemies,* thought the Somehow Nexus. *They're actively raiding places just so the Conqueror can zombify extra Rosies and Servants of All.*

More agreements. *We (champions) (military ranks) are the only ones who have to suffer the brunt of the Giant's rage.*

The elite ranks were silent for a moment, each coping with shame in their own private way. They were all too aware of the many advantages the enemies had. Zombification. Mass-teleportation. The Conqueror had invented some kind of abominable communications network that worked over any distance, like a sickly shadow of the Megacosm. And whenever the Giant arrived in a city? Civilians dropped everything and fled.

The Former Commander commiserated with her peers. She pulled out her antacid bottle and took a pill.

During her last visit to the Death Architect on that forsaken asteroid, she had been unable to suppress her criticism. She had delivered several cases full of NAI-13. Then she'd stood back, wondering if any champion would dare to assassinate this particularly wasteful supergenius.

Why did the Death Architect insist on forcing Rosies to remain garrisoned on Nuss? Surely Rosies were too valuable to waste like that? There was no glory in a stupid, pointless, easily avoidable death.

The Death Architect had actually responded to her unspoken criticism. *I am architecting (building up to) a situation.*

That was vague. The Former Commander wondered if the little girl had any understanding of how outmatched the Torth Empire was. Did she even care about reality?

*Outmatched? No.* The Death Architect had emitted not even a wisp of emotion. *The Conqueror's strategy hinges entirely on him creating hordes of expendable assets. That is a critically flawed strategy.*

Was it really?

The Former Commander felt haunted by the battles she had witnessed in the Megacosm. Zombified victims died by the hundreds every day, gouging out the eyes of Red Ranks or savaging them in other ways. The Torth losses were obscene. The enemies lost comparatively few soldiers.

*Resource allocation is critical to any strategy*, the Death Architect thought calmly. *The Conqueror can no longer win a battle without his disposable bodies. His minions are utterly reliant upon him. They (his minions) are beginning to forget that We (the Torth Empire) can play the same game. And We can do it a lot more effectively.*

*?* The Former Commander had felt lost. She had no idea what the Death Architect was insinuating.

*We have more (far more) throwaway assets than the Conqueror can produce*, the Death Architect thought. *We have a nearly infinite horde of disposable bodies.*

Slaves?

Ha. The Former Commander disdained that idea. Kamikaze slaves could be useful in isolated skirmishes, but a cringing ummin was no match for a zombified Torth. Plus, the whole notion of arming slaves was childish. They were too likely to turn traitor and switch sides.

*You exhibit a marked lack of imagination*, the Death Architect had thought. *Slaves can be used for many purposes, in many ways.*

She had envisioned an example of what she meant. Just a flash. Hundreds of slaves writhed in pain beneath a hot desert sun, staked to metal crosses.

Bait.

Such a sight would enrage the enemies and make them stupid. Especially the Giant.

The Former Commander had remained stoic. She could not guess the full scope of what the Death Architect planned, but she was reassured. The girl did have something planned. Something that the Conqueror would fail to counter.

*???*

Her comrades in the derelict factory sensed her memory and probed for details.

Mind probes used to be rude, but the Former Commander no longer outranked her fellow champions. She allowed them to learn what small hints the Death Architect had dropped.

*Ah.* The Somehow Nexus leaned back, satisfied. *That is interesting.*

*So she is planning something.* The Snap Analogy leaned forward, excited. *The enemies are going to get very angry. Enraged, really. Does this have something to do with that rage neurotoxin the Twins were working on?*

When the Giant was enraged, he made mistakes.

He might even ignore the Conqueror's commands.

That was how emotionally volatile savages reacted whenever they got overwrought. The Death Architect was creating a perfect storm. She was misleading the Conqueror, lulling him into a false sense that the Torth were being wasteful and careless. And she was simultaneously building up storm conditions.

*This is already a fruitful meeting*, the Burning Hilt thought.

The Former Commander did not need praise for ferrying information. Servitude was an honor.

She supposed that the Death Architect was admirably like her in that way, at least. The girl served the empire for the sake of serving. Unlike the Upward Governess, she did not have an ego that needed stroking. She was not greedy for luxuries, art, relics, or delicacies. Her lair was industrial and unadorned.

That selflessness was a good sign, wasn't it?

Only savages felt greed. Only savages yearned to amass art, music, stories, gardens, trinkets, and accolades.

The Death Architect had also brought up another cause for hope. *As long as We are on the topic of resources*, she had thought, *the Conqueror does not have as many advantages as you believe. Do you honestly assume that he is the one and only individual in existence who can control minds?*

The Former Commander had gone still.

Even the rarest of Yeresunsa powers were repeated in a population of more than thirty trillion. That was an unavoidable fact of statistics. There must be other mind readers who could twist minds and brainwash people. But if so . . .

Where were they?

Hidden?

*Brainwashing is different than throwing wildfire or using telekinesis.* The Death Architect's mental voice was intimate. *It is so internal, it is unlikely to be activated by an external crisis. Not even the vigorous training of Servants of All is enough to awaken that power. Brainwashers on Our side of the war are likely unaware of what they can do.*

Yet.

There was an unspoken implication.

The Former Commander had, of course, tried to awaken new powers in herself. Should she try harder?

*The search for brainwashers should be a much higher priority than it has been,* the Death Architect agreed. *If you encounter someone with that power (or if you gain that power yourself), contact Me in private.* She had flashed a mental image of an encryption tablet. *Such a champion might become crucial to saving the Torth Empire.*

The Former Commander had bowed her head in obedience.

Deep down, she felt uneasy. Would such a person—such a monster, really—obey military orders? Once the Torth Empire won the war, would a winning champion with that monstrous power then meekly submit themselves to the Majority for execution?

Or would they become another Conqueror?

*Have no fear.* The Death Architect had regarded her loyal champion with a patronizing lack of emotion. *As a supergenius, I can (and I will) assess brainwashers and determine who, among them, is trustworthy. The fate of civilization is in My capable hands.*

How reassuring.

The Former Commander had bowed and begged for permission to leave. She wanted to place her trust in the Death Architect. She really did. But . . . well, the little girl just seemed so comfortable with hidden dangers.

What was she hiding inside her freakishly capacious mind?

What if . . . well, what if she herself could twist minds?

That idea was too terrifying to consider. The Former Commander tried to reassure herself. If the Death Architect had such a useful power, she would surely share it with the Majority rather than keep it to herself. The little girl was selfless. That was her best quality.

The secret meeting of Servants and Rosies eyed each other askance. Secret mind controllers would be able to hide in plain sight. They would seem ordinary. Mundane. Easy to miss.

Who knew what they were capable of?

*Anyone might be able to brainwash people*, the Somehow Nexus thought. *It could be one of Us.*

*It could just as easily be children on baby farms*, the Forcer Burn pointed out. *It could be literally anyone.*

*It is more likely to be someone with powers*, the Snap Analogy thought.

The Null Distraint touched her forehead, as if reaching to dial up a tranquility mesh. *Ugh.*

The Former Commander agreed with that sentiment. Secrets should be anathema to civilized people.

*I believe that one of Us (in this room) is, in fact, hiding a mind-control power*, the Unsung Spur thought. *It is probably the one who arranged for this private meeting. !?!?!?*

The Former Commander stared at the young Rosy. They all did.

*Also, there is evidence.* The Unsung Spur replayed their journey to Gnar. Their streamship had departed from MoreProgress Orbital with six hundred and ninety-four passengers. It had docked at Gnar station with six hundred and ninety-five passengers.

The Unsung Spur paused, politely giving them time to reach their own conclusions. *And no one seems able to identify the additional passenger who appeared out of nowhere.*

The Former Commander figured that the Unsung Spur was the sort of person who bought into conspiracy theories. Surely the supposed extra passenger was just a clerical error?

She sensed her cohort thinking along the same lines.

*No*, the Unsung Spur thought, defensive. *I got curious and asked passengers and crew members. None of them admit to making a clerical error. None of them remembers anything or anyone odd.*

The Former Commander tried to put aside her doubts. This topic made her profoundly uneasy.

*There is only one conclusion*, the Unsung Spur thought. *A mind controller was aboard that ship and did not want to be noticed, so they edited memories. But they forgot to edit the official record.*

The Former Commander collected her thoughts. She sensed her peers brimming with speculations and trepidation. Was one of them—right here and now—hiding a power to turn the rest of them into brainless puppets?

*So there is a mind controller among Us*, the Burning Hilt thought. *So what? They are on Our side. Right?*

*Right. I'm not saying it's bad*, the Unsung Spur thought. *Like the Death Architect implied, We ought to welcome such a useful champion and make Them feel comfortable.*

His mind held an unspoken invitation. Apparently, he expected the secret mind controller to reveal themselves.

Everyone else's reactions ranged from lukewarm to chilly. The Former Commander personally had no desire to meet another potential Conqueror. One was more than enough.

*Right.* The Null Distraint solidified her own concerns. *What happens if Our secret creepy mind controller goes rogue? What atrocities might another Conqueror be capable of?*

That was such a frightening idea, everyone needed a second to process it. The ramifications were too horrifying to contemplate. Civilization would be caught between two warring supertyrants. What hope was there?

The Unsung Spur volunteered his opinion again. *I think it's paranoid to presume that every mind controller would turn into a tyrant. Few Torth are as power-mad as the Conqueror. Most of Us are loyal to the empire (and civilization).*

Perhaps.

The Former Commander thought of all the low ranks who refused to evacuate their endangered home cities. Rather than flee the instant the Giant showed up, they allowed themselves to be collared by the enemies. It seemed to her that a lot of Torth knelt rather easily.

*We are safe.* The Unsung Spur looked at them, dismayed by their reactions. *If anyone brainwashes one of Us (a valuable champion), surely the supergeniuses would detect it and put a stop to it? That's the job of supergeniuses. Right? To safeguard civilization?*

The Former Commander drummed her spidery fingers on her armored thigh, wishing she could drum wisdom into the Unsung Spur.

*Can We trust supergeniuses, though?* the Snap Analogy dared to wonder. *The Lone Twin is likely a traitor, just like her partner, the boy Twin.*

The Former Commander favored that Rosy with a gaze of agreement. The Torth Empire ought to just launch nuclear missiles at the girl Twin's vessel. Sure, the ugly child was allegedly hard at work inventing rarefied weapons. But the Twins had mirrored minds. Where one went, the other was very likely to follow.

*Well, I choose to be optimistic.* The Unsung Spur gave them each a look, as if he wanted to impart his youthful idealism. *The Twins are no longer mentally synced up. The Lone Twin must realize that a partnership with the Death Architect is superior to what she used to have.*

Skepticism radiated off the others.

*Things will turn around!* the Unsung Spur assured them. *Why are you so negative? The Death Architect must have an amazing plan. Plus: We can teleport! The Torth Empire will prevail, just like We always have.*

The Former Commander scooped out one more antacid tablet and ate it.

But she did not argue with the Unsung Spur. None of them did. The Torth Empire needed whatever advantages it could wrangle. After all, they had thrown their heaviest weapons at the Giant and failed. They had invaded the Conqueror's stronghold with inhibitor gas. They had preemptively destroyed baby farms. None of it worked.

Meanwhile, half a billion Torth were erased, dead or enslaved as penitents. And there was no way to hide that fact from the public.

They must win at any cost. Civilization mattered.

*I will defer to the Death Architect,* the Somehow Nexus agreed. *She has proven herself to be loyal (and clever). But just in case her secret strategy falls short of victory . . . I suggest We practice Our combat skills.*

As if that would win the war.

*Those of Us with teleportation powers ought to figure out galactic teleportation.* He met the Former Commander's gaze, perhaps aware that she had been struggling to surpass her own ghosting limits. *The most powerful among Us should be capable of whatever the Imposter is capable of.*

That stung.

But he was correct. There must be a trick to ghosting across the galaxy. Perhaps she needed to stretch her sphere of influence in some way? And no doubt she would have to memorize star charts. That would entail a lot of rote memorization, which she hated. Torth minds were not suited to rote memorization.

Still, there would be advantages to being able to pop up anywhere.

The Former Commander imagined teleporting directly behind the Conqueror—or the Giant—and slicing off his head with her ionic-bladed scimitar. If she could do that, she would win back all the praise and status she had lost. She would be worshipped for eternity in the Megacosm.

It was embarrassing how much her throat tightened with craving at that idea. She wasn't supposed to want personal glory. She was supposed to serve All. That ought to be reward enough. The mantle of office, the authority and fame . . . those were just perks.

She wondered if she should be more like Death Architect.

*We should all be more like the Death Architect,* the Forcer Burn thought. *Tranquil no matter what.*

They agreed, departing. A few of them marveled at the meeting and the abrupt way it had ended. One or two wondered if brainwashing was involved.

The rest tried to ignore that speculation.

The Former Commander did not ascend right away. Downtime used to feel punishing, but she had begun to develop a fondness for existential silence. Being alone inside her skull calmed her symptoms of stress.

She rode a hoverbike across the factory floor and contemplated her future.

Although she no longer wore her mantle, she was still invited to secret leadership meetings like this one. A few people respected her enough to include her. She was, in fact, alive, which was better than the fates of all previous deposed commanders.

It was remarkable. There were reasons to be optimistic.

She might yet reclaim her glory and die with honor.

# CHAPTER 9

# IRREDEEMABLE COWARDS

Ariock's inner voice imparted truths that his mind-reader friend must be overhearing. Truths such as: *This is not noble.*

This was not honorable. This was sick. This was tyrannical. This was not how wars should be fought.

"Speed it up," Thomas ordered, apparently oblivious to the unspoken criticisms.

He needed a constant infusion of raw power from Ariock. It seemed he could tune out the opinions that came with that power link.

Jailers tugged chains and the long line of prisoners was forced to stagger past Thomas. The next Red Rank in line pleaded for mercy in a babble—then lost his words and bowed his head as Thomas zombified him.

Jailers removed the shackles from the fresh zombie with practiced swiftness. A businesslike govki waved an ocular wand to change the zombie's eye color from red to white. Another govki slapped a spear into the zombie's outstretched hands.

Freshly armed and programmed with instructions, the new zombie lurched toward the horde of zombies streaming along the causeways into Flawless City.

Thousands of brainwashed victims carried halberds, spears, or makeshift clubs. The ones in the best condition were outfitted with discarded blaster gloves that might misfire. Some zombies were wired with explosives. Their Alashani keepers had not thought to turn them into suicide bombers—but Garrett had.

Distant screams carried on the wind as the zombies softened up the city.

"Soon I will see my mate again," a nussian captain said with grim satisfaction. "Kessa's spies say she is still alive. I hope the Torth who took her suffers worse than death."

"We should mount the heads of defeated high-rank Torth onto spikes, like they do to ours," another nussian said with savage righteousness.

The Torth Majority had a knack for picking the most beloved former slaves to gruesomely behead. The victims tended to be folk heroes, smugglers, or well-respected elders. Apparently the Torth Empire thought it was a good idea to torture those captives to death, then let their detached heads dangle from their own severed spinal ridges. They displayed them outside their city walls.

It was as if they wanted to provoke maximum brutality. Ariock couldn't understand it.

"I've rounded up all the Rosies they had in there." Garrett strode along the line of prisoners. "But I'd give the zombies another hour." He gestured to the end of the chain gang. "Let any remnants of inhibitor gas clear up. Then we can send in our sapient troops."

Thomas offered nothing but a curt nod. He was zombifying another prisoner.

Ariock did not need to ghost into the city to know what it looked like inside: a blood-soaked slaughterhouse. Any Torth who'd failed to flee before the transport bays were locked down would now be struggling to fend off zombies. Sure, the Torth civilians were always armed . . . but zombies were immune to pain, immune to fear, immune to inhibitor gas. They would fight until they dropped dead.

So Ariock's people were more than happy to send in zombies as front-line troops. From the perspective of slaves, such a battle looked like Torth versus Torth.

And after Flawless City contended with armed zombies who would fight to the death, the remaining Torth would have to face roaring nussians armed with blaster gloves, plus a handful of shani warriors who could shoot lightning.

Very few members of this Torth garrison would survive to become penitents.

*They refused to kneel,* Ariock reminded himself. *They won't uphold justice. So we have to force justice here.*

His inner self refused to accept that explanation.

His inner self kept asking *why.*

Ariock looked at the nussian captains, at Garrett, and then down at Thomas. Was no one else troubled? Hadn't they seen enough brutality? Did they honestly believe that every single Torth deserved the same savage punishment?

"You don't need to be here, Ariock." Garrett seemed to have picked up on his mood, because he gave Ariock a sympathetic look. "Let us finish up, okay? Why don't you do some cargo runs or something?"

"But I need to boost Thomas," Ariock pointed out.

On his own, Thomas got depleted after zombifying seventy-five or eighty Torth. It was an intensive power.

"I'll boost him," Garrett said. "I don't mind."

Thomas nodded as he zombified another victim. Lately, he seemed to be agreeing with Garrett more often.

"All right." Ariock stepped away guiltily. He truly didn't want to see another city conquered by zombies—but stepping away also felt wrong. He didn't want to find comfort in Vy's arms while his friends and military forces did all the brutal work.

Anyway, at this time of day, Vy would be busy with council matters. Ariock considered his duties. He chose one, put himself into a clairvoyant trance, and ghosted.

He vanished from the planet Nuss before any of the captains could plead for the Son of Storms to stick around to enjoy their tremendous upcoming victory.

Instead of teleporting to Reject-20, he went to a savanna region of Umdalkdul. Weptolyso and Irarjeg sat together in what used to be a slave plantation factory, drinking nectar that was likely spiked with firebomb ale.

Ariock appeared outside the door of their office. He knocked to alert them, then entered without waiting for an invitation.

"Son of Storms!" Weptolyso looked up, startled. "Welcome."

Irarjeg jumped to his feet. Ummins tended to bounce when they did that.

"No need for formality." Ariock waved for Irarjeg to be at ease. He looked from one to the other. "Please tell me, why are you in here instead of working with the recruits?"

This military program for penitents was Ariock's own suggestion. If it worked? Then they could finally ease off on zombifying prisoners and use willing penitent pilots and soldiers instead.

Kessa had claimed the penitents weren't ready, but she had been uncertain enough to backtrack and allow it as an experiment. Irarjeg had volunteered to take charge of four hundred trustworthy penitents. Weptolyso was a consultant.

"How's it going?" Ariock asked.

Weptolyso groaned and gulped his drink.

"There is nothing good to report." Irarjeg stood straight, hands clasped behind his back, exemplifying his years as a hunting captain on his slave farm. "I believed we were making progress at first. But . . ."

"But there are significant hurdles," Weptolyso put in. "For instance, ordinary soldiers refuse to train with them."

"People don't want their minds read." Irarjeg had a placating tone, as if he'd offered a reasonable justification.

Ariock folded his arms. He'd heard it all before. "Having a mind reader by your side in battle can actually be a benefit."

Irarjeg looked ashamed. "Our soldiers are not as brave as you are, Bringer of Hope."

"It has nothing to do with bravery." Ariock felt irked. Why was friendship with mind readers such a difficult concept for people to grasp? If Ariock could tolerate having his mind read, so should his soldiers.

Although lately, admittedly, Ariock was less sanguine about it. Why did he always feel a step behind Garrett in terms of battle tactics?

"There is another aspect to this," Weptolyso said in his gravelly rumble. "I have overheard soldiers joke that they won't be able to tell friendly penitents apart from zombies or Torth in the chaos of battle. They may accidentally shoot our penitent allies."

Ariock had no easy response.

"And the penitents know it," Weptolyso said.

Ariock did want an easy way to delineate Torth allies from Torth enemies, if they ever gained such allies. Color-coded armor? Helmet crests?

The problem was that both sides of the war used essentially the same supplies and styles of armor. It was all Torth technology. Ummins and govki and nussians could not be mistaken for Torth, so they were safe from accidental friendly fire. But if his theoretically friendly penitents wore the black armor of his military, he knew the Torth Majority would mimic that color.

"We will address that issue." Ariock wondered what enemy Torth would be unwilling to wear, or do. Perhaps singing?

Nah, something visual was the only way to be taken seriously. Maybe they could use augmented-reality goggles to point out friend from foe? "Our communications technology is improving all the time."

Weptolyso snorted with acceptance. "Good. But those are not our only hurdles."

Irarjeg sat at the table and took a quick sip of his drink. He seemed ashamed of what Ariock might perceive as a failure.

"Well?" Ariock leaned against the wall. "What other obstacles are you facing?"

He assumed that any other problems were miscommunications. Former Torth tended to speak in rigid, stilted sentences and showed little emotion. Former slaves tended to ascribe the worst of intentions to them. As a result, penitents and liberated people hardly spoke to each other.

Perhaps Weptolyso and Irarjeg were issuing commands in a way that insulted mind readers? Or perhaps their commands were too kind, whereas the penitents wanted explicit orders?

Weptolyso and Irarjeg exchanged a weighty glance.

"I believe it is best if I show you." Weptolyso lumbered to his feet.

Ariock accompanied his friends out of the office, along the factory floor, and outside, into a partly cloudy day. The industrial areas were unattended. No work crews. The barracks looked abandoned, although they bordered a grassy square that looked trampled from recent use.

"Penitents!" Weptolyso bellowed. "Form up!"

There were no penitents in sight. Nothing stirred except for a breeze.

And a face. Ariock noticed a human-looking person peeking through the door of one of the barracks. She or he quickly drew back and the door quietly closed.

Irarjeg clicked his beak in derision and folded his arms. "They are not going to come out even for the Bringer of Hope?"

Weptolyso made a noise of disgust.

Ariock looked from one to the other, needing an explanation. Why would penitents refuse to obey a direct command? He had expected challenges, but he hadn't expected outright . . . well, what was this?

Outright refusal from the penitents?

Or crippling performance anxiety?

"They seemed happy to accept our training when we began," Weptolyso explained, seeing Ariock's unspoken questions. "But a day ago, they stopped."

"They simply stopped." Irarjeg seemed to think he was offering a more complete explanation.

"They won't touch a weapon," Weptolyso said. "They refuse to obey military commands. They all beg to be transferred out of this combat unit and back to ordinary work crew duties."

Ariock wanted this to be a miscommunication. If the best hand-selected penitents were just biding their time, pretending to be rehabilitated while they secretly rooted for a return to their overindulged lifestyles of godhood . . . then they could never be trusted.

That meant zombification *was* the only path forward.

Before the pink inhibitor gas, Ariock's military on Nuss had made headway. They had taken an entire continent. Now? Even with the warriors wearing air tanks and gas masks and taking double and triple shifts of duty, there were not enough to fend off every Torth raid. More than a dozen warriors had died in defense of nussian citizens.

The raids had only slowed when Thomas started sending zombified hordes into Torth cities.

Ariock paced, uncaring if the sky might gray with clouds to reflect his mood. He had been so hopeful about willing penitents. He had figured that if anyone could transform enslaved prisoners into friends, it would be Kessa and Weptolyso and people like them.

It should have worked.

Thomas had promised that it would work.

So much effort was going into the supposed rehabilitation of former Torth. Kessa oversaw tens of thousands of lieutenants. Each one of them worked with a crew of penitents, one-on-one, for many hours every day. Thomas wasted time every morning scanning the minds of hundreds of penitents, declaring them to be trustworthy.

Not trustworthy enough, apparently.

Meanwhile, Ariock's citizens on Nuss were being terrorized. Anyone who soared too far from his territories got shot down. If people dared to ride a hovercart or go for a hike in a slave farm or orchard area, they were likely to get snatched and collared by Torth. Or butchered. The Torth there were basically saying, *"Look at how inferior your species are to us. Your people are disposable."*

"PENITENTS!" Weptolyso roared even louder than before. "FORM UP!"

A few penitents slunk out of the barracks. Perhaps they had noticed the clouded sky.

Only two of them wore scraps of black armor. The rest wore the plain, baggy outfits of penitents. Together, they lined up like recruits, but they only took up a fraction of the square. Hundreds more must remain hidden in the barracks, unwilling to even pretend to be brave enough to face Ariock.

"Where are your weapons?" Weptolyso asked.

The row of penitents looked miserable. They kept their eyes downcast. Yellow eyes. Very few high ranks survived conquests to become penitents.

"Here." Irarjeg peeled off his blaster glove and threw it at the feet of the nearest mind reader. "You can use mine."

Ariock tensed and inhabited the air in front of himself. He thickened it to an impenetrable shield. Irarjeg had just casually tossed them a tool of assassination.

"Pick that up," Irarjeg commanded.

The penitent in question, a masculine-looking woman, visibly trembled.

"Or just bend down and touch it," Irarjeg said with impatience. "Can you do that much?"

The penitent spoke in a whisper. "I will not break Kessa's edict."

Kessa's laws for penitents included a decree that they were not permitted to touch weapons.

"You are exempt from Kessa's edict for training purposes," Weptolyso said in his gravelly voice. "You know that."

Ariock scrutinized the row of penitents. Young or old, fit or not, every single one of the penitents was a sniveling coward.

"What are you afraid of?" Ariock asked.

A few penitents shuffled or shifted their weight. They didn't seem to want to admit to anything.

"Answer the Son of Storms," Weptolyso commanded.

One penitent cleared her throat. "We are afraid of battle."

Soldiers lived with risks. That was the lifestyle. Ariock himself used to risk dying in battle before he'd designed his iconic galaxy armor. He still lived with a slight risk that a Torth might catch him off guard and unarmored.

"I heard you were beginning to train," Ariock said.

Silence.

"What changed your minds?" he asked.

More embarrassed foot shuffling.

The penitents really disliked speech. Either that, or they were terrified to admit whatever the truth was. Maybe they were hopelessly self-absorbed, like Evenjos?

They were probably afraid to admit that they considered themselves superior to mere soldiers.

Ariock turned away in disgust. There was no hope here.

"It was a good idea." Weptolyso's tone toward Ariock was comforting, meant to soothe. "They truly did seem willing to learn, at first. It was as if, all at once, they changed their minds."

Irarjeg nodded in agreement.

All at the same time? It sounded as if this experimental unit had decided to quit combat training, en masse, yesterday.

Ariock turned back to survey the few recruits who had dared to show their faces to him.

A couple of them met his gaze. Most looked downcast, but the ones who looked back were searching. They couldn't read his mind from a distance. They seemed afraid that he would figure something out.

What did the mind readers know that Ariock did not?

Surely Garrett or Thomas would have mentioned any news of note. Anyway, penitents were forbidden from ascending into the Megacosm. That was a core law. Garrett patrolled the Megacosm on a regular basis, and whenever he caught penitents there, he acted swiftly, executing the offender.

Thomas still visited the Megacosm once per day, to invite Torth to join the right side of the war. But he hadn't mentioned anything he found suspicious. Just . . .

"The Torth Empire is taking losses that make no sense," Thomas had explained during their last private hero council. "Why are they leaving garrisons on Nuss? Why not evacuate the planet completely?"

Ariock had dismissed that. Collective decision-making was not always wise decision-making. Sometimes the Torth Empire did stupid things.

"They're letting us defeat tons of Red Ranks and Rosies," Thomas had pointed out. "We're turning their best ranks into corpses or zombies. The Torth Majority is allowing that to happen, confident that their elder supergeniuses have some amazing secret plan that will defeat us. That alone has me worried. But on top of that, the top military ranks are enabling it. Something is afoot."

No one had any answers.

"It worries me," Thomas had concluded. "I can't figure out what their goal is, if there is one, but I don't like it. The Torth have left a lot of nuclear weapons and military ranks on Nuss. You need to be extra wary on that planet."

Ariock stretched out his awareness and floated the discarded blaster glove back to Irarjeg. A feeling of disquiet had taken root. He was definitely missing some vital knowledge.

Did these penitent cowards collectively assume, for some reason, that the Torth Empire was about to reconquer them?

If they had a solid reason to anticipate a major attack, then Thomas and Garrett must know about it. They must have picked up something beyond the obvious nonsensicalness of Torth brutality. Thomas absorbed penitent and Torth minds all day.

Yet he had not given Ariock anything that resembled a concrete warning.

# CHAPTER 10

# FORBIDDEN FRUIT

Riddled by shame, Thomas floated through the alley behind Lieutenant Yolpeen's townhouse.

He shouldn't be here. Between scanning his daily quota of penitents and zombifying hordes of captives on Nuss, he ought to rest in the Dragon Tower. Hide. Let his subconscious marinate in the multitudes of lives he had absorbed today. Bask in guilt.

He certainly did not belong in a residential neighborhood.

These proud rows of apartment buildings belonged to war council members and officials who were highly valued by Kessa. The dignitaries would not want their supergenius mind reader to lurk around their living quarters, disguised as an Alashani.

Thomas parked his hoverchair in an unobtrusive space where people normally parked hoverbikes. He had purposely borrowed a mundane gray hoverchair. No one should recognize it as belonging to the *rekveh*.

He inwardly cursed himself. He was being a complete idiot.

Even so, he slid off the seat. Loose pants hid his leg braces. Hopefully no one would hear the mechanized whirring of his exosuit. It was very understated. Ambient traffic noises drowned it out, mostly.

Penitents were not permitted to wear hats or anything like fashionable clothes. They wore glowing collars, and they had to keep their faces uncovered. So if anyone happened to glimpse Thomas, they should mistake him for a random Alashani in a sun hat. It was a good thing he had the proportions of those slender cave dwellers.

Thomas let himself into the garden yard through a gate.

Right on time, according to the schedule of chores Thomas had soaked up from someone in the household, the Pink Screwdriver trotted outside with a basket of laundry balanced on her hip.

She saw Thomas and froze.

Thomas's face was shaded beneath the big sun hat, but the Pink Screwdriver had the mind of a Torth, trained to look for clues beyond what was visually apparent. She knew that random shani had no reason to visit the Yolpeen household. And she might recognize his gangly preteen proportions.

Thomas pushed the hat back enough to show his face. He offered a harmless smile.

The Pink Screwdriver took a step back.

Thomas had prepared a slew of potentially reassuring things to convince her that he meant no harm. He would not brainwash her.

Before he even decided on which line to open with, the Pink Screwdriver set down her load of laundry. Her yellow eyes flashed as she took a quick look around, searching for voyeurs.

Then, apparently satisfied that no one was watching, she darted into range, grabbed Thomas by his lapels, and yanked him behind a row of shrubs.

Thomas lost his balance. He would have fallen, but the Pink Screwdriver cushioned him. She hauled him into a crawl space beneath the outdoor steps, into a dark little cubby hole.

Hm. Maybe she had picked up on his unspoken desires?

?!?!?! The Pink Screwdriver radiated a wordless demand to learn why the Conqueror had paid her a visit.

The space was only big enough for one person. Together, they barely fit. Her slave collar lent the place a dim glow. Thomas glimpsed a rumpled blanket. The cubby included a few meager personal items, such as a penlight. A hairbrush. Barrettes. A makeup kit.

Vetted penitents such as the Pink Screwdriver were assigned to households and treated like personal slaves. They avoided the worst manual labor. Instead of having to sleep in the filthy, overcrowded penitent barracks, they were given small places to sleep inside whatever household they'd been assigned to. Thomas knew, without needing to ask, that this cubby was where the Pink Screwdriver slept between work shifts.

*I know I should not be here.* Thomas acknowledged that right up front. *It is risky (for both of Us). If you ask Me to leave, I will be gone.*

Visiting this poor, unsuspecting, relatively innocent penitent was a terrible idea. He knew it. People would condemn him if they found out. The undergrounders would accuse Thomas of secretly colluding with the enemy. His friends would assume he was being exploitative, throwing his authority around to gratify his own personal pleasure.

Maybe he was.

Was that so wrong? Did it cross a line of morality? Thomas wasn't sure.

He thought he had detected a sultriness in this penitent when he had vetted her more than a month ago. He had sensed that she found his overly complex mind attractive, despite his freakishness and his monstrous reputation.

But perhaps he had misjudged the degree of her desire? Or she might have changed her mind.

*Oh.* The Pink Screwdriver's thought patterns smoothed into ripples of curiosity. *I see. You want sex?* She walked her fingers up his chest. *With Me?*

Thomas made an unspoken protest. He had not come here for sex. Not exactly.

Well, okay. Maybe he had.

Her touches set off pleasant tingles. His metal braces were not the only hard part of him.

*I only wanted . . .* Thomas gave up on mental articulation. It was so nice to talk without using words. The embarrassing honking octave drops of puberty were a regular thing with him.

He wordlessly let her know that he wanted something like comfort. He wanted a mind reader on his side.

Really, he wanted trillions of mind readers on his side.

But that strategy was proving to be *(a horrific failure)* too slow. It wasn't panning out. So never mind the droves, for now. He yearned for one—just one penitent Torth, if he could have that—who could understand him as intimately and as supportively as Cherise used to.

Cherise had shifted all her creative energy and beauty and love to Flen.

Vy and Ariock had each other.

Even Evenjos had managed to scrounge up love. She and Garrett were a pair.

Why couldn't Thomas have someone who acted as a touchstone in the same way, to ground him, and to help him sort out his emotions? He practically ruled this planet. Shouldn't he be able to procure some semblance of love?

He was so sick of being hated.

He was so tired of being relied upon and distrusted at the same time, while he soaked up other people's terrible lives, while he juggled research projects between planning conquests . . .

The Pink Screwdriver kissed him.

*!*

Her kiss was passionate while her mind fizzed with attraction. She lifted her skirt and straddled him.

Thomas sensed her thoughts, and his own frenzy built in response to her hot desire. She wanted to be on top of the most intelligent and powerful mind in the known universe. She really wanted to *(\*)(\*)(\*)(\*)* the Conqueror. But she feared . . .

She shoved him out of her cubby hole, into the jarringly sunlit garden.

*!!!* Thomas tried to crawl back inside.

She barred the entrance with her arms, her mood a clash of wanton desire versus logical refusal. Her hair was mussed up.

*Go away,* she silently begged him. *Savage sex is (not for the likes of Us Torth) wrong!*

Mind readers could not lie to each other, and Thomas sensed that she had fumbled out an excuse. She was desperately trying to obfuscate the reason for her deep-seated fear.

It had nothing to do with her still-savage lust.

That truth was as obvious to him as the bright-pink bell flowers nearby.

*What are you afraid I'll learn?* Thomas crawled closer, his own mood wilting. His sun hat had fallen off.

*I have nothing important to hide!* She withdrew, trying to avoid his range of telepathy.

Thomas sat in front of the entrance, blocking her escape. She did not quite dare shove past him. It would be a bad idea to assault the Conqueror. Any penitent knew that. After all, the Pink Screwdriver had seen the zombified hordes.

She had actually seen them.

*!*

  *!*

The Pink Screwdriver and Thomas stared at each other.

She shook with the fear of death. *Kill Me,* she begged. *I have transgressed. I partook in forbidden knowledge.*

She waited for him to destroy her with a pain seizure, or to twist her mind and make her kill herself. Penitents were not allowed to know anything that the Torth Empire knew. They were supposed to be separate, and different, from Torth. The penalty for accessing the Megacosm was death.

Thomas hesitated. According to his own laws—the laws that Kessa had set up, and that he had advised—he should kill the Pink Screwdriver.

But he had questions.

*How many penitents are secretly accessing the Megacosm?* he demanded. *It's not just you. Is it?*

She trembled. Fear spiked through her mood.

He graciously did not probe her mind. Instead, he waited for a willing answer.

She quivered. She had witnessed thousands of mindless wretches pour into garrisoned cities—wretches who used to have name-titles and civilized lifestyles. After they were brought before the Conqueror, reason could not reach them. They did not even have a self-preservation instinct. The only way to stop them was to kill them.

The zombies bludgeoned *(people)* Torth to death. If their weapons failed, they used their teeth and fingernails as if they were animals. They caused so much pain! They were pain incarnate.

*Please.* Thomas let her examine his sincerity. He only wanted to find out if he had somehow missed a large-scale insurrection. *If many penitents are accessing the Megacosm without Garrett or Myself learning of it, then We (I) will have to reexamine that law. And I will not (kill) harm you. I promise.*

She considered his offer.

Thomas wordlessly tried to soothe her, although his reassurances meant little even to a fellow mind reader. He was one of the few people in the galaxy who could mislead mind readers with ease.

After a moment, the Pink Screwdriver offered a fearful, hesitant answer. *(Please do not kill me.) I have not accessed the Megacosm.* She radiated sincerity. *Not since I was made into a penitent. I obey all Kessa's laws. Most penitents obey. We are good. I am good. Only a very few bad penitents break that law and ascend, and they are the ones who share their learnings with the rest of Us.*

Only a few.

Not her.

Thomas narrowed his eyes. Penitents were purposely kept apart from each other, in pods of ten or fewer. They were never allowed to congregate in large groups.

So how could eight hundred million penitents swap and share information?

There had better be a legitimate explanation.

# CHAPTER 11

# BENEATH COLLECTIVE WISDOM

It was natural for enslaved people to share gossip. Thomas had, in fact, privately theorized that an impromptu minicosm might have sprung up among the penitents. Too many of them reportedly shared the same outlooks and opinions, even when they lived on different planets.

*It is something like that*, the Pink Screwdriver admitted. *Not a minicosm! We never ascend. Here is how We share information:*

She unfurled a scenario in her imagination.

The Pink Screwdriver carried a trash bag from Lieutenant Yolpeen's house to the dumping receptacle at the corner of the block. On her return, she strolled past a fellow penitent in the street. Neither penitent acknowledged each other in public. They did not look at each other. They merely walked past each other, each one apparently busy with their respective errands.

Nevertheless, an information exchange happened.

It was furtive. It would have seemed rudely curt to a Torth citizen. Apparently, though, this quick exchange was a ritual penitents had developed as a means of sharing gossip. Each penitent dumped a quick summary of newly acquired news upon the other.

Penitents made these furtive little exchanges any time they passed within telepathy range of another penitent.

*I see.* Thomas picked up his sun hat and dusted it off.

In some ways, their mesh network was more dangerous than he had imagined. It was formalized. It was widespread.

He sensed, from the Pink Screwdriver's fearful memories, that any penitent who refused to participate in the information grapevine was shunned. The peer pressure to share information was intense. Those who truly went renegade and cut all ties to collective thinking were castigated.

True renegades became pariahs.

Their meals got confiscated. Their chores got sabotaged. They continued to look and act like any other penitent, but sooner or later, they would get murdered in secret. A mafia of "the unknown" had formed in the penitent barracks.

The Pink Screwdriver had tears in her eyes, making them gleam even more brightly yellow. *Are You going to end it?*

He should.

Their widespread network had an umbilical cord, however tenuous, to the Megacosm. That meant all penitents were listening to news they should not have access to and learning things they should not know.

*It is harmless!* the Pink Screwdriver pleaded. *It is just harmless, empty gossip. We hardly know what is going on among the Torth. The news reaches me hours later. Sometimes a day later. I barely know anything.*

Thomas was hardly mollified. Although the penitents were not currently shar-ing anything useful with Torth leadership—otherwise Garrett would have picked up on it—sharing in the Megacosm was a two-way street. All eight hundred million penitents could be turned in an instant. Sooner or later, the Torth Majority would apply pressure to the penitents in just the right way.

His territories had a gaping hole in their defenses. And he hadn't even seen it.

*No!* Tears spilled down the Pink Screwdriver's cheeks. *Most of Us (penitents) want to experience emotions freely. We want to be good. Very few of Us want to return to the Torth Empire!* She offered a shy admission. *I don't.*

And yet they had collectively broken a core law.

*Out of fear!* The Pink Screwdriver gazed at him, her iridescent eyes reflect-ing her collar's glow against earthy darkness. *You have immense self-confidence.* She reached out and caressed his arm. It was an oddly tender gesture, and a strange new experience for both of them. *You never doubt that You will win the war, because You are the Conqueror.* Her fingernails sent shivers across his skin. *But We?* She meant all penitents. *We are far too small to feel certain.*

Thomas's curiosity was aroused. He craved a more thorough explanation.

The Pink Screwdriver was ashamed, but she wanted him to understand. *I can meekly obey and serve Your loyalists, and that is not betrayal to the Torth Majority. That is survival. It is logical. Pragmatic. It is acceptable, from a Torth perspective.*

Thomas knew that. He urged her to make her point.

*But,* she thought, *if I get ready to shoot Torth? There is a line that gets crossed. If I take a spoken name—if I throw myself wholly on Your side—there is no going back. If I ingratiate myself with Your forces and converse out loud? That is choosing a side. The Torth Majority will never reaccept traitors.*

Thomas leaned back on his hands.

The secret, furtive mesh network explained why the penitents refused to pick up weapons to fight their Torth brethren. It explained why so few of them chose spoken names. They would not cast aside the last dregs of their Torth loyalties as long as there was a possibility that doing so would get them killed.

*You believe that the Torth Empire is going to win,* he realized.

Of course they believed that. They were still Torth in their hearts.

*How should I know?* She hung her head, waves of misery radiating off her. *No one knows who will win. All I know is that the collective wisdom of the Majority is enough (more than enough) to remind me that I am Torth, and that the Torth Empire may yet prevail.*

Thomas felt elated and sickened at the same time.

This explained why Kessa's outreach efforts were failing. The penitents were still Torth in their hearts. They clung to their Torth identities.

He should not allow this to continue. He could not—should not—approve of a secret gossip network that worsened the gap in understanding between former slaves and former Torth. It was too dangerous.

Once Garrett became aware of the mesh network, he would go ballistic. He would make sure that all penitents were eradicated or zombified.

And he might be right to do so.

Fear spiked off the Pink Screwdriver. *You have turned My life into garbage.* She curled up. *(Please kill Me) You ought to kill Me. If You don't? The penitent mafia will do it as vengeance. They will track down who told the Conqueror.*

Thomas had not come here to interrogate and threaten this penitent. He resented the unpleasant turn his visit had taken. *What do you penitents discuss?* he wondered. *Do you chat about ways to overthrow Me?*

*No!* She threw the answer at him.

*So are you simply biding your time and waiting for Me to lose?* Thomas prepared to dive into her memories. This was too important to let slide. He needed to understand how traitorous the Pink Screwdriver and her ilk were.

*You don't understand.* The Pink Screwdriver gave Thomas a pleading look. *Our secret network is as You called it—a tenuous umbilical cord. For me, it is a breath of sanity. It is all I have.* She propped herself up against the filthy wall. *Can You understand that?* She searched his face. *I have lost everything I ever owned. My dignity. My status. My wealth. My sense of belonging. Even the beliefs I grew up with. I have nothing but this hovel.* She flicked her hand around the cubby hole.

Thomas was prepared to harden his heart against her justifications. Instead, he found himself listening.

His foster sisters had suffered a similar loss. He contained Vy's memories of being ripped away from her home on Earth and forced into slavery.

*Whenever I gain a scrap of a delayed glimpse from the Megacosm,* the Pink Screwdriver thought, *I feel a Comfort.* She was flustered. *I am having difficulty conveying it.*

But Thomas understood.

He, too, had quit the Megacosm for long stretches of time. It was like withdrawal from a powerful drug.

He knew that whenever the Pink Screwdriver caught a glimpse of ordinary Torth sharing their minds in the Megacosm, she felt assured that civilization was still going strong. She might hate her hovel. She might suffer from daily chores. Yet she could cling to the notion of a great and glorious galactic empire, and she could draw strength from the notion that someday, she might be part of something great again.

That hope gave her the strength to keep working. To survive. To keep going.

Promises from Thomas or Kessa did not offer the same hope. Those promises were sketchy and dubious. To former Torth, the Torth Empire still loomed. It was larger than Ariock. It was more concrete than love and happiness could ever be.

*I will not take that away from you.* Thomas tentatively scooted closer to the Pink Screwdriver.

He would have to cast this knowledge out of his conscious mind whenever Garrett or Evenjos was nearby. He would need to keep this a secret from his friends. Even from Ariock.

Was it worth taking such pains?

Thomas decided that for now, yes, it was. The emergent mesh network might be dangerous, but it was also fascinating. It kept the penitents sane. In time, all those penitents might betray him and rejoin the Torth Empire . . . or they might fully convert to his side and become his willing allies.

There was still time.

There was still hope.

Anyway, the alternative was mass zombification.

The Pink Screwdriver radiated the warmth of gratitude. *You really do understand.*

Thomas still felt troubled. Now that he was alert to the potential problem, he would be more assiduous about mind probes. The penitents had better not plot a rebellion. If he caught any whiff of a threat . . .

The Pink Screwdriver opened her arms, inviting. *Aside from galactic news, penitents just share stupid gossip. That is all.*

Thomas crawled into the cubby hole with her. The scent of her conditioned hair was pleasant. He even liked the cozy environment. Never mind the scent of dirt, or the occasional crawly bug.

The Pink Screwdriver worked loose one of his upper buttons. *We discuss silly stuff.* She invited him to search her mind. *We experiment with makeup. We practice with emotions and primitive behavior.* She worked loose another two buttons.

Thomas barred her from touching any more of his buttons.

Was the Pink Screwdriver likely to share news of this tryst with her fellow penitents? If this became a public scandal, all his secrets would unravel. Who would trust him afterward? Not even Ariock.

*I am not suicidal.* The Pink Screwdriver laughed softly. *Your concubine (or sex toy, or whatever You wish me to be) would be a military target. I have no desire for that spotlight. I will keep Our encounters a secret, Great One.*

That was reassuring. But Thomas didn't like her self-characterization. *People are not toys,* he thought. *I am not here to exploit you.*

*Whatever.* She understood that he was offering one sort of truth, and she appreciated the sentiment. But she was also painfully aware of how little value her life had. *I will serve You however You wish, Conqueror.*

She ripped open the buttons of his vest and began to aggressively kiss him, on the mouth and then down his naked chest.

She was so pleasant, so soft and warm.

Part of Thomas responded helplessly to her touches. That part of him seemed to have a mind of its own.

His actual mind, however, processed and analyzed incoming data at a rate that was not conducive to the enjoyment of physical sensation.

He could not avoid overhearing her private thoughts. The Pink Screwdriver was academically curious about carnal pleasures. She had overheard other penitents attempting sex, and she wanted to test out the primitive act for herself. If the Conqueror was offering? Yum. That was far superior to screwing the creepy old penitent next door who kept sending silent hints that he was willing.

Yet she was also cognizant of the dank, cramped cubby that she called home. It wasn't exactly welcoming, in her opinion. They were about to act like animals rutting in a den.

And she was so sexually inexperienced, she feared she would accidentally offend the Conqueror. He must know all sorts of human tricks . . .

"Stop."

Thomas used a spoken word. That seemed the best way to break through her anxiety.

*I am just as inexperienced in sexual matters as you.* Thomas slid an arm around her, urging her to lie beside him. *Let's just get to know each other. That way, maybe it can be a good experience (instead of awkward) for both of Us.*

The Pink Screwdriver emanated shame. She had accidentally inundated the Conqueror with her uncontrolled worries, and wasn't that rude? Anxiety wasn't sexy. No wonder he wanted to fend her off.

*You're fine.* Thomas brushed a lock of dark hair away from her pretty face. *I'm the one who interrupted your routine life.*

He held her, enjoying her scent. And he opened his inner self for her perusal.

Spoken language could never equal the way mind readers spoke to each other. Thomas let himself relax some of his own wariness. He kept his military secrets locked up tight. Those were not for the Pink Screwdriver.

But he had well-hidden personal vulnerabilities, and for the first time, he allowed someone else to glimpse them.

# CHAPTER 12

# UNDERGROUNDERS

"Flen!"

Flen turned at the unexpected salutation. Jinishta entered the alley. She was the one who had called Flen's name—and in a friendly tone, no less.

The two undergrounders with whom he had been chatting made quick excuses to leave. Aishel returned to his merchandise stall. Heffen adjusted her Yeresunsa mantle and whispered "Good luck" to Flen before she hurried away, with a deferential nod to the premier of premiers.

"I hope I wasn't interrupting anything important," Jinishta said, walking up to Flen. "I tried to reach you this way." She tapped her wrist, indicating her supercom. "But it seems you're unavailable?"

Flen never used supercoms when he was off duty, but he knew how futile it would be to lecture Jinishta on the evils of *rekveh* technology. She used to understand. Now? Jinishta seemed to embrace everything alien as a good thing.

"Can I buy you a drink?" Jinishta said. "It's been too long, I know." She seemed ashamed of her busy schedule and the distance that had grown between her and some of her oldest friends. "But I have something to discuss with you."

"Certainly."

Flen had been expecting a conversation with Jinishta. Two premiers had died in battles recently, and rumors abounded about who would be promoted to replace them. Flen was a favorite among certain councilors and warriors.

He let Jinishta choose a nearby café, and he did not complain when the person who served them mushroom ale turned out to be a non-Alashani govki.

Jinishta looked as overworked as he felt. There was something unexpected in her countenance. She had a steely determination that overrode any softness.

"The war isn't going so well," Flen dared to observe. "Is it?"

He wondered if Jinishta would admit it. Jinishta never said anything demoralizing. She probably wasn't allowed to.

"I am sure Thomas will invent a way for us to become immune to inhibitor gas," Jinishta said, idly watching pedestrian traffic beyond their outdoor table. "Eventually. And then we can get back to killing Torth and enjoying our return to light and glory."

Although her statements sounded confident, Flen wondered if she hid secret doubts. Their mission to liberate countless slaves on thousands of planets was such a ludicrous goal. It was too big for reality. Surely Jinishta felt that?

She might have heard something about the undergrounder movement.

Had she figured out that Flen was a gateway to joining? Was it possible that she wasn't here just to offer him a promotion, but to make surreptitious inquiries about something that truly mattered?

Flen considered ways to suss out her interests. How much did Jinishta care about Alashani purity? Would she forgive Flen if he chose to stand up and speak in public about the dangerous erosion of Alashani morals and values?

He opened his mouth to ask.

"Flen." Jinishta pushed her brew aside and faced him with an intense look. "I asked to talk with you for an important reason."

Ah. This might be it.

Flen tried to look welcoming. If she asked to join the undergrounder movement, he would not be entirely surprised.

"I'm sure you know, as well as I do," Jinishta said, "that the war's leadership is under intense pressure. Ariock is just barely defending the lands we have conquered. The cities on Nuss are forced to defend themselves without our help."

That was common knowledge. Flen nodded.

"I have heard a troubling rumor." Jinishta met his gaze. "I am unsure whether to believe it. But . . ." She hesitated. "Do you remember Densaava? The warrior who attempted to kill Thomas?"

Flen forced himself to look ignorant. Poor Densaava was not allowed to return to Freedomland. He was stranded in some backwater urban ghetto on one of Umdalkdul's moons, severed from contact with his friends and family. He wasn't even allowed to govern the people there. He had to serve them, and if he resisted, he might be transferred to an even worse outpost.

"Densaava probably did not act alone." Jinishta rotated her mug of ale, reluctant. "My informants say there is a secret organization among Alashani purists. They call themselves the undergrounders."

Flen tried to look surprised.

"They want to return to life underground," Jinishta went on. "And they foolishly believe that the only way to do that is to abandon this war and kill Thomas."

She spoke that unholy name with such casual kindness. Did she truly consider that *rekveh* a friend? Was she brainwashed?

"I came to you because you love Cherise." Jinishta gave Flen a warm look. "So you will want to protect her human family. I mean, her siblings. Thomas is her foster brother."

Flen choked on the brew he was sipping. He knew that Cherise had a *rekveh* in her family—not a blood relation, thank the gods—but it was extremely offensive to blurt it out. If Flen married Cherise, they absolutely must hide that family shame.

He coughed away his disgust and regained his expression of polite interest.

"And I know you love the messiah." Jinishta sounded certain. "You were right there with us when he built the space ark that saved our people."

"Right." Flen had to work hard in order to say that without sarcasm. That spaceship had saved a lot of Alashani, but it had not saved his mother or father or sister.

"You understand what is at stake," Jinishta said.

Flen nodded, although he had no idea what she was getting at.

"We cannot afford to deal with threats to Thomas on top of everything else," Jinishta elaborated. "Thomas is the only reason our species has survived at all. And he continues to protect us. Without him, we would have no supercoms, no space armor, and no warnings of when and where Torth will attack. This entire war will fail without him."

Flen felt sickened by the worship in her voice. Jinishta must be a puppet of the *rekveh* Thomas, just as much as the messiah was.

"And then the Torth will overrun everyone and reenslave them," Jinishta said. "And us."

*Not if we find a cave and go underground*, Flen thought. *As we should.* But he pretended to nod in agreement.

"So." Jinishta clasped his arm. "I'm aware that you have friends among Alashani purists. I would really appreciate it if you could dig deep and identify anyone who might be an undergrounder. I need names."

Flen's sick feeling worsened.

"It would be a huge help to Ariock," Jinishta said. "And to me. If we are going to survive this war, we cannot put up with fake warriors who undermine everything that we do."

"What are you planning to do with the culprits?" Flen asked.

But he knew, even before Jinishta answered.

"Exile," she said. "I suppose we can try a reformation program for some of those on the periphery of the organization. But obviously, we cannot let threats to Thomas stick around."

"Obviously." Flen pretended to be just another mindless messiah worshipper. "Right. I completely agree."

Jinishta's face transformed with one of her rare smiles. "Thank you, Flen. I knew I could count on you."

His return smile felt so fake, it was a wonder she didn't notice.

# CHAPTER 13

# BENEATH THE BAIT

Only the most savvy explorers could find the dugout way station in the red-rock desert between Tempest Arena and Telemetry City. One had to study the way each baobab bush leaned and recognize the faint imprint of what might be a nussian footprint in the loose dust in the leeward shadows of rocks.

Ruuktdmaroochdt found the disguised trapdoor after three days of hiking in harsh conditions. She traveled only at night, with her pebbly golden skin rubbed with dark clay. She had hiked through a haboob, with razor-sharp dust whipping into her large mouth and nostrils, almost enough to make her suffocate. But the violent sandstorm was both a curse and a blessing. It meant her tracks were covered. The Torth could not see her if they were searching.

The first thing she did, upon climbing down into the hidden dugout shelter, was to gorge on water from a keg. Nussians could last for days without water, but she needed copious amounts after her ordeal.

There was enough light streaming through the open air vents in the ceiling to cast the supply shelves in dusty beams of sunlight. Ruuktdmaroochdt ate half of the nonperishable travel wafers on one shelf. It was difficult for a nussian to starve for an entire day and night, let alone for three of them.

She also flicked the signal beam. Her alert would light up on military monitors in the nearby friendly city and its outposts. That would let military officials know that the way station needed tending. Someone would be sent to pick her up under cover of night.

While she waited for nightfall, she reviewed the materials she had smuggled in a pouch affixed to her armpit. That was a place on a nussian body that people rarely saw.

There were a dozen data cubes the size of pebbles. Each one contained a recorded message from an undercover agent. She had also smuggled out a map of the Torth-held city, tightly folded, drawn by a slave with an eidetic memory. She had written the labels on the map herself, since she knew the art of writing. Most slaves did not.

And there was her most prized possession: a tiny camera, designed to appear as a cartilage growth at the base of one of her shoulder spikes. She wore it while pretending to serve the Torth. Her holographic recordings would show exactly where the most dangerous Torth lived in Telemetry City, as well as the city's busiest thoroughfares and weakest points.

Satisfied that her smuggled goods were safe and unscathed, she repackaged them and settled into a nussian crouch for a nap.

Daylight was still streaming through the vents when the whoosh of an arriving hovercart woke her from a doze. The crunch of footsteps above was disappointingly light.

"Hello?" The cheerful voice had a foreign accent. It must be one of those albino aliens that looked vaguely akin to Torth.

Ruuktdmaroochdt snorted in response. She would have preferred to be picked up by a fellow nussian.

It wasn't that she disrespected smaller species. Some of her kinsfolk drew a disturbing sense of superiority from their natural size, but she liked govki and ummins just fine. She just found small folks to be . . . well . . . easy to bump into. They got underfoot. They never thought to make room in crowded places, so she was always forced to slow down because of them.

If she was perfectly honest with herself, their delicateness made them seem a bit too akin to Torth. Frail size was just a tad unnatural for sapient beings.

"I'm coming down," the shani called.

Ruuktdmaroochdt backed up to make room. She thought she recognized the voice. "Chayni?"

"How'd you know my name?" The little shani hopped to the floor and turned, folding back her floppy hat with a grin.

"I have a good memory," Ruuktdmaroochdt said truthfully.

Most people in Tempest Arena had met Chayni, or had at least heard about her reputation. Albinos tended to be insular. Those who weren't stood out. One ugly rumor even said that Chayni . . . well. Ruuktdmaroochdt doubted that a shani and a nussian would ever explore each other sexually, no matter how adventurous they were. That rumor was almost certainly false.

"Whew! It's boiling hot out here." Chayni walked to the kegs and poured water into her canteen. She murmured a strange little prayer over it—something about the Lady of Sorrow watching over her loved ones in the land of the dead—then gulped it down. "Hey. So, what's your name?"

"Ruuktdmaroochdt."

Chayni made a face. "Can I call you Ruuktd?" Apparently, she found a majestically multisyllabic name to be annoying. "There are restock supplies in the hovercart. Would you mind bringing them down?"

"It is dangerous to work in daylight," Ruuktdmaroochdt pointed out. What had possessed her ride to show up in the middle of the day?

"Oh. Sorry." Chayni looked guilty. "Truth to tell, I wanted an excuse to get off penitent duty. They're being especially creepy today." She shrugged. "I heard someone needed a lift, and I thought, hey! I've never been to the way station before." She clasped her hands behind her back, bashful. "I hope I didn't overstep? Were you expecting someone else?"

"It is fine." Ruuktdmaroochdt let out a forgiving exhalation. "We might as well get moving." Daylight work was risky, but she would be grateful to get home in time to share a home-cooked stew with her neighbors. "I will help you restock the station."

She did not complain about being asked to fetch and carry. A nussian could unload a hovercart faster and more efficiently than a shani, after all. She only wished that shani and other small species would stop making assumptions. Why did they never seek a nussian's help for, say, mathematical calculations? Or writing lessons? There was an implicit assumption in the questions that never got asked.

They made small talk while they worked. Chayni was interested in hearing about how city slaves reacted to the legend of Kessa the Wise. She wanted every detail of what it was like to smuggle things between the land of the free and the land of the enslaved.

After a while, Ruuktdmaroochdt changed the topic. "You said the penitents are behaving in a creepy manner. What do you mean?"

"Oh." Chayni shoved boxes of paper goods onto a low shelf. "You know how they do things in sync?" She shrugged. "They're doing that a lot. And now they're talking in sync."

"Talking?" Ruuktdmaroochdt swapped an empty water keg for a full one. "I thought they rarely talked?"

"They usually don't!" Chayni agreed with fervency. "But today? So creepy. They were hissing mean things at me and the other guards on duty. Like, 'Y o u a r e d o o m e d' and 'w e w i l l w i n.' Ugh." The albino shuddered. "I hate them so much. I was supposed to guard them until sunset, but I begged a friend to swap his duty for mine." Chayni perked up, adding supplies to the first aid kit. "He gave me a lesson on how to drive! It was really great."

Ruuktdmaroochdt remembered that shani avoided technology. It went against their religion or something.

A dangerous pickup should not have gone to someone inexperienced. Anyone competent would have waited until sunset to set out.

Chayni looked surprised to see Ruuktdmaroochdt climbing out of the dugout. "Oh, I guess we're leaving now?"

"The hovercart is visible in daylight," Ruuktdmaroochdt reminded her. "We are not safe until we cross the border into our own territory."

Chayni murmured a quick prayer to someone whom she referred to as the Maiden of Candlelight. Then she scrambled up the ladder, which consisted of divots chipped into the rock face. She hurried to join Ruuktdmaroochdt aboard the hovercart.

"Can I drive?" Chayni offered. "I know how."

But Ruuktdmaroochdt was already working the controls.

They sped across coppery sand and rounded rocks. It was a relief to use technology without the terrifying possibility that a mind reader might glide past and pick up some illegal stray thought.

The most difficult part of being a smuggler was—by far—faking ignorance. In the Torth city, Ruuktdmaroochdt could not allow anyone to even suspect that she could read glyphs, or that she understood data tablets, or that she had learned how the Torth communicated long-distance, or how freedom worked in practice. She dared not even allow fellow nussians to figure out who she really was, lest their minds be probed. She had to pretend to be a slave.

But that was the thrill. That was the challenge.

Ruuktdmaroochdt had done it four times, and she would do it again. In her own way, she knew, she was a war hero.

She didn't even care about the respect it earned her at home. She cared about spreading the message of freedom and preparing slaves for liberation. She cared about the lives she changed.

After all, Ariock Dovanack was a distant demigod. He dwelled in some foreign paradise—a world without Torth. People had seen the Son of Storms from a distance, hurling lightning bolts or floating in midair, but no one ever feasted with him, or with Kessa the Wise, or with Weptolyso the Brave, or with any other legends. No one even knew if Jonathan Stead existed, for sure. A lot of people suspected that he and the Son of Storms were the same deity.

If this war was truly going to be won, Ruuktdmaroochdt figured that it would be won by people, not demigods. It would be won by people like herself.

It would not be due to shani war heroes, either. Those albino magicians wore purple mantles of power, but how many actually went into combat? They sent drooling zombies into war zones instead of themselves. Sure, the zombies attacked Torth like rage-fueled battlebeasts, but the shani seemed to have no interest in sticking around after a conquest. They spoke of being transferred to other worlds. Nuss was not their home.

There were rumors that all the liberated people would be evacuated to some faraway paradise, but Ruuktdmaroochdt had trouble believing that. Why liberate so many cities on Nuss only to give up and leave?

Well, she would continue to fight even if the heroes abandoned them. So would many other liberated slaves. They would not let Torth snap collars around their necks, or shackles around their arms, ever again. They understood: It was freedom or death.

"Do you have any family, Ruuktd?" Chayni asked.

"I was a slave." Her origin should be obvious, judging by her scars and the way she talked. There were actually families of nussians who had been born free, but those rare individuals spoke like Chayni, with the Alashani accent. They were far less tough than ordinary nussians.

"Oh." Chayni flounced against the railing. "Well, I'm just sick of my family. My parents act all proud that my brother is a war hero. Like he's the only person who matters in our family. We never see him! He might as well be a stranger. Meanwhile, as far as they're concerned, I'm basically a garbage eater who just vomited onto their rug. They . . ."

She nattered on while Ruuktdmaroochdt used the dashboard holographic display to scan their route.

The overlays were customized with paradise letters instead of Torth glyphs. That way, Torth might have trouble using this technology, whereas any free person who had learned to read could page through menus and make their desired selections.

According to rumors, the radar system was invented by a very smart renegade Torth—the same one who generated all the zombified minions. Ruuktdmaroochdt had trouble believing that such a renegade Torth existed. Yet she was aware that the radar system was clever, and it was, indeed, a step above what the Torth had. It scanned to the horizons and beyond, and it digitized any fast-moving vehicles onto a wire-frame map.

She studied the radar map every few seconds. Its emptiness encouraged her. Meanwhile, she also kept an eye out for tall rocks and fissures in the ground, just in case they might need a fast spot in which to hide. One could never be too careful in Torth territory.

"Weird." Chayni stared at her wristwatch com with suspicion. "No one is answering my calls."

Coms could die in extreme heat. "Is it possible you left it somewhere hot?" Ruuktdmaroochdt asked.

"No, it's working." Chayni held up her com to prove it. "But no one is answering." She tapped the tiny menu. "I've tried calling six people."

Ruuktdmaroochdt held up one large hand to quiet the shani. Motionless shapes dotted the horizon.

She checked the radar. It was clear.

Indeed, the distant shapes were too evenly spaced, and too top-heavy, to be transports. Ruuktdmaroochdt steered wide. But even though she went far afield, the motionless things stood on the horizon. There must be thousands of them.

"Chayni, can you see what those things are?"

The shani squinted. "I don't know. Um, mushrooms?"

Ruuktdmaroochdt snorted. Alashani folks called every plant a mushroom, even if it was a tree or a flower. Anyhow, there were no forests in the desert.

"Let me see your com," Ruuktdmaroochdt said.

It turned out that Chayni was right. The com seemed to be working fine. Yet every call they made, whether to a department or to a friend, went unanswered.

Ruuktdmaroochdt felt her spikes pop out. Something felt wrong.

"You okay?" Chayni asked.

"Hush," she whispered back.

Wretched cries of despair came on the wind.

She saw the wrongness even as she heard it. Chayni saw it, too.

Tortured bodies on crossbeams littered the landscape with such gluttonous abandon, they truly seemed to be a forest that stretched to the horizon and beyond. The smell of blood and sweat-soaked misery carried on the breeze.

Nussians hung in chains from iron loops that looked hammered into their forearms. "Help," one croaked. Others moaned, their bodies hanging unnaturally, their shoulders dislocated.

Ruuktdmaroochdt had seen torture before. As a former gladiator, she had caused more brutality than most people ever witnessed. She had seen some of the worst depravities that Torth were capable of.

Even so.

This was the most grisly display she had ever seen. Many thousands of people were dying, strung up on crossbeams. It might be the population of her entire city.

"Save us."

"Where is the Son of Storms?"

"Please."

Govki hung by their upper pairs of arms. Even ummins had awful stakes hammered through their arms, linking them to chains so they could hang in torment.

Chayni squeaked in horror. "Gechel?"

An albino hung from one of the crossbeams, blood streaking his arms from the iron spikes. He wore a purple mantle.

A war hero.

Those types of shani were supernaturally fast and agile, and they could hurl specially reinforced spears that pierced Torth armor. Just one warrior could singlehandedly defeat a troop of military Torth. But Gechel was defeated.

*We are in trouble*, Ruuktdmaroochdt thought.

"He is alive!" Chayni's hand flew to her mouth.

"Hush," Ruuktdmaroochdt whispered. Torth might still be in the vicinity. Gechel could not have been left out in the desert sun for long, because his skin was only a bit pink instead of red.

"These people are alive!" Chayni cried, far too loud. "We must rescue them!"

"Quiet." Ruuktdmaroochdt widened the radar scan. Nothing. But radar could only pick up vehicles, not people.

Motion in the desert caught her eye. All her spikes popped out as she mentally prepared for something awful.

It was just a tumbleweed. It bounced between the crossbeams.

"I need your strength!" Chayni whispered fiercely. "Let's rescue Gechel."

"Put on your blaster glove," Ruuktdmaroochdt whispered. She herself lacked a weapon.

"I don't see any Torth," Chayni whispered, pulling on her glove.

"They could be hidden." Ruuktdmaroochdt retraced the path of the tumbleweed with her gaze. Tumbleweeds tended to gather in arroyos. Sure enough, she spotted a distant depression—an arroyo. A place to hide. Good.

She steered in that direction.

"We need to rescue Gechel!" Chayni's luminous eyes were wide. "Where are you going? Turn around!"

Ruuktdmaroochdt gave Chayni a look. She poured all her warnings and personal experiences into that look.

Chayni failed to see it. She climbed onto the hovercart railing, entirely focused on her own emotional pain.

Pain was bait.

Any slave knew that truth. Ruuktdmaroochdt had seen many good people die in an attempt to protect or rescue someone else. That was how most slaves died. Even farm slaves, who had a modicum of freedom, knew what happened during reaping time, when Torth came to collect their strongest and most promising children. Sometimes older siblings got in the way. Or parents.

Attempted interventions never ended well. One did not defy the Torth.

Ruuktdmaroochdt refused to feel the full brunt of the despair and horror that the Torth wanted her to feel. Every crossbeam was high up, its dangling victim out of reach, so she refused to look up. She ignored their moans and their pleas for help.

She did, however, activate her tiny camera. She made sure it was affixed in its customary place on her shoulder, camouflaged, and she tilted it for a view of the victims. She started recording.

"Argh!" Chayni glared as if Ruuktdmaroochdt were some kind of insanely selfish Torth loyalist. "Protect your own hide, if that's all you care about. I'm not abandoning my brother!"

Chayni leaped off the vehicle and landed on the rocky ground. Soon she was running back toward the crossbeam that held her kinsman.

Her admonishment lingered.

Ruuktdmaroochdt steered toward the embankment, seeking safety and a way to flee this death trap. But where could she go? Her home city had clearly been attacked. Her neighbors were dying from torture right in front of her eyes.

What if Chayni was right? What if Ruuktdmaroochdt was just a slave, obeying instincts that led to slavery instead of freedom?

Ruuktdmaroochdt nudged the hovercart into the arroyo. It landed on dirt with a soft *whomp*. Instead of following the zigzag fissure, Ruuktdmaroochdt crouched and lifted her eyestalks just enough so she could peer over the embankment. She was hidden by rocks.

In the distance, Chayni circled the base of the crossbeam, frustrated. It was clear that she had no idea how to act as a savior.

Perhaps she would figure out that she could use her canteen strap as a climbing aid? Shani seemed made for climbing. Some of them climbed sheer cliffs just for sport. With that strap, she might shimmy up—

Chayni yipped and flew backward through the air.

Ruuktdmaroochdt covered her mouth to prevent her own cry of dismay. She instinctively knew to be silent.

A group of Torth stood beyond the rise of a hill.

Their armor marked them as Red Ranks, dusty from a hike. But that armor was a lie. At least one of them had Yeresunsa powers.

Ruuktdmaroochdt glanced helplessly down at her naked fist. If only she had a blaster cannon.

The Torth used their powers to erect another huge crossbeam, and they hoisted Chayni up there. The shani kicked and writhed, but she was helpless against their powers. Her screams of agony wrenched at Ruuktdmaroochdt.

She crouched down, feeling like a coward.

She didn't know how many Rosy Ranks might be patrolling this area. For all she knew, more Torth might be hidden in this very arroyo. And if one Torth saw her hovercart, the rest would know.

They would hoist Ruuktdmaroochdt onto a crossbeam as easily as they had handled the little albino.

She could wait and hope for the Torth to leave without spotting her. Then she could act like a hero in a story and rush around, freeing Chayni and other victims. That was the sort of foolhardy bravery that Alashani praised.

But smugglers knew the difference between story heroes and real heroes.

One did not defy the Torth by dancing in front of them. That was a path to death. The best way—the only way—to beat them was to stay low and to look for opportunities. A smuggler recognized opportunities that most slaves would overlook.

Like her camera.

If Ruuktdmaroochdt could get back to the way station, there was a superluminal signal booster there. She could transmit her camera footage to friendly cities. Some of those cities had military fleets with pilots who used to be slaves.

Her footage might even reach someone who could save the entire tortured population of Tempest Arena before they died.

# PART FOUR

*"Equality and justice cannot exist until every person is born with the same powers."*

—Unyat

# CHAPTER 1

# ESCALATION

The holographic recording glowed with eerie, flickering color. Combined with the content, it gave Ariock the impression that he was watching an excerpt from a horror film.

There were so many victims.

A city's worth. An entire metropolis that Ariock had failed to protect.

Lightning flashed, thunder rolled, and rain began to pour down. Ariock didn't care if the whole universe saw his reaction. Apparently the Torth believed they were safe, surrounded by pink inhibitor gas emitters. Idiots. Ariock had been gentle on the planet Nuss, giving each Torth garrison time to kneel and peacefully surrender before he inundated them with zombified hordes.

Here was proof that they didn't deserve mercy.

"If they want violence and death," Ariock said, "I will bring it." He would start with the perpetrators of this latest atrocity. "Where is this?" he demanded. "Telemetry City?"

"Tempest Arena," Thomas said. "But this situation merits analysis."

The little ummin captain, Fayfer, gasped. "The victims are still alive!" She pointed to the holographic projection.

Ariock took a closer look. The recording lacked audio, so he had not heard anyone screaming or moaning. But Fayfer was correct. The Torth on Nuss had purposely strung up millions of living people on metal crosses, the way Ariock had once suffered.

The Torth were reminding him of the power they had once wielded over him.

Power they clearly thought they were still entitled to.

"We must rescue them." Jinishta's tone held urgency. She was already dressed for combat, and she tapped her supercom. "Ariock, there are warriors there. They will burn in the desert sun."

Warriors were indispensable. There were so few of them left, street performers were able to reenact every single heroic name and deed.

Ariock prepared to put himself into the clairvoyant trance, aware that his best captains were already readying troops for teleportation. There was no time to waste.

"Can we stop and think about this for a minute?" Thomas was pleading. "This is setting off alarm bells in my mind. That's why I wanted to meet with you first."

"Out with it, then," Garrett barked.

"What do you see, Thomas?" Evenjos asked with decorum.

"This is a provocation." Thomas paused the holograph so it froze in motion. Rows of crucified victims paused in death throes. "The nussian who sent this footage characterizes the scene as bait, and I happen to agree. This was architected to make us angry." He looked directly at Ariock and said, "To me, it looks like the Torth want you to go charging in there without a second thought."

As if Ariock was nothing but a stupid, mindless killing machine.

That was how the Torth Majority used to view him. Perhaps they still did.

"Everything the Torth do is infuriating." Garrett tightened his armor. "This is nothing new. It's the same crap they've been pulling for months."

"This is an escalation." Thomas looked frustrated, even angry. "What if they have a superweapon they're just waiting for the right time to deploy?"

"I would have picked up some hint of it," Garrett said.

"You sound so certain." Thomas gave the old man a challenging glare. "But you didn't pick up any hint of this mass crucifixion."

It had been months since Garrett had scraped anything like crucial military intelligence from the Megacosm. Either the Torth high ranks had become wiser, or they were outsourcing all their thinking to their top supergeniuses.

Garrett looked affronted. "All right, maybe I'm not getting military intelligence anymore. But I still overhear dumbass chitchats, so I know what the average Torth knows. And I've heard they're poised to evacuate Nuss and cede the whole planet to us." He stamped his staff for emphasis. "They have empty cargo ships ready to ferry the last cowardly assholes away. This"—he gestured at the pain-racked bodies in an otherworldly desert—"has got to be their parting taunt."

Weptolyso rumbled in solidarity. "Yes. This is the act of cowards backed into a corner."

Ariock looked toward his friend. "What do you advise, Thomas?"

It felt unnecessary to ask. If Thomas had a brilliant scheme, he would have already presented it and arranged most of it. He was reliable that way. This meeting was pure courtesy.

Rain dripped off the eaves. A sky croc soared through the downpour, black scales glistening.

Thomas looked pained. "Just . . ." It was rare for him to trail off and reconsider his words. "I'd rather you not go at all. If you fall for a trap, everyone is screwed."

"What's the alternative?" Garrett demanded. "Let our warriors and good allies die on Nuss while we kick back, safe and sound?"

"No, of course not." Thomas spoke reassuringly, forestalling anger from everyone else. "But maybe Ariock can sit this one out? He could send Jinishta and her healers."

Ariock saw his key leaders exchange looks, weighing the optics of bringing hope without the Bringer of Hope.

Well, he wasn't much of a savior. Ariock wished he had evacuated the entire freed population of Nuss to somewhere safer, like Reject-20. Why did he keep struggling to protect so much faraway territory?

Because Thomas said he could.

Thomas promised it was possible.

Just like Thomas promised there were trustworthy Torth in the universe. Ariock studied his friend and wondered if Thomas himself still believed there were millions of secret renegade Torth allies.

"Now, see here—" Garrett began to bluster.

"I will go with my top healers." Tears shimmered in Jinishta's luminous eyes as she turned to Ariock. "Please, just send us now. My sister lives in that city with her husband and children."

Ariock remembered Daichalsa from a party in the cave city of Hufti. Jinishta's sister was plump and friendly. Hadn't her kids sung for him?

They had. Because . . .

"They are your family, too." Jinishta gave Ariock a pleading look.

It must seem like Ariock was purposely ignoring the family who had welcomed him, like a newly raised king trying to bury his commoner roots. What did the genetic distance matter? Jinishta's family were Ariock's only surviving relatives aside from Garrett.

And he was failing them.

Just like he had failed his mother. And his father.

"I'm going." Ariock stood so straight, his head touched the ceiling. "I've gone into risky situations before. I'll be careful."

"You have me." Garrett clapped Ariock on the back, since he could not comfortably reach Ariock's shoulder plate. "I'll keep an eye out for trouble."

Thomas looked unconvinced.

"And we can bring some zombies," Garrett said. "They should trigger any trap."

"Take Evenjos," Thomas said in a rush. "She's useless if she stays here, but she can heal millions of victims."

Evenjos looked ashamed. But when everyone looked at her with hope, she seemed to firm up her courage. "Okay."

Garrett hooked his arm around her waist. Ariock nodded his gratitude to Thomas. It hadn't occurred to him to even ask Evenjos, but it should have. She would not need to fear pink gas in an open desert.

"Be ready to teleport away at the slightest hint of weirdness," Thomas said. "Please. I know you want to save everyone, Ariock, but I think you and Evenjos should prioritize the crucified warriors. Then leave ASAP. Orla and the healers can save everyone else."

"I will stay and help," Evenjos said meekly, "if there is no danger."

Thomas continued to look worried.

Ariock hesitated for one more moment. Was he overlooking some crucial red flag? Some piece of evidence that even Thomas had missed?

No.

Thomas had been fretting about superweapons and traps for over half a year. In all that time, the Torth Empire had only deployed one new superweapon: the gaseous inhibitor. And it was pink.

Whichever supergenius was nominally in charge of the Torth Majority, they seemed to lack innovation. They couldn't even make an invisible gas. The Torth were dull and sadistic and lacking in all kinds of ways. They had no secret renegades. No gems. No one like Thomas.

Ariock took one last look at the frozen image of people hanging from metal crosses, and he knew they deserved a chance at life. Like he'd had.

They should be rescued. Like he had been. Like his mother had deserved to be rescued.

Ariock gave Thomas his own version of advice. "I trust you. Keep the city safe while we're gone."

That said, Ariock vanished, taking his top warriors and captains with him.

CHAPTER 2

# DARK ANGEL

"Yourrr tiiiime is ennndinnng."

Cherise paused on a stone overpass above a culvert. She was heading home, satchel tucked under her arm, but the whispery voices chilled her.

Torth.

Other pedestrians stopped to peer over the parapet. Thanks to the news about mass crucifixions, and maybe due to the rainstorm that had ended as suddenly as it began, people were on edge. No one wanted to hear whispery Torth voices while Ariock was likely away on another planet, saving people.

"Yyyyour leaderssss aaare dooooomed."

People walked on, disgusted rather than afraid, but Cherise wanted to be sure this wasn't an attack. Since when did penitents talk?

She peered down into the culvert.

There was a typical work crew down there, ten miserable-looking penitents, collared and shackled. They raked mud and crap out of the canal. Clearly, these were the unredeemed kind of penitents, not the certified friendly ones who were allowed to work in kinder conditions.

One of them twisted his mud-splattered face to peer up at Cherise.

The rest mimicked the motion, all in unison. Their iridescent eyes gleamed against the filth. Judging by the way they all stared at Cherise and none of the other curious onlookers, they must recognize her.

"Chhheriiiise."

She hurried onward. It was sickening, how Torth still had the power to rattle her nerves even when they were shackled and enslaved. They could compete with Ma for giving her nightmares.

Maybe Flen was right about Torth. They did have an evil aspect.

Except Thomas and Kessa seemed to believe that most of them were worth salvaging.

Who was right? Thomas and Kessa had managed to persuade Ariock and at least half the free population, and Cherise wanted to believe him, as well. But perhaps she only wanted the penitents to be human because they looked so much like herself?

She found Flen preaching to a crowd of several dozen Alashani outside the war fortress.

"Who invented crucifixion?" Flen paced along a raised walkway that lined a row of Alashani-owned shops. "From whence did that sadistic torture originate?"

He was decked out in civilian finery, off duty. His Yeresunsa mantle swung from his shoulders like a short purple cape.

Cherise stood in the back of the crowd. She was taller than the average shani, but with her bonnet, she blended in. Every albino wore a bonnet or a hat over their cotton-fluff hairstyles when outdoors during daylight hours. Sometimes Cherise felt bold enough to wear an outfit from Earth, but today she wore an embroidered outer wrap to fend off the rain and big gold-plated earrings. She might as well be Alashani at a casual glance.

"Our neighbors and family members are dying in an alien wasteland." Flen sounded more passionate than Cherise had ever seen him in public. "Not only are they tormented by chains and dislocated shoulders, but they are staked out beneath a blazing sun, without any sun hats or sunblock to ease their suffering."

Cherise had noticed that every species had a species-specific weakness. Ummins had a problem with intense humidity. Humans depended on hydration and needed to drink a lot. For the shani, it was intense sunlight. Flen's skin used to be a moonlight hue, but it had turned ruddy. He burned in sunlight worse than Thomas ever had.

"So let's be aware," Flen said, pacing the other way, "who invented that torment."

The crowd seemed eager to participate. "The Torth?" someone ventured to guess.

Flen stopped to glare at the speaker. "The Torth are unimaginative," he said, fists clenched. "They cannot imagine ideas on their own. Who gave them the idea?"

Cherise hoped Flen was not going where she thought he was going.

Flen resumed pacing. Static sparks crackled along his lithe body. "It was the *rekveh* Thomas." He shot a look toward the crowd, his luminous eyes hinting that he knew things, or had seen things, that the rest of them had not. "The same *rekveh* who puppeteers our war."

Cherise nearly shouted a defense of Thomas.

She stopped herself, because she had no desire to reenact a private argument in public. She wasn't going to make herself vulnerable in front of a crowd of war hero admirers.

How many times had she begged Flen to be more respectful of the war's leadership? It never mattered what she said. Flen was far too invested in his angry bitterness.

Not that Cherise could judge him too harshly for that. She felt the same angry bitterness toward her ma. She used to feel it toward Thomas.

If anyone could understand what broken trust and betrayal felt like, it was Cherise. She was an expert. Flen had lost everyone he loved, and there was a reason for that, and who was Cherise to tell him to forgive and forget? She knew, firsthand, that forgiveness was not always easy. Or possible.

If Flen wanted to blame Ariock and Thomas for destroying his world . . . well, he was not wrong, exactly. And Cherise wanted him to work through his losses in whatever way got him through his pain.

But she hadn't expected him to hold an angry rally.

"The first time the Torth ever crucified someone," Flen said, "it was because the *rekveh* Thomas whispered in their minds and told them it would be a good idea."

He stomped to a standstill and faced the crowd, allowing them to see his fierce outrage. His dramatic flair was reminiscent of Garrett.

"What sort of a sick mind comes up with hanging living people from crossbeams?" Flen demanded to know.

Albinos on either side of Cherise gave sharp, angry nods of agreement.

It was too much. Cherise knew that she ought to remain quiet. She remembered how dangerous attention could be. Yet she had also taught classes at the academy. Was this so different? These albinos needed to learn a few facts.

Cherise peeled back her bonnet, so everyone could see that she was human. She raised her voice. "Thomas didn't invent crucifixion."

Everyone glared at her.

That was how it felt, anyway. Cherise swallowed. Her throat felt constricted, and she wished that she had stayed silent, except . . .

No. This was not her ma's trailer.

Hundreds of students liked to hear what Cherise had to say. Sometimes she had trouble reaching a student or two, but that was never a reason to give up. If they seemed uninterested, or if they argued, all she had to do was rephrase the concept and say it in another way.

"Humans invented crucifixion," Cherise said, loud and unapologetic. "Not Torth. It is an awful way to die, but it is also famous in certain human cultures."

Flen stared at her in disbelief.

"The Torth got it from humans," Cherise said in a tone of finality.

A moment later, Cherise regretted her defense of Thomas's reputation. She had just admitted that paradise—her homeworld—might be full of substandard Torth cousins instead of angelic sweethearts.

Cherise felt her cheeks grow hot. She wished she could shrink out of sight. Wasn't she an actual Earth representative on the war council? She ought to be fired.

Anyway, did Thomas deserve a defense? He had literally sentenced Ariock to death by crucifixion. Maybe he *had* popularized this method of cruelty for the Torth Empire.

She cleared her throat. "Excuse me." She pushed through the crowd. It was time to leave.

Flen's smile toward her looked forced. "We will discuss this later, my love."

Uncertain laughter from the crowd.

"I am eager to learn why crucifixions happened in paradise," Flen said. "Perhaps I should have taken a few of your lessons."

He should have.

Except . . .

Cherise neglected to teach about the more gruesome aspects of human cultures. She never wanted to think about people like her ma. There were so many wonderful things to cherish, and to talk about, and to teach.

Now she realized that she had painted a merrily false picture.

To her students, Earth must seem as wondrous and whimsical as her paintings of flowers and imaginative critters. Of course they wanted humans to join the war. They did not see humans as flawed. Cherise and Vy were angels.

Most Alashani did despise hearing about human art, music, and joys, but that was only because they envied a sister culture that had lived well for a long time. As far as Flen and most shani were concerned, humans and shani were in the same bucket. They were both in the good category, contrasted against evil.

But they sort of had the wrong idea about Earth.

Maybe Flen and other people needed to hear about the brutal aspects of humankind? Maybe they needed to learn that the Torth did not have a monopoly on evil, just like the Alashani did not have a monopoly on good.

Maybe Torth were just a variation of humans. Maybe humans were just a variation of Torth.

Flen continued to spew his suspicions about Thomas. He strutted across the walkway—a war hero steeped in righteous indignation. He spoke of warriors who had died. He listed funeral processions he had attended or wished he could have attended. He related his grief.

This wasn't an aimless rant, Cherise saw. Flen was pouring forth his soul.

And everything he said resonated with the growing crowd of listeners, whose faces knotted with empathy. This war was hard on everyone, but it was especially hard on the Alashani, who were losing lives without the counterbalance of gaining freedom.

And wasn't that Thomas's fault?

Thomas had turned himself into a zombification factory. What if he needed to take a day off? What if he got injured or sick? Then, it seemed to Cherise, the Torth Empire would swoop in and retake a lot of the ground they had lost. Did Thomas have to rely so heavily on zombies and Alashani warriors? Was that a sustainable strategy?

Flen was making too much sense.

Cherise slipped away, unable to endure his rant any longer. Maybe she would sneak a letter to Thomas. She had to do something. If she remained quiet and meek . . . well, Flen was making himself a target. He was an outspoken enemy of their military state.

For a wild moment, Cherise considered actually confronting Thomas herself. In person.

A video call wouldn't be personable enough. But Thomas was rather unapproachable, surrounded by admirers and bodyguards and probably zombies, and that huge sky croc. Even if Cherise got waved through to enter his tower, people would whisper and talk. There was no way to stop gossip. That talk would trickle through the city and make its way to Flen.

She had no desire to add lighter fluid to that fire.

Besides, she could imagine how Thomas might react to her judgment of him. If he brushed off her concerns after she took a risk to see him? She might scream. It was probably best to avoid calling him or associating with him.

She hoped she was making the right choice.

After wandering the streets for a while, Cherise found a patio where she could sit at a table and order drinks. She flipped open her sketchbook. For the first time since she had escaped her ma, she did not draw natural wonders or pleasing patterns. Her drawings were dark and disturbing.

She drew angels made of mud, shackled and chained.

And she began to draft a letter to Thomas.

# CHAPTER 3
# ANTIHEROIC

Cruelty was always lonely, Ariock thought. Torture only happened if there was nobody in power who cared. That was the Torth assumption. That was the Torth way.

Ariock watched from the air while a dozen zombie dregs bumbled around the rocky red landscape. These zombies were filthy and emaciated, but they should trigger any traps or missiles or whatever. He was ready for anything.

Nothing seemed alive in this desert except for the shambling zombies, the crucifixion victims, and small desert critters.

Ariock expanded his awareness across the desert, hyperalert for any hint of danger.

He did not sense any unwelcome blazes of power. No Rosy Ranks. No Servants of All.

Nothing hidden underground. Just rocks and dirt.

Nothing overhead except for dry desert air.

Ariock scanned for any metal objects that might be a nuclear bomb instead of a cross. Nothing. No unstable wrongness. No military transports. No armored vehicles waiting just out of sight.

Ariock growled at the time he was wasting on being overcautious. There weren't even any ominous satellites in orbit over this region of Nuss.

He exited his body on Nuss, letting it plummet while he spiritually ghosted to Reject-20. His healers and friends waited on the flats. Ariock teleported above them, encompassing everyone within his awareness—Jinishta, Garrett, Evenjos, and all the healer warriors—and mass-teleported them all to the desert on Nuss.

While everyone adjusted to the change in temperature and atmosphere, Ariock landed on his feet. "There's no trap here." He spread his arms, and his voice went cold and distant as he sank his awareness into every piece of metal in the desert. "I'll set down the victims so we can go through and heal them."

In the early days of using his powers, Ariock would have had trouble keeping track of so many millions of metal beams. He would have had to uproot them one at a time, or in small batches. But these days? He regularly encompassed huge amounts of cargo or armies within his awareness. It was a juggling act, to sort living cargo from barrels and crates, and to set things down gently after traversing half a galaxy, especially while shielding himself. Ariock was a lot more comfortable with multitasking than he used to be. Being a titan of power had become second nature to him.

He yanked every single cross out of the ground.

For a moment, they hovered, shedding red dust that billowed across the desert. Ariock made sure that he had a sketchy notion of the uneven terrain.

Then, satisfied that he was aware of boulders and ditches, he simultaneously eased the crosses to the ground. He was careful to keep the organic matter—the people—on top, rather than squishing them underneath each heavy cross.

Now the victims could be healed on an individual basis. That was the only way to do it. Healing was a full-focus power.

"Let's go," Ariock said.

Jinishta shouted orders, and her black-armored warriors spread out amid the downed crosses. They must be searching for sunburned albinos decked in purple mantles. It was common sense to heal warriors first.

"That poor shani!" Orla rushed to a victim with curly white hair whose face and arms were as red as a boiled lobster.

"My sister was crazy to settle in this sunny outpost." Jinishta strode away, no doubt searching for her family members among the victims.

"Evenjos," Ariock said, "will you go overhead and look for anyone on the verge of death?" There was far too much pain here to stick to standard protocol. "Prioritize healing them first."

"Good idea." Evenjos dissipated into dust. As a field of particles, she would be able to spot dying people before anyone else.

She would be an angel today.

Ariock broke chains, removing them. That should be enough to free everyone. He might have missed a few, but his people were armed with their own tools and powers.

The Torth Empire probably assumed Ariock would never rearrange his own personal schedule to conduct this rescue operation. Torth simply did not comprehend kindness.

And Ariock supposed his track record on Nuss wasn't great.

He had failed to rescue dozens of people in an attack on Plateau City last week. And the week before that, there had been six people killed. The Torth kept nabbing people who happened to wander a bit too far from his military outposts. They caught undercover smugglers. They murdered free people almost every day, in terrorist bombings or in raids upon the cities he was supposed to be protecting.

"When are you going to stop blaming yourself for other people's bad luck?" Garrett growled in a low voice. "You can't be everywhere at once. You can't save every single innocent person."

Ariock walked away.

He was sick of that lecture. Garrett brought it up whenever he caught a whiff of guilt from Ariock. Well, if the old mind reader didn't want to absorb spillover guilt, then maybe he shouldn't stand so close.

"Get to work, Garrett." Ariock removed his helmet and made it vanish. He would teleport it back if this place turned into a battle zone, but he suspected that his galaxy armor was overkill here.

He knelt near a moaning nussian. He had to let go of his personal shield, since healing was an act of overwhelming giving. Ariock had more than enough raw power to spare, but healing required his absolute presence in the moment.

He was sure his friends were wrong about his supposed savior complex. Guilt was a trait that mind readers—including Garrett—seemed to have a deficit of. It didn't mean Ariock was power-tripping. Just the opposite. Guilt was a telltale sign that he was human.

No one deserved this much suffering. Ariock, of all people, knew how it felt.

When he leaned over the poor nussian, he heard a mechanical hissing sound. Weird. But Ariock was too busy connecting with her ebbing life spark to investigate. He poured himself into her life.

The nussian gasped with relief. She sat up.

Ariock coughed a little bit. The air had an odd smell, like chlorine mixed with ale or beer.

He stood and the smell seemed to dissipate.

"I owe you my life." The nussian swept her head in a gesture of loyalty toward Ariock. "Are you the messiah? The Son of Storms?"

"I am," Ariock said absently. His hairs stood on end, the way he typically felt before a major battle.

The only rescuer who was neglecting the victims was Garrett. The old man stood in the midst of the atrocity, hands on his hips, like he expected bad news.

He hadn't looked that way a minute ago. Why wasn't he pitching in with the healing?

Well, Ariock wasn't going to waste time coaxing intelligence out of the old man. If Garrett sensed a threat, he would say so.

Ariock went to the next dying victim, another nussian. He knelt and extended his hands over pebbly skin.

But he had trouble feeling the necessary sympathy.

Ariock shifted his position, irked by his own feeling of annoyance. He needed to give healing energy to this suffering nussian. Instead of feeling empathy, all he felt was anger.

He was pissed off that a city full of his people had allowed themselves to be victimized. What sort of defenses had failed? Who was in charge?

When he leaned over the victim, a puff of that scent filled his nostrils, chlorine and beer. It made his eyes water.

Did the cross beam have tiny nozzles embedded in it?

Ariock studied the metal. The nozzles were easy to overlook, camouflaged to blend in with the metal, and they were partially blocked by the nussian's head. But . . . had the cross just sprayed some kind of toxin in his face?

The Torth weren't that clever. Were they?

The air responded to Ariock's frustrated annoyance with a hot, gritty wind. He could still use his powers, so it wasn't the pink gas or any form of the inhibitor. Inexplicable.

Ariock scanned the scene. If every cross was a trap, then a hundred of his best warriors had probably just breathed an unknown toxin. Their space armor made them nearly invincible, but their faceplates were down. They had taken their cue from Ariock.

Well, who wanted to breathe canned air in every situation?

Ariock supposed they might all need healing. Evenjos was impervious to most dangers, and she could fix any illness or injury. After this, he guessed, he would need to wear his helmet from now on, even when he felt safe. Ugh. Air tanks and helmets. They looked so stupid. With so much gear, his warriors would be clumsy.

It really pissed him off.

"The crosses are traps." Ariock straightened to his full height, his armored shadow engulfing the nussian at his feet. "Don't lean over them."

"What?" Garrett braced himself, staff clutched in both hands. "Ariock, we have missiles incoming from three directions." He pointed out the directions: east, west, and above. "I'm beginning to think the boy's warning is valid. We should leave."

"Missiles?" Even as Ariock spoke, shrill whistles brought his attention skyward. He recognized the shriek of incoming projectiles all too well.

All around the desert, warriors snapped to attention. They drew spears, looking skyward.

"Ariock!" Jinishta yelled, sprinting toward him. "Get the victims to safety!"

Ariock began to encompass the victims within his awareness. He wasn't going to fight off a Torth fleet while worrying about millions of injured victims.

The problem? The victims weren't consolidated. They sprawled over a mile or two of uneven terrain. These were not his orderly troops.

They would not all fit on the teleportation flats.

Ariock would need to find a big open space in which to deposit them. Once he found a place? Some of these already-injured people would end up being dropped from a few feet, since the ground in the new location would not match that of the red-rocks desert.

That must be what the Torth wanted. They wanted Ariock to clumsily run away and worsen the injuries of his people in the process.

They wanted him humiliated.

They wanted his own people to scorn him.

Ariock tightened his fists. The wind picked up. The temperature plummeted, responding to his dark mood.

"What are you doing?" Garrett glanced at him. "Mass-teleport the victims to safety!"

Right. Ariock needed to calm down if he was going to detach from his body and teleport people.

The smell of chlorine and beer seemed to linger. He snorted outward to clear his sinuses, then took a deep breath, desperate to calm himself.

It didn't work. He only felt more furious.

Ariock gave up on the trance. He couldn't get in the right mood to teleport. He felt jittery.

"EVENJOS," he said, amplifying his voice with power. "GET OVER HERE AND HEAL ME."

Garrett regarded him with concern. "What's wrong?"

Ariock wondered if his great-grandfather was trying to make him look incompetent. "I told you," he said, measuring out the words to make sure he was understood. "The crosses are traps. They sprayed me with some kind of neurotoxin."

Garrett's eyes went round. "The inhibitor?"

"No." Ariock wondered why Garrett wanted him to explain. "I have my powers."

"That makes no sense." Garrett used his staff to hurl force shields outward. The sky erupted in rings and ovals of fire as missiles exploded far away. "I would think a Torth neurotoxin would include the inhibitor. What could be worse than that?"

"Orla?" Jinishta yelled over the wind. "Shevrael? Why are you fighting?"

Ariock stared in disbelief. His warriors ought to be readying for combat or else healing victims. Instead, they were dueling.

And not in a friendly manner.

Orla's black armor glistened with blood. A spear had skewered her leg. She hurled lightning at an older warrior, who threw another spear at her.

Jinishta whirled to Ariock. "Messiah? I don't know what's wrong, but we need to evacuate. Spears are no match for missiles."

Ariock's jittery feeling refused to go away.

He shook his head, trying to clear the rage that fogged his thoughts. There were millions of injured innocents here, some of them still chained to downed crosses. There were a hundred of his best Alashani with healing powers. These were extremely valuable warriors. He really needed to mass-teleport them all to safety.

Yet he just wanted to kill Torth. He couldn't get calm enough to enter a clairvoyant trance.

"I need to be healed," he growled.

Glittering dust zoomed across the desert toward him. The dust gathered into the regal winged form of Evenjos, complete with her tiara. She held out her hands in the healing pose toward Ariock.

Then she hesitated.

"What are you waiting for?" Ariock demanded. Why did Evenjos always have to look like a fairy queen? She was so fake, so disingenuous.

Evenjos shook her head. "I sense no injury or illness. You are healthy."

"Heal me anyway," Ariock said, just as Garrett spoke nearly the same words.

"Heal him anyway."

Evenjos did so.

Ariock felt some minor aches fade away. He must have been very tense to have aches to begin with. He could only assume that Evenjos had healed whatever problems the neurotoxin was causing.

Missiles flared white-hot, streaking toward them.

Ariock whipped out a shock wave before Garrett even had a chance to react. He sent the missiles spinning away, exploding in fiery rings.

At the same time, he spread his awareness. It seemed to spill even farther than normal, almost against his will. Several miles away, two separate fleets flew toward him. Ariock engulfed hundreds of thousands of life sparks, all aiming in his direction.

But they were all of ordinary intensity. No Rosies. No Servants.

Only weaklings.

Maybe these lowly Red Ranks and civilian Torth thought they could drop some pink gas and take Ariock out that way? If so, they were mistaken. Inhibitor zones took time to set up. Ariock had no intention of giving them that time, and he wasn't stupid enough to let them get in his airspace.

If they had nuclear bombs? Ariock knew they would be limited in number. This planet, Nuss, lacked any stockpile facilities. They had no factories for the assembly of nuclear weapons.

Jinishta's voice was small and faraway. "We can't get through to Thomas! The Torth might have blasted the relay orbital?"

Ariock raised his arms, levitating on a tide of power, ignoring the little people beneath him. He was well rested. He was powerful. Sure, he had apparently fallen for a trap here, but he had survived Torth tricks before.

If the evil cowards who had crucified a city full of people wanted to give him a workout?

Well. Let them hurl firepower at a desert storm.

"Ariock?" Garrett shouted. "Get a grip! You don't even have a helmet. The Torth are coming in fast and confident with one hundred percent of their resources, and I don't know why. This has got to be a supergenius plan."

Ariock had trouble working through the implications.

Well, he understood that he needed to protect his face and head. Since his galaxy helmet was back home, he used his powers to tear chains apart, reshaping and reforging them into a crude helm. He flared its base to fit over his neck guard, leaving enough room to breathe. Slits allowed him to peer forward.

There. Now he was protected.

"The smart thing to do," Garrett yelled, "would be to exit stage left." He levitated, trying to be heard. "Nethroko's cloud fleet will do what they can—"

Ariock snatched Garrett with one armored hand just to shut him up. Did the old man actually want to flee? It was atypical of him.

But it was exactly what mind readers seemed wont to do.

Cowards.

"We fight." Ariock's voice made rocks jitter on the ground. Thunder rumbled.

He dropped Garrett, knowing the old man would land on his feet.

"I can't stay here!" A colorful phoenix bird circled around Ariock. "Teleport us away!"

It was jarring to hear Evenjos's voice coming from an animal. What a useless piece of fluff she was. Really, Evenjos was no different from the cringing penitents who refused to take up arms to defend justice and liberty. Ariock wanted to clamp a hand over her multihued feathers and crush the cowardice out of her. He hated mind readers.

"You'll stay," Ariock commanded. "I need you."

The talking bird landed on one of Ariock's shoulder spikes. "Why aren't you evacuating people? Your warriors are slaughtering each other. Haven't you noticed?" She fluffed her feathers in a cute and innocent way. "I am sorry, but—"

"Shut your beak." Ariock was not in the mood to listen to her blather. "You will take the same risks as me for once."

"Nah." Garrett gestured from the ground where he had landed, waving the Evenjos bird away. "Get somewhere safe and see if you can reach the boy. We really need his advice."

Apparently he had forgotten about undermining Thomas's authority at every opportunity.

"I'm in charge," Ariock reminded everyone.

That seemed to scare Evenjos. She flapped away, moving faster than any natural creature. One of her magenta feathers lingered in the air. It disintegrated to dust and zoomed after the rest of her.

"Let her go." Garrett whipped force fields outward, precluding the possibility that Ariock might chase Evenjos. "We can't use someone who doesn't want to be here. She has her supercom. She'll figure out a way to help us from afar."

Everyone was a coward today.

Ariock wished Garrett would stop making excuses for the birdbrain. Well, the prophet Migyatel had foretold that the messiah should heed his own counsel. Never mind his supposed advisers.

The shouts of warriors faded to meaningless drizzle as Ariock's awareness expanded across the desert sky. He was too enraged to stand still, to root himself in bedrock, to constrain himself. He wanted to connect to every incoming Torth and rip their bodies in half with the power of his mind.

This planet belonged to him.

If murderous telepaths wanted to take it back, then he would eject them like the trash they were.

Ariock inhaled, and the ground swelled with enough force to rearrange the landscape into bizarre crags and canyons.

He glimpsed beings in the jagged landscape beneath him. Some hid. Some ran. Some fought like maniacs, slaughtering each other with spikes or spears or electricity.

"DIE, TORTH." Ariock spoke with so much force, a tectonic plate shifted on its ancient foundation.

Lives vanished. Enemies, surely. If they were friends, then they should have gotten out of his way. Anyone who fought alongside the Giant knew to expect violence.

"What are you doing?" Garrett's voice rippled on the wind, magnified by power. "You're killing innocent people. The ones on crosses. Remember them?"

Although Ariock was sure that he was being played . . . a part of him, deep down, suspected he was truly hearing Garrett.

Was he actually damaging friends and allies?

It was hard to believe. Ariock tried to reason through the situation, but he could not shake off his enraged feeling. All he wanted to do was tear people apart and wreck everything around him.

He tried to lose his stature. He tried to make himself meager and merely an oversize human rather than a storm.

But he could not control his rage.

And rage, he realized, was a major trigger for his storm powers. As long as he felt this way, he was unable to stop—unable to control tidal waves of sand and earthquakes that tore the ground asunder.

He roared in wordless anguish and rage. He hardly knew who he was anymore. Ariock Dovanack? Who was that? Some kind of vulnerable mortal man? Names were human abstractions for lesser people. He was no longer lesser.

He was a storm titan.

He slammed gigantic fists against the desert, spraying sand half a mile in the air. People fell into the blast craters and died.

"KNOCK ME OUT," he pleaded, but even his voice was inhuman. It was the roar of wind and the growl of thunder. He could not actually plead. Not as a storm god. He could barely make the words sound like words.

Life sparks were winking out around him. The horizon was dark with enemy transports, but they banked around his circumference, miles apart. They seemed unwilling to move closer to his mortal core.

He hated the way they circled him, like carrion eaters watching a maddened beast. Was that what he was to them? A beast who ripped aliens apart with his bare hands for a judgmental audience of silent, decadent nonpeople?

Were they entertained?

Were they waiting for him to run out of energy and fall, so they could chain him up and make him suffer and steal him away from anyone capable of loving him?

The storm titan unfurled arms of rainfall and electric energy. His awareness continued to unfurl, driven by rage. Did these stupid Torth believe they could chase away the Giant and win eternal glory in the Megacosm? It seemed like an insane risk.

A fatal miscalculation.

His roar was encased in a bolt of lightning so huge, it would blind and deafen anyone. The impact sent fissures cracking through bedrock. Transports slammed down in fiery bursts, blasted by sand or ropes of lightning. More life sparks winked out. Rocks split with a sound more ominous than thunder. So many cowards. They all fled.

Except one.

A vibrant life spark blazed toward the Giant, wrapped in the scouring winds of a tornado.

Unexpected. An enemy stormbringer.

The Giant screeched sand and wind at it, slamming his enemy until it broke apart.

The enemy tornado re-formed, coming at him from another angle. The clash of their collision sent up massive shock waves of grit.

The lesser stormbringer fell apart again, then re-formed as a towering wall of rocks. The Giant hammered that wall into submission. He destroyed the other stormbringer again, then again, all the while flinging away the enemy transports at his edges. He was a massive sandstorm. No one would survive his rage. These murderous mind readers wanted to make him their clown? Their gladiator? He was done with that.

He would take down every last one of them. He would destroy every mind reader on this planet if he had to.

# CHAPTER 4
# HARDLY INFORMED

Thomas stepped back to admire his handiwork.

Taking steps was still awkward for him, the rocking motion somewhat unnatu-ral. But outfitting Azhdarchidae with missile launchers was not something he could do from his hoverchair. He needed to stretch in order to cinch straps and tighten bolts.

The sky croc arrowed his long head around, eyeing the payloads with mistrust. Mockup missiles protruded from the harness, one on either side of his scaly body.

"You're fine." Thomas sensed Azhdarchidae yearn for reassurance, and he whir-stepped close enough to wrap his arms around the scaly neck.

Not that he could get his arms all the way around the immense beast's neck. Not even close.

Azhdarchidae had gone through a rebellious teenage phase, figuring that Thomas was more like injured prey than a majestic predator. Thomas was more than equipped to handle such challenges. He had stung Azhdarchidae with flames until the sky croc acknowledged his dominance. He'd had to teach that lesson a few times.

But now that Azhdarchidae was on the other side of his juvenile stage, he had settled into a beta role. The animal emitted a long, rattling croak—the sky croc equivalent of satisfaction.

"You're a good friend." Thomas leaned his forehead against the warm, iridescent-black scales.

If only there was some way he could teach certain other friends to quit chal-lenging him.

Thomas tried to remind himself that Ariock and Jinishta were busy, and that must be why they weren't answering their supercoms. If they ran into trouble, surely someone would call him?

He figured he was being overly paranoid.

There was an unending load of work to do in his labs, but he didn't want to overhear what other people, even friendly lab assistants, thought of him. So here he was, with Azhdarchidae.

*I'm no longer sure I'm on the right path.*

Alone, inside the privacy of his own mind, Thomas could admit that.

He had an anemic mind for a supergenius. Technically, he was catching up with his sleek Torth peers in terms of sheer amount of knowledge . . . but it was all garbage. Unlike the Torth supergeniuses, Thomas was not picking and choosing what he absorbed. He had filled his mind with enough depravities and repressed psychoses to populate a planet. He had turned his own mind into a disgusting, monstrous landfill.

What if all that nonsense was interfering with his ability to reason?

Oh, his tactics were sound. His plans still won battles. But long term? What was he doing?

Every time he zombified people, robbing them of free will and personhood, he felt like a demon. The undergrounders sermonized that he was evil.

And didn't they actually have a few valid points?

Deep down, he knew that his path was unsustainable.

It was wrong.

Thomas whir-stepped toward his hoverchair. His thoughts were going nowhere good. The albino undergrounders might be right to hate him. They might as well get in line behind the Torth Empire. All that hatred . . .

It was an almost welcome counterpoint to the penitents who worshipped him.

A not-insignificant number of penitents wanted to become his personal concubines. One in particular kept popping up in his imagination.

Maybe he would risk another visit to the Pink Screwdriver?

A soft knock on the door frame brought Thomas out of his reverie.

"Teacher?"

Varktezo stood there, small and clad in the embroidered garments that many freed ummins wore. His goggles hung around his neck.

"What are you doing here?" Thomas felt irked. The guards at the base entrance must be bored if they were letting uninvited guests into the Dragon Tower. Maybe he should ask Varktezo to tell them to be more vigilant. He didn't want to listen to the things they dared not say in his presence.

Azhdarchidae croaked a rattling threat in solidarity with his parental figure.

Varktezo shrank back. "I just . . . We haven't seen you for three days. I thought you would want to know the results of your experiments? You haven't answered your messages?" He held up a data tablet. "I am just worried about you. That is all."

Varktezo began to leave.

"Wait." Thomas said it on impulse.

He examined his own psyche for the reason why he cared about how Varktezo felt. Maybe it had something to do with friendship?

He didn't quite understand why, but he didn't want Varktezo to feel undervalued. Or disappointed.

"Will you help me unload these missiles?" Thomas asked. "Don't worry. They're fake."

Uncertain, Varktezo stepped closer. Thomas reassured the sky croc so his chief lab assistant could get close enough to help.

"I'm sorry that I've been neglecting you." Thomas heaved one fake missile out of its cradle with Varktezo holding the other end. The mock payloads were hollow and lightweight, but for Thomas, balance was often a problem. He didn't quite have the hang of it.

"No worries," Varktezo said brightly.

"I miss working in the lab." Thomas pulled down the other false missile. "And truthfully, I miss talking with you."

Varktezo looked heartened.

"So, what's been going on?" Thomas patted Azhdarchidae twice, letting the sky croc know their work session was over.

"Quite a lot!" Varktezo began to recap the latest experiments with exuberance. "We discovered organelles within the dust sample from Evenjos. To me, that implies . . ."

Varktezo covered everything Thomas wanted to know about and more. He interrupted his own stream of conversation several times, clambering onto a plush armchair and then later jumping off it to pour himself an energy drink. There was a service table for beverages.

". . . And I am fully fluent in reading English now." Varktezo slurped his beverage with gusto. Ummins could turn their beaks into a straw shape. "Literacy is incredible magic! It feels as if a whole new galaxy has opened up for me!"

"Oh? What are you reading?" Thomas sat in his hoverchair, braced for the yo-yo ride of moods that Varktezo emanated. That was a factor of adolescent hormones.

Not that Thomas was any better. He and Varktezo were the same biological age.

"Everything I can! Your digital library from Earth is the best gift ever!" Varktezo went on to describe textbooks on physics, astronomy, neuroscience, and philosophy.

Torth data marbles contained dry lists of facts or equations. They never told stories or conveyed opinions, and they assumed a baseline of knowledge that could only be gleaned in the Megacosm. Therefore, human libraries were the easiest way for aliens to learn, with the rare exception of ancient alien relics. Varktezo was the first nonhumanoid alien to explore this knowledge frontier. He read more than one book per day, a rate that impressed even Thomas.

". . . I told Hifin there's an excellent primer for learning English," Varktezo was saying. "And I told her where to find it. Twice! But she forgot!" He radiated disdain and sipped from his energy drink, which was neon orange. "I don't know why someone so forgetful is working with the plasma cutters."

Varktezo had a habit of disparaging his fellow lab technicians. He called them forgetful, or too slow, too distracted, too lazy, or too dull-witted. Thomas could relate. He used to do the same thing when he'd worked remotely for Rasa Biotech on Earth.

He wasn't going to judge Varktezo for having trouble winning friends. Neither of them was a pro at it.

"I like what you've done with your animal." Varktezo settled back in the armchair and nodded toward Azhdarchidae. "That is a marvelous harness design. May I look at the blueprint?"

"Sure." Thomas had already digitized his mockup and loaded it into a collaborative online archive. "You'll find it in the mechanics library."

Azhdarchidae was restless. He nipped at the harness around his body, and Thomas made a permissive hand signal, emphasizing to the sky croc that he was free to leave.

"Are you going to teach Azhdarchidae to carry passengers?" Varktezo was enthused, picturing himself astride the beast while soaring over the city. "Will you ride him?"

Azhdarchidae launched off the tower and opened his immense wings.

"No." Thomas shuddered. "I value my life."

His pterosaur friend soared over the academy's central plaza, angling toward the mountainous wilderness that was his usual hunting route. Thomas could

imagine a harness failure. Sure, if Thomas fell off, he might slow his deadly plummet by using his thermodynamic power, but *might* was the operative word. Panic
might overtake him and subsume his ability to control his power. Then he would
end up roasting himself alive before smashing into the ground.

Varktezo crossed one scaly foot over the other. "So." He seemed incapable of
silence. "There was a sudden rainstorm. Now it is sunny. I assume Ariock went to
Nuss to save the people there?" He hesitated, cringed, then mentally gathered his
courage to ask a weighted question. "How many are dead or wounded this time?"

Thomas leaned his head against the headrest cushion. Serious topics were dangerous. He might cause Varktezo to worry.

He might get emotional.

And yet he did want to get away from his own overcomplicated perspective
for a bit and filter his problems through the perceptions of a friend who was less
cynical and more exuberant. That was so hard to do these days. His mind felt more
burdened than ever, with all the penitent garbage knocking around in there.

He missed Cherise.

He missed having an inner audience.

Thomas found himself talking, sharing private thoughts that he probably
should not share. "Ariock doesn't like all the zombies I keep making."

"Oh." Varktezo closed his beak. He knew that if Thomas was sharing secrets
and complaining, it was serious.

"It's not just Ariock," Thomas admitted. "Just about everyone has doubts about
the zombie hordes. You do."

"Pshaw. No. Not really." Varktezo blustered and squirmed in the armchair, trying to shove away the accusation. "I don't doubt that—"

"You're right to have doubts." Thomas flushed, humiliated by the admission. "I
fully believed we would have integrated the penitent Torth into our armed forces by
now. 'Droves,' I said." He stared down at his hands. "I guess I'm not a very reliable
supergenius."

Varktezo looked startled.

Then he studied Thomas, his gray eyes as piercing as a Torth giving a mind
probe. He had never heard his Teacher express self-doubt before. It seemed he'd
thought it was impossible for a mind reader to lose self-confidence.

"Kessa still believes it is possible," Varktezo pointed out.

Thomas shrugged. He wasn't sure if Kessa was acting out of obligation because
it was her job, or if she held a true belief that Torth could be converted into reliable
allies. Kessa had yet to give him permission to get within telepathy range of her mind.

"Perhaps we will integrate Torth into our society," Varktezo said, full of reassurance. "Eventually."

"Eventually." Thomas echoed that word without hope. "Eventually isn't good
enough."

He floundered every day, searching for a sustainable method to grow his army. Every
day gave the enemy supergeniuses more time to perfect their nefarious secret plans.

"Even Ariock thinks I'm wrong about the penitents joining us," Thomas said.
"They should have been on our side by now." He stared miserably at the beverage
counter, wishing that he could ingest something to make his problems seem smaller.
Alcoholic drinks might work.

"So what if it takes a long time?" Varktezo asked. "Didn't you predict that it would?"

"Not this long." Thomas had risked his entire military strategy on a surety that he would gain Torth allies.

And he was wrong.

Devastatingly, horribly wrong.

"Are you saying you have no backup plan?" Varktezo studied him again. Clearly, he flat out did not believe Thomas would enact a strategy without any backup contingency plan.

"Oh yeah, there's a backup plan." Thomas did not hide his misery. "The backup plan is to have me create hordes of zombies."

"As you've been doing," Varktezo realized.

Thomas nodded. "Yes. And I'm working on secret superweapons."

Varktezo reacted as if that was good news.

It wasn't.

"That means," Thomas explained, "we are fully engaging in a weapons race against Torth supergeniuses. They thrive on that sort of science. I'm not in the same league." He rested his forehead on his fingertips. "I really thought . . ." He hated to admit how much he had believed in his erroneous dream about Torth allies. "I never imagined I would be this wrong."

Varktezo put aside his energy drink. His faith in his much-admired Teacher must be shaken.

Thomas knew he ought to feel guilty about dumping his burden of worries onto his lab assistant. He should have told Varktezo to go away. He never should have opened his heart for someone else to examine.

Yet . . .

It was gratifying to see someone else begin to worry about the bigger picture. It was almost a relief.

Garrett was mindlessly smug about victory being preordained. As long as the painted prophecies kept coming true, then everything was peachy fine, as far as Garrett was concerned.

And Ariock? The big guy worried about his next battle or the next crisis. He did not think years ahead. He trusted Thomas to handle overarching strategy.

It was the same with Evenjos. And the war council. And everyone else. Nobody wanted to consider how the Torth might win this war. It was too scary. Nobody seriously analyzed the possibility of defeat except for Thomas.

"I'm trying not to worry right now," Thomas confessed. "I haven't heard from Ariock or his forces in half an hour. They're supposed to be healing the victims on Nuss. But I wish someone would call, just to check in."

Varktezo's brow ridge tented in worry. "Is Garrett with him?"

"And Evenjos," Thomas said.

Varktezo's brow ridge went even more vertical.

"I asked her to go with them," Thomas clarified. "For healing purposes, but also because I'm concerned that the Torth might have set a trap for our army." He hesitated.

But he had already said too much. Varktezo had a curious mind.

So Thomas summarized his misgivings. "What the Torth did this time was exceptionally cruel and large-scale. Yet they left a lot of victims alive. It was a situation crafted to trigger our emotions, to make Ariock go running over there to rescue our people." Thomas faltered. "Um, that's how it looked to me, anyway."

He knew he sounded paranoid. The Torth had largely evacuated Nuss. What could a few garrisons do against Ariock and his army of warriors?

No one else was worried about it. Not Garrett. Not Ariock. Not Jinishta.

Maybe Varktezo would feel obligated to reassure his Teacher. He would probably pat Thomas on the arm and awkwardly tell him that there was no reason for fear.

Instead, Varktezo looked alarmed. "Well, I assume you tried to check in with them?"

He was actually taking Thomas's paranoia seriously.

"I did make a few calls." Thomas eyed his tablet. There were still no notifications, no missed calls. "No one answered."

"Hmm." Varktezo looked ready for action.

"But they could just be busy," Thomas admitted. "There are a lot of people to heal. Thousands."

"Have you checked the Megacosm?" Varktezo asked.

"No." Thomas hunched, embarrassed. "If I go into the Megacosm to gather news, I'd be alerting the Torth Empire to the fact that I'm alone here."

"You're alone?" Varktezo seemed to be weighing the various implications.

"I'm unprotected," Thomas said.

"You mean that *we* are," Varktezo said. "You mean all of Freedomland."

Thomas nodded, accepting that technicality.

"Well." Varktezo sounded brusque. "Don't you think it is responsible to warn people?"

"No!" Thomas stared at him in surprise. "Let's not spread news that the city is relatively unprotected. There are plenty of penitents whom I haven't vetted. We can't trust them unilaterally."

Varktezo's gaze toward Thomas was judgmental, for the first time that Thomas had ever known him.

"I'm sure Ariock and the rest of them will be back within the hour," Thomas said, trying to bolster his tone with reassurance he did not feel.

"Warn your bodyguards, at least," Varktezo said. "Warn everybody in the city with military training."

Thomas began to protest.

"If you're wrong," Varktezo said, "so what? Everybody will feel relief. You might feel embarrassed, and I am sure a few morons will scream that the *rekveh* made a mistake. But everyone with a brain and a heart will thank you for sharing your misgivings."

Thomas closed his mouth. He wondered if Varktezo was right.

"That is most of us," Varktezo added.

Thomas found it hard to imagine. The entire city expected him to be right all the time. They knew his role in the war council, planning every battle. Orators and radio newscasters would shred his reputation if he showed the slightest sign of making errors in judgment.

"Freedom is the ability to make informed decisions," Varktezo said. "It is knowledge. Anyone who values freedom understands that. Your worries sound valid to me. I understand why you cannot be certain. That is fine. But if you keep your concerns a complete secret, you are—"

He cut himself off, clearly struggling against whatever insult he wanted to blurt out. Varktezo regularly insulted underlings and coworkers. His Teacher, however, was a different matter.

"Rumors always spread," Thomas pointed out. "Someone in the know might walk past an unfriendly penitent. Do you really think this is worth that risk?"

Varktezo studied Thomas as if he had never seen him before. "Our military people know the importance of keeping secrets from unfriendly penitents."

That was a fair point. Perhaps Thomas was just making excuses, trying to avoid the shame of being publicly wrong.

Varktezo seemed to gather his resolve. Then he squared his shoulders. "Won't you give our military people the respect they have earned?"

Thomas sensed how much courage that criticism had required. Varktezo was used to being subordinate to his Teacher. This was a new dynamic. This conversation was the first time Thomas had opened up to Varktezo about nonscientific issues, and Varktezo had risen to the challenge.

He was being honest with a friend.

"I'm probably overblowing things." Thomas shrank in his hoverchair. He hated to make himself vulnerable. What if he riled up the city garrison for no good reason? What if everyone found out that he was wrong?

"Probably." Varktezo stated that as if it didn't matter.

And to him, it did not. He was asking Thomas to allow other people to make their own informed decision. If they trusted Thomas's judgment as readily as Varktezo did, then they would arm themselves and be alert for a Torth attack, just in case.

And if the worst did happen? They would be grateful to be forewarned.

Thomas gave in. "Okay."

Varktezo looked gratified. He emanated relief, and Thomas sensed why. Varktezo was relieved that his Teacher was willing to risk his own hubris. That made him worthy of respect.

"Would you convey the message for me?" Thomas was ashamed to ask the favor, but he did not want to face normal people. It was overwhelming to soak up so many opinions about oneself.

He expected disgust. An ummin wouldn't understand. No one could understand except other mind readers.

To his surprise, Varktezo looked sympathetic. "Of course, Teacher."

Perhaps he recognized signs that Thomas felt overwhelmed?

Varktezo had lab technicians demanding his attention every day. He tended to get hyperfocused, and when he was busy, he hated interruptions. Perhaps he did understand how Thomas felt.

"Teacher, you have good instincts." Varktezo headed toward the door. "You draw from a well of knowledge that is deeper than anyone else's. The very fact that you feel alarmed should be enough to worry anyone with sense." He glanced over his shoulder. "Thank you for doing me the honor of sharing your worries."

With that, Varktezo was gone. Thomas sat alone in the aerie and wondered if he had unleashed a flood of paranoia upon the city.

# A STIR OF ECHOES

Varktezo exited the Dragon Tower with a spring in his step and happiness stretching his beak. What an enlightening discussion that had been! Who would ever guess that the Teacher could suffer from self-doubt?

Or that he would actually listen to—and accept!—advice from his lab assistant?

"Told you," one of the door sentries grunted to her companion.

The second door sentry grumbled in concession. "Well, he was gone for a long time."

Varktezo recalled this sentry saying that the *rekveh* would likely roast the ummin alive, then feed his crispy ummin corpse to the sky croc. She must have made it a wager. Nussians had such a weakness for gambling.

"Yup, I am fine, thank you for your concern." Varktezo paused midstep, wondering if door sentries counted as military personnel.

He supposed they did.

"The Teacher asked me to convey a message to you both." Varktezo beckoned.

The nussians had to crouch down, then crane their heads forward as far down as they could go in order to meet Varktezo at his level. Or close enough.

Varktezo did not normally talk to nussians. Sure, there were a few immense candidates who wanted to work as lab technicians, but Varktezo simply did not want any chance of a big, clumsy oaf destroying delicate test tubes and other equipment. He refused all nussian applicants. The lab was no place for people who weighed a ton and who had thorns and spikes on their armored skin.

The Teacher said Varktezo ought to give nussians a chance. He claimed that pre-Torth nussians used to build their own scientific laboratories, where they had used data interfaces built for their voices and hands and machinery as a proxy for delicate operations. Some of them supposedly had a knack for intuiting theoretical mathematics.

Whatever. That was ancient history. Nussians these days were oafs, as far as Varktezo was concerned.

"Be on high alert today and tomorrow," Varktezo told the door sentries. "I am not saying we are in danger. But listen to your dispatch service a lot. If you hear the slightest hint that our city might be under attack . . . um, call a military reserve troop to the Dragon Tower immediately. Remember, your top duty is to protect our Teacher. Your job is important."

The sentries exchanged a look.

"You two have a pleasant day!" Varktezo patted one of the sentries on her pebbly shin, trying to convey that he appreciated her competence. He began to trot away.

"Hold on there," one of the sentries rumbled.

Varktezo tried not to tap his foot with impatience. "What?"

"Did the *rekveh* say anything specific?" one sentry asked.

"Can you tell us anything more?" the other asked.

Varktezo considered glossing over a few factoids, since he wanted to be on his way. He had a garrison to warn. He had experiments and research he wanted to get back to. After the spontaneous rainstorm and the news from Nuss, the guards should be able to infer that Ariock was off-world, which was always a cause for extra vigilance at home.

But he supposed that if anyone had a right to be fully informed, it was the sentries who personally guarded Thomas.

"Freedomland is relatively unprotected right now," Varktezo said, after a quick glance around to make sure no one was eavesdropping. "Garrett Dovanack and the Lady of Sorrow are gone, along with the Bringer of Hope. The Teacher feels more concern than usual. He thinks there is a strong possibility that the Torth will attack us here."

The guards looked alarmed.

"Nothing is certain," Varktezo hastily said. "He cannot guess what the Torth are planning, if anything. But he asked me to convey that to you. I am sure it is nothing to worry about."

The guards both snaked their necks in a nussian gesture of gratitude.

"Thank you," said one.

"We appreciate your information," the other said in a kind tone. "You have our respect."

Varktezo bobbed his head. He walked away feeling remarkably lighter in body and in mind. He had half expected the nussians to roar laughter at him because he was a cowardly scientist.

Maybe nussians weren't so bad? Maybe he just didn't know enough of them.

Varktezo bypassed the doorway to the wing where he usually worked and went through the outer lobby. The reception area was granite and brass, with mirrored surfaces of polished meteorite to keep out teleporters. More than a dozen people sat at stations behind the long, curved desk.

Varktezo considered greeting the cute ummin docent who worked for the research annex. He even had a legitimate reason to talk to her this time. Her job entailed running errands. He might ask her to . . .

The cute ummin saw Varktezo coming, and the smile dropped off her beak. She pretended to busy herself with a holographic display of files.

Varktezo swerved without breaking stride. His innards turned into knots, which he strove to ignore.

So what if most people failed to understand why he spent so much time with a *rekveh*? So what if they failed to comprehend the things he was learning, or the things he was already capable of? He wasn't interested in their mundane prattle, anyway. That docent was cute, but his awkward conversation with her the other day should have been enough to turn him off. She had an empty mind.

Like so many, many, many people.

Well, there were quadrillions of ummins in the galaxy. He would make suitable friends and find a suitable mate, eventually.

Someday.

Clearly not any time soon, but statistically, long-term loneliness should not be a concern for a snazzy youngster such as himself. It was just a matter of numbers. He was a whiz with numbers, so why worry?

Whistling, Varktezo strolled into the idyllic courtyard between the research annex and a wing of lecture halls. He was determined not to waste any more time thinking about that docent.

Which military headquarters should he visit first? The teleportation flats? The war palace? The prison?

Varktezo sat on a decorative bench and tapped his wristwatch, summoning his Rolodex of personal contacts. He would set up appointments. Then he would decide whether to deal with the midday traffic on a hoverbike or pilot Thomas's private transport and deal with the hassle of rooftop docking bays.

Students walked past him in pairs or threesomes.

". . . claimed that Torth attacked Ariock."

The voice was hushed. It was one student speaking to another.

"She only said that to see if she could start a panic." The other student sounded certain. "You can't trust anything that comes out of a penitent's mouth."

Varktezo normally tuned out the blather of foot traffic. He didn't care to overhear chitchat about recipes or clothing fashions or dating. He would much rather discuss cognitive neuroscience or astronautical engineering. Who wouldn't? What was wrong with people, that they didn't find the underpinnings of creation to be fascinating?

"And yeah," the student went on, "I don't care that it's supposedly one of the extra-special obedient ones. They're all secretly rooting for the Torth Empire to win."

Varktezo stood. He stared at the two students, who both happened to be female ummins.

They gave him an unfriendly return stare. He was being rude, blocking their path.

"Excuse me," Varktezo said. "But will you tell me what you heard? What are you talking about?"

One student looked him up and down, as if assessing trash.

The other looked slightly kinder. "Do you take classes here? I don't think we've met." She made a gesture of peace.

"Peace." Varktezo was often mistaken for being a student. "You said that a penitent . . ." He lowered his voice, not wanting anyone else to overhear. "A penitent claims that Ariock got attacked?"

The less friendly student clicked her beak in disgust. "What is your problem?" She confronted Varktezo, hands on her hips. "Do you really feel a need to spread stupid rumors?"

"It's just something I heard," the other student said to Varktezo, her tone reassuring. "Someone I know is friends with someone who lives in one of those big households, you know, with a penitent chambermaid to serve their meals and stuff. And apparently, the penitent chambermaid rushed out of their house and told her that dark times are ahead, because, supposedly, the Torth Empire has defeated Ariock."

"Defeated?" Varktezo hoped this was a joke. It wasn't funny.

"Yes." The student laughed, proving she was not gullible enough to fall for such an absurd tale. "That's what the penitent said, according to my friend. It said something like, 'Dark times are ahead, because the Torth Empire defeated the Bringer of Hope and the Conqueror is going to lose the war.'"

"Woo." The other student was clearly not taking it seriously. "How would a penitent even know? They're not allowed to mentally link up with other Torth." That law was common knowledge.

"Right." Varktezo glanced up at the colorful sky.

Brightly colored butterflies flitted from tree to tree. It was a peaceful and lovely day in Freedomland.

Surely not a day for catastrophe?

He forced a smile at the pair of students and stepped aside. "Well, thank you for the silly rumor. I am sure you are right." Rumors were easy to start and easy to spread. "Have a pleasant day!"

They waved and walked onward.

Varktezo jabbed his wristwatch, now desperate to talk to the head of the Freedomland garrison, but even more desperate to convey the rumor to Thomas. The knotted feeling in his stomach returned tenfold. He didn't believe that Ariock had been magically defeated . . . but if such a travesty had happened, who would protect Thomas?

Which meant: Who would protect everyone?

The call connected. Thomas's face was a tiny image on the screen of his wristwatch.

Varktezo moved off the pathway and kept his voice low. "Teacher."

As Varktezo breathlessly retold the rumor, Thomas's expression hardened. He was definitely taking it seriously.

"I'm going to a bunker." Judging by the motion in the camera feed, Thomas was already on the move. "I want you to contact Zenzaldal—she's in charge while Ariock and Jinishta are away—and tell her to prepare for an invasion. I'll contact you later."

Screams broke through Varktezo's focus.

He lost track of the tinny voice in his earpiece, because a deluge of panicked students were stampeding toward him. Their eyes were wide with terror. They weren't seeing the path or anyone in their way, because they were clearly more afraid of what was driving them than what they might run into.

"Crap. I'll call you back." Varktezo wanted to get away from the stampede, but they were coming from all directions, pouring out of doorways and even spilling out of windows. It looked as if the city had vomited people into the academy.

And the academy was vomiting itself into the research annex.

One did not need a supergenius brain to infer the enemy's basic intentions. Torth could not teleport directly into a room with mirrored surfaces. If enemy teleporters were invading the city, they would likely show up outdoors, then swiftly close in on their top military targets.

They were heading toward Thomas.

And they were probably killing and maiming everyone who got in their way.

Varktezo activated the campus map on his wristwatch. The map app would automatically share his location with his chosen grouping of contacts, including the Teacher. Perhaps Varktezo could be of use? Newscasters might not take life-threatening risks, whereas Varktezo . . . well, he was from Duin.

The Teacher, and even the great Bringer of Hope, had once relied on the slaves of Duin for protection. Varktezo had not forgotten.

He called Zenzaldal as he rushed back toward the research annex. The shani who answered the call looked harried.

"Torth are attacking the academy," Varktezo reported. "I think they're going for Thomas."

"I'll send warriors." Zenzaldal ended the call.

Varktezo wished he had a blaster glove stowed in his vest pocket, but he rarely carried weapons. All he could do was scan for a hiding place. The annex had lots of doors, as well as oblique tunnels that led to restrooms or utility rooms. Varktezo threw himself into one of those.

He flattened himself on the floor of a restroom. Here, he could peek around the privacy wall and spy on the hallway. It was a risk, but knowledge was worth risks. Wasn't that what everyone said?

The Teacher was the embodiment of knowledge.

If they lost Thomas, they lost the war.

Varktezo set his wristwatch camera to "live stream and capture" mode. The Torth Empire were collectively uncreative, but they might have learned from their last mistake. They had wasted forty teleporters on their first invasion of Freedomland's academy. Their surprising gaseous inhibitor had not been enough to overcome the Teacher's brilliance and his power to zombify.

So what new tactic or weapon had the Torth brought this time?

Varktezo intended to live-stream footage directly to Thomas. His daring communication might make the difference between freedom or death for everyone in this city. He was ready.

The stampede died down.

There was a lull as panicky people cleared out of the hallway. Anyone with sense wanted to find a hiding place.

Varktezo prepared to withdraw farther inside the restroom, in case any Torth showed up and made a threatening move toward him. Surely he was too insignificant to be a military target? He was just an adolescent ummin. And if any Torth dared to probe his mind, well, he would have a severe panic attack. That usually put them off.

Shadows stirred in the hallway.

Varktezo was so keyed up, he nearly forgot to aim his wristwatch camera in the right direction. He would scramble to retreat if any armored Torth approached his hiding place.

But the creeping, shambling figures were not Torth.

They were ummins.

And govki. And other types of people. But why did they look so lost and confused? Former slaves stumbled through the hallway with their hands held out in front of them, as if they were blind. Their gazes tracked things that were not there.

Lost-looking people walked or stumbled past Varktezo.

He gawked. They couldn't be zombified. Could they?

One of the staggering ummins turned toward him. She must have been a city slave in the past, judging by the ring of scar tissue on her neck. When she stumbled around the corner, she seemed unsurprised to find the restroom occupied. She squatted next to Varktezo.

"What happened?" he whispered.

She looked at him. She did not speak.

Varktezo truly envied the Torth power to read minds. As he debated ways to convey the importance of getting answers, though, he began to have the strangest sensation.

It was worse than double vision.

He saw through his own eyes, yet he also saw himself as if he was peering through the eyes of this stranger who squatted next to him. Somehow, he also felt her limbs. It was almost as if he wore her body in addition to his own.

And he felt her fear.

He was himself—Varktezo—but he was also this middle-aged ummin who had been teaching a class on industrial hydraulics. How did he know that? The knowledge seeped into his mind as if they were merging. She had been exhibiting different ways to diagnose a bad solenoid, showing her students practical examples in different types of engines, when a mass panic swept through her class. Torth were invading the academy!

And now? She suspected the Torth must have released a neurotoxin into the hallways, because she felt extremely disoriented and confused.

Varktezo stared at her.

She stared back at him.

Their mutual fear and confusion seemed to build toward a silent crescendo, like they were caught in a feedback loop. Varktezo struggled to hold on to his own sense of reality, but the nearby ummin's disorientation and fears kept seeping in. She stood, and Varktezo felt like he was standing and edging away, except he was not.

When he checked his wristwatch, the other ummin glanced at her naked wrist.

Their movements were synced up. They were hardly individuals.

Other people meandered in the hallway, and jagged bits of their perceptions showed up inside Varktezo's head, like crazy reflections thrown by shards of glass. Feet moved that were not his own. Stray thoughts distracted his own efforts to diagnose the problem.

The walls were not trustworthy.

Angles kept shifting.

Nothing was what it seemed.

Varktezo pushed his fists against his head. He needed to remember which body was his and which head was his.

Unspoken voices begged for an explanation. Varktezo alone thought that he might be able to guess what was happening.

Except it was nonsensical.

It should be utterly impossible.

He needed to tell the Teacher.

# CHAPTER 6
# FROM GREAT HEIGHTS

Evenjos floated above the apocalypse.

Below her, the planet Nuss turned, streaked with black smoke instead of white clouds. Oceans overflowed their shorelines. There were lava geysers. Tsunamis. Tectonic shifts, all caused by the mad titan.

She did not need to see the red-rock desert to guess that Ariock had tossed it into oblivion. His rage was wrecking entire cities and industrial facilities. She did not wish to see how many innocent people were dying.

Most living beings would suffocate way up here, in the frigid heights above the stratosphere. Few people ever ventured out an airlock, so there weren't enough spacesuits to outfit a fleet, anyway. But Evenjos did not need that protection. She did not need to breathe.

Although she was corporeal, wearing her default goddess-empress form, it was a hollow shell. Frostbite did not touch her. She was composed of ice crystals. Her dust could withstand extreme temperatures.

If only she could transform herself into something useful, like a swarm of rescue shuttles.

She was doing her best to repair the damaged orbital relay station. It would be easier for her if a supergenius would walk her through it.

But Thomas wasn't answering calls, and Evenjos lacked an in-depth knowledge of engineering. She could not transform her body into mechanical objects. She did not have the advanced molecular chemistry needed for nuclear fusion reactions or bombs and drugs. She could not become a starship and evacuate refugees.

Anatomy was a different matter. Evenjos had studied biology for more than a century, and she had gained intimate knowledge of how bodies functioned. She could repair bodily organs. She might even give herself the titanic strength of a leviathan or some other monstrosity.

She could attempt to wrestle Ariock with pure strength.

Or she could try to smother the storm titan with air pressure, or make him dizzy with tornadoes.

But Ariock would win any of those fights. And everyone within three thousand miles of them would die a horrible death.

So Evenjos merely welded wires and hammered out dents on the orbital relay station. It was all she could do. Garrett was valiantly failing to stop Ariock right now. Once the titan depleted himself, Evenjos supposed she would dare to seek out survivors and heal the injured.

By the time Evenjos had figured out that the problem was a weaponized neurotoxin, it was too late. Many warriors had breathed the invisible gas and turned into rampaging berserkers.

But there was no question, in her mind, about the intention of such a drug. It was the sort of ingenuity that Unyat had been capable of. This neurotoxin was specifically designed to take advantage of Ariock's greatest weakness: his self-loathing.

Evenjos could only guess at which one of the Torth supergeniuses was responsible for this epic catastrophe. The boy Twin had used a version of insanity gas on his own people in order to pull off his vanishing act. Clearly, he had been developing it in his laboratory. His partner, the girl Twin, must have disseminated the evil recipe to factories on Nuss.

If Evenjos ever got her hands on either one of the Twins . . .

Her fists became icy-hard rocks, spiky with blades. Never mind the fact that they were fragile little children. Some crimes were too heinous for excuses.

Tens of thousands dead.

The death toll would likely be millions by the time Ariock depleted himself.

Evenjos had been a mad titan once. Ariock had been unable to restrain her. Now that their roles were reversed, she was all too aware of the futility of trying to stop him—and the guilt he would suffer afterward.

Jinishta wasn't answering her supercom. She was likely dead because of Ariock.

If he survived his own mad apocalypse, he would cease to be any sort of threat to the Torth Empire. They would rampage through Ariock's territories and reconquer them and reenslave everyone. The death toll would rise to billions or worse.

Thomas, Garrett, and Evenjos herself might not survive the massacres.

So it didn't matter how frail the cute little Torth supergeniuses were. They had not merely crossed a boundary. They had shredded the boundary into a bloody pulp, and then they'd blown up the remains with grenades. The masterminds behind this attack did not deserve to live.

A tinny voice from her earpiece startled her. "Evenjos? Can you hear me? It's Garrett."

Evenjos pressed the earpiece closer. She did not technically need ears in order to hear, but the vibration of his voice was a comfort even when filtered through an electronic device.

"I hear you," she said.

She had shut off the local newsfeed. It was too depressing, just losses and devastation. She couldn't listen to it. But her personal channel remained open. She was ready to hear from anyone in command.

"Have you heard from Freedomland?" Garrett asked. "I just received an emergency signal. The boy is in danger."

That shook Evenjos. She was more alarmed than she had felt since . . . well, since Elome had jabbed her in the back with an injection of the inhibitor. "Maybe I managed to repair the orbital relay station," she said numbly.

They had been fools.

They had left Thomas alone on Reject-20 a few times before, but it was always in an unscheduled, spurious way. This time? They had played right into a Torth trap.

A trap that Thomas had warned them about.

Evenjos cursed at herself. It was all too easy to dismiss dire warnings from powerful children. If she survived this, she vowed to treat the young supergenius with respect worthy of an emperor. A Conqueror. Because that was the truth of who he was.

"I'm going to Freedomland." Garrett sounded beyond exhausted.

"To help Thomas?" Evenjos reached out as if she could touch Garrett and stop him. "Aren't you close to depletion?"

"No choice." His voice grumbled in her earpiece.

The fate of the galaxy was at stake. Ariock might survive. He might even recover from this attack, someday. But without Thomas? No one else could possibly outthink the Torth supergeniuses.

If they lost Thomas, this war was over. They were done.

"Then I'll come with you." Evenjos felt frozen with fear, saying that. The last thing she wanted to do was face combat, but she owed the heroes, especially Thomas. "I'll help."

"You can't," Garrett said.

He could not bring an adult-size passenger when he teleported. But Evenjos was malleable and could make herself as light as a cloud. She could wrap herself around someone else's body, and . . . well. Anyway. She felt sure she could hitchhike across the galaxy using Garrett as a vehicle.

She scanned the roiling planet below her. "Where are you?"

"You don't understand," Garrett said. "Even if I can bring you to Reject-20, I won't have enough power to make a return trip to Nuss. Ariock will be alone here."

The implications began to sink in.

"The Torth are circling him like vultures," Garrett said. "They're waiting for him to die from his rage or reach depletion. They have forces everywhere. Waiting."

Evenjos remembered how Audavian had kept her alive, like a snack in his cellar, ready to be used as a weapon of mass destruction against her own allies.

She did not doubt that the Torth would use Ariock that way if they could. They would keep him alive. Depleted, inhibited, possibly injured, but alive.

Until they found their own mind controllers.

Zombified victims could not access their own Yeresunsa powers. Such powers required the free will to explore emotional nuance. But even if the Torth did not zombify Ariock . . . if they only threatened him with it . . . that might be enough to control him.

Or they might use the lighter form of brainwashing, the fourth magnitude instead of the fifth. They might lightly brainwash Ariock just enough.

Just enough to turn all his power against his friends.

"Someone needs to protect him." Garrett was begging. Evenjos heard the thickness in his voice. He was either in immense pain or on the verge of tears. "Please. I would never ask you to fight. But I'm begging you to keep an eye on him, and as soon as he starts to wind down? Grab him. Bring him somewhere safe. You've got to get him before the Torth do."

Evenjos felt inadequate. She didn't think she could outsmart whichever Torth supergeniuses had masterminded this trap.

"I see," she said.

"And heal his brain if you can. Please. I'm afraid the insanity gas is deadly." Garrett sounded final.

This was a goodbye.

Garrett was weakened, probably near depletion, yet he intended to pit himself against an unknown invasion force bent on destroying Thomas. As if he was invincible.

Because he put far too much trust into the paintings of that damnable child oracle, Ah Jun.

He refused to believe her paintings were nothing more than hints and hopes. He assumed everything was preordained. But he was wrong. Unlike the past, the future could transform.

"Wait." Evenjos's voice cracked. "Let me say goodbye. Where are you?"

Garrett told her.

Evenjos sank into the atmosphere. She flew through turbulent clouds of smoke, where the air was acrid enough to choke a normal person. CloudShadow MetroHub was unaffected by earthquakes. A decadent array of electromagnetic thrusters kept the city aloft. Storm winds shoved buildings into one another and caused wreckage, but the grand edifices had strong walls. They were merely damaged rather than wrecked.

Evenjos streamed through the broken windows of a rotunda.

Below her, worried people filled an indoor pavilion where Torth used to shop for luxury items. There were no Torth here, of course. Some of the people were armored for battle. Most looked battered. There were a lot of nussians with broken spikes, their lips tight with despair.

A cleared area, raised like a dais, included a few obvious leaders. Evenjos recognized the enormous red nussian Nethroko.

Garrett was a broken wreck.

He lay against a retaining wall, crumpled as if crushed, both legs broken despite his armor. His chest plate looked smashed. A blood-soaked bandage wrapped his head, but blood still seeped into his beard and hair.

"You are injured!" Evenjos coalesced next to him, so quickly and forcefully, she had to readjust her balance in order to get into the healing pose. "Why didn't you tell me?"

*I did.* Garrett added wry humor to his thoughts, letting her know that his tone was not serious. *Why else would I have enticed you to come to me?*

It was a wonder he had enough good humor left to be obnoxious. As Evenjos delved into his body, she sensed that every part of him was pulverized. He barely had enough consciousness for speech. Calling her must have taken heroic effort.

"I tried to knock Ariock out," Garrett mumbled, on the verge of losing consciousness from blood loss and pain. "Tried my best."

Evenjos poured energy into his life spark.

Garrett writhed, his body arching. He momentarily lifted off the ground from the force of her healing.

When she was done, Garrett dropped back to the floor, and she sensed his ravenous hunger in the aftermath of healing. His bones were set and mended. His blood was replenished. His wounds were gone.

"I love how you do that." Garrett gave her a rakish look as he struggled to sit up.

He ripped the filthy bandage off his head, using his hands like a child. No doubt he wanted to conserve what little raw power he had left.

Evenjos left his armor uncomfortably dented. She rose to her feet. She did not care if she loomed over the old man. She was shining and proud in her opalescent dress, her nacreous wings framing her statuesque figure. Was it possible to impress upon Garrett that he was a foolish twit?

"You could have gotten yourself killed," she said. "You nearly did."

"Yeah, I'm fine now, thanks to you." Garrett extended a hand, wanting help to get to his feet. It seemed he had lost his silver staff. No doubt he would make a new one when he could.

Evenjos hauled him up.

Behind her, the huge nussian rumbled. "Someone had to try to stop the Son of Storms."

Was that a passive-aggressive rebuke?

Aimed at her?

A goddess? A perfect being?

Evenjos nearly turned to give Nethroko an arch look. But she could not quite manage to feel self-righteous. This floating pavilion was filled with injured pilots, battered soldiers, and people who were mourning dead loved ones. They were terrified and grieving.

Ariock might accidentally destroy their world in his mad rage.

Even if their world survived—would they be enslaved?

She could not meet their gazes. At least Garrett had tried to save them. True, he had stupidly put his life at risk. He could have easily died fighting Ariock. There was a vast power differential between the craggy old warrior and his great-grandson.

But there was something noble about the way Garrett was willing to throw everything he had into an endeavor. It made a statement. It left no room for doubt.

Garrett cared about winning. He would do anything to defeat the Torth—to "kick their asses," as he colloquially put it. He would even attack his beloved great-grandson.

"The alert from Freedomland has me worried," Garrett told her, apologetic. "I need to go."

"Of course," Nethroko rumbled. "Do not let Torth take Kessa the Wise. Or Thomas."

Garrett's armor was stained and battered. His beard and hair remained dirty. He looked ready to keel over, and Evenjos sensed his exhaustion and hunger.

And his unshakable faith in his destiny.

His determination to win, no matter what.

Evenjos realized that she would not be able to talk Garrett out of running headlong into danger again.

And perhaps she should not.

It was improper to show obvious affection in public. It would start a million rumors if the people here survived. If she threw her arms around Garrett, commoners might see them as ordinary—

Garrett roughly seized her and crushed her against his armored chest. He kissed her with savage abandon.

Evenjos's feet were off the floor. She kissed Garrett back, and never mind who watched.

She flexed her wings, enjoying the unfamiliar sensation of being unexpectedly embraced. Garrett didn't seem to resent her for being afraid to battle Ariock. Instead, he emanated trust. He cared about her in totality, without reservations.

Love.

So this was love.

The fierce hug ended, as all things must.

Garrett set her down and gave her one last look that was all promise. Then his eyes glazed into the clairvoyant trance.

He vanished with a faint popping sound and a trace of ozone.

Evenjos remained alone in the overcrowded pavilion, with thousands of gazes aimed her way.

# CHAPTER 7

# OUT OF IDEAS

Emergency klaxons blared, warning everyone that the Freedomland Academy was under attack. Thomas ignored his own blurred reflection in multiple surfaces as he sped through the Dragon Tower's grand lobby. His overclocked perceptual senses enabled him to note every unique shadow, every distant sound.

"Yes?" Thomas answered a call on his supercom wristwatch.

"You must get to safety." It was one of his door sentries.

"On it." Thomas had already switched his tower to lockdown mode. Nerve gas protected all possible points of entry, and reflective quicksilver transformed large surfaces into makeshift mirrors. That should prevent teleporters from surprising him.

He considered commanding the sentries to go home and defend their own families. Perhaps if they went somewhere safe, the Torth might jump to the wrong conclusion: that Thomas was elsewhere.

An incoming call from Varktezo interrupted his thought processes. "Protect anyone who needs you," Thomas said, and switched to the next call.

"Teacher?" Varktezo's beak filled the tiny viewport video feed, as if he had forgotten how wristwatch cameras worked. "The Torth have a new gas."

He was whispering.

The camera moved, and Thomas squinted at footage of lab technicians staggering down a familiar hallway. Varktezo was in the research annex.

"Get to safety!" Thomas urged.

"I think I'm hearing people's thoughts," Varktezo whispered.

"It's chaos," another ummin voice moaned in the background. "We are hallucinating."

"Shh," Varktezo whispered. "Torth are coming."

The figures in the hallway acted drunk or drugged. Thomas heard wet blasts in the distance, yet no one ran. Were his people brainwashed? Or hallucinating?

Or reading minds?

That made no sense, even if such a miracle were possible. Why would Torth empower their enemies with telepathy?

"Take care of yourself," Thomas whispered at Varktezo. "Use your wristwatch to scan for neurotoxins." He had installed sensors on their supercoms in order to give warnings about any substantial compositional change in the air.

No response. Varktezo must be in danger.

"Stay safe," Thomas whispered and ended the call. He could not help Varktezo from afar.

Or anyone else.

If only Ariock or someone on his team would respond to emergency calls. Thomas might actually be able to do something with solid facts instead of guesswork.

". . . invaded the academy."

"No one knows where the Bringer of Hope . . ."

". . . say he's defeated."

Thomas wore an earpiece over the ear that had been mangled and chewed by wild zoved. He listened to the citywide broadcast channel. Since his earpiece was bone-conducting, it was virtually inaudible to anyone else.

". . . They have some kind of hallucination gas?"

". . . probably heading toward . . ."

"Let them have the *rekveh*."

"That wouldn't bode well for . . ."

On it went. Thomas dialed the audio down, needing facts rather than rumors. How he hated to feel mentally blind.

The Megacosm glowed just above his perceptions.

It was a beckoning siren, a promising trove of useful data. But Thomas knew better than to hand his enemies an advantage. The instant he ascended, the Lone Twin, the Death Architect, and others would plunge into his brain and fish out his exact location.

He needed to go somewhere unpredictable.

Thomas stopped at one of the many hundreds of electric torches in the grand lobby. He raised his hoverchair and stretched up, grasping and yanking a lever hidden within the torch's wall bracket.

A portion of the stone floor dropped away, facilitated by oiled tracks. Thomas went down with it.

The trapdoor above him slid shut, concealing him inside the secret passageway.

One could never go overboard with defensive measures when one had supergeniuses for enemies. Thomas had engineered the city's infrastructure to include bomb shelters, passageways, even an underground backup control room for the spaceport. Other than himself, only Ariock knew the locations of every underground bunker. Ariock was the builder. Thomas dared not entrust the secrets to anyone else.

So no one had ever used this passageway until now. It smelled musty.

Thomas sped along a corridor lit by dimly glowing stones at intervals. His earpiece continued to ding with notifications.

A chime overrode the rest of the noise. That was a top-level incoming call. Maybe it was Ariock?

Thomas eagerly answered the call.

"Where are you, boy?" It was Garrett's gruff voice.

"Safe," Thomas said. "But Freedomland is under attack. Where are you and Ariock?"

Garrett groaned, and Thomas knew it would be bad news.

"Ariock got hit with insanity gas," Garrett said. "He's on a rampage, wrecking everything in sight."

Implications ran through Thomas's mind. Most were devastating scenarios.

"I tried to stop him." Garrett sounded exhausted. "Couldn't."

Thomas felt stricken. Suddenly he didn't feel safe at all. These stone walls might as well be flimsy paper.

His precautions against a Torth invasion seemed pathetically inadequate. Secret passageways? A standing army? Superluminal communications? Ha. He should have locked himself away in a secret lair off-world. Maybe he should have surrounded himself and Ariock with zombies, the way Garrett kept urging them to do.

Poor Ariock. What had the Torth done to him?

Thomas dared not ask how many allies Ariock had harmed by accident. Funerary processions would come later. But one thing was immediately clear: This attack was not just against Ariock's forces, but against Ariock's psyche.

The aftermath would have long-lasting effects.

The bottom line was that a Torth supergenius—or maybe a secret coalition of them—had launched a horrific attack. And sure, Thomas had half expected something like this, but he had failed to predict the specifics of when and how.

"Where are *you*?" Thomas figured he ought to set up superluminal trackers for the heroes in the future, so that he'd be able to find them anywhere. "Are you injured?"

"I'm near depletion," Garrett said.

That was bad.

"I left Ariock." Garrett sounded ashamed. "Maybe Evenjos will be able to stop him or save him. Let me help you."

He was offering to save Thomas's life with the last of his strength.

"Where are you, exactly?" Garrett asked.

Thomas hesitated. Torth must be pouring into the academy, threatening everyone who worked with him. Shattered equipment could be replaced. But people? No. Friends and colleagues? No. The proud sense of security that his citizens had, living in these seaside mountains? That was being tromped upon.

"Look after Kessa," Thomas told Garrett. "Keep her safe. And Cherise. And Varktezo, if you can."

"I need to protect *you*." The old man sounded thwarted, no doubt prioritizing the Wisdom of the prophecies. He was obsessed with those prophecies.

Thomas imagined himself protecting his friends. Could he be useful in a war zone? His translucent hoverchair had a top speed that was illegal under Torth rule. Might he be able to speed past hundreds of invading Torth and twist their minds in quick succession?

Could he do so without running into pink inhibitor gas?

Or the insanity gas that had gotten Ariock?

Or whatever gas was getting to Varktezo?

"What's the situation in the academy?" Thomas demanded. "I need intelligence. Where are the Torth forces deployed? What chemical weapons are they using?"

"How should I know?" Garrett sounded grouchy. "I'm not crazy enough to go into the Megacosm right now."

Thomas had hoped for actionable intelligence. But he would make do.

"You shouldn't go after them." Garrett's voice was adamant. "They've been crafty today. You need to stay hidden. Please. I don't want you to take unnecessary—"

"I'm at full strength," Thomas interrupted. "It sounds like you're on the edge of depletion?" Even if Garrett had some juice left, he would lose it in coming to Reject-20. Teleportation was a massive drain on raw power.

Garrett spluttered. "Don't count me out. I can—"

"Do what I said." Thomas didn't care if he sounded commanding. Someone had to be rational and mature. "Beware the insanity gas. Protect our friends. I have a way to detect neurotoxins in the air. I'll be careful."

He let Garrett bluster and protest for another second.

Then he said, "Take care," and ended the call.

Thomas silenced the other dings. He floated alongside the wall, listening with his telepathic sense.

He reached the end of the long passageway without encountering any other minds, unless the negligible synapses of alien rock mites counted. Thomas hesitated to press the activation plate that would rotate the secret passageway exit. His embroidered kaftan was not armor. He had no weapon other than his mind.

He pressed his forehead against the cold, rough-hewn stone, and listened with all his senses.

Fear.

Thomas sensed the mind of a military-trained nussian. The thorny soldier stood in the utility closet on the far side of the wall, hidden. Terrified. Certain of death.

Well, some risks were worth taking.

Thomas firmed up his resolve and opened the passageway.

The terrified nussian leaped aside and slammed into shelves. Supplies rained down. Thomas ignored that and scanned the soldier's mind, ascertaining that there was no pink miasma outside.

He checked his wristwatch to be absolutely sure. The faintly glowing readout told him the air composition was within normal parameters. No neurotoxins nearby.

The soldier stared down at Thomas, emanating a volatile mixture of fear and crazed hope.

"Shh," Thomas whispered.

He floated out of the secret passageway.

As the wall rotated back into place, silent on its oiled tracks, the thorny soldier seemed torn between a duty to protect Thomas and a desire to hide in the secret passageway. Blood spattered his lower plates. It seemed he had escaped a war zone.

"You'll be fine here," Thomas whispered. Having soaked up the soldier's recent memories, he could guess where the mayhem was. Red Ranks had invaded the lobby of the research annex.

Red Ranks? Those were hardly a threat.

Thomas floated onward, confident. His wristwatch would vibrate in warning if the air exhibited the least hint of becoming toxic.

It was no surprise that the Torth Empire had sent invaders to the research annex. Thomas had become too predictable in his habits. He would need to remedy that.

He rounded corner after corner. Soon he floated toward the massive lobby . . .

. . . and into a massacre in progress.

A nussian tried to gallop away on all fours and bellowed in agony as his lower body exploded in bloody ropes of gore. An injured govki moaned as an ummin dragged her, trying to escape the mayhem. The ummin fell in a wet explosion.

The stench was carnal and fresh.

There were heaps of bodies. Hundreds.

Blood pooled on the floor. Blood painted the walls and reception desk. Blood dripped from the orb lights, painting the light red.

Thomas backed away, searching for threats. All he saw were a couple of Red Ranks. They swaggered with so much confidence, they didn't even wear helmets.

Why had none of the nussian and govki soldiers shot them down?

The few survivors in the lobby moved as if unsure whether they could trust their own eyes. They seemed confused about where to place their feet. And they exploded in gore as the Red Ranks walked up behind them and casually shot each one in the back.

They died without even fighting to defend themselves.

Thomas flicked his gaze to his wristwatch. His display showed no problems. No neurotoxin. So why were the people on his side acting intoxicated?

Both Red Ranks strode toward Thomas, and he saw their pink irises. Their armor was misleading. These were Rosies. They had powers. They might be able to infuse their bodies with extra speed and shoot him, or throw grenades, before an ordinary person could even think to react.

But Thomas was sure he could dodge them using his power to project illusions.

His overclocked brain gave him advantages. All he had to do was zoom at the nearest threat and twist her mind. That would enable him to start amassing a daisy chain of zombified Torth.

*The Conqueror is dead meat,* one Rosy Rank thought.

*The Conqueror is Ours,* the other silently agreed.

*We—*

*—win.*

They were beyond Thomas's range, yet he heard their thoughts.

That ought to be impossible. Was he imagining things?

Worry wormed inside him. Why weren't these two Rosies fleeing from him? Why did they radiate triumph? They clearly believed they were about to become immortalized in the Megacosm as the champions who defeated the *(former)* Conqueror.

While his consciousness struggled to understand the wrongness of this situation, his mind collated clues. Whatever drug or illusion was affecting the aliens did not appear to affect telepaths. That hinted at something specialized. Something tailor-made. It wasn't affecting the Rosy Ranks—and it wasn't affecting Thomas.

Why spray the room with something that did not affect Thomas? Something that merely confused soldiers rather than killing them? It seemed pointless . . .

. . . Unless he was only noticing a mere side effect of the drug.

There might be a main purpose that was eluding him. After all, the drug was not setting off any vibrations on his wristwatch sensor.

He was missing something.

The Torth were not acting afraid of Thomas's mind-control power. Was that merely an attempt to psych him out? Or did they have a legitimate reason to be confident? Did it have something to do with . . .

*!!! (Teacher) !!!* "Teacher!"

Varktezo skidded into Thomas's range of telepathy, emanating determination to shoot at Torth. He had grabbed a blaster glove.

But he seemed confused as to where to aim.

Varktezo aimed at one Torth's head, only to waver and shift his aim elsewhere, as if she had teleported. But she had not. Varktezo was apparently unable to believe his own perceptions.

The pair of Rosy Ranks grinned like twins. *Let's kill the Conqueror.*

*Together.*

They had closed in on Thomas. They were too close, within his range.

Easy targets for zombification.

Thomas prepared to plunge into an abhorrent Torth mind and twist it.

Varktezo fell on his backside, staring at Thomas. His beak gaped open. His eyes bugged out. "Whoa."

Thomas helplessly absorbed the ummin's perceptions. Varktezo was perceiving not just with his eyes, but the way a mind reader would perceive things. Part of Varktezo saw the way Thomas looked. Most of him saw a towering monstrosity that contained hundreds of thousands of lifetimes worth of life experience, snapping with lightning jabs of inspiration, thundering with revelations.

*Teacher?* Varktezo scrabbled back. "Teacher?" He was uncertain whether the enormity of thoughts had any relation to the frail boy who guided his experiments in the lab.

Thomas sensed all of that.

Varktezo sensed Thomas sensing it. He stared in awe and terror, feeling as small as someone meeting a god.

That was when Thomas understood the function of the mysterious neurotoxin. It wasn't a chemical at all. That was why it hadn't registered as a threat on his sensors. It did not change the air.

It changed brain waves.

It acted like a tranquility mesh.

Like telepathy.

Thomas wanted time to work through the implications of telepathy gas. But the Rosy Ranks had their blaster gloves readied. Thomas's capacious mind continued to collect and assess hints, and the final piece of the puzzle slammed into place with breathtaking clarity.

This new gas enhanced telepathy.

Thomas and these Torth were not immune, but since they were already telepathic, they hardly noticed the fact that their thoughts were skating along a dark energy matrix and mushrooming beyond their normal boundaries. They hardly noticed that the four-yard range was rendered meaningless.

It was like fog. There was no sharp beam of light. Instead, the light was everywhere.

Thomas overheard the thoughts of people beyond his normal range. Not with exacting precision, but random perceptual data and thoughts drifted here and there, as indirect as echoes. Even nontelepaths could sense the widespread thoughts and perceptions and moods.

And if Thomas twisted a mind?

Everyone in the vicinity would be affected . . . including Thomas himself.

. . .

*Ooh,* one Rosy Rank thought. *He gets it.*

*He recognizes his Defeat.* The other glowed with triumph.

*Sweet victory is Ours!*

*Do We even need to shoot him?*

The moment of shock lasted an entire millisecond.

In that instant, Thomas understood he was screwed.

He could not brainwash or twist a mind or he would suffer the effects.

He could not give a pain seizure or it would be reflected back upon him.

His mushrooming thoughts would give away his location even if he projected an illusion to try to fool their senses.

He could try to flee, but the Rosies had enough power to rope him back.

This new weapon was specifically designed to nullify his unique advantages, in the same way that insanity gas had been designed to defeat Ariock.

*Checkmate, little Yellow.* He could all but hear the gleeful whisper from his Torth opponents. They weren't the Upward Governess, but they were the ones who had inherited her scientific research. The Death Architect and the girl Twin wielded double the brainpower and social influence that the Upward Governess used to have.

Wildfire was an extracorporeal power. Unlike telepathy, it shouldn't get reflected back on him. Thomas summoned a fireball and hurled it at the Rosy Ranks.

One of them casually raised her gloved hand and sucked the heat out of the fireball. It died in midair.

She thumbed her trigger.

Thomas flashed back to his first day in the Torth Empire, when the Swift Killer had aimed a blaster glove at his face. He had peered into that black aperture and known that his death was imminent. Except it had been postponed.

Till now.

Thomas sent a silent apology to Varktezo, and to anyone else who might overhear his defeat and death. Some Torth supergenius or two had finally outmaneuvered him, and there was absolutely nothing he could do to save his own life. He had put up a good fight—the best fight in galactic history—but he should have anticipated this ending.

No individual could hope to stand against the collective might of the Torth Empire. The Torth were always victorious.

Lightning flashed.

There was a crash of thunder and a smell of ozone. The blast whizzed past Thomas's head, burning his scarred ear and disabling his earpiece.

Garrett landed out of nowhere, robes billowing, hair and beard flowing. He held a makeshift staff in one hand. When he flicked it, stone pillars cracked and buckled. The Rosy Ranks went flying as if hit by invisible fists.

One of the Rosies slammed against a stone wall with enough force to liquefy bones. The other cushioned her landing and backflipped in midair to land near Thomas. She triggered a blast at him.

Her blast should have killed him. Instead, it exploded against an invisible shield of solidified air.

The Rosy spun and force-slammed Garrett against the wall. Thomas could see, now, that Garrett's armor was dented, and he had a nosebleed. The old man seemed to gather his strength before whipping a miniature shock wave at their attacker.

She aimed another blast at Thomas. The shock wave hit her at the same time, and her blast went wide and slammed into the passageway. Chunks of granite rained onto the inert bodies of victims.

Garrett force-slammed the Rosy against the ceiling. Cracks formed. Blood leaked from the corpse before she fell in a crumpled heap, dead.

"That was amazing," Thomas said.

Garrett sank to one knee, clinging to his staff for support, wheezing. "Yeah," he said. "Thanks for saving your *I told you so*s for later."

Judging by the ruination of his armor, he'd had a hard day.

Thomas wanted an update about Ariock's situation on Nuss, but there was no time. The Torth Majority knew his exact location. Garrett seemed entirely depleted. A horde of champions could easily finish both of them right now.

"Ariock and Evenjos are in trouble," Garrett confessed.

"So are we." Thomas did not hide the shakiness of his voice. More Torth invaders would show up at any second.

*The Torth will have to get past me first.* Varktezo stood with a blaster glove on each hand, radiating determination. He looked ready for anything.

# CHAPTER 8

# WINNER OF NOW

*WINNING*
* \* ! \* ! \**
  *We are winning!*
*  ! \* ! \* !*
   *!!!!! Yay !!!!!*
*   ! \* ! \* ! \* !*

The Death Architect had to tune out a lot of jubilation and praise. Evacuees on Bountiful chorused, *The Death Architect is the most genius supergenius ever!*

*(Yes) We owe Her everything!* That came from evacuees on Sunbeam Orbital. *We will do anything She ever requires!*

  *She has saved civilization!* A congregation of Torth on Vagary silently rejoiced.

   *She is the savior of the known universe!* That came from Verdantia.

    *She is incredible!*

     *She must rule Us!*

     *She is the best!*

*Death Architect! Death Architect! DEATH ARCHITECT!* The victorious chant began with a few hundred thought leaders on various worlds, but they quickly picked up thousands, then millions, then billions of Torth throughout the Megacosm. *Death Architect! DEATH ARCHITECT!*

They loved her.

With nasty, uncouth, slave-like emotions.

The Death Architect would have vomited in disgust at the servile minds squirming all over hers, except she'd never felt disgust. This much *(praise) (worship)* emotion was unbecoming for any self-respecting Torth. How could billions of them lose their collective superiority?

They had better regain their decorum soon. Otherwise she would think of ways to make them stop.

Her stray thought shut a few million of them up.

Good enough for now. The Death Architect was too busy directing battles to dedicate her mental resources toward anything petty. Even while she endured the worshipful billions, she peered through the eyes of an ever-shifting panoply of Servants of All and Rosies.

She whispered in their minds.

She guided their hands, instructing them on where to go, what to do, and where to aim.

Her troops shot enemies on sight. They sabotaged enemy equipment. There were headquarters to bomb, battle leaders to assassinate, launchpads to destroy, and enemy consuls who should be terrorized. Her troops waded into slums where temporarily embarrassed Torth—those known as penitents—survived in nasty barracks amid trash heaps. They removed shackles, unlocked slave collars, and broke doors.

Millions of enslaved Torth were set loose.

*Rampage,* the Death Architect urged the few penitents who dared to ascend and orbit her mind. *Remember your Torth dignity? You can have it all back. All you have to do is (discard the enemy's laws and) pick up weapons. I don't care what rank you used to be. My orbiters will promote you to Red Rank the instant you kill an enemy for the great and glorious Torth Empire.*

Her orbiters chorused an assent.

Penitents who yearned to become Torth again leaped into action, spreading her offer, making sure that all penitents understood they had a great, albeit undeserved, opportunity.

*Why are so few penitents rejoining Us?* Red Ranks asked each other.

*Why are they hiding?*

Instead of rushing out to sow mayhem, most of the penitents cowered inside their barracks or cubby holes. Their minds remained silent beneath the Megacosm. Were they afraid to take a risk?

How shortsighted. Didn't they value civilization?

Didn't they have any sense of self-preservation?

They might need some external motivation.

*Kill any uncooperative penitents,* the Death Architect decided.

The Majority quickly ratified that as a decree, and the troops obediently incorporated it into their list of objectives. Reluctant penitents got shot in the face, the chest, or the back. There was no reason to show mercy to traitors.

*(!?) !? (!?)*

A substantial minority *(44.19643 percent)* of Torth protested the elimination *(murder)* of *(flawed ones)* penitents. Was it really necessary to massacre fellow mind readers? After all, the penitents were not shooting at Torth. Inaction was not a crime. Wasn't punishment a bit premature?

The Death Architect ignored the small-minded protesters. They were ignorant of the larger picture.

Her version of the victorious empire would be flawless. In the future, there would be zero tolerance for emotions. Zero tolerance for protesters. She would never allow another Conqueror to arise.

She sent out a new directive in order to distract the unruly masses. *Commence the reconquest of Umdalkdul!*

*!!!!!!* A jubilant cry went up in the Megacosm.

　　　* * *

　　*YAY!!!!!!!!*

Trillions of Torth agreed that they must retake that hub planet. Umdalkdul never should have been snatched so easily. Soon, that embarrassing sequence of losses would be merely an aberrant blip in galactic history.

A space armada surged through various temporal streams and converged toward Umdalkdul. The Death Architect leaped from mind to mind, directing navigation crews, positioning dreadnoughts and swarmships. She never felt anything like triumph. Nevertheless, she understood that she ought to feel triumphant.

Victory was inevitable.

The Giant had decimated his own allies in his drug-crazed efforts to kill anything that looked like the merest hint of a Torth. Local fleets pounded him with nuclear bombs. He was still more deadly than a nuclear meltdown, coasting on his massive raw strength. Nobody could get close enough to spray him with inhibitor gas.

Yet.

As soon as he showed signs of losing strength? An extraction crew, operating on covert instructions, would swoop down and airlift the unconscious titan out of irradiated clouds of toxic ash.

And the Torth Empire would then own a new sort of weapon.

The Death Architect could not fully rely on that optimistic outcome. Her daydreams of the future blurred with too many possibilities. Every decision made by every military pilot bifurcated each second of the battle into a million facets, generating an exponentially expanding number of ever-shifting potentialities.

She didn't really care. The Giant (that colossal pain) would likely never threaten anyone again after today.

Anyway, netting him was only an afterthought. She was after the biggest prey.

The Conqueror had blundered straight into the telepathy-gas trap the Death Architect had engineered especially for him. He was supposed to have lashed out in self-defense. He should have accidentally twisted his own gigantic mind.

It had almost happened like that.

Almost.

The Death Architect had foreseen that future as an extremely strong possibility. With the Conqueror brain-dead, all his runaways would give up and quit. The galaxy would settle into a new regime of peaceful civilization, overseen by her.

He should have made that fatal mistake.

Instead? The Conqueror had stopped short at the last second.

He had defied probability and made a fateful decision. Somehow—how?—he had deduced the thalamocortical mirroring possibilities engendered by a dark matrix encephalographic distortion zone.

Just how had he made that intuitive leap?

He was older than any other living supergenius except for the Lone Twin, but his brain was withered from a decade spent on the backwater planet Earth. He should not have become smarter than the Death Architect.

Perhaps his gross overconsumption of random Torth lives had boosted his intellect above everyone else's?

That seemed unlikely. He was absorbing trash, not scientific ingenuity.

The Death Architect figured she had simply made an unfortunate miscalculation. She probably should have piled all her forces toward her primary target rather than splitting her invasion across multiple targets. Really, Kessa didn't matter. Neither did those Earth women, Vy and Cherise.

She sent out mental commands to redirect her champions.

The Conqueror was a wily nemesis. It was a mistake to underestimate him, even by a smidge.

Comprehending one's opponent was often a vital key to winning. That sort of psychological analysis had empowered the Upward Governess to predict Yellow

Thomas as a threat. That was why the fat girl had been so eager to research dark matrixes and encephalographic distortion fields. She had put a lot of thought into the best way to defeat her former mentee.

The Death Architect, on the other hand, had not foreseen Yellow Thomas as a danger until well after he went renegade.

Her lack of firsthand knowledge of his mind was a blind spot. It made for potential flaws in her schemes, even when her visions of the near future held the clarity of virtual certainty.

It was a good thing she had so many other advantages.

She could intuit the future enough to create her own luck. In contrast, the Conqueror could not even fully control the minions he called friends.

The Death Architect ruled most of the galaxy. Her resources were nearly infinite, and more and more, they were increasingly under her complete and total control. A desperate populace yielded to her whims.

Also, she had much smarter colleagues than what the Conqueror could muster. His lab assistants were mere runaway slaves. They were probably illiterate, ruled by bestial whims and groveling before their mental superior. Meanwhile? The Death Architect farmed work out to her polymath colleagues. The Lone Twin, the Rind Topographer, the Geodesic Flux, and the Spin Overture were all supergeniuses who had ripened into their full potential.

There was one dud in that age bracket, the Stalled Proofer, but that was to be expected. One out of every four supergeniuses died by suicide. Mental idiosyncrasies were just part of their bioengineered nature.

The Lone Twin was formidable above and beyond the rest. Sure, her mental twin had betrayed the empire and gone rogue, but before that, he had helped to provide the winning weaponry. Together, the Twins had improved upon the Upward Governess's notes. They had zeroed in on antineutrino desorption as a technique for amplifying ambient thalamocortical resonance, and together, they had brought her invention to fruition.

Their collaborative brilliance had also moved the rage-inducing insanity gas beyond a trial phase and into production. The Death Architect wished she could take credit for the insanity gas, but most scientists knew she was less of a chemist and more of an architect.

And the phase-shifting inhibitor gas? What a clever concept. What a paradigm shift! The Torth Empire also owed that battlefield neurotoxin to the Twins.

*We never found Kessa,* her champions on Reject-20 reported. *And We cannot find the Conqueror.*

They rushed from room to room, leaking frustration and killing the few living beings they saw. They would have pleased the Majority by taking high-value hostages, but all the laboratories and closets were empty. Much of the city's populace had disappeared.

*Your targets are hiding in bunkers (underground),* the Death Architect surmised. *Or in secret passageways.* That seemed obvious to her. *Any supergenius would design a city full of safe havens.*

The champions praised her for her brilliant insight. They began to search the academy in a more methodical way, tapping on walls and listening for hollow echoes. They leaned their heads here and there, listening for minds that might be hidden from sight. They spread their awareness and searched for concealed spaces.

It was only a matter of time.

The most powerful champion on Reject-20 stood in a lobby piled with corpses. He spread his awareness, searching for life sparks. Since the enemy powerhouses were on another planet, this champion Servant of All was able to explore his own sphere of influence without interference. He was able to expand throughout a large portion of the academy complex.

*I do not detect any outstanding life sparks*, he reported in the Megacosm. *If the Imposter or the Conqueror are here, they are not standing out.*

That probably meant the Imposter was depleted. As for the Conqueror . . .

No one knew how he received power boosts. He siphoned off a minion, usually the Giant, but linking was a mystery. No Torth could figure out how it was done.

Anyhow, without minions to boost him, the Conqueror was no more powerful than an average Rosy Rank.

*He is highly vulnerable right now.* The Death Architect pictured the Conqueror quivering in the dark. *Terrified. Cornered. He cannot best Our champions in a fight (and he knows it).*

Her orbiters chorused with melodies of bloodlust. The Conqueror dared not use his power to brainwash or twist minds. Not with all the telepathy-diffusion zones that their champions had set up.

*Conserve your powers*, the Death Architect instructed her champions within the Freedomland Academy. *Save your strength for when you see the Conqueror. Then? Crush his skull.*

The champions reacted with respectful determination. They looked for a way to drill underground, to get to the hidden life sparks.

The Death Architect sank away from the Megacosm and explored her own intuitive sense of the future. Was victory preordained?

Nuss was falling, Umdalkdul was falling, and Freedomland was invaded. Even if the Conqueror surprised her with some unpredictable strategy—which he was likely to do—she just needed to lock down his city for seven days. That was how long it would take for Torth dreadnoughts to arrive and nuke everything on the ground.

The Giant was defeated. They only had to kill the Conqueror.

The hunting champions knew the Majority would force them to take much more deadly missions unless they succeeded today. So they were highly motivated.

Satisfied, the Death Architect made an eye gesture at one of her slaves. There was a bowl full of fermented, prune-like fruits on a counter, between scalpels and blood-soaked rags.

She did not care about treats. Yet she wanted some visceral way to celebrate her triumph over the enemies, because the fools beneath her *(the Majority)* expected such rituals. An influencer had to humor her constituents. For now.

And perhaps . . . well, perhaps she might feel something like actual satisfaction, once she won?

Soon.

She ascended again, ready to orchestrate far-flung battles. But she became peripherally aware of distant, nearly inconsequential cries of alarm.

*!?!?*

It was just a handful of mental voices reacting to something in the deep space beyond Vazza. But they were amplified by exponentially larger audiences, and soon the Death Architect sensed her own orbiters tugging her attention.

Whatever this was, it was news.

*The Twin!*

It seemed the Lone Twin, formerly known as the girl Twin, had done something inexplicable. She had ascended into the Megacosm for a split second—although she had scheduled this time for sleep—and she had emitted a cryptic string of seemingly random symbols, icons, and glyphs, interspersed with numbers.

Then?

She had promptly dropped out of the Megacosm.

Hm.

The Death Architect did not waste time trying to parse the code. She could guess it was a subversive signal, and she could guess whom it was meant for. The Twins had earned their shared name-title. Thanks to their long-time cohabitation plus their supergenius processing speeds, their minds were nearly identical. They were grossly obsessed with each other.

The pertinent question was: How could the other Twin receive the mental code?

Supergenius minds were too enormous to hide amid the normal ebb and flow of conversations. Ripe supergeniuses in particular—those who were as old as the Twins—could not hide. If the boy Twin ascended into the Megacosm, even for a nanosecond, someone would notice and it would become public knowledge.

Quite a mystery.

The Twins must be conspiring with a lesser mind. One of the rogue Servants of All, perhaps? Someone who could blend in with Megacosm choruses, like the Imposter?

*It was not a code meant for Me*, the Death Architect confirmed for her billions of orbiters. *Or for anyone loyal to (civilization) the empire.*

Nuclear launchers swiveled to lock onto the Lone Twin's scientific vessel.

Ever since the boy Twin had disappeared, the empire had taken extra precautions with his erstwhile other half. The Lone Twin was under constant, unbroken surveillance. Camera drones monitored her at all times. Three Servants of All had devoted themselves to round-the-clock watchfulness over her, in person.

*The Lone Twin must be defecting*, the Majority chorused in a crescendo of agreement.

*DESTROY HER!*

*NUKE HER!*

The Death Architect emitted a small sigh. She would regret losing her smartest work partner, but . . . ah well. Neither Twin showed up in her daydreams from this point forward. They had served their purpose.

*Go ahead and kill her.* The Death Architect turned her focus to her invasion force on Umdalkdul.

How had the Conqueror trained so many slaves, in such a short time, to pilot military swarmshuttles? And where did they get such bravery? Slaves were usually cowards.

Before she could immerse herself in the firestorm that was one fleet pounding another, her orbiters interrupted her again.

*!!!!!!!*

The Servants of All who were supposed to kill the Lone Twin were gone. It seemed they had died quite suddenly.

The nuclear warheads, although launched, remained undetonated. Something had gone awry. The Majority seethed in confused disquiet.

*A mechanical failure?* That was an investigating Green Rank. *But We were very thorough with our daily checks. How could all nine guidance matrices have failed simultaneously?*

*SABOTAGE!* the Majority chorused.

There could be no other explanation. The scientific vessel that had also been a prison was gone. During the excitement of glorious wins over the enemies, during the short window of time in which the Death Architect had absented herself from the Megacosm, the Lone Twin had enacted some sort of plan.

And escaped.

Given the evidence, the Death Architect suspected that someone close to the Twins had secretly done their bidding. Perhaps that someone was the instigator? Had someone persuaded—or brainwashed?—the brilliant scientists into turning away from civilized progress and toward primitive sympathies?

The saboteur needed to be rooted out.

*Launch an investigation*, the Death Architect urged the highest ranks who were close to the situation. *Report your findings directly to Me, in person. Make it a private report. Do not share your findings in the Megacosm.*

One could never be too careful when dealing with enemy supergeniuses.

*Trace routes the Lone Twin is likely to choose*, the Death Architect added. *Double the watchdog forces at all temporal stream gates. Prepare to nuke either Twin when their vessels show up.*

The Majority relayed her commands. Military ranks set out, eager to outdo each other in their race to prove their loyalty to the empire. They would obey any command given by the Death Architect, who was the unequivocal ruler of the known universe.

The Majority agreed that she had proven her loyalty and her capabilities beyond any doubt. They had already held a quick election to ratify her rule.

As they should.

The Death Architect turned her attention to Reject-20. The Twins were irrelevant. The planet Umdalkdul was irrelevant. The Conqueror was her true enemy, the only nemesis that mattered, and he must be hidden somewhere inside the ridiculously eclectic city known as Freedomland.

When her troops dragged him out of hiding, would he weep like a slave? Would he bravely try to protect his slavish friends? What was he most likely to do?

She wished she had insight into his mind, as the Upward Governess used to have.

*Find him*, she urged her underlings. *And show the enemies that the Torth Empire cannot be defeated.*

# CHAPTER 9

# MORE THAN SUPERFICIAL

A weak beam of sunlight pierced the roiling, apocalyptic clouds. That was all that remained of the natural state of the weather.

The mad hurricane of Ariock was a thousand miles from this floating metropolis, but he was getting madder. Wind shrieked past floating tower tops. The scudding clouds were so thick, day was as dark as night. Earthquakes rippled the wrecked remains of the lower city.

Yeresunsa powers were tied to emotions. Quitting was literally impossible for Ariock right now due to the insanity gas, yet he must be holding on to a shred of sanity. He wasn't roving all over the planet.

Yet.

Evenjos paced.

She ignored the thousands of people who watched her beneath emergency lights, some of whom chanted prayers to the Lady of Sorrow. In an era where a galactic empire wielded unlimited power, how could anyone worship a lone Yeresunsa? She supposed they prayed because they were drowning and grasping for reeds.

"Lady?" That was Nethroko.

She thought he spoke with respect, but it was difficult to tell, since the nussian was beyond her range of telepathy. His voice was so deep and gravelly.

"Garrett said insanity gas is a death sentence," Nethroko said. "He wants you to heal the Son of Storms."

Evenjos paced the other way, wings shielding her back. Did Nethroko and his cohorts want her to approach Ariock right now? She would fail and die. She would use up all her vast power in a futile attempt to wrestle Ariock in all his strength.

If only she had studied neurochemistry more assiduously.

Evenjos could imitate anything on a superficial level, but she could not magically regenerate part of her body into becoming a functional tranquilizer, let alone an antidote to the mysterious insanity gas. She would not know where to begin. Thomas might be able to guide her, if she could reach him on a supercom. Then again, it would probably take years for her to understand anything beyond the basic principles.

"Is it possible you can stop him?" Nethroko asked. "These might help."

The big nussian offered three gigantic hypodermic darts. The darts appeared cruel enough to punch through armor if shot at high velocity.

"Torth used these to stop berserk nussian gladiators," Nethroko explained. "It might work on the Son of Storms. We filled these with a mixture of inhibitor serum plus tranquilizer."

Another nussian leaned in. "Jonathan Stead tried to inject him, but he missed."

"He could not get close enough," Nethroko corrected. His small eyes fixed on Evenjos with unspoken significance. Plainly, he wanted Evenjos to do what Garrett could not accomplish.

Evenjos walked over and plucked one hypodermic out of Nethroko's grasp. Its contents could kill her. One brush of that liquid would make her lose cohesion forever.

She studied its sharp tip.

The Torth pilots were likely guided by an enemy supergenius or two. She would be risking her life just to get close to his core body. They might saturate the area with deadly inhibitor gas. Even if she survived that gauntlet . . .

Would the enraged Ariock allow her to get close enough to his mortal body to poke him with a needle?

She remembered her own furious shock and pain after Elome had stabbed her in the back. That sense of betrayal. Her own unthinking rage once she was resurrected.

She would have to reassure Ariock in some way. She could not allow him to see a needle.

Could she trick him? Make him trust her, if only for a short time?

Then, if she succeeded, she would need to immediately haul his unconscious body to a safe place while Torth shot missiles and inhibitor at her.

What if she missed?

Evenjos rolled the deadly needle between her fingers. Ariock had excellent battle instincts. She would only get one attempt to surprise the enraged titan.

The indoor pavilion trembled from a violent burst of thunder. Glass shattered. Urns and decorative elements fell.

Evenjos had already manipulated Ariock, pretending to be his human lover. How could she even consider doing that again? She would be making a mockery of his tenuous trust. She did not want to become his Elome.

And yet.

Evenjos surveyed the desperate people all around her. No one else had a chance of pulling off a rescue. The cloud fleet was decimated. Individual pilots had no chance to get close to the furious stormbringer, let alone airlift him to a safe haven.

She considered the love Garrett had shown her.

Garrett must be in grave trouble right now, but Evenjos could not teleport, so she could not aid him. All she could do was honor the trust he had shown her. Garrett cared about Ariock, probably more than he cared about anyone else in the universe. If Garrett survived only to learn that his great-grandson was dead or captured by Torth . . . ? He would never forgive himself.

The old man would take any number of stupid risks to rescue Ariock. He had already done so.

Evenjos was his last hope.

She transformed one of her legs, making it hollow. It became the simulation of a prosthetic.

"I will do what I can," she said, placing the hypodermic dart into her simulated prosthetic leg. "I will only get one shot." She refused to carry the other tranquilizer needles. If Ariock smashed her, the broken contents of a needle would unmake her forever.

Nethroko and others watched her with hope in their beady eyes.

Evenjos could not afford to think too hard about what she meant to do. Otherwise she would talk herself out of it.

Quivering with fear, she launched herself skyward.

Evenjos arrowed through clouds so thick they were nearly solid. Magma oozed in runnels along the distant ground, like veins flayed open. Buildings crumpled between sharp new crags of rock. The wreckage of crashed transports burned here and there. Ariock had become destruction incarnate.

There were ancient tales about this.

Stories about destructive incarnations were long forgotten in this era, but the Yeresunsa academy had been full of cautionary tales. A powerful Yeresunsa who lost touch with their own sense of self—who lost track of their core, becoming wholly enveloped by some runaway emotion—could become a gross embodiment of a specific power, or a set of powers. Fire. Flooding. Quakes. Tornadoes.

Stormbringers, with more than one extracorporeal power, were particularly susceptible to losing control. That was why many of them led celibate lives.

They used to, anyway. Back then.

Evenjos reminded herself that Ariock's rage was not his fault. He was a victim, and she might just as easily fall victim to that insanity gas. She had to be extra careful.

She stopped breathing. She erased her own nose and mouth and ears, sealing all orifices, subsuming cloth and hair and anything soft into her body. Her skin became as metallic and inhumanly opalescent as her wings. She was impenetrable.

She was a bullet. This was how she would get through his shrieking winds of insanity.

As she zipped through the pulverizing hurricane, traversing miles within seconds, she knew that no transport could withstand the forces here. Ariock had surrounded his core self with bladelike crosswinds that destroyed anything larger than a pebble.

Evenjos encapsulated the hypodermic needle inside her hardened self. She held her impenetrable body together with the power of her mind as she whipped past ashes and pebbles of debris, determined to get to the other side.

A colossus emerged in the core of the hurricane.

He was the size of a volcano. He was rock and sand and liquefied torment, and he was moving. One of his enormous, hollowed black-hole eyes focused on the tiny bullet that was Evenjos.

Oh no.

Evenjos summoned all her shapeshifting expertise. She kept her skin hard and impenetrable, yet she also morphed into the soft, feminine form of Violet Hollander. Only one leg remained visibly chrome-hard. Her false prosthetic contained the dart. She needed to protect that dart from destruction or she was dead.

"Ariock?" At least she did not need to fake being scared as she fell and bounced in vicious crosswinds. "I love you. Please don't hurt me?"

This was so unnerving. Was her voice the right timbre and pitch? Was her hair the right shade of coppery red? Had she forgotten any crucial details about the way Vy looked and acted?

Winds died down.

Magma hardened to rock.

Oceans realigned themselves.

A much more human-size titan emerged from the eye of the storm, floating on a wave of pressurized air and crackling lightning.

His galaxy armor wasn't even scratched. Every diamond of the galactic spiral on his chest plate remained in place. His mismatched helm was crude and ugly, but also thick and solid. Between the eye slits, Ariock's bloodshot eyes were narrowed with suspicion.

Raw power radiated off the superhuman titan like the strength of a supernova.

No wonder he'd dared to expose his mortal body. He was a juggernaut, not even remotely depleted. If anything, he must be fighting to contain his rage and power.

Evenjos acted as fast as she could. She spread her arms like she wanted to hug the giant even as she fell toward hellish fissures in the wasteland below. Vy could not levitate or fly, so Evenjos pretended to be a helpless victim of gravity.

But a ribbon separated from her back—a serpentine appendage of immense strength.

Evenjos liquefied her false prosthetic long enough to seize the hypodermic. And she plunged it toward the gap between Ariock's gorget and helm. She aimed for the tiny gap that exposed a bit of his throat.

He saw it coming.

Ariock twisted away, and a cliff-size sledgehammer rocketed toward Evenjos. She let go of her bodily cohesion and his titanic strength tore through her without effect.

Ariock shielded himself with rocks, cascades of sand, and a cage of electric energy. Evenjos tunneled through his shields with a million tiny drills. Boulders plummeted through the air she occupied. She formed makeshift blades and used them to rip through his solid defenses.

He chopped at her with sand-infused wind.

She hardened her appendage against his furious forces and threw all her focus into hitting the target.

The oversize dart stabbed the naked skin of his throat.

Ariock shoved her harder and harder. His strength was inexorable. Unstoppable. She was not going to be able to hold the needle in place . . .

But it was emptied.

Ariock threw her with so much force, it was all she could do to hold on to consciousness.

Evenjos surrendered, letting herself become ashes and dust, letting crosswinds disintegrate her body. The emptied needle fell. Evenjos was scoured. She fought to remain conscious, because consciousness was life, and if she lost it . . .

The insane hurricane winds began to ebb.

And the whole world changed.

Boulders dropped out of the sky and splashed into magma that was already hardening to black rock. Tectonic plates shifted, no longer gripped by an outside presence. Ash fell like sleet.

The unconscious, mortal body of Ariock fell, too.

Evenjos coalesced into her default form, the winged goddess-empress she had practiced for more than a century. She caught the giant in her strengthened arms. She had to stretch herself just to hold on to him.

Ariock was breathing. Good.

Blood leaked from the corners of his closed eyes, and the veins of his neck looked swollen and dark beneath his helm. He was fighting even while unconscious.

Corpses and wreckage littered the wasteland below. The two of them were the only living beings for hundreds of miles.

A nuclear detonation ripped the atmosphere apart.

The shock wave would have vaporized Evenjos and Ariock if not for the airtight shield she threw around them at the last second. Corpses burned to cinders. The ground became a scorching-hot zone of death.

The second bomb turned the night-dark sky into blazing, blinding light. It would deafen anyone with eardrums. No doubt it was damaging Ariock.

Shuttles swarmed out of the ballooning mushroom clouds, and Evenjos knew that she would be insane to stand her ground. The Torth armada seemed to consist of relatively ordinary pilots—with Ariock's raw power nullified, she was able to sense life sparks when she expanded her awareness—but they had the insanity gas. And inhibitor gas. And who knew what other weapons.

They were shooting missiles, and they were likely being choreographed by a supergenius.

Evenjos hauled the behemoth that was Ariock high into the air. Thousands of missiles targeted them, speeding as fast as bullets. She had to dodge and twist, faster than any game she'd ever played, with Ariock as a dead weight that she was unaccustomed to.

CloudShadow MetroHub was a bad idea. Evenjos would not lead the Torth armada toward any populated areas.

A cave, then? Or a glacial crag in the distant mountains?

She must find some obscure shelter. She must do everything she could to race away from the monsters of this era.

Evenjos plunged through storm clouds that still looked violent, webbed with continuous bolts of lightning. Deadly radiation blew across what used to be a desert. Without his powers, Ariock was as vulnerable as any human. His ability to heal and recover would be impeded.

Would he even be sane when—or if—he woke up?

The Yeresunsa of her time used to pray to their illustrious ancestors as if they were deities. Evenjos might have considered praying to her grandmother . . . but when she'd been trapped in the mirrors, on the twilight edge of life for an eternity, she had sensed the endless barrier between life and death. No one crossed over until their last breath left them and their heart stopped beating.

The dead never returned. There were no ancestors listening.

Evenjos flipped above a spinning projectile that emitted pink gas. She used her powers to vacuum the deadly air out of her way, tunneling forward. The Torth had guessed her weakness. They were shooting inhibitor.

She needed safety. She needed peace. If she could stay hidden for a while, she would explore the misfirings in Ariock's neurons and try to diagnose the problem. And cure it.

# CHAPTER 10

# EQUAL FOOTING

There was a lot more to Thomas than emotional immaturity, but for the first time in ages, the child aspect of his mind was ascendant and the various masterminds were buried. He was scared.

He had nothing to say. Radios crackled. Battle leaders reported mayhem and death.

He had nothing to see. It was dark inside the secret passageway. The frightened expressions of his companions were illuminated by glowing bricks and wristwatch displays.

Garrett leaned his forehead against the wall in a posture of defeat. His craggy face sagged with exhaustion. With his power entirely depleted, he looked as if he had aged by four or five decades.

Dust sifted off the ceiling every time the passageway trembled. The Torth must be trying to break into the network of secret passageways, throwing grenades into the warren of scientific laboratories. Destructive bastards.

But they were not idiots.

That was a fact Thomas really should have kept at the forefront of his mind at all times.

"Can I ask you about their new gas?" Varktezo asked, his voice low.

The passageway was stuffed with frightened lab technicians and soldiers. Thomas had invited hundreds of people to join him in hiding, since the invaders were pumping telepathy gas everywhere and wreaking havoc upon anyone they encountered. Torth forces dominated every possible exit from the academy.

"Was it . . ." Varktezo hesitated. Then he whispered his outlandish guess. "Telepathy gas?"

Nearby people fell silent.

The air in the passageway was stuffy from overcrowding. People pressed against the walls, against each other, and against Thomas's hoverchair.

??? Varktezo sidled closer. He emitted cloyingly sharp curiosity.

"Yes," Thomas admitted. "The Torth invented a telepathy gas." His people would learn the truth one way or another if they survived, so he might as well alleviate the overwhelming curiosity all around him. "It seems like some kind of desorption technique that amplifies brain waves."

Garrett sighed, depressed.

Varktezo's beak fell open in delight.

Thomas wished he had time to theorize about how telepathy gas worked. It must utilize stochastic supersymmetry, but did it rely on a fermion matrix? Or antineutrinos? If only he could interrogate the inventor. It was disgustingly brilliant.

"I think it's a matrix of dark energy," Thomas went on, "created and spread by emitters. Anyone within an artificial telepathy zone will experience each other's experiences, whether or not they can read minds."

"Was that really what telepathy feels like?" One lab technician exchanged dubious glances with another.

"Yep," Thomas said.

Another technician seemed to gather her courage, and she faced him directly. "Is it what you experience all the time? Like, right now?"

"It is," Garrett said.

Thomas nodded.

"But why was it so confusing and disorienting?" another technician asked.
*???*

    *???*

        *???*

People practically held their breaths, driven mad with their eagerness for explanations. Dust sifted down. Curiosity pressed against Thomas, cornering him.

Garrett must likewise feel cornered by all the unspoken questions. "It's not confusing for mind readers," he explained.

"Right," Thomas added. "Our brains are adapted to handle multiple viewpoints and inputs. You're just not used to it."

"It's like," Garrett said, "if a person who was blind from birth suddenly gained eyesight."

Thomas added, "The formerly blind person would not yet be able to associate words with images. It would just be a jumble of new data."

The listeners emanated dismay.

Except for Varktezo, who was ecstatic. His beak hung open with joy. "Are you saying we can actually learn to read minds?"

Thomas did not want to falsely stoke that wistful passion. "It's possible," he admitted. "If we survive the next hour. But it would take a lot of time and practice." He tapped his leg braces. "You've seen how long it's taken me to learn to walk."

Telepathy gas was, specifically, a guarantee against mind control. Thomas figured the Torth would only release it where their Conqueror nemesis might be present. They would never allow nontelepaths to get used to it.

Because they feared a universe where they no longer had a power advantage.

Such a possibility must haunt their darkest nightmares.

Varktezo tapped his earpiece. "Try to confiscate any mysterious equipment the Torth leave lying around," he told the garrison dispatcher. "Please. Look for . . ." He gave Thomas an inviting expression. "What do the emitters look like?"

"I have no idea." Thomas had failed to soak up any extraneous mysteries while those Rosies had tried to murder him.

"Just any unknown boxes or cylinders," Varktezo told the dispatcher. "If people experience confusion or double vision? There will be weird equipment nearby. Grab it. Switch it off, if you can, but keep it safe. We will need to study it."

He ended the call and grinned at Thomas.

The passageway shook as another grenade went off. People drew closer together, scared.

Thomas wondered if any of them would survive long enough to reverse engineer the weaponized telepathy gas. The Torth were going to blast their way into his hideout. It was inevitable. And then they would find Thomas as helpless as the weakest ummin.

His thermokinetic power was the rough equivalent of a blaster glove. It would not stop a bunch of Rosy Ranks.

He could create illusions, but any halfwit of a mind reader would see right through that sort of thing.

In fact, Thomas's powers might actually be a liability right now. What if his life spark stood out? He might glow like a beacon to the most powerful invader. He should go dark.

Yet he could not bring himself to press a blaster glove against his skin and inject himself with inhibitor. Losing his Yeresunsa aura might be a smart gamble on staying hidden, but it might also entail his doom. He just didn't know.

He hated guesswork.

"I hope Ariock is all right." Garrett spoke in the dimness. "I can't reach anyone on Nuss. The relay stations must be wrecked."

The next bomb was closer. Walls quaked and people murmured with fear.

"Can Ariock destroy a planet?" someone whispered. Perhaps their loved ones were on Nuss.

Garrett's mouth thinned. They all knew how possible it was.

As Thomas imagined the passageway filling with telepathy gas and all these people braving their fears together—as he imagined Varktezo navigating volatile emotions as a fledgling telepath—he reconsidered the capabilities of his allies. Was he misjudging them?

The Torth certainly assumed that nontelepaths would bumble around like disabled children.

But disabled children could be surprising.

Thomas's allies were armed with blaster gloves. They possessed as much determination and will to survive as Thomas himself. This was their city, too. To write them off as disabled children, ignorant and incapable . . . wasn't that a mistake?

A mistake the Torth Empire kept making, over and over and over again?

"There is a way we might survive," Thomas said in the silence.

People regarded him, inquisitive or skeptical. Garrett looked at him with incredulity, but also with suppressed hope.

"I was wrong," Thomas admitted. "The obstacles you face in learning telepathy are not insurmountable. You're all capable."

The lab assistants and soldiers exchanged looks of surprise.

And hope. And goodwill.

Thomas did his best to mentally erase the supposed power differential between himself and his allies. He was not better than them. They were not his inferiors.

It was difficult. It was a paradigm shift, a reevaluation of core beliefs that would not occur to most Torth, not even to Torth supergeniuses.

But it was necessary.

"I can give everyone here a significant advantage," Thomas said. He manipulated light and vapor to project a holographic golden arrow. Motion was guaranteed to draw attention, so he made his arrow pulse with a liquid flow. It glowed against the darkness. "I can project hyperrealistic objects or scenarios."

Thomas had used fiery arrows to train Azhdarchidae. Vapor projections really weren't much different from fiery projections.

"Our enemies can't do this," he explained. "Not spur-of-the-moment. They won't be expecting me to guide you."

Ummins, govki, and nussians stared at the holographic arrow. The quick-witted ones gasped in understanding.

"The Torth will use telepathy gas whenever they think I'm around," Thomas said. "So they'll expect you to lose track of what's real and whose perceptions you're seeing. But—"

"You can give us beacons!" Varktezo brimmed with excitement.

"Exactly," Thomas said.

"But," someone said, "there are hundreds of us. How will you keep track of who is supposed to go where?"

"Trust me," Varktezo put in. "The Teacher can track all of us."

Thomas remembered the way Varktezo had fallen backward in shock and awe upon perceiving his mind. People already whispered rumors about him behind his back. How much worse would those rumors be, if hundreds of people gained an intimate and up-close view of his naked psyche?

"It's a good idea." Garrett admitted that begrudgingly. "But the Torth have excellent imaginations. They'll just copy the boy's arrows and make them point in the wrong direction. They'll fool everyone."

Soldiers groaned.

"I can counteract that." Thomas projected customized arrows in front of each technician or soldier. He changed them, morphing each one to a new shape or a different color. "I'll customize the icons and make them individual for each soldier."

Garrett's bushy eyebrows raised in admiration. It seemed he had not expected Thomas to be able to multitask like this.

"He can track of hundreds of us?" A lab technician sounded skeptical. "And give us each custom-tailored information?"

"Yup," Varktezo said with definitiveness.

Thomas avoided their stares. From now on, people would only see him as a freakish mental colossus. They would know that his brain was as far from normal as it was possible to be.

Or . . .

Not necessarily.

Telepathy gas could spread far, but within its penumbra, only the nearest neighbors caught intimate glimpses of each other's minds. Everyone else was just a vague impression in the murk. Thomas figured he would hang back. He would orchestrate the battle from its farthest fringes and project his neon guideposts visually. He would resort to mental tactics only if he had to.

Few people would see an up-close, naked view of who he really was.

"I still don't think this will work." Garrett sounded strained, like he was fighting an uphill battle. "The Torth are masters of telepathy. They'll band together and imagine super-vivid but false scenarios. They can trick any soldier or lab technician!"

Normally, yes. But . . .

"They can try." Thomas let his holographic icons fade. He replaced them with his own vividly imagined scenario, and he played it like a movie in midair.

A holographic ummin soldier ran with determination, armed with a heavy-duty blaster glove.

In his projected scenario, the ground split apart. The holographic ummin skidded to a halt before she could career over the apparent cliff.

"I promise," Thomas said, "I won't lead you astray."

A neon arrow appeared in his holographic scene. The holographic ummin stared at the arrow, which pulsed, urging her to cross the apparent chasm.

She tentatively placed one foot over the edge of the abyss. Instead of plunging, her boot landed on invisible, yet solid, ground. The figure gained confidence and proceeded to run across what seemed to be thin air. As she ran, the truth was revealed. Her boots touched plaza flagstones instead of nothingness.

Beaks clicked in worry.

"If you fail even one of us," someone commented, "you will lose a lot of public trust."

Thomas could scarcely afford to lose the public's goodwill. Even so . . .

"The trust I am asking of you matches what we're up against," Thomas said. "The Torth are masters of telepathy. You have to be prepared to see disturbing things. You'll encounter perceptions that aren't yours, and hallucinations that someone else wants you to see. That's on top of getting inundated with thoughts and ideas that don't belong to you."

He tried not to despair. Every one of the nontelepaths had a whole new obstacle course to run. For them, telepathy gas would be as deadly as a minefield and more difficult to traverse. And all because their minds were not adapted for navigating reality like a telepath.

The Torth were exploiting their lack of telepathy.

It was no different from a bunch of schoolyard bullies shoving disabled kids around because those kids could not physically fight back.

Thomas firmed up his resolve. "The only reason you'll have trouble," he said, "is because you're not used to it. That's all. The Torth are counting on that."

They listened. Varktezo, in particular, paid attention.

"One battle, or one day of telepathy gas, isn't enough for your mind to adapt to a flood of alien perceptions," Thomas said. That was an unavoidable truth. "But don't let that discourage you." He rapped his leg braces. "Five months ago, I couldn't have stood up or walked."

He gathered his courage. It seemed dangerous to reveal one of his secret hopes, but it might make his point. So he said, "I expect to walk unaided soon."

The soldiers exchanged looks.

Thomas tensed up. They probably thought his goal was pathetic. After all, most people could walk without any problems.

Instead of whispers of derision, they looked hopeful. Determined. A few soldiers actually gave Thomas glances of admiration.

Thomas sat up straighter in his hoverchair. "I'll give everyone signs that are personal. They'll be signs you recognize, like a meaningful object, or some item that means something to you or your loved ones."

He demonstrated.

The soldiers and technicians went silent. They contemplated their own uniquely personalized icons.

"And I'll point out any Torth in the area," Thomas added. "So you can kill them." He projected neon dots arcing toward a neon target. His holographic soldier aimed her blaster glove to shoot the target. A Red Rank materialized in that spot, already keeling over, dead. The blast had exploded his helmeted head.

"I can't predict how this day will turn out," Thomas said, "or what the Torth will do. But I do know their invasion force is limited. Very few of their champions will have enough raw strength to teleport away from this planet within the next few hours. They used up a lot of power getting here."

The soldiers understood the implications. They had a window of opportunity in which to rid their city of the invaders.

"Won't the Torth just send more Servants of All?" someone shouted.

"They don't have an infinite number of teleporters." Thomas raised his voice, clarifying the stakes. "Their commanding supergeniuses want to keep throwing all their resources at me, but if we kill enough Torth military ranks? That will stir up objections within the top ranks of the Torth Empire. The Servants and Rosies themselves will refuse to be used continuously as expendable weapons."

"He's right." Even Garrett stood straighter. "He's absolutely right. We need to make this a dangerous environment for the Torth."

The soldiers understood. Most of them had learned that the Torth Empire functioned by Majority vote.

"I see," a nussian soldier rumbled. "Our goal is to create doubts among the Torth. We do not even have to kill all the invaders. We just have to kill enough of them."

"Exactly," Thomas said.

His idea was catching on. He could see that they were afraid, but it was a ray of hope in an otherwise hopeless situation.

"The Torth Empire is trying to buy seven days for themselves," Thomas said. "That's how long it would take for a Torth armada to glide through slow space and reach our planet. They want to destroy Freedomland before Ariock can recover and come back to us."

Everyone grumbled with defiance.

"But we don't need Ariock," Thomas said. "We can destroy the Torth here. And we can destroy their incoming armada, if we have to."

His allies exchanged glances. These people all had families, spouses, or networks of close friends. They would take risks to protect their loved ones.

"We should imprison a few Torth, if we can," Varktezo suggested. "For later use." He gestured at Thomas. "As zombies."

That would work as a terror tactic. Thomas nodded in approval.

An official pushed his way up through the crowd. He was a self-important young ummin in an embroidered outfit, and Thomas recognized him as Gralet, the son of Councilor Deschuba.

"Let us say we defeat the invaders." Gralet tugged on his lapels, straightening his outfit. "What about the millions of penitents? Are they not a threat? What is to stop them from turning against us?"

It was an unfortunately good point. Perhaps Thomas had seeded his own destruction by showing mercy to former Torth, who might now regain their positions as masters of the galaxy. Had he been too idealistic?

He thought of the Pink Screwdriver. He didn't want to imagine her turning against his allies.

A govki bustled to the front of the crowd. "I am a lieutenant of Kessa the Wise." She faced Gralet and tapped her pendant watch. A holograph of Kessa glowed in the darkness. "I received this message from her."

Thomas and others watched in amazement as the recording played.

Kessa's image glowed in projected light. "I expected many penitents to join the invading Torth," her recorded voice said. "And it seems a few of them have."

Soldiers grumbled.

"But," Kessa's recording went on, "the vast majority of penitents are abstaining from combat. It is possible they wish to wait and see which way the battle goes."

Thomas let out a breath and realized that a tense part of him had expected to hear that the penitents were all a bunch of murderous traitors.

They were not allies.

But they were not enemies, either. That was something.

"I think it is notable that they are hesitant," Kessa's recording went on. "They are not rushing to rejoin their Torth brethren. Instead, they are remaining in their barracks and in the households of their sponsors." She paused. "I want you to leave them alone unless they pose a threat. Anyone who kills a nonthreatening, unarmed penitent will face banishment."

The recording ended. Kessa's image vanished, and the lieutenant dimmed her pendant.

"Is Kessa safe?" Thomas asked amid the growing buzz of discussion.

The lieutenant faced him. "Last I heard, she is hidden. She has protectors."

Thomas let out another breath. He wasn't sure how much bad news he could handle, but if Kessa got hurt or killed . . . the very idea was devastating.

He hardened his jaw. He didn't want to float into danger, but Kessa's safety was worth taking risks for. "We need to get the Torth out of our city."

Multiple people assessed him. Some thought he was not the most ideal military leader in the galaxy—but he was far from the worst.

Others considered him more impressive than the Bringer of Hope.

Varktezo raised his voice. "Remember to shield the Teacher!" he shouted. "The Torth want to kill him more than anything. Without him, we are blind."

And without these brave soldiers and technicians, Thomas was just a vulnerable target. He would be utterly reliant on these ummins, nussians, and govki, just as much as they would be relying on him. It was mutual. They would all be going into danger together.

But that was justice. Maybe it was a semblance of equality.

A grenade shook the walls. Thomas nodded to his people, showing that he was ready for danger.

Soldiers checked their blaster gloves. They prepared to survive phantom sensations while following personalized holographic arrows.

And they would kill Torth.

"I am ready." A nussian soldier snorted with determination. Other echoed the sentiment.

Thomas was glad that none of his people could read his mind right at this moment, because he was scared.

## CHAPTER 11
# INSIDE A MENTAL OCTOPUS

Pung took careful aim.

His academy classmates had called him paranoid for carrying a deadly weapon in his school satchel every day. He was taking a workshop for optics technology because he loved holograph recordings and he wanted to learn more about how they got made. Yet even though Pung attended classes on a leafy, sunny campus—even though he lived in a friendly neighborhood with housemates who treated him like a brother—he carried a blaster glove everywhere.

One did not survive as a smuggler in a Torth-ruled city without being ultraparanoid.

Or perhaps his paranoia came from his travels? Unlike most of the free population, Pung remembered when the Bringer of Hope had been far from invincible. He had seen Ariock crucified. He had seen Thomas blindfolded and kept in a dungeon pit. Sure, those two had become powerful enough to establish a happy little empire, but power could come and go.

Ummins used to be powerful, eons ago.

Mind readers used to be peasants, eons ago.

Those were lessons Pung remembered. And so he took nothing for granted.

When Torth invaded the campus? Pung had not joined the throngs of panicked students. Who knew whether the supposedly trustworthy penitents would simply stroll outside and join their brethren? Instead, Pung dived under a desk. He gambled that the invaders would not investigate every single empty classroom.

He had been right. Torth invaders passed him by, homing in on wherever they believed Thomas to be.

Pung listened to his newsfeed. He learned that the Bringer of Hope was "in trouble"—that was vague—and that Jinishta, Evenjos, Garrett, and even Weptolyso were unreachable. A miracle seemed unlikely. Zenzaldal, the premier who was in charge of defending Freedomland in their absence, was leading a siege on the academy. She told noncombatants to stay home or in bomb shelters and to bar their doors.

That was common sense. But it really wasn't enough information. Approximately how many Torth were in the city? More importantly: What made the Torth brave enough to risk confronting Thomas up close? That hadn't gone well for them last time. Anyone could guess that the Torth must have shown up with new weapons or tactics.

Pung wanted to know if Kessa was all right.

So after a while, he got tired of hiding, and he began to take chances.

He sneaked out of the classroom. He tiptoed down the corridor, his eyes and ears on high alert for anything out of the ordinary.

He did not rush out of the doorway, of course. He went to a window and peeked outside . . .

And he recoiled at the sight of body parts and blood everywhere. The grassy courtyard was a slaughterhouse.

Pung forced his throat to close up. Silence meant survival.

Torth strolled around, murdering people with leisurely aim. Several Torth in armor stood a distance away. They wore heavy-duty blaster gloves. Whenever a terrified person sneaked out of a doorway or a window, they blasted that person to pieces.

Pung didn't understand why people were stumbling out into daylight. Did they fail to see the Torth? Weren't all the corpses a rather obvious warning sign?

Pung skittered away, toward another exit.

But the next exit was just as bad as the first. Pung hesitated at the doorway, staring at slaughtered students. Maybe he ought to go back inside and cower under a desk?

He caught sight of a black-armored shani warrior.

There were two—no, three—warriors, their armor blending in with the shadows behind colonnades. The warriors held spears ready to throw. As they crept closer to the unsuspecting Torth, Pung silently cheered them on.

It was enough to inspire him to ready his own blaster glove. He was nowhere near close enough to take a shot, but perhaps he would station himself behind this door? If one of the armored Torth happened to bolt toward him . . .

. . . *(Hiding) it's an ummin (he has a glove)* . . .

Pung looked around, unnerved by the flurry of whispers that seemed to come from everywhere and nowhere.

Not just whispers. For a moment, Pung glimpsed a hallucinatory vision of himself. It was as if he was outside his own body, peering through that bush over there.

Someone was inside the bush. Pung saw another ummin peering through the leaves at him.

As he tried to reason out what was happening, another flurry of whispers surrounded him, stronger. Impossible to ignore. Insistent in an alien sort of way.

*There.*

*Just ummins.*

*(So many ummins in this place.)*

*(Idiots) Think they can hide?*

*Kill them.*

Whatever these whispers were, they were not friendly.

Pung whirled around, blaster glove ready. He only saw the harmless, bland stone wall.

His sense of imminent danger was tingling.

If this was a Torth-ruled city, he would have tried to blend in with a crowd, pretending that he was innocent and harmless. If this was the slave village of Duin, he would have faked panic. But where were the Torth?

His body thrummed with a feeling humans called adrenaline.

On impulse, he threw himself to one side and rolled down the stone ramp, onto flagstones.

A blast exploded where his body had been an instant ago. Rocks rained down.

Pung scrambled to his feet. He needed to flee . . . but he was shocked to discover that nothing looked right.

The buildings were gone.

Or were they just in the wrong places?

Pung ran, but was he running toward the next building? Or back the way he had come? Was he about to crash into that wall? Was he even on the flagstone path?

*I can't do this anymore (all is lost).*

That morose vibe seemed to come from one of the black-clad warriors. The warrior *(Haz)* stood behind a column. Although Haz was hidden from sight, Pung somehow knew he was there.

And that he had just heard awful news.

According to the supercom network, Orla and Jinishta were both dead. It was word of mouth, but it was likely true. Haz was devastated.

Pung knew all this even though Haz had not spoken a word or even looked at him. Concepts seemed to float, disembodied, in the air.

*Stupid slave.*

A Torth with a stiff crop of hair leaned against a wall, watching Pung with empty eyes. He casually aimed his blaster glove.

It was strange. Until now, Pung had never met a Servant of All with a personality. This one had the typical blank eyes and slack facial expression . . . yet somehow, Pung knew that he was facing *(the Morph Mopper)* a smugly superior attitude. The Morph Mopper believed that he *(Pung)* was a useless moron.

A dead useless moron.

Pung felt the aim of that weapon. He felt as if he was peering through the Morph Mopper's eyes, tracking himself as a hapless, doomed target.

He was going to die.

*. . . !!!*

*. . . BLAM!*

Pung jumped, certain that his spirit was detached from his body and that he was now dead. He must be. How else could he see so many points of view? He couldn't be inside a body anymore.

A pile of body parts lay where the Morph Mopper had been, beneath a bloody blast pattern on the wall. The Morph Mopper was dead. A friendly soldier—an ummin *(Eerkhet)*?—had shot the threat from behind.

"Run," Eerkhet advised.

Pung felt the advice in the depths of his soul. The word seemed to resound, as if he had known what Eerkhet would say even before he spoke. With that one word, Eerkhet conveyed that more Torth were rushing toward them.

Pung ran.

But running was no simple matter. He was seeing double. His feet were only partially connected to his body. They were also someone else's feet.

He managed a few hasty, stumbling steps.

Then reality seemed to fall apart completely.

Pung was running on nonsense, toward a blue sky. He could not even tell whether up was down.

A nussian soldier thundered past him. Pung felt the breeze from her passage.

*"Torth are trying to confuse you, ummin."* Her voice rumbled in her wake, seemingly imbued with extra meaning, as if the words resounded in his heart as well as his ears. *"Follow the arrows."*

Pung began to complain. There were no arrows. He had no idea what was . . .

A picture of Kessa floated in midair, attached to an arrow.

Pung stared.

What was holding that sign up? And why did the rippling arrow look as if it was cut from cloth—the exact same woven fabric that his mother used to wear?

The arrow rippled toward that crazy blue-sky area. It pointed, slightly off-kilter. Pung wondered if he would fall off the edge of the world if he dared to follow the appealing beacon.

A familiar voice spoke next to his left ear flap. *"Pung."* It was Thomas. *"I'm projecting an auditory hallucination for you. Can't keep it up. Directing too many people. Plus I am far away, relying on the telepathy gas zone to convey my words to you."*

Telepathy gas?

The arrow remained in front of Pung, beckoning like a friendly helper.

Pung took a step in that direction.

It seemed like he was walking upward into the sky, yet he felt grass under his toes. He was walking on what felt like solid ground.

Weird.

Pung sped up. As the ground remained solid beneath his feet, he gained confidence. He began to jog.

The sky illusion vanished, and suddenly, Pung was back in a semblance of the recognizable courtyard. His perceptions were still a sickening jumble. A confusion of whispers filled his mind. He hoped to hear Thomas again, but there were no clear voices. Only intrusive double vision. Another Kessa arrow pointed toward the right.

Pung followed it.

He became aware of other arrows floating in midair. Each arrow had a different theme, and people seemed to use them as guides. One govki vanished into a doorway that had been nonexistent a second ago. Other people dived behind flowering bushes or columns.

Every person who sprinted past Pung emitted their own nausea-inducing panoply of thoughts and emotions and perceptions. Pung could hardly keep track of his own limbs. He used to wish he could read minds, but if it was anything like this . . . well. How could Torth stand to be Torth?

He might have given up and fallen over if not for the friendly arrow rippling ahead.

There was a blast next to him. An armored Torth appeared out of thin air and fell over. That Torth had been invisible just moments before. Pung would have run straight past her, within grabbing distance, but now he was able to swerve around her body. Someone had shot her.

Wildfire flared.

Pung skidded to a halt and backpedaled. There was a *(die, albino minion of the Conqueror!)* Rosy Rank battling *(evil rekveh!)* a determined shani warrior, right in the middle of the corpse-strewn courtyard.

The albino gathered an electric ball of energy in her armored hand. It glowed like an orb light, reflecting on her black armor. The warriors had really honed their powers. She had fine control of the orb as she drew her hand back, ready to hurl the makeshift weapon.

The hulking Rosy Rank suddenly blinked out of sight.

There was no smell of ozone, yet Pung wondered if the Rosy had teleported away.

A cluster of ivory-white bone arrows appeared. The arrows twisted and clacked against each other, all pointing out an invisible moving target.

The armored warrior let out a primal scream of rage and hurled her orb toward the targeted outline.

It smashed into something solid.

The Rosy Rank materialized out of thin air, doubled over in pain and emitting *(!!!)* shock. The warrior drew three spears from her quiver and shot them all, bullet-fast.

That ended the Rosy Rank. He fell over, his armor pierced, blood leaking from his wounds.

*!!!*

*Kill*

*Kill*

*KILL!*

The ground trembled as three more Torth rushed toward the shani warrior. They wore metallic-red armor, yet Pung sensed their hidden powers as clearly as if they had advertised it. These were Rosy Ranks.

He needed to get out of harm's way.

His personalized Kessa arrow appeared, showing him where to go.

Pung ran in that direction, and never mind his questions about how the arrow maker *(Thomas!)* knew where he was or how to direct him. He would ask questions once he survived.

The flagstones beneath Pung's feet became treacherous holes. He nearly tripped on one.

Yet the Kessa arrow never wavered. Pung firmed up his beak and kept running. When he accidentally stepped on one of the holes to infinity, it felt normal and solid beneath his foot. That was proof enough. The holes were an evil illusion. The arrow was his friend.

A hedgerow appeared. Pung followed his personalized arrow and flung himself behind the shrubbery. It might not be a place of safety—was any place safe in a war zone where everyone could overhear each other's thoughts?—but he needed to catch his breath.

He peeked out at chaos and death.

Illusions crawled and blinked all over the courtyard. It was worse than a Torth city. Free people sniped at armored Torth and vice versa.

It should have been an easy victory for the Torth. They had every advantage, with their powers and their heavy-duty blaster gloves. They had come to this fight prepared. Some of the free people lacked armor. They had to dodge around the corpses of students and friends. Clearly, the Torth had been winning not long ago.

Yet now the battle seemed evenly matched.

Flow charts and moving hallucinations guided the free people, showing them where to hide, what to avoid, and where to shoot. An ummin blasted a Rosy Rank in the back even as Pung watched. The mind reader had apparently failed to anticipate the threat.

Wow.

"Oof!" The shani warrior landed near Pung with bone-jarring violence. Her fear and her rage were as unavoidable as colors and scents. Her pain was monstrous. This warrior *(Nulshta)* was badly injured. Pung sensed her broken ribs and her blinded eye as easily as he sensed his own health.

He wanted to tug Nulshta to safety. But there was nowhere to go. Three Torth stalked toward him and the injured warrior.

Pung tried to steady his gloved hand. He was a decent marksman. He had learned how to shoot from Thomas himself, on another world, in what seemed like a different era. But if a veteran Yeresunsa war hero couldn't defeat these Rosy Ranks, what chance did a slightly overweight ummin have?

Arrows appeared. They glowed and flowed in a sparkly way, with animated urgency. The arrows remained even though the three Rosy Ranks blurred into dark shadows and dissipated.

*Ugh. Another (ummin) slave.*

*Right. Well, don't underestimate it.*

The invisible Torth communicated in abstractions rather than words. How strange. Yet Pung understood their silent conceptual conversation.

*She (the Death Architect) should have armed Us with insanity gas as well as telepathy gas emitters.*

*Agreed.*

*Well, be fair. She did not expect the Conqueror to actually join a battle.*

*Well, She should have (since She's allegedly the smartest supergenius).*

*Do Her tactics seem (insufficient) cowardly to You (also)?*

*Kind of.*

*Yes.*

*Nothing We can do about it. We're just pawns to the Death Architect (the Conqueror) (supergeniuses).*

*Ugh. The Majority ceded way too much authority to Their ilk. Supergeniuses were never meant to conquer their own illnesses or invent weapons. We (champions) ought to kill the Death Architect once She takes Her final victory (destroys the Conqueror).*

*Agreed.*

*Yes. (In fact) I would argue that the Death Architect is actually worse than the Conqueror.*

*Oh, come on! (That's ridiculous.)*

*You exaggerate.*

*Clarification: I only meant in terms of personal honor. The Conqueror is definitely awful, but at least he is brave enough to stand with his minions (troops). Meanwhile, Our commanding mastermind (the Death Architect) hides on Her asteroid, shielded by battlebeasts and dreadnoughts and whatever else She wants. She—*

Pung sensed one of the Torth targeting him. He triggered his blaster glove.

An armored body thumped to the ground.

The artificial shadows lifted, and Pung thumbed his trigger again, targeting another Torth. He missed. Or rather, the Rosy Rank shielded herself with an icy blast of air.

*!!!* Surprised gratitude emanated from Nulshta. She had not expected an ummin to heroically defend her.

She threw her iron spears and the ice-master Rosy Rank fell. Pung had given Nulshta enough time to use her weapons.

Pung felt some chagrin as he sensed how Nulshta felt. Disposable. Vulnerable. She was hurt and scared.

That wasn't right. Everybody knew that warriors were the primary guardians of freedom. They were here, striving to protect the campus and everyone trapped inside. They were here even though Ariock was not. They were here even though many of their best *(Jinishta) (Orla) (Dishra) (so many healers)* had died today. They were ready to defend Thomas and Kessa.

Yet no one befriended warriors. They kept to their own neighborhoods and enclaves.

Perhaps they deserved more than the disdainful distance that Pung and other free people showed them?

"Come on." Pung tugged Nulshta's hand, helping her to stand. "Let's make sure you're safe."

She leaned on his shoulder, her emotions tinged with gratitude.

The third Rosy Rank turned to flee.

Together, Pung and Nulshta took aim. Pung triggered his glove and the Torth's head exploded.

# CHAPTER 12

# THE UNDERCARRIAGE
# OF A FIERY BEAST

Vy knew she ought to hide in the nearest bomb shelter. Each neighborhood shelter was mirror-paneled so not even Ariock could find them easily, although he had built them. Their trapdoors were camouflaged. They were reinforced with the same near-indestructible ionic tungsten used for spaceship hulls. It would take more than a few grenades to wrench them open. And inside? The shelters were loaded with rations, survival gear, and weapons.

So Vy knew she ought to join the hidden throngs. Ariock would want her to use common sense and stay out of danger.

But Ariock was missing in action.

There were rumors on news channels, but Vy refused to believe the speculations that he was defeated or captured. Ariock was the Strength. There was no way a mere army could knock him out. That didn't make any kind of sense.

Thomas would likely know the truth.

Vy just wasn't sure whether Thomas was safe. No one seemed particularly concerned about him. All the concern was for Ariock, and Kessa, and Jinishta, and Weptolyso, and various war heroes. Those were the people everyone talked about. But *rekvehs*? No one cared.

How ironic that Cherise never even asked about Thomas. Vy wished her well, and then ended the call.

She hurriedly grabbed a hooded overcoat and a scarf that could double as a warrior's veil. She would never pass as an Alashani up close, not with her undignified height. She just didn't want to be immediately obvious.

She rode a hoverbike past intense-looking soldiers. If anyone recognized her, they did not shout out. But she had to stop at Recruitment Plaza, where soldiers formed a blockade at the academy archway entrance.

Vy jumped off her bike. "Where can I find Thomas?" she asked the nearest soldier.

The soldier, a tan-furred govki, stared at her.

"The Teacher?" Vy hoped that would clarify whom she meant.

"Lady of Paradise." A warrior addressed Vy with reverence. "Please go to the nearest shelter. This is a battle zone."

"Is Thomas okay?" Vy wanted to believe that he was busy defending the academy. That might be why he wasn't answering calls.

The warrior seemed to be inwardly debating what to tell her.

Vy tried to banish imagined scenarios where Thomas was cornered or, worse, captured by Torth. "Where is he?"

"This is a dangerous place." The warrior sounded stressed-out. "We cannot protect you. Please, go somewhere safe?"

Vy leaped onto her hoverbike and zigzagged past startled soldiers. No one dared to threaten her. They shouted warnings, and a few cursed at her. They went running toward their own parked hoverbikes. Maybe they would follow Vy onto academy grounds?

She sped past decorative shrubs. The plaza she traversed was empty, but as she approached the main classroom buildings, she heard distant sounds of violence.

Wet blasts.

Cries of pain.

Vy parked her borrowed vehicle in the shade of a class building. She was not entirely useless in combat, having practiced with Thomas's recent gift. She pressed two fingers to a specific spot on her leg prosthetic. The spring-loaded compartment door popped open.

For now, Vy ignored her collection of hand grenades and inhibitor gas emitters. She donned her custom-tailored blaster glove.

Armed, she sneaked around the granite flank of the building. She intended to peek in on the battle, just to ascertain that Thomas was elsewhere. Then she would sneak toward the research annex.

She paused when she heard footsteps behind her. There were a lot of swift-moving feet, all running toward her.

Vy turned, expecting to see friendly soldiers.

Instead, she saw a mob of scabby, filthy Torth.

They could have been mistaken for zombies. The only difference was the burning sapience in their gazes. That, and many had eerie red irises, denoting their former status as Red Ranks. They resembled demons from a nightmare.

And they were coordinated, the way telepaths could get.

Penitents.

Vy's skirt had a slit that went up to her hip. All her clothes were tailored for combat. She threw off her hooded robe and exposed her upgraded leg prosthetic.

She could have released inhibitor gas, but these rebel penitents would have attacked her already if they'd had any powers. Instead, they wielded rocks and other items they must have raided on their way through the city. Pitchforks. Scrap metal. Makeshift clubs.

Vy tapped her prosthetic to ready the blaster charges. She finalized the auto-fire activation sequence by drawing her knee up, balancing on her natural leg.

The first wave of overeager ghouls tried to mob her.

Vy sprayed blasts with her gloved hand and her prosthetic knee, and penitents went down in bloody lumps. Not fast enough. There seemed to be about a hundred enemy mind readers hurling themselves at Vy, their alien eyes narrowed with collective determination.

Well, they had to prove their valor to the Majority, didn't they? Having broken Kessa's edicts, they could not expect mercy from Kessa's side of the war. Nor could they expect mercy from the Majority if they failed here and now. They had to win. Otherwise they were dead.

No wonder they attacked as frantically as cornered animals.

Vy couldn't spare any sympathy for the plight they had made for themselves. She had more important concerns, such as surviving long enough to find out what had happened to Thomas and Ariock. She could not balance on one leg forever.

*(!!!)*

*Take her.*

*Pretty girl is vulnerable.*

Vy had a crazy sensation, like she was overhearing silent comradeship and seeing herself from various *(superior)* points of view. Penitents clawed their way past others, trying to take *(one-legged girlfriend)* her as a hostage *(for the glory of the Torth Majority)*.

Vy yanked two hand grenades out of her leg compartment. She triggered the grenades, and as their countdown strips morphed from blue to green toward yellow, she hurled them at her attackers.

*!!! * !!! * !!! * !!! * !!!*

Vy felt as if she was torn apart herself. As the explosions went off in the mob, she reeled backward, enveloped by *(!!!)* phantom agony. Maybe fear was causing her to hallucinate? Were friendly soldiers rushing to rescue her?

*That's Vy!*

*Going to save her.*

Friendly voices resounded inside Vy as though she was imagining conversations. They were vibes rather than sounds.

One of the friendly soldiers, a govki, wore blaster weapons on all six of its limbs. Traitorous penitents exploded with every ripple of the govki's body.

*Get her.*

Vy sensed Torth coming up from behind. They held shovels and clubs, but she sensed that they *(the Majority)* wanted to take her alive *(for later use) (to motivate the Giant)*. These penitents yearned to *(get her) (get her!)* please their telepathic overlords.

Vy whirled away from grasping hands. She reactivated her prosthetic, having given it enough time to recharge.

*Uh-oh*, a penitent thought.

Vy aimed her prosthetic knee and blasted his lower body. Viscera sprayed outward.

** ! **

Vy whirled this way and that, destroying sneaky penitents. Chests ruptured and body parts went flying. The heaps of corpses grew.

But there were so many.

Every rebel penitent in the city seemed to run at Vy. She was a helpless target facing an endless attack. Her prosthetic's blaster gun needed time to recharge again. Perhaps this was why she was overhearing thoughts and seeing emotional auras? She was a dead woman.

*She (Vy) needs to survive for the final prophecy*, a gruff voice said without sound or words. He sounded armored yet eroded, like a barren rock scorched by a lifetime of seasons full of wind and rain and ice.

Vy was unsurprised to see Garrett riding a hoverbike toward her. He ruthlessly shot unarmed penitents in the back with his blaster glove, leaning heavily on the handlebars with his other arm.

Yet Vy was seeing Garrett in a way that she had never seen him before.

Veins of black fury radiated off him. Gleaming sparks showed valor. And his age! She could actually see a mantle of knowledge and practical experience swirling around him like a cape, as multilayered and complex as a tree's growth rings. Garrett was thoroughly armored with scaly bark that implied years of experience. Compared with these penitents, he was a tank.

But then a foreign force slammed into Garrett.

*!!*

Vy absorbed Garrett's shocked pain as if it was her own. The feeling crippled her.

He went flying off the bike, survived a brutal collision with a stone wall, and crumpled to the pavement. Vy felt his unspoken vulnerability. He felt . . .

Scared?

Depleted?

Mystified? He seemed to believe his death was not preordained for today. He expected to be beheaded on a future occasion.

Three blank-eyed Torth approached Garrett *(the Imposter)*, baring their teeth in a parody of human grins. Although they wore the armor of Red Ranks, waves of power blurred their outlines into massive hulks. These *(Rosy Ranks)* Torth were titans. They were like Ariock.

Well, no, they were not as colossal as Ariock. But in this battle zone? They had no peers. They were going to crush Vy and Garrett with ease.

"Run, Vy!" Garrett yelled. His voice was only a crust on top of urgency aimed at Vy. He struggled to regain his feet, radiating desperation. In normal times, he would have outclassed any of these Torth, but a short respite *(hiding with Thomas)* wasn't enough time for him to recover from depletion.

"I m m m p o s s s s t e r r," the Rosies whispered. Their voices were echoed by rebel penitents creeping out of bushes and shadows.

"Y o u r r r e n d d d i s n i i i i g h."

Vy felt an undertone to their whispers, a certainty of victory. The Imposter should have stayed hidden. Out here, he was dead meat.

*Get them!*

The mob surged.

*!!!!!!!!!!!!!!!!!!!!!!!!!!!!!!!!!!!!!!!! *** * * . . .*

Enormous bony jaws stabbed down from the sky and crushed penitents between needle-thin teeth.

Vy gaped. She kept seeing and hearing and even smelling and feeling things that weren't there. Was this scaly black sky croc part of some hellishly complex hallucination?

But it could only be Azhdarchidae. He wore a harness with a lot of straps.

Azhdarchidae flapped his gigantic wings, steadying himself over the flat plaza. All the razor wires overhead had long since been removed. There were no gigantic predators gliding through the urban skies these days, other than Thomas's pet.

Azhdarchidae sized up the mob with his orange eyes.

Then he went into shred mode.

*! ***

   *! ***

> *! &ast;*
>
>    *! &ast;*
>
>       *!! &ast;*
>
>          *! &ast;*

Azhdarchidae chomped on penitents, ignoring the rocks and metal scraps their comrades threw at his scaly hide. His jaws, as long as a semitruck, scissored open and shut, and his many, many teeth caught flesh and cloth.

The penitents scattered.

Vy's grenades had hardly fazed the mind readers, but this beast was a different matter. Maybe they didn't like his predatory thoughts? Or maybe it was the fact that his carnage made the piles of corpses around Vy look like nothing?

*!!!*

Garrett stared at a neon arrow that hung in front of him. It pointed straight upward.

The three Rosies backed off, apparently intimidated by the deadly beast. Vy sensed their self-preservation instincts. They wanted to conserve their powers *(for escape) (for a return to civilization)*.

Azhdarchidae landed, yet he still blotted out a lot of sky. He towered. And that neon arrow? It seemed to point at the straps that encircled the animal's silver underbelly.

"Wonderful." Garrett sounded sarcastic. "That boy and his brilliant ideas." He hobbled toward the sky croc. "Agh, come on, Vy. Here's our ride."

Vy understood, without needing to ask, who had projected the holographic arrow *(Thomas)* and what it implied *(safety) (escape)*. It was just, well, incredibly hard to believe.

She jogged toward the straps that dangled from Azhdarchidae's underbelly. She wanted to know where Ariock was, and she would never get answers if she got killed.

Fireballs roared across the courtyard at her.

Vy threw up her arms as a reflex, but her human limbs could not stop fire. She was about to die—

Azhdarchidae lunged between Vy and the fireballs. The sky croc bellowed in pain that Vy felt as much as heard.

Garrett staggered. Vy sensed his weakness. He didn't even have his staff to steady himself.

"I've got you." Vy hefted Garrett into the harness. Her ultrastrong leg prosthetic gave her enough leverage to lift him. She held that position long enough for the old man to fumble straps and buckles into working order.

"Ariock is alive," Garrett mumbled as he secured himself in the harness. His thoughts overlapped his spoken words. *But he's going to have psychological damage.*

Vy gasped as Garrett replayed a tornado. She caught vague impressions of Ariock.

It was enough.

It was staggering.

"Climb into the harness," Garrett urged her. "Hurry! Ariock will need you."

Vy was pretty sure she must be insane to trust her life to a sky croc. Then again, if Thomas was directing his pet to make pickups . . . and if telepathy gas was an actual thing . . . and if Ariock had accidentally killed one hundred of his own war-riors . . . who was she to judge what was normal and what was insane?

The harness had just enough room for two passengers. Vy hoisted herself next to Garrett and strapped herself in. She wasn't the bravest of pilots, but—

Azhdarchidae launched himself into the smoky air.

Vy screamed. Garrett screamed. The sky croc banked to one side, and Vy kept a death grip on the harness, feet dangling. She cinched straps until she felt somewhat secure.

Torth glared at them from the ground, eyes burning with frustration. Two of the three Rosies hurled fireballs, but they were too distant to be effective. Their fire-balls died as harmless embers in the wind.

The third Rosy vanished.

Vy assumed that one had teleported to a swarmshuttle in orbit, or farther away.

Until Azhdarchidae roared and banked violently, trying to shake off an unwel-come and sudden burden. The armored Torth fell off the sky croc's wing.

Vy could not overhear thoughts anymore, but she could guess why this Rosy had risked depletion. So many Torth were shortsighted glory hounds. No doubt the plummeting Rosy believed she would be immortalized in the Megacosm for accomplishing what no one else could: assassinating the Imposter. She would serve the Majority or die trying.

Sure enough, the falling Rosy tracked Garrett with her blaster glove. She thumbed the trigger.

With a flap of his wings, Azhdarchidae veered away. He angled toward the fiery flare of Thomas's training signal.

The Rosy screamed with frustrated rage as she plummeted toward a patio gar-den roof. Her blast missed Garrett by inches.

Azhdarchidae lifted Vy and Garrett even higher, skimming the undersides of low-hanging clouds as he circled toward the safety of the Dragon Tower.

# CHAPTER 13
# UNRECEPTIVE

Every time Evenjos thought she'd escaped the enemy missiles, another bomb dropped out of the clouds or rocketed up from the faraway ground. The Torth forbade any sort of artificial intelligence technology or drones, but perhaps a supergenius had swayed the Majority into changing the law to allow for guided missiles?

At least the Torth here seemed short on nuclear weapons. Nuss was a hub planet, not a militarized outpost, and the empire had failed to stockpile enough weapons locally to seriously harm or destroy the world.

Evenjos jerked higher and lower, all the while aware that her burden—Ariock— needed to remain within habitable zones. She would not drag him underwater. She would not take him into the stratosphere or higher, where he'd be unable to breathe.

She tried to lose the guided missiles by careening through mountain passes, canyons, and forests.

And then the missiles stopped coming.

Not for long. But Evenjos took advantage of a short respite to fly closer to one of the polar ice caps, seeking glacial crevices. Whichever supergenius was in charge of this attack must be distracted by something.

Thomas, perhaps?

Evenjos's earpiece crackled continuously with distant voices. They spoke of illusions and insanity.

". . . another weaponized gas?"

". . . makes everything seem unreal. The ground can vanish beneath your feet."

"That's how it looks."

Evenjos used her powers to melt an ice burrow inside a glacial ravine until it cascaded in a waterfall. Once Ariock was safely inside the burrow, she joined him and iced the entrance shut. Soon she and Ariock were sealed inside a bubble of thick, solid ice.

She blanketed him with her wings, transforming her metal feathers into something like a warm pelt. But the alteration required focus she could not spare during a healing procedure. So she sought scraps of lichen and other fuel and used her powers to bring them inside the cave. She carved bowls from rocks and sparked flames inside them.

Soon her makeshift lamps gave the ice cavern a cozy glow. The walls began to sweat. Her gathered bits of fire fuel would eventually burn out, but she would worry about that later.

Evenjos traced the strong line of Ariock's jaw with a nearly insubstantial finger.

It seemed risky to be cooped up alone with him, surrounded by smoldering lamplight and the purity of snow. He would jump to the wrong conclusion if he woke up.

Oddly enough, Evenjos found that her sexual desire for the giant had waned by quite a lot. She required unapologetic bluntness. Ariock was not that person. He might be an avatar of war, yet his baseline nature was ridiculously constrained and reserved and gentle. He had never learned how to let loose safely.

Also, he was a magnet for trouble. And nuclear warheads.

Ariock was going to be an emotional disaster once he recovered. He would be infuriated at himself, or worse—what if chemically induced brain damage left him with a propensity for extra mood swings?

What fun.

Evenjos had enough problems without absorbing someone else's extremes. She would be okay with letting other people—like that one-legged nurse—deal with his relentless self-loathing.

Ariock's life spark guttered. His veins were turning black against his ashen skin as the Torth poison began to overwhelm his drugged body.

"You will get better." Evenjos said it out loud, making it a promise.

She delved into his sleeping brain with her diagnostic sense. She crept past astrocytes and investigated neuronal ensembles with the greatest care. She traced axons through cellular nuclei to the branching ends of their dendrites. She studied ionic voltage levels and transduction proteins.

There.

Nothing natural would bind so tightly to postsynaptic glutamate receptors yet slip unnoticed past the reuptake transmitters that should clear them from synapses. This must be the cause of his out-of-control rage.

The neurotoxin had spread throughout his entire brain.

Evenjos solidified, tapping her chin in thought. Brains were so delicate. So difficult to work on.

She yearned for the teachers and colleagues she had lost. This would be a tricky operation. She might pull it off on her own, but she would have felt much more capable with at least one expert neurosurgeon by her side.

Might Thomas offer his expertise across light-years of distance? Could he be useful without reading her mind?

". . . hiding in the hills outside the . . ."

". . . only a few penitents turned. Most of them are . . ."

"If Kessa is still in charge . . ."

". . . lost contact with Freedomland again."

Thomas must have his own emergencies to deal with. This was too much to ask.

Evenjos set her earpiece aside on icy ground. She tried to give herself a pep talk. She could do this alone. Surely she could?

She had to act now, as the neurotoxin was busily wrecking its way through Ariock. Cleansing it molecule by molecule would not be efficacious. It would cause irreversible brain damage—and likely death—before Evenjos could complete that arduous process. She had to take a risk and expedite the brain cleanse without damaging her patient.

Making precipitous decisions all by herself was nothing new. She used to be a goddess-empress.

But she'd become infamous for her terrible decisions.

Garrett and Thomas and Ariock had shown her other ways to rule, though. Ariock, in particular, had sacrificed his own strength and blood in order to resurrect a mysterious winged prisoner. No one else would be so recklessly kindhearted.

Ariock had bypassed all the obstacles that prevented uncounted heroes from rescuing her in the past. He had shown up for her and caught her in his arms after smashing the mirrors so she could finally reenter the realm of the living.

She owed Ariock every bit as much as she owed Thomas.

Evenjos sent her awareness tiptoeing through Ariock's neurons. She must take risks to give him back what he had lost. She experimented with warping a reuptake transmitter, trying to make it drain the neurotoxin into intracellular spaces.

No good. That could cure his rage, but it wouldn't save his mind.

Well, might a lysosomal deaminase eliminate her warped transmitter after it had done its job?

That might work.

Evenjos synthesized a string of mRNA code and replicated it. Ariock was running out of time. His mind was shutting down, closing off avenues that led back to consciousness. Evenjos began to lace the replicated mRNA through every instance of her modified neurotransmitter.

As long as she was messing with Ariock's functionality, she figured she would keep him unconscious. The best thing to do, she thought, was to make sure he slept until someone with the capacity to deal with huge, Ariock-size problems—Vy, she supposed—was available.

He would need a lot of counseling once he woke up and realized what he had done.

# CHAPTER 14

# FREEDOM

Weptolyso wasn't sure why he was still alive.

He had been on his way to Tempest Arena, leading a flotilla of hovercarts laden with crucifixion victims, when the apocalypse began. Everyone heard Jinishta beg the messiah to stop. Even over the radio, her voice had resounded with power. She'd been desperate to make herself heard.

Everyone heard the warriors scream curses of rage.

And, in groups, they had gone silent.

Weptolyso had intended to ready the beleaguered city for victims in need of aid. If he had carried out that duty, he would have been vaporized. But when the warriors ceased responding and the very earth rolled like water, he had recalled Thomas's warnings.

*"Evacuate Tempest Arena,"* Weptolyso had commanded.

The inhabitants of Tempest Arena refused to leave. They had faith in the Bringer of Hope. Demigods, they said, should be trusted to know what they were doing. The Son of Storms never made mistakes.

*"The Son of Storms can make mistakes."* Weptolyso had contradicted local leaders. *"I have seen it. Anyhow, he may be fighting a new enemy or weapon. Why is he reacting in this way? The Torth here on Nuss were supposedly too weak to attack him."*

Weptolyso had prepared to be humiliated for wrongly criticizing the Son of Storms. The risk was worth it. If he was right—if Thomas was right—then he might survive and be able to help others. So he had commandeered a cargo transport and fled toward the wetlands. Only a few people joined his flight away from the desert hurricane.

Those were the ones who remained alive.

Together, they skated away from the initial destruction by the width of a shoulder spike. Tempest Arena was now a glassy, smoldering ruin.

Next, Weptolyso should have died when violent earthquakes tore apart the base levels of CloudShadow MetroHub. Who knew how many penitent Torth had died in those upheavals? Millions, Weptolyso felt sure. The slave tunnels had been crammed full of penitents who were forced to serve as slaves.

Weptolyso had docked at a bay that was soon wrecked. There were survivors in the upper city, and he'd managed to join them.

The whole planet seemed to be in danger of being torn apart. Anyone who had survived the annihilation of the Torth Homeworld recognized the insane winds and unceasing earthquakes of an apocalypse.

But the storm had subsided.

Weptolyso had no idea if it would resume, or if it was over for good. He wasn't sure if it mattered anymore.

Because now the Torth were attacking in force.

Torth shuttles descended through the roiling skies as soon as the earthquakes ceased. Their multipronged invasion was swift, smart, and overwhelmingly coordinated. They bombed the major pedestrian causeways that fed into the spaceports of every freehold city. That gave Torth shuttles enough opportunity to land without much interference.

Other shuttles airdropped weapons, such as fissile materials, gaseous inhibitor emitters, and ionic-bladed knives, into penitent barracks. The weapons gave a critical number of penitents the means to free themselves.

Now there were rebel penitents running through various cities, restored to status as Torth citizens, armed and full of spite. Some had gone on murder sprees. Others committed acts of sabotage. Some engaged military leaders in battle, while others used those battles as distractions so they could tear down communications relays or blow up knowledge depots.

Weptolyso had tried, repeatedly, to contact Jinishta and other Yeresunsa on Nuss.

They weren't responding. The calls were not connecting.

Weptolyso had a dark suspicion that there would be a lot of funeral processions in the upcoming days. Or worse. Would there even be any Alashani left to mourn the dead war heroes?

But Weptolyso had his own people to mourn. He heard, through radio newscasts, that the free cities on Nuss were not the only cities under attack. The planet Umdalkdul had been invaded. Nussian captains—friends whom Weptolyso had spoken with only this morning—were dead.

Even the populated moons, Morja and Jerja, were under threat.

And Freedomland itself?

That so-called reject planet was not easily reachable through space travel, so the reports of invasion there were hard to believe. But Weptolyso knew the Torth Empire had one very high-value target: Thomas. They would go to any lengths to destroy their Conqueror. If they had sent hundreds of teleporting high ranks into the Freedomland Academy? That would not surprise him.

So he had no idea whether Thomas was safe.

Or Yuey.

Before the supercom network died, his life mate had assured him from afar that she was hiding in a bomb shelter. Yuey had been raised as a shani nussian, but she was no fool. She would avoid any deadly battles where she could not win. Even so . . .

Reports from Freedomland had been hectic and filled with impossible claims. A sky croc was supposedly devouring marauding penitents. The newscasters also claimed that up was down, and right was left, and anyone who faced one of the Servants of All or Rosies in battle was sure to lose their hold on reality. One reporter kept babbling about weird, magical arrowlike symbols that glowed in the sky and guided people to safety.

Weptolyso tried hard not to think about what dangers Yuey might be facing. His questions and worries would have to wait until the superluminal relays were restored. He was not on Reject-20.

He was in an underground bunker beneath the Lava City industrial complex.

"Weptolyso," one of the senior captains nearby said. "We suspect the Torth Empire is tapped into our communications network, listening in."

It made for an ironic mental image: Torth, who hated vocal speech, forcing themselves to listen to former slaves chatting away. But Weptolyso supposed they would if they wanted to win. There was a lot of information zooming back and forth. Survivor groups kept trying to locate each other, or help each other with weapons and fortifications.

"We need to stop communicating through the radios and coms," Weptolyso said.

The captain looked shocked. His spikes drooped. "Can't we just develop code words?" he suggested. "I'm sure the Torth will be too lazy to figure out our verbal system of code phrases if we put some effort into it."

Weptolyso flared his nostrils in a regretful way. "We can try that. But I believe the local networks will stop functioning soon anyway. We need to prepare to lose that advantage."

For uncounted generations, slaves had communicated in person, while Torth relied on a long-distance network of knowledge. Now that liberated slaves had begun to get used to a long-distance network? They liked it. Of course they did not want to give it up.

It seemed the liberated refugees would need to rely on old ways again. Non-Torth ways.

"I agree that we must hold together," Weptolyso said. "We will need smugglers and runners, people who are willing to take risks."

"But . . ." The captain stared at Weptolyso as if he had lost his grip on reality. "If the Torth destroy our local network, can we not repair it?"

"Even the local radios rely on relay stations," Weptolyso said. "We don't have access to the spaceports anymore, or to a lot of our territory." He could imagine Torth aiming missiles at each satellite. They would wreck the network soon.

"Well, can the Son of Storms not repair our satellites?" the captain asked.

Apparently, this captain needed to check his own grip on reality. Was he one of the fools who believed that victory was preordained?

Weptolyso met his stare with a level look. "I fear we may be on our own for a while."

The captain looked horrified.

Several other captains listened in, and they exchanged doubtful glances. Former slaves ought to accept bad news as normal, but these captains were clearly unwilling to believe such a dire proclamation.

Perhaps their lives had turned into too much of a fantasy tale?

Every slave grew up hearing legends about heroic runaways. Weptolyso collected such tales. He knew all about Mirk the Bold and Lanselmyuthrul of the Mountain Tribe. But to him, only one heroic tale was more than mere mythology. Weptolyso knew Kessa the Wise personally. He had traveled with her.

And he had learned that legends made everything sound simple and easy when, in fact, nothing worth doing was that way. Too few stories clarified that truth.

"Let me tell you about the time I carried the Son of Storms over my shoulder," Weptolyso said, "when he was gravely injured and we were in a toxic wasteland full of sludge serpents and telepathic cannibals."

The other captains gathered around. They seemed stunned and amazed that even a hero as mighty as Ariock Dovanack could have weak moments.

"I knocked a Servant of All off a tower top. Like this." As Weptolyso demonstrated how he had fought to protect himself and his friends, the captains seemed to recognize an inner nobility within themselves. They straightened.

Slaves did not have to be helpless victims.

If anyone knew the value of freedom, it was them. And anyone could make a difference. A child. An arthritic, elderly ummin. A hall guard who had taken a stupid risk instead of carrying out his duty.

Anyone.

The captains sat in silence after Weptolyso concluded his tale. They processed it like sentinels learning the approaches to their fortress.

"We may be on our own," one captain rumbled. "But we remain free."

# HONORING KNOWLEDGE

Sabotaged vehicles smoldered, their smoke columns tinged red from the coastal sunset.

Kessa stood on a veranda and surveyed a panoramic view of urban sprawl. Evenings usually entailed a lot of traffic in Freedomland. Shopkeepers liked to offer last-minute bargains, and people sought entertainment after work. But right now?

A few furtive pedestrians hurried through otherwise empty streets. They must be checking on loved ones or treasured belongings.

The immediate threat was over. The invaders were slaughtered.

Yet Kessa guessed many residents still hunkered in bomb shelters. People were miserable with uncertainty. Torth had bombed the delicate satellites around Nuss and Umdalkdul, ending all friendly communication from those planets.

According to Garrett, the Torth Empire had not managed to retake any cities. But wasn't that just a matter of time?

The Bringer of Hope was missing.

No one, not even Thomas, knew where Ariock or Evenjos were.

Kessa's pink-cheeked assistant, an albino shani named Yanyashta, emerged from the doorway. "Um . . ." Yanyashta always hesitated before saying anything remotely controversial. "Um, Kessa, is it not dangerous to stand out in the open like this?"

She looked ready to guide Kessa back inside the cavernous war palace.

"Perhaps." Kessa admired the banded planet that shone through parted clouds above. She could imagine Torth ghosting through the air in front of her, invisible, intangible, and targeting her with silent malevolence. The ghosters could then send teleporters directly to Kessa. They could have her murdered within seconds.

If the Majority of Torth considered an elderly ummin to be an important enough target.

If the Majority collectively decided to send yet another wave of invaders.

"Ariock can ghost for up to seven minutes at a time," Kessa said. "He can do it again and again. But most Servants and Rosies can only manage once. If they try it again, they are in a depletion coma."

Yanyashta looked slightly mollified. As an Alashani, she had grown up with concrete knowledge about the abilities and limitations of Yeresunsa, but her albino variety could not ghost or teleport. Their species had completely lost that power during one of their population bottlenecks, probably during the Age of Starvation.

"So . . ." Yanyashta moved closer, her tone full of suppressed hope. "You think the Torth are taking a break?"

Kessa recalled a holographic recording that Thomas had sent her an hour ago.

He clearly didn't trust the bad times to be over. He had taken up residence in a secret bomb shelter, and he'd urged her to do the same.

"*Stay hidden,*" he'd said. "*Take care of yourself.*"

But that wasn't a conversation. Thomas had not invited Kessa to report her own opinions and observations.

She had not shared with him, for instance, the fact that dozens of penitents had forewarned her about the invasion.

It was hard to believe. Kessa would not have believed it herself, but all her lieutenants had clamored to talk to her. Thanks to their warnings, most of the city population had gone underground minutes before hordes of penitents wreaked havoc.

Kessa pulled a tiny, colorful marble out of her pocket.

"*I used to oversee the manufacturing of blaster gloves,*" one sad-looking male penitent had told Kessa during one of her routine inspections. "*This data marble contains primitive engineering tips. I downloaded the data before your people collared me, figuring I might gain access to materials to create a makeshift bomb. Maybe I could make the Torth Majority proud.*"

The penitent had offered the marble to Kessa.

"*I no longer trust the Torth Majority to fight for justice,*" he had said. "*I'm not one of them anymore. I have no status or name. But I recognize you as the mother I never had.*"

Kessa folded her hand over the marble.

She had never had the opportunity to incubate eggs or to raise hatchlings. City slaves were not permitted such wondrous things as families. To be considered a mother . . . to have someone see her that way . . . it touched a yearning part of her soul. It reminded her of youth.

Kessa carried the marble in acknowledgment of her quasi motherhood.

She wondered how many reformed penitents wished for parents. And how many liberated city slaves wished for children?

There was a possible bridge across the chasm that separated nontelepaths from telepaths.

"The Torth penitents are wayward children, lost and alone," Kessa told her assistant. "Slaves are now finding their way out of eons of confusion and loneliness. I think both former slaves and penitents are maturing in ways the Torth Empire cannot comprehend."

Kessa still yearned to know everything, to see everything that mind readers could see.

The data marble fit inside her small hand. Her impossible dream was likewise within her grasp. She would make use of telepathy gas. She would learn to be a mind reader.

"I am not afraid," Kessa said.

# ACKNOWLEDGMENTS

Thank you so much for taking the time to read *Greater Than All* and prior books in the Torth series. The next book is the finale.

If you enjoyed this, please let the Majority know, or at least some random readers you might encounter in the wild. I'm one of the smaller fish in the sea, and I would be much obliged if you can take the time on Amazon, Goodreads, or Audible to post a rating or a review.

Special thanks to my subscribers and former subscribers on Patreon: Nyroe, Wrath, Godlyskeleton, ryan ukeiley, volpol, NoteOfE, G O L I X T H, KarenSampson, John O'Connor, Adil Riggs, Bunny Waffles, Zak Pr, Josh Cothran, Aqua, Pokey Equation, Xavier Lamphere, Ceagle, The Dargon, JC, Tyler Smith, Sparkie, A. Brown, Pietro Simone, JJBlack, Certa, Jason Gross, Isaac Boyles, faisal, Mitchell, Gres, Grosbilljunior, Orion Mitchell, LiraGuitar-, luke, MrNobody, John Hurley, Chikkane, Jonathan Williams, mythic, TurtleOfRainbow, Andrew Webb, Dave The Technician, Gavin Olsen, Scott Southworth, E, Alexandre Ablon, Conor lennon, Adam Moore, bensorme, Naorke, Sherriff kadir, Corella, Dvn, George Waller, Jack, Jackson Ragland, Derrick McDowell, Philldoran, Alric Good, Joel Wells, Jerry, Notlimah, Timecrafter, Ithri Benamara, F M, Frightful6_7, Jason Denzel, Теодор Жечев, Aph, and my parents. Your support means a lot, and it's hugely helpful to my writer lifestyle. You help me feel legit!

Huge thanks to my readers on Royal Road and Wattpad. I only know you by your usernames, but I've learned to recognize those names. Especially commenters: Cjenx, General Peaceful, Shadow of Marethyu, Zombie Unicorne, Miss Nomer, Smoarville, dishtv, EatMoreVegetables, The Lord of The Cookies, Ghosti, sid_cypher, UpsilionEnlightened, Omni-Origin Perfect-Inheritor, Banarok Lionrage, Raszhivyk, Ars404, Mofy, Megapooz, MicahLM2, playr543, Ceilingfanenvy, Whiplash246, V6ct9r, micpanda, IcefireStarfire, biravincent, _mehatepizza_, ShaunKZ, Rhandyabao5, Joey-Jay_Spooner, Marysiak14, SubZero_005, Kafui27, MelissaKimFernandes, AGENT_88, Art3miss777, DeSmiley, ko0025, lisadavis910, and a whole lot more. I appreciate you very much!

I'm grateful to the following consultants: Benjamin C. Kinney, neuroscientist and author; Anatoly Belilovsky, physician and author; Carl Frederick, physicist and author; Rebecca Roland, physical therapist and author; Kayla Whaley, disability consultant and author.

The following readers offered constructive advice on the first draft of this novel: Ellen Van Hensbergen, Leigh Berggren, Brian Rappatta, and Sarah Kelderman. Thank you!

Especially, as always, thanks to Adam Robert Thompson, my wonderful alpha reader and husband, who is actually Thomas and Ariock combined (minus their flaws, of course)! He's the reason the Torth series goes noblebright instead of spiraling into grimdark.

And here's a shoutout to some excellent online communities for readers and authors in this genre:

Royalroad.com (and its many associated Discord servers)
Facebook.com/groups/scifiandfantasybookclub
Facebook.com/groups/LitRPGGroup
Facebook.com/groups/LitRPGsociety/
Facebook.com/groups/LitRPG.books/
Facebook.com/groups/LitRPGReleases
Facebook.com/groups/349808165619256
Reddit.com/r/ProgressionFantasy/
Reddit.com/r/torth/

If you'd like to hang out in the Megacosm, join the Torth Discord server at https://discord.gg/gDYVXdS2qz, or subscribe to Abby Updates at
https://abbygoldsmith.com/subscribe/
https://www.patreon.com/abbygoldsmith

# ABOUT THE AUTHOR

Abby Goldsmith is the author of the Torth series and other works of fiction. After receiving a critique from George R.R. Martin at the Odyssey Fantasy Writing Workshop, she sold short works to Escape Pod and Writer's Digest Books. She is qualified for SFWA, with starred reviews from *Booklist* and *Kirkus Reviews*. Abby continues to serialize as AbbyGoldsmith on Patreon and AbbyBabble on Royal Road and Wattpad. You can also find her on YouTube and the *Stories for Nerds* podcast. Abby is credited on more than a dozen Nintendo games as an animator, and she currently enjoys life in Texas with her game dev husband who doubles as her alpha reader.

Website: AbbyGoldsmith.com
Newsletter: AbbyGoldsmith.com/subscribe/
Twitter: @Abbyland
Facebook: AbbyGoldsmith
YouTube: @AbbyGoldsmith
Reddit: AbbyBabble
Store: Redbubble.com/people/abbyland/
Patreon: AbbyGoldsmith
Discord: https://discord.gg/gDYVXdS2qz

# Podium

DISCOVER MORE

PodiumEntertainment.com

Printed in the USA
CPSIA information can be obtained
at www.ICGtesting.com
JSHW021903291124
74528JS00002B/2